# Eclipsing the Tide

## Book One

D1738948

## C.G. Jaquish

Cover by Fahad Ejaz

ISBN: 979-8-571108-33-1

# DEDICATION

In loving memory of my Aunt Nancy
Her will never wavered.
Her heart knew no limits.
And her legacy lives forever through the lives she touched,
Both animal and human.

# CONTENTS

# CHAPTER ONE

"NO!"

The ten-year-old boy fought against the soldier holding his upper arm, but the man was too strong, and he couldn't free himself. He shot a panicked glance to his older brothers on his right, finding them in the same predicament. As a last resort, he looked desperately to his left. His little sister was already crying when the soldier holding her golden hair jerked his arm to make her hush. The four children watched the leader of the invaders, helpless as he slit their father's throat and let his writhing body splash into a puddle on the cobblestone road. The heavy rain sent his blood coursing across the ground. He desperately tried to hold his wound closed, but it was pointless. Drowning in a pool of his own blood, choking on it as it gathered in his throat and seeped endlessly through his fingers. His eyes met his son's one last time. Then, suddenly, he was still, and a glossy emptiness took them over.

The boy felt tears burning in his eyes. He wasn't sure if he was angry or devastated. His father and mother were the only ones who stood up to the invaders when they came. It was midnight, the night before, when they marched into town. They didn't attack. Instead, their leader gave some speech about how the north was too busy fighting itself to realize its potential if everyone banded together. The western hemisphere of Asylum had been absorbed in chaos for thousands of years, and he claimed to have a way to fix it. All they needed to do was bow and accept his rule. He couldn't have been more than 16, but still commanded a large enough force to frighten everyone in the small town. His name was Victor Monohue.

The boy's village was a peaceful one, with not a sword in sight. In fact, this entire portion of the northern free lands was nothing but farmers and shepherds. They all fell to their knees and submitted to this *Victor*. Only the boy's father and mother refused, and they begged their people to see reason. The townsfolk outnumbered his men three to one, why should they bow to a king they neither needed nor desired? The same people they considered friends then watched as Victor's men seized the couple and their children. Since then, his father had been tortured before their neighbors, and now murdered, and his mother's screams could be heard throughout the town as Victor's men held her in their own home. Their cowardly neighbors, who they had spent their entire lives with, did nothing.

The children stared in horror as they brought their mother forward and threw her at her husband's lifeless body. She was naked and bleeding, bruises forming where they beat her. The boy watched her scoop his father's head up against her bosom and hold him tight as she wept. He couldn't bear to see anymore, his father beaten and killed, his mother naked, ashamed, heartbroken. He turned away and clenched his eyes shut, listening to her sobs and praying to The Ancient for strength to break free and end Victor's life.

No sooner had he looked away, then his mother screamed and begged for them to leave his father at peace. He turned back to see Victor cutting the corpse's torso open with one long slice from his neck to his crotch. His mother stood and pulled on the villain's arm with every bit of strength she had left, eventually falling to her knees beside her mutilated husband once more. Victor ignored her until his cut was finished. Then he turned to face her, gently placing the tip of his sword on the cobblestones and folding his hands over the pommel. For a long time, the only sound was that of the rain falling. Finally, the mortified woman spoke.

"Yer a monster." she choked. "What right do ye 'ave to rule the north?"

"The right of intelligence and justice." he replied calmly.

"*This*," she snapped as she waved her hand toward her husband. "isn't justice. This is barbaric and cruel."

Victor grinned at her. He turned to face the crowd and gave his answer to them.

"This *is* justice. There are always those who stand against progress. Our villages have been raided by mountain men from the north and the mystic riders from the east for centuries. Our people have been raped and tortured, left for dead or slaughtered, kidnapped and used in rituals that tore their very souls from their bodies. Yet we always choose a path of submission and cowardice. I can save you all from the carnage that sweeps our homes! We can unite to defeat magic once and for all. Bring peace and prosperity to the entire north. Anyone who stands against that deserves the fate they would sentence all of us to."

He turned back to face the naked woman on the ground while her children heard a murmur of agreement spread through the spineless crowds behind them. Victor crouched down and reached into the chest cavity of the corpse. The woman sobbed and shook her head, knowing what he was searching for. It was an old, barbaric form of punishment, one that was only used on the most morbid of criminals. Yet her own people began to clap their hands as Victor removed her husband's heart and held it out to her. She wept as she watched the blood drip from his hand to the street.

"Eat it." he commanded.

She shook her head miserably, and the crowd cheered louder for Victor. Her vision blurred with a mix of tears and raindrops as the metallic scent of blood reached her nostrils. She cringed. Victor leaned in so he could whisper in her ear. Only she heard his words as she sobbed and trembled in the cold rain.

"Eat it, or watch your children die." he warned.

Her eyes snapped to them as he stood back up and held out the heart once more. They were still struggling against their captors and already looked traumatized from what they had seen so far. She couldn't imagine the help her sons and daughter would need to push past what they were about to witness. Victor decided she was taking too long and snapped his fingers. The soldier holding her youngest son kicked his feet out from under him and pinned him to the ground by the back of his neck, dangling his knife above his temple. She didn't have any other option. Her son was crying in terror as the tip of the dagger dug into the side of his face and made him bleed. She quickly grabbed the heart from Victor and took a large bite from it as the crowd cheered. Victor stood with a sick grin on his face and watched as she chewed and swallowed the entire organ, gagging with each bite through her weeping. When she forced the last bite down her throat, Victor gripped a hand full of her hair and raised her to her feet for the crowd to see. They cheered at her submission and humility. He then threw her back to his men. They tied her hands together with a long rope, attaching the other end to one of their horse's saddles. They were taking her with them, as an example for anyone else who stood in his way.

Victor approached the boy on the ground and knelt beside him. He was trembling from cold and terror, but the boy evenly met his gaze. He only cringed when Victor wiped his blade off on the back of his shirt and then sheathed it, nodding to the men who held him and his siblings. The eldest of the brothers jerked his arm away from Victor's lackey and rushed to help his brother off the ground. His little sister flew into his arms and buried her face in his shirt. He glared at Victor as he held her and his younger brothers close.

"Someday, when you rule the world and lay fat and secure inside your palace walls, I will be there" he growled, stroking his sister's hair. "and I will kill you. I'll make it last days and hurt a thousand times more than anything you've done to my family."

Victor stood from his crouched position and drew up face to face with the eldest. He guessed they were about the same age, but Victor was far taller. The siblings looked away or hid their eyes. They didn't want to watch their brother die as well. Victor met the boy's gaze with unwavering confidence.

"I welcome a challenge." he smirked.

And then they left, Victor, and his men. They mounted their horses and rode away into the sunrise, leaving four children behind to plot their revenge.

ΩΩΩΩΩΩ

Victor woke from his slumber and sat bolt upright. His room was empty, and the door was still closed. No little boys were waiting to slaughter him tonight. Slowly, after looking around the room once more, he laid back down and pulled his blanket up to his chin. He had just gotten comfortable and sighed deeply when his alarm bell resounded off the metal walls. With an angry grimace, he threw his blanket off and hoisted himself out of bed. *Every damn time.*

It was a miserable day in Chrosia. This happened every spring, the rain fell in sheets from the sky and turned everything below into mush. Fayerien was one of the wettest months of the year on Asylum. Already the flood reports were filing in without pause. And they were only 13 days into the cursed forty that would complete the month! Buildings of metal stood a better chance of not being wiped out with the rest of the mud and shite, which was why most of the capital was built of the sturdier stuff, including the streets. It helped that Chrosia was home to almost unlimited resources.

Victor Monohue, now the supreme ruler known as the promontory, fought his way through the blinding rain, with his personal guards following closely behind. He cursed the day he had scheduled to be at the academy for the annual inspection. He had more important matters to attend to. The torrents were soaking him to the bone, so he just stared at the road to avoid the drops pelting his eyes. *I'll have to get Acre to work on this,* he thought, *I need to control the weather. Maybe he already has a plan for that. If not, he will by the time I get finished with him.*

He reached the entrance to the school with an ironic smile pressing itself on his face. It was funny, really, the way he could... persuade... people to make his every desire come true. As he entered, water pouring onto the floor from his clothes, the four cloaked men who had followed him there immediately dispersed. They were the best-trained warriors on Asylum, with nerves of steel and minds of sheep. One stood at the door to make certain no one else entered the school, two preceded on the Promontory's next path to ensure it was safe before his arrival, and the fourth shadowed the man himself. Victor's Elite were always on top of any situation.

4

Victor stood in the dark, semi-circular atrium. The outer structure of the building was, of course, made of metal, resulting in the thunderous noise of rainfall that echoed around him. Doors lined the rounded walls with signs designating which rooms were behind them, branching out from the central atrium, where Victor stood. The room had a few light sconces on the walls, but no overhead lighting, so it was still rather dark. Wringing the water out of his long, royal robes, Victor glanced impatiently at each of the ten doors that fanned out before him, and his anger burned. He was expecting the child he based his entire future on to be born at any minute, and these commoners at the school were keeping him waiting inside the door, dripping wet. Heads would roll for this, and bodies would burn. Disrespect was not to be tolerated. He wasn't used to waiting and that was only more apparent when he was in a rush.

Finally, the door farthest to the right opened and a secretary emerged, her eyes fixated on her clipboard. She didn't look up until she stepped in the puddle left by the Promontory, inches from him. She froze in terror as she met his gaze and then fell to her knees and slunk into the doorway she had exited, crawling backward on the ground. The Promontory folded his arms behind his back. Exactly two seconds later, a large man in a floor-length robe entered and advanced quickly to the dictator's position. He too fell onto his knees.

He was older than Victor, and his gray hair was slowly falling out leaving a bald spot on the top of his head. A rather pudgy fellow, he looked very much like a sweet old grandpa at first glance, but only at first glance. If you looked deeper into his eyes, there rested a vast wasteland of fear and self-preservation. The look was well known in Chrosia, and there were some who were far worse off than the old man on his knees, with his nose pressed to the ground. It was all because of the figure glaring down at him. He struck fear into every heart and every tongue, for that matter, which is why the poor principal stayed bowed and trembling, silently waiting for him to speak. The Promontory waited a full minute before addressing the terrified wretch before him.

"You do realize, Principal, that you have kept me waiting for five whole minutes, don't you? I hope you know how this kind of behavior threatens your position."

His voice was strong and deep, greatly hinting at the speaker's displeasure with the man lying prostrate before him, who got the idea that his 'position' didn't refer to his job as principal, but rather meant that he was currently alive. He truly did not want that position to change, though most preferred death to Victor's alternative punishments.

"You have my sincerest apologies, Your Excellency." the man trembled as he answered. "I was not aware that you had arrived. You're here an hour early and…."

"I, early?" the Promontory bellowed, stepping toward the crouched figure, who quickly scrambled backward out of his reach, staring up into Victor's eyes with terror. "You are to be prepared for me *always*! From now on, I will no longer schedule my appearance as I have graciously done in the past. You will learn to expect me constantly, then. Now take me to the first class and pray you don't disappoint me anymore today!"

The Promontory thought the punishment fit the crime, considering it made his life easier and that was all that truly mattered. The pale principal stood, with great difficulty, and hobbled across the atrium to the first door on the left. He fumbled nervously with the knob as his trembling hands tried to open it. Victor made it even harder for the poor man to concentrate as he glared directly at his face until he finally succeeded in opening the door. The two men who had gone on before jumped to attention as the Promontory entered. After he nodded to them, they moved on to the next hallway, leaving Victor in the current one with the principal and his last Elite bodyguard.

The hallway had four doors on each side. The doors were labeled by class: two for one-year-olds, two for two-year-olds, two for three-year-olds, and two for preschoolers. The hall went on for another thirty feet before stopping at a dead end. On that metal wall, there was a booth with a strange light bulb spiraling around on the ceiling inside of it. A preschooler sat on a bench within, staring directly up into the center of the light. He was motionless. Only his eyes darted around after the light as it moved in and out along the spiral contour of the bulb. He looked dazed and flushed, perhaps even feverish.

The Promontory ignored whatever the principal was saying about his infant class and walked slowly toward the booth. It was honestly the only reason he was here. The principal was looking into the room he was talking about and didn't notice Victor moving away.

"Has it been working?" the dictator asked.

The principal jumped at the question, confused by the direction it came from, but recovered quickly and jogged up to the inquisitor with a great deal of heavy breathing.

"The discipline machines? Your Excellency, they work fine. I've had less and less trouble with my students since they were installed." he answered with a shrug.

Victor rolled his eyes at the disinterest the principal displayed and watched the boy for a while longer. It was Acre's design, stemmed from his own idea. The scientist had pointed out that killing every child that even mildly tested the rules would decrease his subject population, which would also decrease the size of his army exponentially. Not to mention how it would turn his people against him as they lost their children. Therefore, altering their minds would be far more profitable. Even the Promontory had to admit Acre was incredible as he turned back to inspect the classrooms.

The computer system that taught all the children was displaying lessons on the translucent screens in each classroom, just as it should have been. The children were strapped into their seats. At this age group, most of them just screamed. The Promontory shrugged his eyebrows dismissively. They were still being brainwashed appropriately and that was all he cared about. The corner of his mouth twitched up when he realized the rooms were all soundproof. Nurturing was not a large part of Chrosian culture.

Victor slipped into the preschooler room just as the boy from the discipline machine was returning. The youngster stumbled into the class and sat wearily in his seat at the back of the room. The straps wrapped themselves around his torso, crossing his chest in an X. The dictator grinned; the machine really did work. That little boy would no longer remember the attitude that caused the offense he must have made earlier. Acre was a genius.

The Promontory lightly and quickly inspected the rest of the rooms in that hall and all the other halls as well. His main concern was that the discipline machines were working and that they were actually being used. He was about to announce his departure when the lunch bell rang. He groaned inwardly. If he didn't inspect the lunchroom, word would get out and the educational system would grow lax around the entire country. It's the little things that matter in a dictatorship.

As Victor spun around on his heels and sped toward the cafeteria; the poor principal almost had to jog to keep up with his long stride. He huffed and puffed but managed to stay only one step behind. The only thing running through his head was how to save his own skin. Not that Principal Fowler was a bad sort of fellow, he was just afraid to die any earlier than he had to. He already knew that his days were numbered. Once any person reached seventy in Chrosia, they were immediately drafted into the army and few survived the training, but if they did, they normally died in the front lines less than a week later. The elderly were viewed as wastes of resources to Chrosia, and Fowler was already 57.

Something entirely different was running through the head of the man in front of him. Victor was thinking about a different, glorious future, though it was technically the same future as the principal's. The promontory just wanted to be there when his fifth son was born. Acre had spent a lot of time choosing this particular concubine. Both Victor's and her genetics combined into one person would make an incredible warrior and an incredible warrior was an incredible heir. The Promontory had the strength, will, and the intelligence: his concubine had the agility, flexibility, and the looks. The dictator smiled to himself. His son would be a handsome devil. His plans for this child were beyond count.

And it wasn't that he was overly fond of children; in fact, he hated them. Messy, sloppy little imps with no form of discipline. His youngest son would be different, like all his sons were. They each learned discipline and warfare at a very young age, and they trained hard daily to ensure that they would never forget it. There were no jokes, no arguments and absolutely NO girls. If there was anything the ruler hated more than children, it was female children. Beyond childbearing, he saw girls as a complete waste of time and often had the unborn females forcibly cut from his concubines to avoid dealing with them. The number of lives he had ended before they had seen light was unfathomable. This was the type of man who walked through the halls of a school, deciding its students' fates.

They reached the cafeteria after all the children were already seated, and Victor's ears began to pick up several conversations in the room. Kids had their purpose, he supposed. No secret is kept in a home where a child lives and listens. If someone was plotting against him, their offspring would definitely know and might just let it slip. Their conversations were about various subjects, all harmless and controlled by the government. Only one truly caught his ear. It was among two arguing sixth graders.

"No, you idiot, the Promontory makes all the rules and prints them in the daily paper!" one said.

"Why would he do that rather than just print the new laws?" his friend retorted.

"So that no one can claim they simply forgot them and disobey!"

"My dad stopped reading the paper years ago because it was too big. He couldn't read it and hold a job at the same time."

The first boy's face grew deathly pale as his friend said this. Everyone knew it was mandatory that every citizen of Chrosia read or be read the daily paper.......... every day. Blatant disobedience like this warranted death. Victor walked up behind the boy who had spoken last and stood still. Either his shadow or the looks of terror around him alerted the boy, who rose to his feet and spun around, immediately striking a trembling attention. The Promontory smiled in mock kindness and placed his hands on the boy's shoulders.

"What's your name, son?" he asked in a voice smooth as honey.

Victor was an expert at dealing with people. He knew what they liked and hated, what they feared and what they deemed safe. He carefully observed the young boy before him. He was broad-shouldered and tall for his age. His skin was a deep, rich, brown, maybe the darkest Victor had ever seen, and his bright green eyes were wide and focused on him. His hair was shaved close to his head and none of it had sprouted on his chin yet. All in all, Victor could see how this boy might become a very capable warrior and didn't want to jeopardize that. No child should suffer for the sins of their parent. His father needed to be punished, though. Victor kept smiling at the child and waited for his response.

The boy in front of him saw little to fear. Maybe the promontory hadn't heard the conversation and was just coming over to see what was happening at the table. He seemed to be in a good mood and just visiting to check on everyone's progress. Maybe it didn't really matter that his father burned the daily paper each morning. After all, the school taught that Victor was a caring and benevolent ruler and wanted everyone to live their best lives. The poor boy knew no better, unless his parents had warned him as fiercely as his friends' parents had.

"Harrison Drum, son of Jonathon Drum, Your Excellency."

"Well, Harry," the promontory continued in the same voice with the same smile, "will you go to this nice man's office after lunch?"

He nodded toward the principal and Harrison's eyes followed the gesture.

"Yes, sir." he answered with a slight shrug.

He didn't want to appear disrespectful by breaking his attention, but he had no reason to fear the principal. Everyone went to his office now and then and poor Harry just assumed that he had left something there. He *was* missing his favorite knife. The Promontory's fake smile widened.

"There's a good lad. Now go ahead and finish eating."

As soon as the boy's back was turned, Victor's smile disappeared. He made eye contact with one of his bodyguards and jerked his head toward the door. The hooded figure nodded and slipped unnoticed across the room and out the door. There was no doubt in Fowler's mind that he was on his way to end the Drum father for his insolence. Then, Victor swung back to him, and the principal forgot all about the boy's parents, as his own life had to come first.

"Use the discipline machine to make young Drum believe his parents died in an accident six months ago. Also make him think he's been living here in the school barracks ever since and that you have found a position for him in a program for me. I'll send you details once I decide which program it will be." Victor ordered quietly, straightening his sleeve with casual indifference.

The principal nodded his understanding before the Promontory glanced at him out the top of his eyes and continued.

"Your school passes inspection. Now, get me a damned horse."

As the man hurried away, Victor looked around the room once more and muttered to himself.

"There's no way I'm walking through that cursed rain again."

# CHAPTER TWO

Victor burst through the door to his fortress and bellowed Acre's name. His voice echoed off the metal walls and resounded like a thunderclap. Within seconds, there was the sound of a door slamming on a higher floor, then the middle-aged scientist rushed down the stairs.

"I'm glad you're back, Vic. We need to talk." he started, but Victor Monohue held up his hand.

"Not now. First, I need to know if the baby has been born, yet."

"Well, yes, it was, but…."

"Dammit!" Victor growled. "I wanted to be here. Well, whatever, I want to see if he will make the cut. I suppose you already analyzed him. Is he strong and capable?"

Victor, obviously not waiting for an answer, began to leap up the stairs, taking three at a time with his long legs.

"Victor, wait!!" the scientist cried out urgently. "I have something to tell you."

"Later, Acre. I've been waiting for this day for years. And I had that ridiculous inspection this morning, a total waste of my time if you ask me." Victor called back. "I don't see why someone else can't do these damned inspections and---"

"It's about the baby!" Acre yelled hopelessly with a cringe; he knew what was coming.

Something in his voice clicked in Victor's mind. He knew the scientist well enough to know that something was off. Normally, Acre never opposed him more than once. He stopped mid-step and put his foot down slowly. A slight wave of concern swept through his thoughts; he had heard Acre use that voice before. It was his I-have-bad-news-I-don't-want-to-tell-you voice. Unfortunately for him, Acre was often asked to deliver bad news to the Promontory. They had a complicated relationship, but it was friendlier than any other one Victor was involved in now adays. It was a miracle that he hadn't murdered Acre in a fit of rage yet, based on all of the disappointing things he had heard from his mouth over the years. Rather than continue to walk up the steps, he turned around slowly and deliberately, walking down the flight he had leaped up only seconds before. He looked straight into Acre's face.

"Yes?" he demanded, meaningfully.

Acre took another deep breath and winced at the thought of what Victor would do when he had the answer. He held his breath too long and had to draw a second before speaking. It would be best, he decided, to break it to Victor slowly.

"Alright. So, the baby is in excellent condition; very strong and healthy. It was born less than an hour ago."

Acre paused. The impatience on Victor's face told him the ruler was not in the mood for his tactics, and his soul groaned. This wasn't going to go well.

"In fact, I believe it will be everything you want... except for one.... very.... *tiny* detail."

"Get on with it, Acre!" Victor snapped.

The scientist closed his eyes and took another deep breath, making the promontory roll his eyes impatiently.

"It's a girl."

At first, there was nothing but absolute silence. No yelling or screaming or foaming saliva. No hand grabbing his throat to kill the messenger. It was so quiet, in fact, that Acre risked peeping open one of his eyes. He immediately wished he hadn't. Victor was glaring at him. His face was red, no *scarlet*. He was shaking in fury and holding his breath for the explosion. Eyes widened to the max and nostrils flaring, Victor finally opened his mouth. The look on his face told Acre what was coming before his eardrums rattled with the explosive sound.

"WHAT!?!!???"

Victor's voice thundered through the great hall, reverberating off the metal walls. Acre closed both his eyes again, squeezing them tight as he recoiled a step and wiped Victor's spit off his face. After a little consideration, he decided that the Promontory's question had been rhetorical.

"Every single doctor has assured me that it was a boy!" Victor continued, angrily pacing the floor. "*Every single one!!!* It would have been taken care of if I had known. What use could I possibly have for a weak, emotional, idiotic......... *female*?!?"

He spat the last word like it was poison to his tongue; it was the best insult he could offer the child. He grumbled on and on as he stormed back and forth for several minutes, using language that Acre had grown used to over the years. Then he slowly ran out of curses and exclamations of anger.

His face paled back to its regular cold features. Victor finally fell, exhausted, onto the bottom steps like they were an easy chair, breathing heavily and staring into space with intense hatred. Only then, did Acre dare to look upon his infuriated ruler. Deceiving him was the worst crime imaginable in Chrosia. For all of his doctors to accomplish it, they would all have to be in cahoots with each other, which meant they would also have to meet secretly, the second-worst crime in the country. The Promontory rested his elbows on his knees and buried his forehead in his hands.

"How, Acre?" he asked with intense heat in his voice, "How could every single doctor conspire against me like this? How *dare* they?"

The scientist sat down beside him with a sigh. He was the only one who wasn't completely horrified of the ruler. He didn't ever take advantage of him, of course, but he was frank and honest. He wouldn't even say he was entirely comfortable around him, but they had fought alongside each other in the war to unite the north and were about the same age. That made them some sort of friends, he supposed. Acre had burned a lot of bridges from his past for the man beside him and Victor knew and appreciated that.

"They didn't. I looked at McKenzie only a week ago and didn't see it."

"How's that even possible?" he groaned again, and Acre decided it was time to drop another bit of bad news on Victor.

"Equipment isn't always a hundred percent reliable, Vic. Sometimes we can't see everything happening. No one saw the girl because she was hidden perfectly behind her brother."

Victor blinked a couple of times before turning and staring in disbelief at his head scientist. What brother? The thought wasn't sinking in, not at all.

"What?"

"McKenzie was carrying twins. The boy was a big, strong, healthy baby. The type you always wanted. The girl was hiding behind him, because she was only about half his size. Even now, she is only about five pounds. The boy came first, but he was dead before he even crowned. The nearest we can guess is that the girl was so desperate for nutrients that she stole them from him in the end. Hence, he died... and she lives."

Acre ended with a shrug. He didn't really care either way. He wasn't as close-minded about girls as the ruler was. She would still serve his purpose just fine. He only had to convince Victor to let her live and let him raise her. Otherwise, he wouldn't have the control he needed over his secret weapon, but it had to be Victor's idea, or it could give him away. The scientist waited patiently for the dictator to process all the information he just received.

It was all too much for Victor. His genetic masterpiece, his strong, impregnable weapon, had been killed by a weak, premature infant! He slowly stood up, walking over to one of the braziers on the edge of the room, and calmly folded his hands behind his back. Acre stayed in his seat and watched. He knew the plans Victor had made and he knew that his friend was far from pleased with this situation. Most likely, the dictator was just trying to control his anger and frustration. He excelled at that when he wanted to.

Victor was tall for most men, standing at six foot nine inches with broad shoulders, which rose and fell in his anger at this moment, and a tall thin head. His dark brown hair was pulled into a tight ponytail at the base of his skull and it hung to his mid-back, straight as a board. But the most interesting thing about him was his eyes. They were dark and deep-set, closer together than most. His pupils were black, but they did not look like other eyes at all. Rather than appearing as a dot on the iris, they looked like pits that drove deep into his mind. There was never any light reflected in them and they made many think of menacing black holes that consumed all in their gaze. Acre watched these eyes narrow in anger in the reflection of the metal braziers, as Victor decided his daughter's fate.

"Kill her." he said calmly.

Acre hoisted himself up with a sigh. Of course, that was Victor's first choice. It was easy, simple and there was no one to stop him. The scientist had to convince him to change his mind and keep the girl alive.

"Victor......"

His voice cut out as Victor swung around, stormed back to the steps and yelled at the scientist, towering a foot above the poor man. His face flared back into its furious scarlet, and his saliva sprayed onto Acre's face, again. So much for controlling his anger.

"I SAID KILL HER! Slit her throat, rip her into pieces, drown her. Do whatever it takes to get that pathetic, little bitch out of my life! I'll start over with McKenzie."

He began to stomp back up the steps again, until Acre's next words flew after him.

"You can't--"

Victor spun around and pounded down the stairs to yell one more time in Acre's face.

"Now see here, Acre, you're the damn bastard who found that dirty, worthless whore in the workhouse and convinced me that she was my perfect genetic partner *and* that my son would be the perfect heir. Now give me one, not even five, just *one* reason why I can't use her until I get exactly what I want!!"

Victor's voice and look challenged Acre's patience. It wasn't often that the two of them bashed heads so fiercely, but he had to have the child, this girl in particular, even if it meant defying Victor a little to get her. He gave vent to his anger with a bit of sarcasm.

"Is the fact that McKenzie died less than an hour after your son a good enough reason?"

Victor's face softened into an annoyed look. He backed down away from the scientist and folded his arms across his chest, showing his complete disregard for his concubine.

"You could have brought that into our conversation a little sooner, don't you think?" he pursed his lips.

Acre shrugged. Vehemently angry as he was at the dictator right now, he was used to this type of response. How could he not care about the poor girl more? They had been together for years........ he swallowed his anger and watched Victor sit back on the steps in defeat.

"You were more concerned about the child."

He forced himself to reply calmly as he sat down next to the Promontory again. Victor gave an exasperated groan and ran his hands down his face, pulling his lower eyelids down as he rolled his eyes.

"The child." he moaned bitterly. "What the hell am I supposed to do with a girl?"

With relief, the scientist realized that meant Victor was going to keep her alive. That was a start. Acre saw his moment.

"The same thing you would do with a boy. Turn her into the weapon you wanted your son to be." Acre pushed, controlling his excitement, but Victor shook his head forcefully.

"Oh no, if I'm going to keep this girl, she at least better be the gem of the country. Maybe someday her body will at least be of use to some man. I could marry her out to some dignitary over the Foam Sea to avoid conflict with them. Otherwise, why keep her? I'm not slapping huge muscles on her; she would look like a freak and there is absolutely no way any child of mine will ever look like a freak. It would ruin my reputation."

"That's not what I meant, Vic." Acre rolled his eyes.

"Then, what would you suggest? It's not like I can have a girl fighting my battles for me. I would lose all the respect I've spent years building. No one would fear me, and I'd become a laughingstock. Besides, no female warrior could rival a well-trained man."

"Perhaps not, on their own, but I've been working on a special serum that increases brain function by 300% and also increases agility, flexibility, and dynamics."

Victor dramatically gave the scientist the most unimpressed look he could muster and rolled his eyes.

"How fascinating." he growled sarcastically.

Acre shot him an annoyed glance. He was trying to prove a point and Victor's attitude was somewhat impeding his progress. He knew the Promontory would be pleased with what he had to say, if only he would be open to listening to it, rather than brooding over this unfortunate turn of events. They had talked about the possibility of this unorthodox enhancement many times. He took a deep breath and continued.

"Victor, enhancement of the mind is an extraordinary achievement and the added advantage of increased elasticity in ligaments and muscles would place almost boundless opportunity in your hands."

"So, I would have an excellent circus performer to entertain me when I'm not busy. When is that? Oh, never."

Acre smiled. This time, the sarcasm didn't bother him as much. He was about to win the attention of his very critical audience.

"A circus performer with telepathic abilities."

At first, nothing happened. They sat in silence. Victor knew Acre had been working on a model that could read minds and move objects with their thoughts, but his last update on the subject was a list of why it wasn't working on their test subjects. Victor thought of the many applications of having such a person at his command. Still, it wasn't possible.

"You said a year ago that you didn't think that was actually possible." Victor said his own thoughts out loud.

"A year ago, I didn't have all the information from Arcane." Acre replied enthusiastically. "I believe they have the edge I need to make this work with their ma---"

"Don't say it." Victor warned, continuing to stare straight ahead thoughtfully.

"You don't want me to try it?" Acre questioned, worried. "Even if I think I can make it work?"

Victor was silent for a long time. He rose to power fighting the very thing Acre was discussing. People believed he could save them from its savagery and chaos. If rumors were to leak that he was just twisting it for his own purposes, he would lose all his support. But he couldn't bear the idea of not pursuing this series. Telepaths bursting into existence would write his name in the historic annals forever. He looked up at Acre's face and the scientist recognized the familiar glint of greed in his friend's eyes.

"Do it."

# CHAPTER THREE

Precisely 2,328 miles south of Holux, Chrosia, another child was being introduced to the world. There, lay a much smaller country than Victor's kingdom named Central Liberty. It was so called because of its location. This particular country was completely surrounded by five other kingdoms on the western hemisphere of Asylum. To the North sat the massive expanse of Chrosia. To the East lay Dormiat and Arcane. To the west lay Ashtar and to the South of all these countries lay the wild lands of The Warden's Wood. It was in the capital city of this country, which had been built in the exact center of the continent, that another baby was born, a little boy.

His father, Josane Rogers was the war strategist of Central Liberty. However, when the country was not at war, he was the main foreign diplomat as well. So naturally, when a rider arrived in Kaysor, the eighth month on Asylum, requesting help for their ally, Arcane, it was his job to travel there and determine how severe their condition truly was. The war strategist was reluctant to go because his fairly new wife was expecting her first child within a few months of the time he had to leave. Besides wanting to be there for his child's birth, he had an extremely important reason for wanting to stay home. He and his wife were both over 40 and their doctor had informed them that the pregnancy would be a huge risk to her health. There was even a not too slight chance that neither the baby nor the mother would survive. Though the father would much rather have stayed, he knew his duty and, worse yet, so did his wife, Anna Belle. She had unconditionally demanded that he went, so he obliged. But he was not back in time to fetch the doctor for his wife. His older brother did it for him.

The young doctor rushed up the stairs and into the stone-walled room in the capital building where the older woman sat cradling her expanded stomach and rocking back and forth on the wicker couch. She was in the living room of the suite she shared with her husband.

"Anna Belle, if you're having contractions, we should probably consider removing the child who so badly wants to come out. It's not too early, why did you tell Marcus not to send for me?"

The woman's entire face crinkled in pain along her regular wrinkle lines, delaying her answer for a few seconds.

"I'm all right Alexander. He said he would get back in time and I know he wants to be here when the baby is born. I'm sure it's just normal indigestion."

Her voice was tight and she hesitated periodically, but when she had finished speaking, her face crinkled again and turned red. She held her breath, knowing that if she didn't, her voice would break through in a scream. The doctor looked at her doubtfully. He sat down beside her on the couch and began feeling her stomach, pressing on it in several places with his hands. Finally, she took a breath again after jumping with every prod he gave for several minutes.

"You have to do that?" she asked with a little heat.

The doctor straightened his back indignantly and sharpened the tone of his voice.

"Anna Belle, if you keep trying to hold that child in there like that, you're going to blow your brains out the top of your head! You almost just passed out from not breathing!!"

"I can wait---" another spasm of pain interrupted her sentence. "--- Joey will be here soon. I can wait, like he waited for me."

Alexander could only assume she meant that he had waited to get married. Joey and Annie had been best friends for twenty years at this point. Everyone thought they were just that, friends, and nothing more. Neither of them seemed interested in more with the other. They were completely platonic. Then, two years ago, Joey just up and proposed, shocking everyone. Alex could understand her determination, but he was a little tired of trying to reason with his overly sentimental patient. They were supposed to obey him without question, not reduce him to a begging fool. All the same, he knew this particular patient well enough to not order her around.

"This isn't about whether or not *you* can wait--I know you can. This is about the child inside you that has already developed your stubborn habits and *won't* wait." he urged with a little impatience showing through his voice.

Anna Belle smiled weakly before bending over with another contraction. Alex was pretty sure they were getting closer together now and he knew he had to convince her to let him help before something awful happened to her... or the baby.

"So, it's a battle of wills, is it?" she asked as soon as she could breathe again.

"Anna Belle, they're getting closer together. Please, *PLEASE*, let me deliver the baby."

He was trying to ask her permission one more time, hoping she would give in, but inside he was adamantly getting ready to try against her will, if necessary.

Her answer was an agonized scream that made up the doctor's mind for good. He was tired of playing inferior to a pregnant woman with no medical knowledge. He picked her up in his arms and carried her from the living room of her suite to the master bedroom down the hall. He laid her in her bed, huffing after carrying a struggling pregnant woman all that way, and then darted back into the hallway, to the door that led into the main castle's stairway. His apprentice should be close behind him

"Drew!" he yelled down the stairs at the top of his lungs. "Bring my gear up here, now!"

It wouldn't be long now, he knew, or at least he thought he knew. As he began to prepare his crying patient, he thought of everything that had led to this very moment, the patience, the hope, the care and preparation. Everything had been so perfect, so ready, then the summons from Arcane had come. He would never forget the look of concern on Joey's face when he had learned that he was leaving with four months to go until his wife was ready. *As if this pregnancy hadn't been risky enough already*, Alex thought moodily.

Naturally, he had warned the couple about this when they came to talk to him about it, but Anna Belle had decided that she was going to have a baby if it killed her. That was the first time Alex learned not to say impossible in front of her. She took it like a challenge. Now he was here with Anna Belle and neither of them had the slightest clue where Joey was. Alex almost wished their places were swapped, but he also knew that Joey would rather have him there. It was safer for his wife and child this way. Alex knew what he was doing and the strategist trusted him.

Alex wasn't even sure Joey wanted a child. His family seemed very distant from the world. Marcus, Joey's older brother, never even married and claimed he was perfectly happy that way. Joey had waited so long and, though he never seemed thrilled about having kids, no one doubted how much he loved his wife. Yet, he always sided with anything that the doctor said about the risks of pregnancy for Annie. Alex often wondered what happened to the brothers to make them so jaded against the world.

Once Annie became pregnant, Joey was very supportive and tried to be excited, but he wasn't used to portraying that emotion. Most of the time, he was just nervous and concerned for Annie's health. Alex noticed that his drinking picked up, subtle as it was. Despite it all, he was devastated when he had to leave.

"I'll be home in time if I have to gallop the whole way." Joey had told Anna Belle at their parting.

She had smiled and brushed off his cape.

"Oh, I know you will be, but I'll wait for you, in case you're held up."

"I won't be." was his confident reply, sealed by a gentle kiss. "I won't be."

"Promises, promises, idle promises." murmured Alex as he snapped back to reality upon hearing his patient cry out in pain.

He growled and strode back out the door into the hallway. Drew was always in slow motion and Anna Belle simply didn't have the time he was taking. As he reached for the suite's entrance door, preparing to yell again, it flew open on its own and thudded against his forehead. Though he staggered back and fell, he was pretty sure he didn't go unconscious, but rather went unfocused. At first, he only saw a shadow that seemed unable to stand still. Then there was a blur that slowly came into focus as Joey, holding his medical bag and bending over him, asking if he was alright.

"You're late." the doctor rebuked, ignoring whatever it was the older man was trying to say.

"I was…"

"Never mind, you crazy old bastard! Just help me up and give me my damn bag!"

Joey pulled him to his feet and handed him his tool bag, which he had grabbed from Drew on his way up. He then jogged to his room, pulled a chair up to the bed and sat by his wife to comfort her. She was overjoyed to see him, but a bit distracted. He shot a concerned glance at Alex when he walked through the bedroom door. The doctor caught it and briefed him about the last twenty minutes; how Marcus had run to get him and tell him that Anna Belle was crazy, how he had run up to see if Marcus was being exaggerative again, how he had discovered that he wasn't, and how he had ended up where he was with none of his tools. As he began working, he started a conversation with the war strategist as if this was just a part of everyday life for him.

"So, how did you end up with my bag?" he asked.

"I saw Drew flirting with a few girls at the fountain with it in his hand. I asked him why he had it and he told me he was taking it to you. I pointed out that he was taking his good old time getting it to you and he pinched the chin of the blonde in front of him and said that it was because he had no idea where 'the good ole' doc was'. Well, you know me, Alex. I put two and two together and got four hundred, grabbed it from him and ran up here." the older man answered in one breath, uneasily watching the doctor take his time putting his gloves on.

Unlike Alex, this was not normal for Joey and he felt as if everything was taking far too long. He wanted his wife in perfect health as soon as possible because he was afraid that he would lose her if it took too long. He had never even been present at a birth before and had no idea how it went.

On top of that, his trip left a great deal of disconcerting issues on his mind, and he hadn't slept in days. While all this worked on his head, the doctor finally leaned over his wife and told her to push, which she did. When she stopped to breathe, Joey frowned.

"Why is nothing happening?" he asked impatiently.

Alex looked up at him in disbelief.

"Joey…. it could take a couple of hours. Just relax and hold her hand. If you lose your decorum, so will she." he hissed through his teeth, keeping a smile on his face.

Anna Belle gave a forced laugh.

"Alex, don't worry; I'm not going to lose it. I just hope it's over fast."

"Me too." the men said in unison with Alex adding another command to push.

ΩΩΩΩΩΩ

"I never dreamed it would take that long." Joey huffed. "She seemed so ready!"

"Well, it would have been faster if the kid hadn't tried to come out backward."

Alex plopped down into an armchair in the war strategist's living room, grumbling. He was exhausted, but years of practice had still taught him to calculate the time.

"How long was it?" Joey asked, sitting down on the couch across the room, even more tired than his friend.

"14 hours, fifty-eight minutes and some odd number of seconds. Born on the 13th of Fayerien, late in the evening. It would have been sooner if the kid hadn't tried to strangle himself on his own cord and slide out the wrong way."

"I think 15 hours would have worked, Alex." Joey replied with a little exasperation. "And you already said the bit about him coming in backward. When will I get to see the baby? When will Annie? How is Annie? Did everything go right?"

The doctor closed his eyes, slamming his head back against the back of the chair. He was used to younger men panicking when their first child came along, but Joey was 42. He desperately prayed to The Ancient for a little more maturity from his friend and yawned while answering him.

"Take it easy, Joey. You've got a healthy little boy and plenty of time to get to know him, but let the nurse take her time cleaning the crap off him first."

Joey sighed impatiently, pacing. He did pause and look directly at Alex for his next question.

"And Annie?"

There was a long silence, in which the doctor opened his eyes, lifted his head off the headrest of the chair and made sad eye-contact with the war strategist. He watched his friend's face fall noticeably and knew he didn't have to say anything, but he did just for the technicalities of it.

"I'm sorry, Joe."

"Oh." the strategist gulped after a long time.

There was another silence. Joey slowly sank back onto his couch and tried to put all the pieces together. If he had only been here...... maybe everything would have been different. Alex honestly didn't want to say anything else and, technically he didn't have to, because Joey didn't ask. However, Alex also knew that Joey wanted to know and wanted to ask. He just couldn't bring himself to do it. Alex's heart fell as he realized that he had to talk about it more.

"She knew, my friend." he said softly. "She just knew, somehow."

"And...... that's supposed to help?"

Alex got up and went to sit on the couch beside his friend. He knew that this was hard for anyone, but he also knew how overwhelming it could look if you were a man and you suddenly found that you would be raising a child on your own. Joey had always been what most people call stiff, heartless, or cold. It was amazing that he ever got married at all, but what made the loss of his wife hurt so badly was that she was the only one who had chosen to look past the outside and see a man whose love was all but spent on his country and she was the only one that had ever chosen to love him. The reason for this was that her love was also in her country, which is what had made him love her over their decades together.

So, they were kindred spirits, and she truly was his soulmate. It was losing his own life to lose her, and Alex honestly wondered if he would have died the same hour as her if his duty to raise her child had not pumped new life into him. But it was different life, driven by duty and regulation, not by love, loyalty and devotion. Only one thing in the future would be able to pull him out of this attitude and help him remember the joy of love again, but it would be years and it would come from the most unlikely place in the world. For now, Joey sat and stoically listened as the doctor tried his best to comfort him.

"It was always a possibility, Joey, but she wanted that baby more than anything, even if it cost her own life. You knew that. She was far beyond normal birthing age, and it was the risk you both took. You asked me, remember? And for all my warnings, she still wanted that baby. She never would listen to me. And she was right, Joe. She was right. At 43, she just gave an incredible effort to bring a life into this world and now.... she has an incredible son. And she'll be able to meet him before she goes."

Joey slowly turned and stared at Alex's hopeful eyes. The doctor could almost see Joey's deadened spirit in the muted reflection of his pupils.

"And…" the war strategist gulped. "that's supposed to help?"

The nurse brought in the baby just then and Joey took him in his arms. He gazed into his face for a moment before nodding good night to the doctor and walking out of the room. Alex bit his lower lip as he thought he recognized a slight look of disgust on the old man's face as he saw his own son. The doctor knew that Joey may blame the baby for the death of his beloved wife, but to see your child for the first time and frown at him was cold, even by that standard. Alex pushed up off the couch and gathered his bag in his arms. He suddenly felt the need to go home, hold his own son and kiss his wife.

Joey walked slowly down the hallway of his suite and opened his bedroom door, where Annie lay uneasily waiting to see her child. She looked up and smiled feebly at him as he approached. Her face was pale, and the sparkle was gone from her eyes. The very sight of her made him feel miserable and helpless, so extremely helpless. It was a few seconds before he could bring himself to move at all. He walked over to her and laid his small bundle in her arms.

"Oh, Joey!" she whispered, tears of joy running down her cheeks. "He's perfect!"

Joey sat beside her again, like he had for the previous 15 hours, and held her free hand. His other arm wrapped completely around the baby and her, helping her weakened muscles support their child. He didn't even look at the infant but gazed into her eyes as she did.

"Annie, there's something I need to tell you."

Annie took her eyes off her baby boy, lifted them and the hand Joey was holding to her husband's face and smiled.

"I know, dearest, I know. I can feel it."

She was quiet for a while, all along keeping her hand near his face to wipe away the tears that streamed down his cheeks. They had been married just over a year and a half, but their friendship was decades old. How dearly this man had learned to love her in all that time. She smiled slightly as she remembered how he snapped at her when they first met. She had bumped into him while he was in a hurry for work. It made him seem like a bit of a monster at first. Then she had learned to see him for who he was and discovered how his political life was the only thing insensitive about him. Now she knew that it was also what he resorted to when he was worried or afraid. He had good cause to be both right now, though he wouldn't show it to anyone, especially when she was gone. Her smile faded as she realized how hard it would be for him over the next few years.

"Joey, thank you." she whispered as he closed his eyes and held her hand on his cheek. "Thank you for the chance to live the only dream I've ever had; to stand by my man and hold my own child. Thank you so much for everything you've ever done and everything you're going to do. Now, please, please promise me just one thing. That he will know his father well and that you will never give the privilege of raising him to anyone else. You will be a good father Joey, don't ever doubt that, just give him all your love and teach him well. You'll see. There won't be anyone in all the world like little Duke."

Joey opened his eyes and looked into her smiling face.

"Is that okay?" she asked softly.

He bent down and wrapped his arms around her and the little bundle in her arms.

"Anything you want." he whispered into her ear.

"I love you, Joey."

"I love you, too. So very, very much."

He gently pressed his lips against hers and knew that it would be the last time when she stopped kissing him back. He drew back and looked at her face in silent passivity. It was white and cold. Her eyes stared at nothing.

Just space.

The 42-year-old man closed his eyes and laid his head on her chest as his son broke into tears and screams.

He ignored him.

# CHAPTER FOUR

"And you're sure it will work?"

Acre sighed and shot an annoyed sidelong glance at Victor. Luckily for him, the Promontory missed it.

"Vic, you know I can't be perfectly sure about any of my experiments, but I'll test it before I use it on the baby."

Acre had at least learned that a disgusted disfigurement came over his friend's face if he heard 'your daughter' or 'the girl'. 'The baby' was entirely safer. They were in the science lab overlooking Acre's notes, data, and sketches for the enhancement machine. Each folder was labeled by model or series. Most of the models were made for only one person; a type of super-powered soldier, but the series were all designed for 500 men. Women had been used in models before, but never in a series. Sometimes, it helped to have the certain distractions women possessed on their side. Of course, they were never advertised, to avoid embarrassment on Victor's part, and none were alive anymore. There were the abandoned Jaspar and Horace series and then there were plans and names for series that did not yet exist. Victor picked up one of these files and stared longingly at it. Acre peeked over his shoulder.

"Ahhh, the Logan model. Well, maybe we can turn it into a series instead. It won't be as significant as having your son as the only juggernaut out there, but it will give you the power you need to defeat the rest of your enemies. Though, I truly believe this next model will be the last one you will ever need."

"Don't think that your scientific voodoo can make me see her as anything more than a thorn in my flesh, Acre. She'll have to prove that on her own and mark my words, it won't be easy." Victor replied as he tossed the file back onto the desk in front of him.

Acre watched him lean on the desk with both his hands and then went back to flipping through the files in his own hand. Victor was still lost in his angry thoughts when Acre spoke again.

"I found it."

The Promontory looked up and walked over to the desk Acre was standing at and looked at the file in his hands. 'Model Emily' it read. Acre laid the file on his desk and flicked on the lamp above it. Then, he opened it. At first, he panicked. Everything, all the sketches, charts, and notes were blurry, completely unreadable! Then, he remembered his lenses. He reached up and pressed on his right temple. His reading lenses lowered out of his eyebrows and covered his eyes. Victor shivered in disgust.

"That's still creepy." he told the scientist.

Acre grinned.

"Everything you have done in your life and *this* is what finally sickens you?"

It was true, Victor had done some despicable things, always justifying them with his higher purpose and longing for a better world, but terrible things just the same. He remembered waking up in sweats just this morning over the biggest mistake of his life.

"I dreamed about them again last night." he mused to Acre.

The scientist withdrew his glasses to frown at Victor.

"Who? The kids? Vic, it's been over three decades."

"Yes." Victor nodded. "I was prideful to let them live after making a threat upon my life. Wouldn't it be ironic if one of them actually ended up killing me?"

"Well," Acre hesitated. "you did brutally murder their mother and father......"

"To save so many more!!" Victor ejaculated in his defense. "Two people died and millions upon millions submitted and got to live. Isn't that better than killing all of them? I united that entire region peacefully, rather than taking valuable time away from conquering the southeastern region. Filthy mages and horsemen, but I even allowed some of them to live, any that submitted and weren't involved in sorcery. I'm not some vile monster, Acre, I just wanted peace. Besides, who would there be left to rule if I slaughtered the world? And, technically, I might add, *I* didn't kill their mother."

Acre raised an eyebrow.

"Really?"

"Yes, really. I let my men keep her and use her as they pleased, but she went crazy. She would laugh hysterically at air and somehow rubbed a hole in her own head. She just scratched right through the skin like it was nothing. Then one day, she went limp, got ill and died. I never once touched the woman and I let her damn children continue to breathe. What more could any *female* ask for?"

"Vic, I'm pretty sure you just described the symptoms of a disease passed through eating human flesh. She died because she ate her husband's heart. It has a delayed effect, anywhere from weeks to years."

Victor sucked in his lower lip and bit it. Acre was the smartest man in the world and Victor almost always went with what he said. It was foolish not to, since Acre was either always right or close enough to right that no one else's opinion mattered. So, it turned out he did kill the woman, by extension.

"Oh." he muttered. "Well, I can't very well fix it now. My entire kingdom is built around the fear that spawned from that one moment. I could never regret it. I'm the first person in history who ever managed to unite the north into one kingdom and maintain control of it. My sixteen-year-old self killing those two nobodies was how all of it started. They get to forever be part of the legacy that is Chrosia. That's more than most simple shepherds get."

Acre grimaced and turned back to his folder, lowering his glasses again. He needed to get the promontory back on track with why they were here. He didn't have time to discuss the past, there was too much future to focus on.

"It will take about a month-long period in the Enhancer on max strength. It should strengthen every part of the mind and the serum is meant to enhance muscle performance, so it will also increase agility in other muscles besides the brain. They will be exceedingly flexible, almost contortionists and they will have the highest mental capacity in the world, plus just a bit of added strength, not enough to even show, though." he informed Victor.

The Promontory dragged his brain out of deep thought and forced himself to listen to Acre. He had never despised someone more than he hated his daughter in that moment. All of the politics and tactics he had to focus on daily were now on hold for a premature infant with little to no future. Maybe there was a chance he could convince Acre to see his way of things, but the scientist was far too stubborn and proud of his newest plan. If nothing else, at least the baby would be an excellent experiment for the man.

"And... what if it doesn't work?"

Victor's tone produced an exasperated sigh from the scientist.

"Vic, if it doesn't work, then you can kill her just as easily when she's ten as when she's an infant. And who knows? If it fails, the enhancement may kill her anyway. Even if it succeeds, she may die from the stress of it all. All brain science is theory. She may even over-respond to the serum and blow off her own head! Why do you care anyway? It's not like you want to be overly involved in her life."

Victor thought it might actually be amusing to watch his daughter blow her own head off, and Acre could literally see him picturing it in his mind.

He was hoping the dictator also heard his last statement. If Victor would only give him the responsibility of caring for the child, Acre would be much closer to achieving his goal. The ruler's brow furrowed.

"I know it's a risky procedure," he said. "I just don't want to waste time raising her if it fails and it all comes to nothing, Acre. Normally, I just hand off the raising to the concubines, but hers went and died."

"Oh, for Ancient's sake! Fine! I'll raise her and train her for the treatment, and you won't have to worry about a damn thing."

Acre could hear his heart thumping in his chest. He had been trying to steer the conversation this way all day and was worried he might give himself away. Did he sound too eager? Or would his friend buy it and agree? The long silence that followed set his anxiety to boil. He stared intently at Victor as his eyebrows shot up and he fell into deep thought, folding his hands behind his back.

The Promontory turned it all over in his mind for a while. It would be Acre's wasted time if it all proved pointless, not his. His other sons would be able to be part of the Logan series and his life might not be as impaired by this unfortunate biological mishap as he originally thought. Acre would raise her, take care of her, and put up with her. His job would simply be to sit back and watch. But he wanted her to know what a burden she was to him. It would inspire her to be more than anyone else if she knew her whole life depended on her being absolutely everything he desired. Then, a thought struck him.

"Acre, if you're so sure this will be the greatest enhancement of all time, why would we waste it all on one girl, instead of hundreds?"

Acre frowned. That wasn't the answer he was hoping for. In fact, that could seriously endanger his plan. It was easy to manipulate one little girl, even into womanhood. If he added 499 other telepathic women into the equation, there was a far greater chance that someone could stop his telepath. For a brief moment, he thought of flat out refusing the dictator, maybe lying about him only being able to create one enhanced Emily, but if he was caught in a lie, it would cost him his life. And as of right now, there was no ultimate human being to protect him. He didn't want hundreds of telepaths, he only needed the one, but there was no way to convince Victor to keep it at one without drawing suspicion. He would have to play along and think of another way to make his girl superior. Of course, he would need to show a little surprise at the sudden change of plans.

"You want an entire Emily series? Is that really necessary?"

Victor snorted.

"You don't think I'm actually stupid enough to leave the future of my country in the hands of *that* thing, do you?"

"Yes, of course, I did! Vic, I've been planning this whole time on having only one telepath. You really want 500 of them? What would be the point?

You maintain control with fear. It only takes one mentally enhanced soldier to strike fear into every man alive. To make more would be expensive and even dangerous if they figure out that we can't control them. On top of all that, to be honest with you, I think it will be more... impressive, and therefore, effective, to leave this enhancement with, with---- oh damn it all, what's her name or title or........ number for all I care? Something to call the damn thing!"

"Eclipse."

Acre raised an eyebrow at him. He hadn't expected Victor to have a name already. Honestly, he was expecting the girl to be raised as a number or something worse than that even. Not only was that an insanely fast answer, but it also wasn't anywhere near as detestable as he had been planning on. It humanized his weapon, giving her a full-on name. That could bode ill for him.

"Eclipse? That's........ unusual." he asked doubtfully. "Why Eclipse?"

Victor, who had barely even listened to the scientist's complaints because he had known that he, as the Promontory, would get his way in spite of them, stared off into space as he answered.

"A name is a powerful thing, Acre. One of the greatest insults we can give our fellow man is to call one a nameless whoreson. It is what defines us while we live and for thousands of years after we die, if we lived correctly, that is. A name should always stand out, be bold, and remind you who you are. Can you imagine if I had a bland name like John Smith? Who's going to take a John Smith seriously? But Victor Monohue is strong, denoting my power and achievements. That girl is going to know what she is, my friend, a darkness overshadowing the brilliant sun of my future and nothing more until she makes it so. Eclipse Monohue has great potential as a notable name. An eclipse can be fleeting and mundane, or it can burn itself into the memories of all who see it. Time will only tell which my daughter is going to be. Just in case I'm wrong and she becomes something just.... unimaginable..... she at least deserves a name that swings either way."

Acre had withdrawn his lenses in the middle of Victor's overly-dramatic monologue. He looked at the serious face that stared into space before him. There was no talking Victor out of that name, but he might be able to spin it to his advantage. After all, it wasn't really a name, more like a space anomaly. He would have no problem convincing the child that her father hated her and a girl with daddy issues could be a powerful weapon. A better one would be if he could remove her emotions altogether, but even he couldn't accomplish that. Who knew what Victor had planned for the infant wailing in his castle right now? Her life would probably be a miserable tale, one that made jaws drop in horror, much like his own. He glanced at Victor's clenched fists, and he almost felt sorry for Eclipse.

Almost.

Then he shook off the hint of a feeling and activated his glasses again.

"You won't be disappointed, Vic. Eclipse will be the best weapon you have ever gotten your hands on, which is why I think she will be more useful if she is the only one of her kind. No one will fear telepaths if they become a mainstream thing."

Victor's eyes lit up evilly as they always did when he was about to win out over someone else.

"Arcane has fallen to me Acre. Our forces will rally and we will continue development on the Logan series and the Emily series. I can raise taxes to cover the cost. Dormiat and Ashtar will not be easy and Central Liberty will prove our worst enemy yet, but I'm a patient man. I can wait till my series are fully developed and then hit them all at once. Central Liberty will undoubtedly send aid to its neighbors, weakening their own defenses. Then, my Emilies and my Logans will end the chaos of the world and we will all be united under one banner, my own. I don't need to establish fear anymore. What I need is a massive army of unstoppable troops to help maintain it. The war is *finally* coming to an end, my brilliant scientist."

Acre furrowed his brow at that. His friend was once again staring into the distance with a look of delight on his face. A slight amount of concern triggered in his mind. He and Victor were both 48. The Promontory had no wife, but several concubines, who he had killed more and more of as time went by. McKenzie had been a strong, capable young woman when Acre sent her knocking on Victor's door. She was tall and thin, but a master with a spear and bow. Acre had spent years watching her train and hone her skills and her genetic code was perfect for the weapon he needed. When he had last spoken to her, he was surprised she even managed to grin at him with the corner of her mouth. She was an entirely different person after Victor had forced her to abort six pregnancies, because the outcomes would have been girls. Her body was destroyed and her mind was barely hanging on. Victor had sucked the life out of her soul like a vortex.

His three other living concubines raised their sons in his fortress. Victor had four sons. The oldest was Shane at eighteen, then Erican at seventeen, then Aidan at fifteen, and finally, Sean at nine. None of them had the same mother and Victor had executed the nine-year-old's mother three years ago. Her name was Leanna. Acre had insisted that Victor teach Sean the most basic techniques of torture, assuring him that the boy would make an excellent torturer.

Leanna stormed into the dungeon during their first lesson and screamed into Victor's face, right in front of all the prisoners, who cheered her on. Unfortunately, those same prisoners cheered for Victor when he threw her into their cell moments later. Sean tried to save her, screaming and crying for the villains to leave her alone and Acre quietly asked Victor to put the woman out of her misery, rather than leave her to be torn apart before her son's eyes. Victor did, of course, since Acre suggested it, but he left her there for five days first. Sean had to be yanked away from the cell door for his own safety. Despite what his people wanted to believe, most of the men Victor threw into prison actually deserved it. Leanna did not deserve what they did to her.

No one ever stood up to Victor, so killing his concubine was not enough since every mother would readily die to protect her son. He couldn't risk turning her into a martyr and rallying the public opinion against him. They had to fear her consequence more than they were enraged by it. So, he had her son watch her death from the executioner's block. His was the last face she saw in her life, and it was the most horrified as well. None of the other concubines would ever forget that execution. And neither would the 6-year-old boy who stood and watched his mother being beaten and tortured. Sean wore her only possession, a plain gold ring, on a chain around his neck from that day forward. He would never forget the broken hand that set the trinket in his own or the bloody face that tried to apologize right before the ax fell to her neck. He would never forget it. It glared out at him from his nightmares. Sean knew that he could never be like his father, if only to honor that face and that hand.

Victor loved power. He thrived on it. His crusade may have started as a plan to unify the north, but like many dictators, he had lost sight of that goal years ago. Now all he wanted was to expand further and further, till there was nothing left to conquer. He had an incredible police and Elite task force and a prosperous harbor on the shores of the Foam Sea to the east, though he rarely did anything with the sea, besides take from the merchants who sailed across it for goods. His land was agriculturally productive and his people totally submissive because of their fear.

None of this concerned Acre. He saw his friend as an incredibly talented man. In thirty years, he had accomplished what no one could in centuries. The northern tribes were now all one country. If he never received credit for anything else, Victor would always have that to boast about. What concerned him was Victor's newest plan. World domination. It was the next obvious goal for someone who had gained so much power so quickly, but Victor sometimes set the bar too high, even for himself. He believed he was saving the world from conflict and poverty, as well as the evil of magic and the unknown. His people were his sheep, and he was their shepherd. He cared for them and taught them how to think and feel. If every now and then, he needed to punish the disobedient sheep in his flock, their death served as a warning to the rest of them and they grew in knowledge and understanding.

Rebels threatened his flock, as did free thinkers, revolutionaries, false shepherds, and other countries. If Central Liberty allowed refugees from

Chrosia, everyone would leave to embrace the freedom they boasted. Victor knew the truth they couldn't bring themselves to face, though. Being free was torture. His people needed him to make their decisions for them. Otherwise, they would make mistakes and ruin themselves. If he let Central Liberty take in his people, they would be destroyed within hours! All governments besides his own had to end or there would always be a chance that his people would suffer.

He had a simple plan, really, it would just be ugly, uncivilized, and brutal. But, if a little brutality could bring about his vision of perfect peace, it was worth it. The plan was to begin a long and bloody war with each individual country, and then wipe them out suddenly with one fell swoop. He wanted them to suffer first. Of course, anyone who pledged allegiance to him as a result of that suffering would be welcomed to Chrosia with open arms and given a new home and life. Everyone else died after struggling against him for years. It gave him an excuse to build up his army and prod his people into further obedience. Then part of the enlarged army would relocate Chrosians into the empty countries and keep them in line there. It was a simplistic form of infusing the other countries into Chrosia and expanding Victor's resources at the same time.

Acre honestly did not understand why they couldn't just wipe all of them out at once and quickly or just nationalize those who really meant no harm. It would be just as demonstrative and cheaper. But as he watched the light dancing in his friend's eyes, he knew that all of his own ideas were nullified by the fact that Victor's was working. It could have been the worst plan in the world, but if Victor had come up with it and it was working, nothing would convince him to change it. Acre sighed inwardly and, once again, tried to pull his friend's mind back to the matter at hand.

"All right, so it's the Emily series, now. I hope you're impressed with them when I've finished." he said glumly.

"I had better be Acre, for your sake." Victor pointed a menacing finger at the scientist and winked.

Acre smiled reassuringly. Victor threatened him all of the time but had never once raised a hand to harm him. The scientist never tested to see how far he could push him, but he doubted that the dictator would actually kill him if the series failed. Maybe if it were a male series, Victor would take it more to heart. Anyway, it wouldn't matter in the long run if he never angered him in the first place. He was sure about this series; they would be the crowning jewel of his career, the greatest of his inventions, and the epitome of scientific discovery. Then a thought struck him just as Victor turned to leave.

"Wait! Vic?"

Victor turned around and folded his hands behind his back, waiting for him to continue.

"Do you want her to know all of this?"

Victor's eyebrows creased in confusion, and Acre realized he would have to explain further.

"Do you want her to know that she is your daughter and that she was bred to kill or shall I raise her as an orphan child and raise her..... normal-ish?"

Acre wasn't sure he had made his point, but Victor got the gist of it.

"I want her to know everything Acre. In fact, I want you to purposely set the bar for her to fail. Tell her who she is, how I let her live only to become a weapon, how she is totally subject to me. Tell her everything about this day, but never let her forget my high expectations and how her life will forever depend on her fulfilling them. After all, she must remember why she is damned with that name."

Acre nodded thoughtfully. He just wanted to cover all of his bases before continuing with his plan. If Victor approved of keeping Eclipse as a pawn, it would be easier for him to do so without looking suspicious.

"So, I need to train her as a soldier, more than raise her like a child?"

The corner of Victor's mouth pulled up.

"That's the basic idea."

"In that case, I think you should be worried about Axl."

The promontory frowned.

"What about Axl?"

"He was there, remember? You ordered him to stand guard with the Elite?"

"Yeeesssss." Victor drawled. "Why does that matter, though?"

"He just seemed......." Acre sought for the word with his lips pursed. "...overly attached to her. To the point where he almost refused to let me take her from his arms after Kenzie died. There was some connection there, I don't know how, but I think it's dangerous. He may pose a slight problem in the future if it's not nipped in the bud."

Victor just stared at the scientist. Acre waited for his response, hoping he understood the issue at hand. After blinking monotonously for a few minutes, the Promontory finally responded.

"He's three, Acre!" he cried mockingly. "And she's an infant! *Neither* of them are any threat! And there are certainly no connections taking place between them. I don't even think either of their brains are fully connected to their own bodies at their age. But I'll talk to the boy if he frightens you."

He ended with a chuckle and shake of his head. Sometimes, Acre seemed more paranoid than himself, a feat of epic proportions. Victor watched a dejected Acre nod a few times before turning and leaving the scientist to himself.

Acre sat down at his desk and rested his head in his hands, relieved. If Victor wasn't worried about Axl, he was probably right. He knew the boy better, after all, and Axl did listen to him. Finally, he could focus on the task at hand. He was absolutely thrilled with the Promontory's decision to make her nothing more than a soldier. Acre had no idea how to actually raise a child. Oh, he knew enough to keep her alive, but that was different than raising her. Feeding her and teaching her science and math and such things would be easy, but school was only half of any normal kid's life. If Victor had wanted some humanity in the girl, he would have had to teach her how to make friends and have fun and fall in love; what right and wrong were and how to think for herself.

Acre lifted up his head and rubbed his hands together. Now, he didn't have to worry about any of that. He could raise an emotionless, duty-driven weapon, who only had to know how to follow orders. He would have to teach her about hate and fear since it was the basis of all of her father's actions and Acre needed her to feel them, but that was easy. She would be stronger and less vulnerable if she was never concerned with protecting her loved ones or doing the right thing. She would never understand the emotions in her head and would therefore suppress them all of her life, as long as her sense of duty was stronger than her curiosity. That could easily be obtained with discipline and training. Her mind would be entirely devoted to logic and following orders.

A knock on the door interrupted his thinking and he got up to answer it. He expected it to be Victor with his baby. It wasn't. Acre opened the door and looked out with a smile. No one. He glanced back and forth, and then shrugged his eyebrows. He was about to shut the door when a voice piped up below his eye level.

"Hi, Acre!"

The scientist's smile faded as he looked down at Sean. The 9-year-old beamed up at him as he held his new little sister in his arms. She was fast asleep. Now, Acre didn't really like any kids, but Sean was the worst of them all. He was talkative and spunky. Although, it had died down a lot since his mother's death. In fact, if Acre had cared, he would have realized that this was the first time the boy had smiled since. But all Acre knew at the moment was that the little brat in front of him technically ranked higher than he did. In other words, he had to humor him. Thankfully, Sean didn't know it was his fault Leanna had been sentenced to death.

"Ah, um, hello, Sean. I thought your *father* was going to bring Eclipse up to me."

"Is that her name?!?" the boy asked excitedly.

"Yes." growled Acre.

Sean didn't even seem to register the aggravated tone to Acre's voice, but bounded, carefully because of the baby in his hands, right into the lab and laid the sleeping girl on Acre's own desk. That's when Acre registered it. There was something about this little baby that made Sean's heart come back to life. The scientist watched the boy with concern as he gently wrapped the blanket he had brought with his sister around her so that she couldn't roll off and hurt herself, talking to him the whole time.

"Oh, I like that name! It sounds cool and an eclipse is an amazing scientific doodad, isn't it? She is amazing, isn't she?"

Here Sean paused to breathe and stare lovingly at his little sister laying on the table. He sighed happily.

"Anyway, Acre, Victor didn't want to bring her down --something about it hurting his ego too much-- so he told me to, but I don't mind. And I'd hate for Victor to hurt his ego, he gets very upset when he's injured. I've been the baby of the family for sooo long that I'm glad she's here to relieve me of duty. That was kinda funny, huh? I think she's pretty. Do you think she's pretty Acre?"

The scientist didn't answer for a moment and his brow furrowed deeply.

"Sean, since when did you decide to call your father by his first name?" he demanded.

Sean's joy faded into angry shame and he looked at his feet.

"That man is *not* my father."

Acre just sat wearily at another scientist's station and pursed his lips.

"I was there when you were born and yes, he is. You can't change that by changing what you call him. Besides, I can't imagine the Promontory approving you speaking to him that way."

Sean nodded his head.

"He was very angry."

"Then why, for the love of all that is Ancient, would you continue?"

"He doesn't deserve to be called 'Father'!" Sean lashed out. "And he knows it!! He yelled at me, but that's it. I'll never call him by any other name than Victor for as long as I live!!"

That was actually untrue. It turned out, that as Sean grew, he learned a great many new words. He used them to describe Victor quite often.

The scientist groaned inwardly and slammed his forehead down on the desk beside him. He didn't have the energy to deal with this boy. He sincerely hoped that his new charge would be easier to handle, since he would put up with absolutely no outbursts like Sean's.

"Acre, you really shouldn't bang your head like that. You could break your.....um.... goofy glasses things."

Acre sat bolt upright and answered a bit indignantly.

"My spectacles, Sean, are tediously manufactured from a completely indestructible substance which, I'll have you know, was tested in this very laboratory and now assists in the construction of several structures of massive capacity."

Sean stared silently blinking at the scientist and Acre had a distinct feeling that the boy had no idea what he was talking about.

"Neat?" he answered uncertainly.

Acre groaned and laid his head back on the table as Sean shrugged and continued to prattle.

"Anyway, Victor says I can come see her whenever she's not busy and that I'll be helping train her. So, she has to have some free time, Acre, otherwise I won't be able to visit. Let me see her schedule as soon as you have it. Of course, you can't start training her yet, she's just a baby." his tone changed to a higher pitch before he continued. "Aren't you, little sister? You're just a baby girl, huh? Well, goodbye, Eclipse."

She awoke at some point in his narrative and was beginning to cry till he spoke to her. Now, it was more of a whimper. The boy planted a gentle kiss right on the tip of her nose and she became instantly silent, reaching her tiny hands out toward his face. Sean let her fragile fingers wrap around his own pointer finger. He sighed happily and changed back to his normal voice.

"I like that name." he cooed.

Acre looked up at Sean. He was just standing by the baby stroking her hair, which she had very little of, and staring happily into her contented face. Finally, he sighed again and walked away from her, not before again making sure she was not going to roll off the desk.

"Well, Acre, I have to go to my drills, but I'll come back right after they're done."

"You have lunch then." Acre quickly interrupted.

"Awww." Sean moaned sadly. "You're right. I guess I'll have to come back this evening. Well, I'll see you then."

He walked to the door and began to shut it behind him, but before it closed, he leaned his head back in.

"Bye bye, little sis. I'll come see you later… Eclipse."

Acre slowly helped him shut the door all the way, leaned against it, and sighed. Eclipse began to weep for her brother's attention once more. So, Sean was going to spend time with her whenever she wasn't busy, hmmm?

"I'm going to have to keep that little girl very, *very* busy."

# CHAPTER FIVE

It was midnight before the war strategist reported to the young Premier. Joey briskly walked up the stairs with his head held high and his shoulders square. The landings were empty, and a dark chill surrounded the only moving being in the castle at that hour. Torches lined the walls about every twenty feet, so it was inevitable that anyone ascending the stairs had to deal with the dark spots between them. The torches didn't mind the dark, though. They flickered as intensely as ever, licking away shadows in the empty stairway for as far as they could, only to dim and let the darkness take over once again. Then it began all over as he continued upwards. Joey was overly used to the dancing battle between torch and shadow, and he normally enjoyed watching it. Not tonight.

Tonight, he was focused on getting where he needed to be, on exerting all his anger and sorrow into strength to almost jog up the many flights of stairs leading to the very top floor of the castle. He reached the top breathless, having to bend over to allow his lungs to work better. Another horrid reminder of his age. It had been too long since his last battle to retain his old stamina. There were only two doors on the top floor. Right beside the door Joey was using was the door to the debate hall, used for informal meetings and debates. It was a way around the law system since law required everything in the great hall to be recorded. When the council had something to discuss that they didn't want written anywhere, they used this room. Or if one council member wanted to meet with a select few of the other councilmen, here is where they'd meet. Honestly, he hadn't seen anyone use it in years.

Joey straightened back up and took a deep breath, to ensure no one on the other side would know his plight, then placed his hand on the computerized scanner beside the council chamber's metal door and waited. Central Liberty did not have anywhere near the amount of metal structures as Chrosia, but it had even less computerized devices, like the scanner. In fact, the scanner was the only known mechanical device in the country. It was stolen from Chrosia several years ago, when they had tried to place a government building within Central Liberty's borders, expecting very little resistance from the nation. The building had been destroyed, but this one scanner had survived with its instructions for installment. Three years later, the Central Libertarians had just figured it out enough to install it, but not enough to duplicate it. Running the electricity was the most difficult part, but they had figured out how to use another stolen device, a windmill, to power the lock.

The scanner gave its approving beep and an automated voice welcomed him into the room. Joey pursed his lips indignantly at what it labeled him. The scanner had come with a keyboard to type in the list of names that were permitted entrance. So, one person had to sit and type in every name in the council. Since it was a rather unimportant job, a private was given the task. Each council member walked by and placed his hand on the scanner and the private typed it in. Then the councilman moved on. The private did an exceptional job for someone who had never seen a keyboard before, except with one name he made a funny mistake in the process. The keyboard was set up in alphabetical order. Well, the private hit the letter before 'j' and the letter before 'o' in Joey's name, so the voice welcomed an 'Insane Rogers' instead of a 'Josane Rogers'. It became a popular nickname behind his back, with the commoners all referring to him as 'Old Insane Rogers'. Joey could never believe that the boy had done it completely by accident.

The door finally opened, and he walked into the dark room and waited for his eyes to adjust to the lack of light. At least in the hallways there were torches and the occasional window, which let in starlight and moonlight. Here there was nothing. Well, there was a large picture window in the room near the ceiling, but a thick tapestry was pulled over it to keep out the cold, even in summer. The council chamber wasn't the largest room in the capital building, but it was the most important. Its ceiling stood twenty feet above the floor. The window had to be reached by a ladder. It was previously a hole in the wall, put there by an earlier attack from the northern tribes long before Victor came to power, hence its awkward position in the room. Stonecutters had chipped away enough to make it look rectangular and purposeful. The tapestry was pulled into place by a large rope attached to a pulley system. They may have filled the window in with stone, had they known what troubles it would cause them.

In the middle of the floor sat an immense circular table, made from the rare metal few other people had. Central Liberty was not as fortunate as Chrosia in their list of resources. They used a lot of stone and wood. There were large wooden chairs all around the table for the numerous council members, but as far as Joey could see, no Premier. Then his scanning eyes caught sight of the tall shadow standing by the large chair on the far side of the table. The figure leaned over and lit a small candle sitting on the table next to his chair, the only one lined in fur. Then he turned and went to light an oil lamp on the wall.

Joey continued to observe the room in the very dim flicker from the candle on the table. He could see the scribe on duty in the corner by the lamp, ready to record every word spoken. On the table lay two tidy stacks of official papers. Joey knew Edward Vantage enough to know that the ones on the left were waiting to be read and the ones on the right had already been handled in the Premier's very organized way. Obviously, his former candle had burnt too low, and he was just replacing it when Joey entered.

Ed was the result of one of Joey's best movements in the council. Two years ago, the old Premier was murdered by one of Chrosia's trained assassins. His heir was highly capable of the position, but Joey knew that Central Liberty needed someone with more of three things: self-control, abstinence from wine, and organization. The council was ready to place the old Premier's heir, whose name was Vincent, into position, when Joey made a motion to call someone else. Aside from offending and enraging Vincent, Joey got the council to vote on whether to give him the position. For a vote to pass, it had to be unanimous. Only one person refused to get on board with Vincent, but no one minded pushing Joey's opinion under the carpet. The council decided, for the first time in history, to ignore one of its voters.

Joey was furious, of course, but he showed it to no one. Instead, he drastically, and falsely, accused Vincent of treason. He was proven innocent, but under Central Liberty law, no one accused of treason, whether proven innocent or guilty, was allowed to assume the position of Premier. Obviously, Vincent burned with anger, but the law stood, and Joey nominated Edward Vantage. The entire council sulkily agreed, rightly assuming that Joey would just keep accusing other nominees until he got his way, so Ed was the new Premier at 23, the youngest age ever, and Vincent was reduced to the status of Major General. He never forgave Joey, though most of the council had by now, because truly, Ed was the best thing they could've asked for. And now he spoke before Joey could even fully focus on him.

"You have my congratulations, Joey.............. and my sincerest condolences."

He was focusing hard on lighting the oil lamp by the scribe.

"Thank you, Your Honor." Joey answered. "I'm here to give my report from Arcane."

The Premier turned from the lamp he had finally lit to face Joey. Everyone knew that Joey was stiff, maybe a little insensitive. Actually, everyone pretty much believed that he was heartless, but Ed couldn't believe that he wasn't aching inside at the loss of his wife, the one person he had sucked up enough of his pride to openly admit that he loved. At least, he didn't want to believe that Joey didn't care she was gone.

"It's past midnight, Joey," Ed answered gently. "and you've already had a long day. Why don't you go ahead and wait till morning?"

He gave the war strategist a sympathetic smile, hoping to give him a break. Joey was entirely uncooperative.

"Do you believe I am incapable of performing my duty, Your Honor?"

The Premier stopped smiling before Joey had even finished talking. Recognizing the other man's tone, he sighed, knowing it had been a long shot. Anything he said now would only insult the older man in front of him. If he said yes, well... that was obvious; and if he said no, Joey would ask why he thought he shouldn't report tonight, and Ed would be stuck either lying or mentioning the events of earlier that day. Finally, he decided just to play along. Of course, that was nothing new, everyone eventually gave into the war strategist. Sometimes Ed wondered who really was the Premier.

"Go ahead." he groaned as he sat down in his chair.

Joey nodded his head sharply in approval and began his report.

"There is no need to send any support to the Arcanards at this point in time, Sir."

The Premier's eyebrows shot up in surprise for two reasons. One, he had been under the impression that Arcane was desperate and two, Joey didn't normally give such short and blunt reports. No, there was more to this that the strategist was hoping to avoid talking about, but Ed knew him well enough to know that if he asked questions, Joey would answer fully and honestly.

"Really?" he asked carelessly, trying to avoid appearing reliant on his war strategist's cooperation. "Why do you say that?"

Joey didn't say anything for a minute. He knew that the Premier was trying to conceal the fact that he desperately wanted the whole story, but he also knew that no one would be ready to hear how bad their situation was. Everything that he had witnessed sent chills up his spine and made him fear for the continued existence of Central Liberty. Nothing prepared the Premier for his next statement.

"Your Honor, Arcane has been wiped out."

Ed just stared at Joey's face. The full impact of what he said hadn't sunk in yet, but the Premier knew that his previous banter with the war strategist ended there. Politics were often fun and games to the men on the council, but when something real went down, they always found a way to unite. Arcane had been doing fairly well in the fight against Victor. How was it possible for Victor to wipe them out so suddenly? It didn't make sense.

"What?" he whispered.

"We saw the battle, Sir. The Arcanards didn't even have a slight chance.

There were thousands of Chrosian soldiers and on top of that, there were giant metal men, the likes of which I've never seen before. Victor had them beat from the moment the first blow fell, but..." Joey stared into the distance.

"What, Rogers, but what?" the Premier prodded.

Slowly Joey's eyes fell back to meet Ed's. They were as unreadable and insensitive as ever.

"He didn't let the battle play out, Ed. He killed most of the Arcanard army, and half of his own, with some sort of explosion."

He sounded distant as he watched the terrible scene play out in his head again. He had been in the command tent with the King and his highest officers when there was a loud, vibrating explosion out on the battlefield. They all covered their ears and waited for the noise to end. It rang through their minds like a bell for several minutes and a few people passed out from the pain it caused. By the time Joey managed to stand and look out to the field, there was no battle, or field, really. Whatever Victor did, it left a massive crater and no bodies.

"They all just...... disappeared." he whispered to Ed, seeing the rest of the battle in his mind.

Even Victor's own men were in shock and didn't charge the tent for the first few minutes. Joey had time to bid the King farewell and escape on his horse in the deep snow. He had to warn Central Liberty and return to his wife, otherwise, he would never have left them all to die alone. It was King Ruohart's final rally against the Chrosians, and Joey turned around to watch him and the rest of his men, numbering barely 1000, mount their steeds and charge Victor's forces. They had to protect the keep behind their lines, where the last of the Arcanard women and children hid in terror.

Joey watched them hit the Chrosians like water on rocks. Victor had placed his enhanced soldiers in the back on purpose. These men were un-killable. Even if they were stabbed through the heart, they rose back to their feet in seconds and kept fighting. Joey had never seen anything like it, but he assumed it was the Jaspar series he had heard so much about. Once they defeated Ruohart's army, they invaded the keep and slaughtered his people. Joey had to flee just as it began to snowstorm. A small force mounted horses and gave him chase. His trip home was delayed by how long he had to hide and avoid main roads, even though he wasn't sure they were still pursuing him. It took him almost two months to reach Feldon's Peak safely.

The Premier closed his eyes and sat down in his chair. It was moments like these that made him feel ten thousand years old rather than 25. They reminded him how helpless his own people would be against a Chrosian attack. They would fall quickly and fall hard. No one would come to their aid. Everyone else would be busy fighting their own battles, losing their own homes to the fierce warrior in the north. He rested his head in his hands and his elbows on the table. He too, could see the scene.

Hundreds of soldiers fighting for their lives screaming dreadful things, begging for mercy and then........ silence, complete and utter silence. He also thought of the Chrosians whose lives ended with their victory. He wondered how many of them had planned on returning home. He began to wonder if all of them were truly evil. Then, his head stopped wondering and became infuriated. No, they were evil, all of them. He swore right then that no Chrosian prisoners would ever survive while he led this country. He would kill them all as they killed the helpless people in Arcane. Yet while his head cursed them, his mouth focused on the issue at hand. He shook off his regret and sat up straight.

"What about civilian rescue teams?" he asked, grabbing a quill and a clean sheet of paper to print his instructions on. "How big of a force will you need and what supplies can we send to-------"

"They'd have no one to save."

The Premier's mouth dried in an instant as he slowly looked up at Joey's face. It was completely passive. His voice did not break, and his eyes did not water one bit. In all, the strategist appeared as if he could care less about the words he had just said. On the other hand, Ed was shocked into immobility. How? How did Victor find within him the strength to end lives so carelessly? How could he have completed a total genocide maneuver without anyone suspecting it? *No one to save.* The words echoed through the empty trains of thought in his mind.

His anger burned as he again thought of the soldiers who helped such a man complete such horrific actions. Where were their consciences and their morals? How could they..... how dare they? The premier's resolve grew stronger as his anger compounded. The only way he would ever win this war was through annihilation of the enemy. On top of all this, Joey's complacency annoyed him. How could he not care about the death of thousands of innocent people, most probably little children who never had the chance to live life. How could he be so apathetic? Especially now, when he had his own innocent, defenseless child to protect. Vantage took a deep breath and came back with a helpless, but calm answer.

"Were they all..... killed?"

"No."

The premiers head shot up to look Joey in the eyes. If there was anyone left at all, he felt as though he needed to save them, even if he had to walk into the very capital of Chrosia.

"Then, why wouldn't we send a rescue team? Assemble as many men as you need and get them out of there!"

The premier stood up and headed for the door, expecting to carry out his own orders, but as he walked past the war strategist, Joey grabbed his shoulder and held it. As soon as Ed looked at his friend, he knew something was wrong. Joey sighed as he let go of the Premier and looked at the floor. Ed felt his gut dropping into his toes.

"What, Joey?"

"No, they weren't all killed but we can't do anything to help them, Sir. According to Ruohart, before Victor even began his initial main attack on Arcane, he had his men sweep through the nation and kidnap a bunch of their children. Every child under the age of two. This was back when there were only skirmishes and Ruohart truly didn't see Victor as much of a threat. Then these 'Jaspars' were introduced, and they began wiping everyone out about three years ago. They were ordered to slaughter everyone, including any new infants. So, it wasn't Victor's love for children that made him save them. The other children were all taken to Holux. We are nowhere near ready to mount an attack into the center of Chrosia. Our best course of action right now is to fortify and strengthen our numbers. We need to wait and see who Victor's next target is before offering assistance. I know both Dormiat and Ashtar are begging us for support, but we need to watch our own borders until Victor makes his next move."

The Premier bit his lower lip and reflected on his former resolve to enter the capital if needed. It dissolved before Joey's logic. He was right, they didn't have anywhere near the number of troops they would need to complete the march to Holux, the Chrosian capital, let alone attack it.

He nodded to Joey and walked back over to look at the lamp burning on the wall.

"I'm sure you're right, Joey. There is absolutely no way we can save any Arcanards from Victor now. Dammit."

He sighed and watched the flame dance. It reminded him of how fragile his country's existence was. One breeze from the north and they would fall. Then it would be Central Liberty's infants being hauled away. His eyebrows creased as he tried to imagine what Victor wanted with the girls. He voiced his thoughts.

"Why in hell would Victor want the baby girls? I would understand boys as forced laborers or forced soldiers, but *girls*? Why not just wipe everyone out and move his own people in? It's not like he's having issues with population and needs more people."

A weak grin split Joey's face. During war, girls almost became a burden to everyone. They had to be protected and fed and other such things while their men died to save them. Almost everyone ended up with a negative opinion of females during war, not quite as bad as Victor, but along those lines. Joey was no different. He often thought it would be best to just send the women and children south till the war ended and at least give them a chance to live and a chance for their men to fight, knowing they were safe. Then, he thought about a specific girl he had just lost, and his grin disappeared. He felt as if he had underestimated her and under-appreciated her......... and now he could never fix that. He swore if he ever got the chance again, he would do better and look at the good, not the burden. His eyes stared off into space as he slowly and deliberately answered the Premier.

"Girls have their uses, Your Honor. Maybe Victor has a new trick up his sleeve. I doubt they will serve his army as soldiers, but there are other ways......"

Ed was thankful he stopped there. He had recently had his very first child, a little girl. He desperately hoped that she wouldn't become a plaything for Victor's army one day. He tried to focus on Joey instead of that. The war strategist was squinting, like he had forgotten something in his report. Then he remembered.

"By the way........ we have to repair the dam again."

Vantage frowned at the war strategist to see if he was joking. He wasn't. Ed stared through Joey with pure hatred in his eyes. He was tired of this war and the casualties and the mass murders, but he was absolutely *sick* of repairing that stupid dam!!!!! He spun around and clenched his fist, looking for something to take his anger out on. The oil lamp was his only outlet. As he threw it to the ground, he envisioned it as the kingdom of Chrosia and guessed that it was as close as he would ever get to defeating it. The scribe used his cape to put out the large flame that resulted from the lamp breaking while lit. Joey and Ed watched him calmly. Then the Premier took a deep breath and ran his hands through his hair before heading back to his chair and plopping down into it.

"Why'd you sign me up for this, Joey?" he asked as the scribe lit a new lamp.

The war strategist went and sat next to the young man with a sigh.

"Because you were the only chance we had of getting rid of Vincent."

The Premier snorted with a grin. Vincent *would* be an awful premier, he admitted to himself. Joey was wise to get him out of office. Ed leaned his head back with his eyes closed and moaned.

"We've repaired that dam three times in the past five years."

"Victor has all this worked out to a science. His system allows him to keep his people thinking that he's protecting them, that he's actually on their side. He uses that ravine because it's within our borders. The Chrosians believe that we are killing countless of their kin. Not in their wildest dreams do the people believe that their promontory would be murdering his own troops out of fear of what he's turned them into. It's genius, though barbaric. Victor doesn't have to take any blame on himself, and he turns his people against us, which keeps us from helping them."

And therein lay the problem. Victor controlled every part of life in Chrosia: education, outside information, news feeds, military training.......

everything. No one in Chrosia ever assumed that they didn't have the absolute best life imaginable, because they were never taught anything else besides what they saw on a daily basis. Vantage knew this. For a while he was formulating a plan of invading Chrosia and turning Victor's own people against him, but that plan was crushed when spies reported that Chrosians were all rather submissive and held Central Liberty in absolute disgust. They had been trained from birth to loath their southern neighbors.

Central Liberty would have to conquer the entire nation to win the war everyone knew was coming and there was no possible way to do it. Chrosia was more than ten times larger than them, and their population count was even exponentially higher than that. No one could beat the northern terror unless it became divided against itself, but Victor made sure he had a tight hold on his own people before he began his conquests. In a way, the war was won already, before Victor had even attacked Arcane officially. Everyone had let him come to power in the north without resistance because they thought it would be healthy for all the northern tribes to be united. Victor was regaled as a visionary when Ed was a kid. Then he turned south, and everything changed. At this point, the Premier saw his job as procrastinating annihilation as long as he could and praying to the Ancient for a miracle. All this ran through his mind as he answered Joey with a far-off look.

"Well, we can't keep stopping soldier drills to repair the dam and we can't spare the men to guard it even if we do."

"Your Honor, we have to fix it. That dam holds our emergency reservoir and right now its draining into an empty ravine where no one can use it. This is the wet season. It will fill our irrigation system just fine, but unless we get that dam up, we won't have a chance this summer. We have too many dry weeks to risk being left without a source of water large enough for the entire capital." Joey pushed.

The Premier took a deep breath and sighed. He didn't really want to think or talk about it at the moment, but he couldn't come up with any way to appropriately change the subject without sounding like he was avoiding the problem, which he knew Joey wouldn't let him do. Joey sensed his intention and decided to help him out. They didn't really need to talk about it anyway. They would end up using the same system to rebuild the dam as they had the last three times. The soldier unit would put training on hold and rebuild it in the next year. Then they would go back to training. Their men were just as efficient at construction as they were at fighting, sometimes better at the first. Joey decided to talk about his future instead.

"About my boy...." he waited to continue till the Premier looked up at him. "I think I'm going to make him my apprentice."

The Premier's eyebrows furrowed as he realized what this meant. Every person on the council got to pick their own apprentice and the council had no right to object or change his choice, unless he became a traitor or committed a crime. However, the apprentice usually had a say in the matter.

"Sooooooo........ you're going to pick your own son's career?"

"Not really," Joey shrugged. "I'm just thinking practically. I'm going to be a single parent and I can't risk letting him out of my sight. I want to make sure he's raised right....... the way his mother would have wanted; so that he uses his brain more than his muscles."

The Premier stuck out his lower lip thoughtfully and nodded as Joey stood, gave a slight bow, and walked towards the door. He hesitated till Joey reached the door and then spoke up.

"So, you're going to pick his career?" he asked again.

Joey turned around and answered with a slight grin.

"Basically."

Vantage said goodnight with a shake of his head. Who was he to teach Joey how to raise a kid? Joey answered with a cordial 'good morning' and then bowed again and walked out the door. He paused after he shut it behind him. The council chamber was on the highest level of the old stone castle, the tenth floor. So, he had plenty of time to think as he walked back through the stuffy stairways to his suite on the third floor. The castle had the Great Hall on the very first floor through the main double oak doors. It took up three-quarters of the surface area, the rest of the floor being occupied by the kitchen behind the back wall in the hall and the staircase. The Great Hall was capable of holding about 2000 people comfortably, but they had packed in double that at one time when an enemy raid left thousands homeless and lost without a thing in the world. There were ten massive fireplaces to help heat it, but it was normally rather cold. On the right wall just inside the door was the first staircase. It was big enough for five men to walk up shoulder to shoulder. When it reached the second floor, there was a hallway that led to the opposite side of the building where it continued up to the third floor and switched sides. It continued this pattern all the way to the top, where Joey now stood.

There were eight floors in between the two most important rooms in the castle. Each floor had two suites for members of the council who did not live on the fiefs they governed. These unique individuals included the war strategist, the doctor, the treasurer, the premier, who actually had the entirety of the ninth floor to himself and his family, the major general, the head psychiatrist, the head mason, the four head trainers, the citizen officer, the stable master, the head cook, the head housekeeper, and the head blacksmith. The only rooms not in use were the major general's quarters, who was the lord of the Honor's Oasis fief, so he had a smaller but separate castle approximately 250 miles to the south, and the medic's quarters were empty, since Alex and his family lived in the house adjacent to the infirmary, so they could be more accessible to everyone in the capital. Every other room was inhabited by the proper individual and his family.

Family.

Joey refused to focus on that word, but it still clung to his mind. He was a politician, which meant he believed that he had to be eight-faced. Only with Annie had he ever truly been himself. He told her things that would horrify anyone else, but she smiled and nodded through it all. Everyone else saw him as a stoic, uncaring, old grouch, as brilliant as they knew he was. He was ever so slightly more agreeable with his closer friends like Alex and his own older brother, Marcus, who was the citizen officer.

Joey's biggest problem was that he had absolutely no idea how to be a father. He could only assume it was like being a general. All good generals loved their men, but they expected perfection of them. Likewise, Joey loved his son but also expected perfection of him. Had he asked for advice, he may have realized his many mistakes, but he didn't really know anyone experienced in the art of raising children. Alex only had a two-year-old son. Antilles was the doctor's first child, and the Premier had a new baby girl, also his first. Joey sighed. He was an old man with a bunch of young friends. He didn't think he had anyone to seek help from.

As Joey reached the oak door with his name engraved on a brass plate screwed to it, the most unearthly sound met his ears. He burst through the door and quickly shut it behind him to try and contain the noise, which was twice as loud on the inside. Every suite had half a floor's space for five bedrooms, a living room, a dining room, a study, and a bathing room. But Joey didn't see any of these inside his door. He saw a long hallway with four doors on each side and one at the very end, all of them labeled with brass plates telling which room it was. All the suites were built this way. Joey knew the awful noise was coming from the one labeled 'living room' and decided to risk opening that door. Marcus was walking around the room, gently bouncing the screaming bundle in his arms, trying everything in the world to get it to stop. Naturally, the baby screeching was the awful noise. As soon as Marcus saw Joey he rapidly strode across the room, handed the baby to his father, grabbed his hat and coat off the wicker couch, and walked out the door, talking the whole time.

"Well, Joe, it's been screaming like that ever since you left. Won't eat, sleep, or even shite. I've done my hour of babysitting for the year. You can schedule me for any time next year, and I will make it a priority on my calendar. Good night, goodbye, and good luck."

With that he walked out the door and slammed it after him, leaving Joey alone holding a screaming infant. Joey looked around hopelessly for a second before clearing his throat and addressing his child.

"Now, Duke, this behavior is unacceptable and unnecessary. It is nothing more than a disgusting display of temper."

The baby stopped crying and looked at the new man who was holding him, only just then realizing it wasn't Marcus by the change of voice. He stared at his father for a whole two seconds, in which Joey decided that parenting wasn't as hard as he thought, before he burst right back into his 'display of temper'. After four times of trying to correct the infant and not even getting the precious two-second response anymore, Joey decided that it would be more logical to try to appease him instead. But Marcus was right, he wouldn't eat, sleep or........ anything. Joey kept trying till the alarm bell began to ring to wake up the soldiers.......... at five in the morning. The baby once again silenced at the new sound piercing the air. It rang four times and in his own silence, the infant fell asleep. Joey stared at him in shock, He couldn't believe it!!!!!!! After bursting his lungs all night, he only fell asleep when there was something louder than him!!

"You scream when I want to sleep and sleep when I have to go to work. How am I ever going to sleep myself?"

It took him a second to realize that he was asking a question of a sleeping infant and probably wouldn't get an answer. Even if the baby was awake, he wouldn't respond. Joey sighed. He was far too familiar with not being answered; few people had the guts to do it. He walked out of the living room and down three doors in the hallway to the one labeled 'Baby' and opened it. He had never been in this room, but he knew the engraving on the door would be changed as soon as possible to 'Duke Justice Rogers'. He looked around the room. There was a wooden cradle about chest high just to the right, against the wall, a swing and crib to the left, and a huge sanitary rug covering the hard, stone floor in the middle. Joey nodded approvingly. There was nothing overly elaborate about the room and it was neat and organized. *Just the sort Annie would design*, he thought. Immediately, his mind darkened. He had a sickening suspicion that this wouldn't be the last time he would wish she was there. His thoughts were interrupted by the doorbell ringing.

Joey jumped when it pierced the silence and shot a panicked look at the baby, praying with all his heart that it would stay asleep. Duke stirred but slept on. Joey gently laid him in the cradle and ran out into the hallway, hoping to reach the caller before they rang the bell again. He swung open the door and barked at the lady on the other side with a little more heat than he intended.

"WHAT!!!"

She jumped back at Joey's sudden appearance. Instantly, he regained his composure and stood up straight and tall, brushing off his clothes.

"Yes, Clara, how can I help you?"

Clara was Alex's very beautiful wife. She was chubbier than most women in the capital, which made sense because she was the best chef in the country. Her pies were to die for. Her light brown curls were normally pulled up in a tight bun with several fly-away strands protruding over her entire head. She was short, 5 feet or so, and he had never once seen her with a bad attitude. Clara raised one eyebrow and looked doubtfully at the war strategist.

"Rough night?" she asked with a slight smile.

Joey shrugged his eyebrows and shoulders, trying to act as though he had everything under control, but either from the circles under his eyes or her female intuition, Clara saw through him like glass. But knowing Joey, she very skillfully hid her chuckles in her throat. He stepped aside and held his arm out into his house with a beckoning bow. Clara nodded politely and walked in, letting him close the door behind her.

"What can I do for you, Clara?" he repeated.

She took a deep breath and spun around to face him.

"Well, that's what I came to ask you, Joey."

Joey paused. He had a gut feeling that he knew where this was going. She was going to offer to do all the things a mother normally would, and he appreciated it, but he remembered promising his late wife that he would do those things himself, whatever they were. He very coolly walked past her and welcomed her into the living room.

"Whatever can you mean?" he asked, avoiding eye contact.

He shut the door behind them and turned around to see her tapping one foot with her eyebrow raised and arms folded. He sighed.

"I'm fine, Clara. I think I'm fully capable of raising my own son." he pointed out.

Clara rolled her eyes and shook her head.

"Joey, no man is capable of *having* kids on his own, so I would say there's a pretty good chance that no man is capable of *raising* kids on his own. It's just a simple fact of nature. It takes a couple."

"Clara, I'm 42! I can't get married again. Not now."

Clara thought briefly about reminding him that he had just gotten married for the first time last year but decided to drop it and press her point.

"Joey, I'm not telling you to get married again. That would be an unfair opinion on my part. All I'm asking is that you let me help you. I'm not trying to take her place or her son, Joe, I just want to help."

"Hey, you only have one child as well. How much can you know that I can't guess?"

Clara could feel his defensiveness more than she could hear it and it upset her. She began to play defense, too. She was just trying to help the stubborn old coot. He didn't need to be such an ass about it. Her voice changed from a plea to a matter-of-fact.

"You were the baby of your family. I have four little siblings that I helped take care of. I think I know just a little more than you. And my mother died when my youngest sister was born, so I did *everything* for her.

Goodness, Joey, Marcus probably has you beat since he's older!!! He at least watched your parents raise you, which I imagine was terribly difficult."

Joey looked at her adamant expression and considered what she was saying. He had to admit to himself that it was tempting. He would have someone to watch the boy and do all the less-inviting jobs for him. He was angry that she brought up his mother and father, but she didn't know not to. He didn't share stories of his childhood if he could help it. Joey stretched his back out as he realized how exhausted he was from the previous night. Maybe he could use the extra help. After all, he couldn't ask Annie for it.

Annie.

*Now, please, please promise me just one thing. That he will know his father well and that you will never give the privilege of raising him to anyone else.* Her words echoed relentlessly in his head. He had made a promise. If he got too relaxed and let Clara do things for him, it was only a matter of time before his son drew closer to her family rather than to him. He wasn't as fun as them and he would lose the 'privilege' of raising his son to them. And Joey had never in his life broken a promise. And the last one to his dearest love was not about to be his first to break.

"No." he said forcefully.

Joey watched Clara blink in disbelief at his sudden tone change. She opened her mouth to object, but he held up his hand to stop her.

"I said no." he repeated. "He's my son and I'm going to raise him. Please, Clara, this is something I must do. I promised Annie."

Clara sighed. She knew she had lost with that. She couldn't ask him to break that promise, no matter how much she doubted that Annie made him promise to turn down all help. If that's what he believed he promised, she wouldn't change his mind. Joey saw the look of despair on her face and walked over to her, placing one hand on her shoulder. The other he used to lift her chin. Small tears streamed down her cheeks, but Joey's voice didn't soften at all when he spoke again.

"You have to understand. I want to do this. It's my responsibility, just as it's my responsibility to keep this country safe. You would never ask to help me do that job, so you must never ask me if you can help me do this one."

Clara took a deep breath and then let it out.

"Can I at least bring Antilles up to visit him often? Alex and I were hoping that he and Duke would be good friends."

Antilles was her two-year-old son.

"I have no objections to that. However, don't pull the bell anymore. He almost woke up when it rang."

Clara gave a slight smile and nodded. Then, Joey walked her to the door and watched her walk down the hall till she turned, and he could see her no more. Then he went and plopped down into the wicker chair in his living room. He needed to rest before he went to work in his study, but his mind reflected uncomfortably on what had just happened. Slowly, his regret turned into resolution. He was sure he knew how to raise a son. After all, he had been one once and he knew all the mistakes his parents made. Duke would follow him everywhere and learn his future job from him. It was only logical to make his son his apprentice. What he didn't realize was that he was placing the world on his infant's shoulders and turning into a master not a father.

"Yes," he said to himself. "we'll be just fine."

If only he had remembered the rest of his wife's words. *You will be a good father Joey, don't ever doubt that, just give him all your love and teach him well.*

'Love' was swiftly downsizing on the war strategist's list of priorities.

# CHAPTER SIX

"Monohue, get back on your damn feet right NOW!!!!"

Ten-year-old Eclipse knew that voice. She opened her eyes and swiped the blood out of them with the back of her hand. Then, feeling every muscle in her back, she kipped up to her feet, only to have her opponent's foot land squarely on her chest and knock her right back down. She decided it would benefit her to use a different strategy. This time, she rolled backward, pushing the floor away with her hands, and landed on her feet......... in a crouch. Amy Gershon, her opponent, assumed that Eclipse would stand up, since that was the standard next move. So, she swung around in a circle to add more power to her kick. This would normally knock the other person out and the match would end. The only problem was that when Eclipse did not stand up, Amy's foot, expecting to hit resistance, traveled past the point she had calculated and threw her off balance. Eclipse took advantage of that very second to make her move. She sprung up and drove her fist into Amy's right jaw, just below ear level. That punch had all the strength of her legs, back, and arm in it. Amy flew backward and fell unconscious on her back.

Though she could hear the technician in charge of the gym clapping for her victory, none of Eclipse's muscles relaxed. She had been burnt before by letting her guard down too soon and decided never to let it happen again. Standing several feet above in the gym's overview orb, Acre subtly lifted his fist in front of his chest and pulled it down in triumph.

"What?" the voice made Acre jump and straighten up. "She has to fall twice in order to actually land a single hit? After dodging and blocking for an hour and a half? Why is that so impressive?"

Acre swallowed and cleared his throat to hide his enthusiasm before answering the voice, which happened to belong to Victor Monohue.

"Victor, Amy has already been through the Enhancer. She has accelerated mind activity and advanced agility and flexibility. Theoretically speaking, there is no way on the face of the planet that Eclipse should have been able to beat her. But Amy is too impulsive. She flies into action too quickly, trying to constantly rely on her feelings and instinct..... her 'gut', if you will. Eclipse was raised to use her head and follow drills. She just beat someone who should've been able to wipe her out in two seconds. And she even used physics to do it. How is that *not* impressive?!?!"

Before Victor could answer, the buzzer went off, signifying the end of the match and hailing Eclipse as the winner. Only then did she relax out of her ready position: fists up, shoulders hunched, legs apart, knees bent, and up on the balls of her feet. She stood up tall, casually turning around, and headed for the gym door. She only knew that she had ten minutes to get to archery practice. Her mind was in the future, the past was forgotten. Victor watched curiously as she walked away a champion. It was getting harder to beat her. He had promised Acre at her birth that he would prove her a failure and, so far, he couldn't. She excelled at almost everything she did. She had just beaten someone twice her status in a battle he had personally set up for her to lose.

Amy was one of his favorite Emilies. He liked her anger and hatred. It fueled her to try and best Eclipse at every turn and, normally, she was the only one who could do just that. Her attitude was very close to his own, making her even more agreeable to him. He could appreciate her impulse and rashness. She had the very things he thought his daughter lacked, when in reality, his own strict rules and criticism held Eclipse back. His gaze drew in on his daughter like a hawk on a mouse. He would prove her useless, yet. Then he looked back across the room at his favorite. She was up!! He almost visibly jumped at the sight. Her right arm was drawn back by her shoulder, a glowing purple orb dancing in her hand. In one smooth movement, she pushed her hand out in front of her and the ball of translucent color flew at a very unsuspecting Eclipse.

That orb was nothing other than visible mental energy, or telekinesis. It was the extremely valuable outcome of a month in Acre's masterpiece, the Enhancer. The person's preference designated the color unconsciously. Purple and pink were immensely popular among the young telepaths, but these orbs were not just flippant girly toys, they were weapons. A carefully thrown orb could feel like a thirty-pound sledgehammer driving into its target.

And Eclipse took its full force on her back.

This was radical cheating and Amy knew it. No act of aggression was permitted after the buzzer rang and enhanced students were not permitted to use their powers against their un-enhanced colleagues. The Emilies had one girl left to go through the process, which was the one Amy had just used her telepathy on. If either of these rules were broken, the perpetrator was immediately accused of cheating in a war-prep game, which could be punished by death, depending on the severity of the injuries the victim sustained. However, Chrosia did not condemn cheaters. Victor had cheated his way into his position and saw no reason to kill those who acted as he did. He only killed the weak and unsuccessful. So cheating was perfectly legal, one was only punished if they cheated......... and then lost. The idea of these games were to get to the top and crush everyone else at all costs. So, as long as you won, you were allowed to use any method you chose. The end justified the means, and Amy was starting to take advantage of the system.

The force of the orb threw Eclipse right into the gym wall. Acre and Victor watched in silence as a sickening smack rang throughout the room. The wall itself displayed a large red splatter as Eclipse bounced off it and thudded onto the floor. Victor rolled his eyes and looked right down his nose at the scientist, who was grimacing at the wall as if it hurt him just to look at it.

"Oooooohhhhh, yes. Verrrrrry impressive." Victor snorted.

Acre turned his head slightly toward his friend, but his eyes were riveted on the motionless girl.

"Wait for it....."

Unless Eclipse was dead, Acre knew she would be up and moving any second now. She was trained to ignore her pain and finish the fight, no matter what. It helped her develop a high pain tolerance over the few years of her life. Victor rolled his eyes upward but looked obligingly back at his daughter. He *almost* gasped.

The small, beat-up figure was dragging her own dead weight through the room by her arms. She crawled away from the wall and managed to prop herself up on her hands and knees just past the place where she landed. She sat there, gasping for every breath she took for almost a minute and then, while everyone in the room watched in shock, she forced herself up to her feet.

Eclipse stood at attention and stared straight ahead. Her clothes were shredded, her face swelling from impact with the wall. Her right eye was so swollen, it was shut and bulged out from her face like a ball. She was covered in blood and dust. Everyone in the room thought it was the most hideous sight they had ever seen. But there was beauty there, too. She was calm and collected. Her common sense told her not to fight back, as that would be cheating and she knew she couldn't win, but her stance told Amy that she had also not won, and she was therefore a losing cheater. Amy could not have picked up the signal any clearer and decided to remedy her situation.

She channeled her telekinesis through her out-stretched arm and picked up Eclipse with her mind. Then she swung her arm across the room toward the opposite wall. Her victim moved with her hand. The wall dented this time when Eclipse flew into it, and the impact was too much for her. She fell ten feet to the floor and lay motionless, too exhausted and damaged to move. Amy waited. Waited for her to get up or roll over or......... anything really, but there was nothing left for her opponent to do but lay there, a defeated warrior. Amy smiled. Now, she had won and was therefore guilt-free.

Eclipse's eyes fluttered open just in time to see Amy through a haze of blood. She spun arrogantly on her heels and stalked out of the gym, with a flip of her long, golden curls and a nod at Victor. Of course, she made sure Eclipse had woken up enough to catch her smug smile before turning to go. That was just her way. Win by cheating, and pretend to be better. Eclipse groaned and struggled to push herself up onto her knees, slowly trying to stand, but her hand slipped on a pool of her own blood, and she slammed right back onto her face. Above, Acre couldn't bring himself to look at the arrogance he knew would be dancing in Victor's eyes. He knew that Eclipse was in for some intense punishment. Not because she did anything wrong really, just because she lost. Still, Acre grinned inwardly. His plan became more of a reality when Victor constantly put her down, trying to make her feel like a failure. It helped him deal with the monarch's cocky attitude. Someday he would prove the man wrong. Little did he know that Victor was actually impressed that his daughter was still awake. Perhaps she was stronger than he gave her credit for. He couldn't show it, though. He was trying to win a bet against Acre.

The overview was a huge glass sphere that moved around the gym using anti-gravitational forces. It allowed officials to view the battles below from all angles without putting themselves in harm's way. The controls were inside to direct it, like the dispatch button, which lowered the ball slowly to the ground. Victor punched it with determination. When they touched down, the door opened, and he stalked off toward his daughter, who had finally managed to reach attention and had wisely stayed where she was. She knew the drill. She fought an opponent and whether she won or lost, her father came down afterward to tell her what she did wrong. Leaving meant facing his inquiry later. She quickly learned which way was less painful, but today she wasn't so sure. Her body ached and burned as she stood straight and tall for her father, but she had been taught from birth to keep a poker face in any situation. Her eyes remained stoic and passive as Victor stopped two feet away from her. She looked past him into space, knowing better than to make eye contact.

"What the hell was that?!?" he asked angrily.

*Huh...... he didn't yell*, Acre thought, a little too quickly. Maybe Victor was warming up to Eclipse after all. He looked desperately at the dictator's face, hoping to see it strewn with the usual disgust. He had to admit, Victor didn't look as red as he normally did. Acre bit his lower lip. He was going to have to deal with this.

Poor Eclipse swallowed hard twice before she could muster up the courage to respond. She already knew she had the wrong answer. No matter what she said, it would be utterly incorrect because no matter what, she had still failed. But, of course, not saying anything was just as bad and would cost her dearly. She took a deep breath and answered.

"I failed, Your Excellency, it will never------"

"HAPPEN AGAIN!?!?!?"

She jumped and made her second mistake. Eclipse looked into his eyes. They were on fire. It drained every lick of courage she had in her entire body. He stood over her and screamed straight into her face, his saliva spraying onto her. She had to look away before he continued.

"You're supposed to be ready for the Enhancer in a week.... a WEEK, Eclipse!!!! And you still can't even handle a little duel!?! If you can't win without telepathy, you'll never be better with it. So, here's the deal."

He paused to let his voice calm down and she looked directly into his eyes in shock. Had Acre been paying attention, he would have realized that this was the first time Victor had ever called Eclipse by her first name to her face. Normally it was 'Monohue', 'Private' or 'soldier'. Acre missed it entirely, but Eclipse didn't. She stared up at Victor's face in surprise, a nice kind of surprised. The 'maybe in the future we will get along' kind of look. He wasn't used to seeing hope in his daughter's eyes and he realized his mistake. Victor bit the inside of his lower lip in shock at himself. He didn't make mistakes. He hadn't in 40 years. Suddenly, he slipped up because of Eclipse?

He was actually a little worried about the small girl in front of him. She was bleeding in multiple places and most likely had damage inside he couldn't even see. His throat struggled to swallow as he realized that he might just care about her a bit. There was something about her that kept nagging at his will to remain distant from her. He couldn't tell her, though, so he had to find a way to get her some help without admitting any of this. It would be fine if he got her to archery quickly, where Sean would dote on her as much as he legally could. A quick glance at Acre told him the scientist was oblivious to his name-calling mishap, so Victor had to do something drastic to distract him from it before he noticed.

"You will face Amy every day this week, and by the time your treatment is ready on Firstday of next week, if you have not beaten her....."

Here he grabbed her chin and forced her to look into those horrid eyes again, though she was already staring into them with such excitement. It made him hesitate to hurt her so badly with his next words, but it was necessary. Just imagining her physical pain at the moment Victor jerked her head around made Acre wince ever so slightly, but not as much as Victor's next words.

"I will personally execute you."

Victor's heart groaned inwardly as her face drastically fell, including her jaw dropping a bit. She had spent her entire life trying to prove that she had a right just to live in his fortress with him and her brothers. A right to be called family and be treated as such. He had raised her hopes just to dash them against the floor and let them shatter into pieces, and she didn't even know what hope was! She gulped a few times and let her pain fade into numbness. There was still a stabbing in her chest, but she assured herself it was just a wound. Emotions had no place on the battlefield, Acre always said. And her entire life was a battlefield. She forced her face into its regular stoic state.

Acre's mouth and eyes both widened in shock. Victor meant it!!! If Eclipse couldn't beat Amy in ten tries, he would kill her. She was so close to being exactly what he needed. Acre looked at the little girl's face in horror, afraid to lose all his progress on his scheme, but Eclipse took it much better. Her facial expression did not change. Only her eyes showed the disappointment in her heart.

"Do you understand me?" Victor demanded.

"Yes, Excellency." she answered evenly.

Victor jerked his hand away and stepped back.

"Good." he said in the same tone.

He knew he had to hurry the process along to get her medical attention.

"Now get to archery practice."

Eclipse grit her teeth and began walking across the gym to the door at a strong, dignified pace, pain searing her flesh with every step. It was all she could do not to pass out. She said the alphabet backward and forced her mind to focus on anything but the agonizing pain.

"And you better not be late!!"

She ran.

By the time Eclipse stumbled into the archery range, the other girls in her series had gone through the daily briefing and were getting their bows. All 500 members of the Emily series had been through the Enhancer already, except for Eclipse, so she was viewed as an inferior. She entered the range and turned to the computer screen on the right to sign in. Her right eye was swollen completely shut by now and she couldn't see through the blood running over her left from her forehead. She glared at the screen, trying to see her name when a flash of movement caught her eye, and a computerized voice assigned her to her booth number. She looked up.

He stood there smiling at her; his scraggly blonde hair twisting and turning all over his head like vines. She could always recognize the image of her nineteen-year-old brother, blurry as it was at the moment.

"Hey Sean." she muttered, and his smile widened.

"Hey." he answered, pulling a bottle out of his coat pocket.

Sean always wore a heavy, leather trench coat, even when he was fighting. It set him apart from all the other soldiers who wore basic gear and gave him a little added protection since it was thick, strong leather. The tails of it fell to just below his knees.

"Here, put this on your eye, it'll help you get it working again."

He handed her the bottle of salve, and it took a few tries for her to grab it from him. Then he reached into a different pocket and pulled out a sweatband for her.

"Wrap this around your forehead, it'll soak up the blood till Acre can help you at lunch."

"Alright."

She grabbed it from him and walked toward her locker. Sean turned and watched her go. He sighed. No 'thank you' or nod of appreciation, just an 'alright, I'll follow your orders'. He waited till he was sure no one could hear him, especially her.

"Love you, too, Eclipse." he grumbled.

Eclipse passed half of the girls in her series. Her locker was the last one on the right side of the range. The building was one huge room divided into individual firing booths. They were all numbered, so each person knew where to practice. There were 250 lockers on each side with 500 booths following, each divided by ropes hung on poles.

As she walked by the girls, rubbing salve liberally on her eye, she could hear their nasty taunts and remarks. She didn't really want to deal with them right now. Archery practice started in five minutes. She did turn to watch Amy point out something about her to the other girls. The entire group giggled and covered their mouths. Eclipse grit her teeth till they scraped and forced herself to look away. She just didn't have the energy.

Eclipse looked at her clothes as she turned toward her locker. Surprisingly enough, all the Emilies were allowed to pick their own styles and colors for their daily clothing. It most likely had something to do with the fact that Victor really couldn't care less what the girls wore. Most girls picked pretty things with their favorite colors vibrantly displayed. Eclipse was the only one who dressed for practicality and chose black and gray. Of course, her clothes right now were tattered and stained with blood, but she had learned long ago to keep a change at each training station. She walked up to her open-faced locker and pushed a button on the side.

Vision screens slid out and blocked the three sides that her locker did not. Then she stripped everything off, except the sweatband Sean gave her. Everything was ripped or soaked in blood, so it was useless. After putting on her cotton underwear, she pulled a black tube of material out of her locker. It slipped over her head and covered her torso from the armpits to her hips when placed correctly. It was as tight as it could be without causing health issues or discomfort, which helped her maintain good posture. It also added a little more protection to her stomach and chest because it was made out of a sturdy material. The next thing she put on were her pants. They were also black but with tiny white thread lines running horizontally across them. They were snug but did not restrict any sort of movement. Then, she slipped on her black crew socks and boots. Their black leather was form-fitted to her feet and calves and stretched all the way to her knees where they folded down to reveal the gray insides. The white laces crisscrossed up the sides with perfect x's, so all Eclipse had to do was tie them under the portion that folded down.

She pulled on a black tank top. It helped hide certain things when she didn't wear her top shirt, which she threw on after her chain mail. Her chain mail was not big and clunky as one might assume, it simply looked like a long sleeve shirt that matched her pants perfectly. If someone looked very closely, they could see that the entire shirt was made of tightly woven metal links. They had tested this shirt and not even a spear driven into her stomach at point-blank range could penetrate through. The inside had a comfortable lining that prevented the mail from scratching her arms. It was form-fitted to keep it from snagging.

Her gray top shirt was her own design. It was functional, but it added a feminine touch to her outfit. The quarter sleeves ended in graceful droops that gradually grew larger from her elbows down, like angel wings. They weren't large enough to get in her way, just enough to reveal some of her mail shirt underneath, coordinating her entire outfit together. The top shirt was knee-length, and the bottom was rugged, as though the true bottom had simply been ripped off. The neckline was wider than most shirts, but she had several layers beneath to hide what needed to not show. This shirt's only purpose was appearance, and she knew it, but she had made up something else when Acre asked why she needed it. Then, she finished her outfit with a wide black belt that wrapped around her hips. It was empty for now, but Eclipse knew that one day it would hold her swords and daggers. She practiced with them daily but was not permitted to carry them till after her enhancement, which meant she was the only member of her series who did not have weapons on her belt at all times. It was mortifying.

It normally would have taken her less than a minute to change, but every bone and muscle in her back groaned with the slightest move, doubling that time today. *Three minutes left,* she thought, as she reached for her bracer. The girls all had archery bracers, which were simply guards that covered most of their lower arm so the string didn't snap them. Eclipse had the only black one in her series. Normally, she hated the differences between her and her peers, but this one was actually on her side. The bracers were color-coded. The color showed the level of the wearer. Green, the color most of the Emilies wore, was only level three of ten. Black was ten.

Technically, no one was ever supposed to reach level ten, because the qualifications were that you beat all of your instructors. No one had ever accomplished this, so most people ended on level nine, dark red. Eclipse, however, had been practicing archery since she was three when Jackson, the head archery instructor, gave her a stick with a string attached. Exactly a week ago, she amazed her instructors with an unusual shot no one had ever seen. They simply labeled it 'the Terror' and not one of her instructors could pull it off. Knowing her father would be displeased, Jackson had reluctantly exchanged her red bracer for the black. Not because he didn't think she deserved it, but because Victor would make her life more miserable because of it. She slipped it onto her arm now and tightened the laces, remembering that day. It had been the best in her life so far, but Jackson was right, every day since had been a nightmare.

The bracer looked more or less like a fingerless leather gauntlet. It fit snugly on her left arm under the gray shirt but over her mail. Its white laces formed x's on the inside and outside of her arm and tied off on the outside to stay out of the bow's way. It extended into points on the back of her hand and her palm with a thin, leather strand running in between her pointer and middle fingers holding those two points together. Eclipse tightened and tied the bracer with her teeth. Then, she pressed a button in her locker and the back wall of it spun around to reveal a mirror. Her hair was a mess. It fell sloppily out of the low ponytail she always held her brown strands back with and the sweatband only made matters worse. Eclipse pulled both it and her hairband out and ran her fingers through her hair. With her vision back to normal, she replaced the sweatband and divided her long hair in half, pulling it over her shoulders. Then she looped both sections through the band and out the bottom of it by the back of her neck. The extra she pulled back into a low ponytail and braided over her right shoulder. It was simple and slightly uncomfortable, but it incorporated the sweatband into her hairstyle, so it didn't just look like a blood rag.

She had one minute left. She didn't have a clock, but training had taught her to estimate time well since she was just a toddler and Eclipse had perfected the art. She grabbed her two quivers, which were connected together in the shape of an x, out of her locker and slipped them over her upper body, with the straps crisscrossing comfortably over her chest.

"Electrified on the left and normal on the right." she muttered to herself as she grabbed her 50 lb. bow and set her locker back to normal.

The mirror flipped back, and the vision screens sucked into the wall. Then she spun on her heels and jogged down the range to the last booth before the drill room at the end of the building. Most of her series were already trying to hit their targets, and Sean was frustrated with one girl who kept yelling at him because she couldn't hit anything. He pursed his lips and raised his eyebrows at Eclipse as she passed. Technically, Sean outranked everyone in this room, since he was Victor's son, but that didn't keep the

Emilies from blaming him for their lack of skill. He smiled at his sister through his frustration and Eclipse let the corner of her mouth twitch up in reply. She was getting used to the pain of moving any body part now and jogged the whole way to her spot. Booth 500 was hers every single day. She liked being on the end, if only Amy didn't have booth 498, beside her.

Electrified arrows were the crowning achievement of Acre's military inventions, minus the Enhancer. Unfortunately, his design was based on mathematical equations and science, not what's convenient in an actual battle. At first glance, they looked just like any other broadhead arrow, but the head was larger than normal. This alone made them more difficult to fire. When the arrows were in their quiver, they were dormant, and each of them had a socket inside the quiver where their points rested when not in use. However, as soon as an arrow was removed it began a countdown and the archer had an exact amount of time to fire the arrow at a target before it activated. A dial on the quiver changed the amount of time the arrow counted down.

These quivers generated a magnetic field within them, fueled by the many tiny solar panels that covered the outside, and caused a chemical reaction with the arrow to activate it. When they finally activated, the arrowhead split open into four triangular sections that often fell uselessly to the ground. Inside were eight minuscule, but highly charged, darts that fired spontaneously at different angles when the triangular panels opened. Then the arrow, with a smaller head, also hidden under the panels, continued on its original course.

The trick was to plan your timing so perfectly that the darts hit eight people and the arrow hit one, killing a total of nine people with one shot, but no one could ever manage this. It took a gifted eye to envision the perfect situation in which all nine targets would be lined up exactly by the time the arrow reached them. Perfecting the timing to have the arrow open before it hit something was hard enough for most people. Often, more than one dart hit a single target, wasting potential for the weapon. And even more often, the arrow opened inside its target, electrocuting an already dead man. The reason they were standard issue was because it was impossible to miss, and most people at least got one or two soldiers. Eclipse hit all nine...... every time. This was the Terror. No one else had ever accomplished this once, let alone several times a day. Even Jackson and Sean struggled with the electrified arrows.

Eclipse fell into position 100 yards from the ten targets at the end of her booth. Made of microscopic shards of metal, they were shaped like soldiers, some short, some tall, some thin and some wide. A technician controlled their movements like they were actual people and they fell like one when they were hit. Acre had designed a type of magnetic field that only affected that particular metal, so the tech could control them and move them, but they were solid enough that weapons stuck in the targets still. It had no impact on the metal arrowheads.

Out of the corner of her eye, she caught Amy firing and grounding her arrow 10 feet short of the target. Most of the Emilies had only been practicing for two years versus Eclipse's seven. They could usually hit their target, but they struggled with difficult shots. Amy normally fell short. All of them were highly inconsistent, which made them unreliable. It was part of why many of them picked on her. She was the instructor's pet in archery, and most of them were failures. She didn't care. Archery was her one escape from everything going on in her life and she wasn't going to let a bunch of jealous little girls ruin it for her.

"Monohue!"

Eclipse spun around at attention for her drill master, Jackson. She wasn't sure why he was here instead of Sean, but she knew better than to let that change her responses. He was the head archery instructor. Even if she technically outranked him, he deserved her respect.

"Yes, sir."

The master let a smile crack his lips apart. The Emilies were assassin trainees. They were definitely of more value to Victor than him, a forty-year-old drill master. Technically, Eclipse was of higher rank than everyone else in the room, besides Sean, not just because she was Victor's daughter, but because of that black bracer. So, she had the right to ignore him or treat him like an inferior along with the rest of her series, but no, with her he had always been 'sir'.

"I'm calling out your drills today. Make ready!"

His last words were a command. She nodded and spun around to face the targets again. Then she turned to her right and spread her feet precisely 18 inches apart with her bow in her left hand, held perpendicular to her body, which was perfectly erect. Her left hand tightened and loosened eagerly on her bow. The drill master nodded approvingly. She was ready.

"Draw!"

Eclipse raised her bow and nocked a barbed arrow from her right quiver, holding the end between her first and second fingers on her right hand as she drew the string back to her shoulder. *DAMMIT!!!!* She sucked air sharply in through her teeth. Pain shot through her spine with the draw-back action. She stopped there, slowly brought the string back to its normal position, and lowered the bow. Jackson watched, confused.

"You alright?"

He managed to keep his concern buried, for the most part. Honestly though, he knew something was wrong and he was worried. He liked this girl. Most people who knew her did. Sure, she was a little stiff and arrogant at times, but she was good at everything she applied herself to and she was simply...... naïve. That was a unique combination to find. He'd never seen her take advantage of anyone. She seemed less and less like her father every day.

Eclipse glanced at Amy. Of course, she was watching right then, a smirk on her face and an evil spark in her eye. Eclipse decided she was just going to have to push through the pain today. Again, she pulled back her bow, grimacing through it till she could easily rest her right pointer finger under her right ear. She focused on controlling her breathing to ignore the stab in her back. Jackson managed an uneasy smile and cleared his throat.

"Aim!" he ordered, continuing with, "Fire!"

Twang, hiss, thud!!

"End!"

One of the computerized targets fell as her arrow thudded into the center of his skull and she yelled her ready-for-action call. Jackson grinned and nodded to himself. She was just fine.

"Alright, Monohue, I'm going to call out your drills. Perform them perfectly and sound your call when you've completed them. Be sure to listen for specific target numbers."

Again, he noticed the hand action on her bow. She was always like this at archery. It was like she couldn't get enough practice. *Anticipation*, he thought. That could be an assassin's worst enemy. He decided to test her in the area. He took a deep breath.

"Three, two, si---"

"End."

Jackson almost jumped. Each target fell before he even finished saying the last one's number, and he spoke quicker for her than some of his pupils twice her age. He shook his head, trying not to compliment her, since Victor forbade this. He had to wait for the targets to pop back up before giving his next exercise. Jackson rolled his eyes. It took the technicians longer to reset the targets than it took Eclipse to drop them. Finally, the booth was ready once again.

"Three, two, si-"

"End." And they waited again.

"Three, two, si-"

"End."

More waiting.

"Three, two, s-"

"End."

That was exactly what Jackson was waiting for. She expected his next call and fired earlier than she had before. She was anticipating his calls. No doubt she thought the next one would be 3, 2, 6. He had a little surprise this time, though. The targets all rebooted, and he yelled out the next drill.

"Three, two, ei-"

"End."

This time Jackson just stared. He had changed the last number and with no hesitation, she had fulfilled his request and not shot the six at all, but hit the eight squarely in the throat. The master deemed that worth the risk of a low whistle. *Nope,* he thought, *no problem with over-anticipating.* He shook his head and placed his hand on her shoulder to get her attention.

"Eclipse, I think you just need to spend your time freelancing it from now on. I'm not sure what else to do for you."

"Just a minute, Jackson."

Again, Eclipse knew that voice. So did her drill master and neither of them liked hearing it in the range. Jackson winced before turning around to face Victor. Eclipse watched her father and Acre walk toward her with Sean close on their heels. She looked at her brother, trying to read his face. Victor had never come to watch her at archery, probably because she was actually good at it and Amy wasn't. She wanted Sean's eyes to tell her why he was here today, but her brother wouldn't even make eye-contact. He was worried about something, and it made her uneasy. Victor didn't address her, he spoke only to Jackson, but his tone made her heart tremble, though her face remained stoic.

"I'd like to see this 'terror'." he challenged.

And just like that, Eclipse suddenly knew what was wrong. He had come to take her one success, her golden feat, and turn it into a mockery. He had come asking to be impressed but never planned on becoming so. He was there to crush her, and Sean knew it. As did Jackson, but no one questions Victor. She felt her breathing pick up in anger. Archery was her safe space, as much as anywhere could be safe for her, and she wasn't willing to let her father take that from her.

The drill master bowed to the dictator and turned around to face Eclipse. He gave her the same smile Sean always gave. It made her feel small and helpless, as if that was how they all saw her. Had she ever heard the word, she would have known it was sympathy, but her emotional education was limited to hate and anger. When Jackson finally nodded, she was relieved to turn around out of his gaze and take her position. She stood flexing her fingers on her bow as usual but didn't make a move to fire. She had some time while the techs set up her targets again and she put it to good use.

Something felt out of place. She had a gut feeling that she was about to fail, but that didn't make any sense. She hadn't missed this shot since the very first time she had made it correctly. Why would her father's presence change that? The targets rose and started to charge. No big deal, she still had a few seconds before she had to fire. Her quiver was set for a short distance. Her gut told her something was still wrong, but her head reasoned out of it. Jackson mistook her hesitation for nerves and tried to help cover for her.

"Fire at will, Monohue." he said reassuringly, hoping to make it appear to Victor that she was obediently awaiting an order.

He actually made things worse. Now, Eclipse knew she had to act before her debate finished. She took a deep breath and reached over her left shoulder, grasping the feathered end of one of the electrified arrows. Anyone who could have seen her face knew she was counting down. Her eyes closed as she hit three. Two, ONE!! With one smooth motion, she opened her eyes, drew the arrow, and fired it. The moment she released, she knew she had it, but that gut feeling spiked as she watched the arrow fly.

It spun off to the left and fell worthlessly to the ground. It then proceeded to activate. One dart hit a target's foot. That was the only kill. Eclipse stared at it, visibly shocked. There was no possible way that arrow could do that on its own!! She knew she shot it correctly, she felt it the same way she always did. No, something was wrong with that arrow. She took one step toward it and then froze. No one had access to her locker but her. No one could've tampered with her arrow before her shot, but she was standing in a room full of spiteful telepaths. And furthermore, she was pretty sure she knew who had the guts to tamper with one of her shots as she fired it. Then, she became enraged. Eclipse spun on her heels and shot a barbed arrow straight through Amy's foot before anyone even realized what she was doing.

# CHAPTER SEVEN

Four voices filled the air simultaneously, drawing a crowd of curious Emilies.

Amy screamed.

Sean, Jackson, and Acre all yelled at Eclipse in unison.

She ignored them all, strode over to the rope dividing her booth from Amy's, and dropped her bow over her colleague's head so that her neck was between the belly and the string. She turned the belly parallel with Amy's shoulders and pulled the girl's head toward her own till their noses were only an inch away. She grasped the bow, one hand on each side of Amy's head, with her own fists facing herself. Then, she braced her elbows against Amy's shoulders. She applied just enough pressure on the back of her archenemy's neck to keep her from struggling. Amy yelped and glanced at Eclipse's eyes. She should have never made eye contact; she couldn't break it after that. She stared into Eclipse's eyes and realized that she definitely was Victor's daughter. Her eyes caught fire, just like his. Even though her eyes were ablaze, Eclipse kept her voice calm and even.

"Do not *ever* interfere with one of my damn shots again."

Not only was it the first time the girl had ever used strong language out loud, but the order also demanded a reply, and when Amy didn't give it Eclipse pulled harder on the bow. Her rival cried out in pain and burst into tears. She was terrified.

"Okay, okay!!! I won't, I swear!"

Her eyes never left Eclipse through her pathetic plea or through the shorter girl's next movements. Eclipse backed up and spun the bow counterclockwise, flicking it off of Amy's head with her left hand, while her right hand grabbed the shaft of her arrow. Only then did she blink, and the fire extinguished right before she yanked the arrow out of Amy's boot... and the floor. The action raised Amy's foot so high, so swiftly, that she lost her footing and flew onto her back with her feet still in the air. Eclipse spun around and walked back to the center of her booth as she twirled the arrow around in her fingers and slipped it back into her quiver over her shoulder. Amy was furious and mortified, a dangerous combo. She scrambled to her feet and fired a purple orb twice as big as the one in the gym straight at her attacker's back with an enraged scream.

Eclipse knew it was coming this time. She ninja-rolled to her left, dodging the orb, but she accidentally bent her bow backward at the same time. It snapped. She didn't have time to care. Instead, she jumped up and, like everyone else in the crowd, watched the orb. It flew at tremendous speed and blew a hole in the wall that separated the range from the drill room at the end of the building. It didn't stop there either but blew a hole in the end of the building, too. Bolts of telepathy ran across both walls like lightning and finally collapsed the entire end of the building. The girls all screamed at the loud crash. Everyone else stared with wide mouths and eyes.

Victor was the first to recover. He pursed his lips angrily and glared at Acre, who was lucky to be staring at the end of the building rather than his friend. This series was getting expensive. He swore he would kill them all if they didn't start making up for it soon and spun on his heels to face Jackson. The drill master was still staring in amazement at the visible sky and ground out the gaping hole in the building.

"A-HEM" Victor growled through his clenched teeth.

Jackson jumped and fumbled with the whistle around his neck. He blew on it fiercely.

"Penalty!"

The crowd's attention snapped back to Eclipse and Amy as the latter stomped her foot down on the ground in fury.

"Oh, you *think*!!??!?!" she bellowed. "She falsely accuses me! She *shoots* me, and you're only NOW calling a damn penalty!?!?!?"

"You're absolutely right, Amy!"

Everyone turned and looked at Sean as he butt into the conversation. His face was red with anger, and he wasn't about to let Amy get Eclipse into more trouble than she was already in. He was at least going to make sure she got into just as much trouble.

"He should have called it a while ago..... when you interfered with a colleague's shot!" he grimaced.

"I didn't!!" she snapped back. "And there's no proof that I did. I'm the victim here!!!"

Sean pursed his lips. One accusation was hardly proof. Technically speaking, Eclipse could have just made a bad shot. *Technically*. Anyone who knew his sister definitely believed that something interfered with her shot. Eclipse didn't miss. But Amy was right, they had nothing on her, and it made him furious. There was no way to prove what a telepath did or did not do. He knew she did it, but he had no evidence. Luckily for him, Eclipse remembered his tip about really listening to what people said and turning it against them. She spoke up for herself, calm and collected as usual.

"If you didn't interfere with my shot, why would you swear never to do it again?"

Amy's face melted with guilt and rage as she slowly looked back toward her nemesis. Eclipse continued.

"You've already provided proof yourself; I was simply the means used to obtain it. You shouldn't worry too much about your failure," here Eclipse risked taunting her rival. "fear often causes cowards to give themselves up, one way or another. It's a staple part of Chrosia's success."

Amy's jaw dropped indignantly. The little brat was actually implying that she was afraid of her! And deep down inside, she was a little, but no one could ever know that. Certainly not the promontory, who was feeling closer to his daughter than ever after that last bit. It was incredible how much she picked up on as a ten-year-old. He was starting to see how intelligence could be as important as strength. He wasn't ready to welcome her into his life, yet, but he gained a bit more respect for her. Amy desperately tried to find a way to drag her reputation.

"I am NOT afraid of anything, YOU least of all. You are an inferior creature. You have no enhancements, no abilities, no life, and therefore absolutely NO value! I'm not afraid of failure. YOU are!"

Eclipse was good at hiding her thoughts and feelings, but that last part hit home. She was afraid of failure, because she was afraid of it being the only outcome of her life. Her every breath depended on her ability to kill and to win. If she was failing at these, she became more and more worthless in her father's eyes. And right now, she was losing an argument and knew it. Victor bit the inside of his lip, actually hoping Eclipse could win this fight. That bit about fear she just said was gold. She just needed to prove that she could shut down Amy. Unfortunately, Eclipse couldn't think of anything to retort; she was too focused on what was just said. Reluctantly, she mentally added another tally to Amy's wins. Then she turned the subject back to the actual problem.

"You still interfered." she muttered, to Victor's disappointment.

Amy's smirk said more than any words could. She knew she had won and that was good enough for her,

"All right!!" Jackson finally cried out. "You can stop arguing over who's to blame because I'm penalizing both of you."

"But---" Amy protested.

"You," he cut in, pointing his finger at her, "are charged with interrupting an associate's drills, using your telepathy against an un-enhanced associate, and destruction of government property."

He waved his hand toward the end of the building before continuing.

"Your penalty is an extra hour of archery and five laps."

Amy nodded sulkily. She hated archery and running. Her punishment fit her well. However, her heart lightened as he began to address Eclipse.

"As for you Eclipse, you are an entirely different matter. You are charged with destruction of government property ---because of your bow--- interrupting your associate's drills, and injuring an associate."

Eclipse's eyebrows shot up in surprise.

"With all due respect, Sir, I didn't injure anyone." she said defensively.

And the whole room stared at her. No one had any doubt in their minds that injury occurred. Jackson turned around and looked at Sean, who looked over at Acre. All of them seemed to think she was crazy. After all, everyone had just seen her shoot through Amy's foot. Perhaps her injuries from the gym were affecting her mind? Acre cleared his throat and walked up beside Jackson, hoping to jog his girl's memory.

"Eclipse...... you shot her through the---"

"Boot." she finished for him. "I shot through her boot."

Several surprised faces greeted this claim. No one thought it was possible, but Eclipse was known well for honesty, even when it was slightly, or highly, inappropriate. It was a trait many valued in her. And she really had nothing to hide. But could anyone fire through a boot without hitting its wearer's foot? Jackson just had to know. He spun and pointed at Amy. His false respect for her died in his search for truth. This time, he was going to give the orders, not take them.

"Gershon, give me that boot!"

Amy snorted indignantly. She had absolutely no intention of obeying the orders of someone with a lower rank. He had the authority to penalize her, yes, but not shout out orders to her. Instead, she spun around and picked up her bow with a flip of her head.

"No."

Jackson rolled his eyes and looked at Acre. Acre shrugged. He was only a personal trainer and a scientist, so his authority was of no use against Amy either. She could just as easily ignore him. They looked at each other for a second and then both spun around and looked at Sean. The boy jumped slightly and gave them both a questioning look, but not too noticeably. Victor saw it anyway and bit his lip to hide his grin. Sean finally got what all the adults figured out. He was a member of the Logan series. That meant he was on the same status as Amy, except he was the promontory's son. So, he had her outranked........ by a lot. Sean stepped forward threateningly and stood beside Acre.

"Give it here, you little snake."

Amy turned around and stared straight at Sean's face. She knew her place here. She knew that she would be rebelling against authority to refuse.

She also knew that Victor was the only authority she had to answer to for her plan to work. The girl was actually quite brilliant. At 12, she had a plan already in motion to take over all of Chrosia. All she needed to do was gain the promontory's respect. Being as rebellious and obstinate as he most likely was as a child was the start.

Answering to his authority alone was a risk that she didn't want to take yet, but more was riding on keeping her boots safely on her feet than anyone knew, because Eclipse was right. She hadn't touched Amy at all. She had simply anchored her boot to the floor. As of right then, Amy was the only person who knew this, and she wanted to keep it that way. Her plan required always besting Eclipse and she didn't know anyone who could pull off that shot as spontaneously as she had. If she let everyone standing there know that at 10, Eclipse was the absolute best archer in the country, her plan would take more effort. Plus, she couldn't risk Victor being impressed with his daughter. So, she took the lesser risk. She kept steady eye contact with Sean as she answered.

"No."

It seemed as if the entire room gasped and then held its breath. Even Victor lost his stoic composure for a brief second and raised his eyebrow in respect. He guessed that his daughter was telling the truth based on Amy's behavior. That's what shocked him the most, her skill. He knew Amy well enough to accept her behavior as natural. The problem he was faced with was similar to hers. Did he want everyone in that room to know that Eclipse was exceedingly gifted in archery... in anything really? No, he didn't, not yet. He wasn't ready to throw out his own plan of replacing her with someone better. But something else was complicating the situation for him. As soon as Amy told Sean no, Victor knew he would be the next person they all turned to. His decision would affect the way his people thought of him. Victor honestly vied for the approval of his people. He wanted them to love him for saving them and hold him dear in their hearts. Right now, that approval was centering around someone other than himself.

He was smart enough to realize that any time this happened, the people chose a new leader in their minds. Normally, he would destroy the reputation of the favorite and people would begin to hate him or her more than they ever hated Victor. Of course, the other guy was framed, but the plan often worked. This time was different. Every person in that room was rooting for Eclipse to the point where putting her down was no longer an option. It would only serve to make her a martyr and anger them into higher action eventually. By now everyone was staring at him, waiting for his call. So, Victor could either risk an uprising now or in the future or he could play the good guy just this once... and support his daughter. Maybe it was fate telling him to give her a chance. This could be the turning point in their relationship that ended both their problems. Curiosity won him over.

What would it be like to have a relationship with his daughter?

"Take it off, private."

Amy's face went deathly pale. Disobedience now warranted death. She didn't understand!! He didn't like Eclipse any better than she did. She knew he didn't! Amy looked angrily at Victor, but he gave her a slight nod of reassurance, a very slight nod, so she removed her boot and dropped it in Sean's hand. His whole arm sunk with the weight of the boot.

"What the--" he muttered flipping it over.

Sean observed the bottom of the boot for a few seconds, poking his pinkie finger into the hole. Then he yanked it out and shook it. It was bleeding. He sucked the blood oozing out of his finger before freezing as he realized what had just happened. He looked up angrily at Amy.

"You dirty little cheater!" he snarled.

Amy looked up at the ceiling in mock innocence and the idea made itself clear that she was not going to respond. Jackson held out his hand for the boot. When Sean didn't see it because he was still glaring at Amy, he just yanked it out of the boy's hand. Jackson took one look at the hole in the boot and tilted his head to Acre. Victor also walked over to join the huddle.

"Look at this shot, Your Excellency!!" Jackson whispered, handing the boot to Victor. "She angled it through the toe and sole but didn't touch Amy's foot."

Sean walked over just as Victor flipped the boot over to try and insert his pinkie finger.

"I wouldn't do that if I were you, Victor!" Sean muttered to his father.

Victor grimaced at Sean. He had never won the boy back from calling him by his first name. It was embarrassing and infuriating, but nothing would convince him to kill his own son, idiotic as he was.

"Well, you obviously aren't me since you *did* do it, but would you mind explaining to me why it was a damn fool idea?"

Sean started by pursing his lips to make sure he used the correct tone, despite what he wanted to say.

"I cut my finger when I reached in and I'm pretty sure rubber isn't sharp so here's what I think is going on. I think Amy has metal plates of some sort custom-built into her shoes to help her kicks feel more solid in the gym."

Again, Victor's eyebrow rose. He knew Amy could be rather devious, but he had no idea that she was also so intelligent.

"It's a rather ingenious idea, don't you think?" Victor glanced up at Sean, who snorted derisively before answering.

"Only if you don't have the skill to win without cheating."

Victor shrugged his eyebrows as if conceding the point.

"Soo...... what do I do, Excellency?" Jackson asked Victor, who simply shrugged and handed the boot back to him.

"Penalize her the same way you were going to. Just charge her for aggressive behavior rather than causing injury."

Jackson nodded and took a deep breath as he turned back around and cleared his throat. He was at least going to make sure the whole crowd knew Eclipse missed Amy's foot.

"Private Monohue, you indeed did not injure your associate but you are still pressed with the former charges..... and aggressive behavior."

Jackson hesitated to observe her reaction. Eclipse simply waited for him to continue with utter apathy. She knew he had to do something. Whatever it was, she was going to have a harsher punishment than Amy, so she would rather just get it over with.

"Your penalty is 15 laps and an extra hour in throwing practice."

Amy shot Eclipse a haughty smile. If there was anything Amy bested Eclipse at, it was throwing weapons. Eclipse simply ignored her and nodded gracefully at Jackson without the slightest change of expression. Jackson eyed the two girls suspiciously for a minute. He was rather old-fashioned and liked to see repentance after he corrected someone.

"Is there anything else you two would like to say?"

Both girls knew he wanted to hear how they had learned their lesson. Neither cared to give him that answer. Amy shrugged her shoulders and answered 'no' before turning back to her practice. Eclipse, on the other hand, saw a chance to have the last word and took it. The corner of her mouth twitched up as she answered.

"I'll see you in the gym tomorrow, bitch."

Sean, Jackson, and Acre were taken aback!! This was a whole new side to their calm little girl. Eclipse was normally the one to accept her lot and never complain, but this time she willingly fired back. Worse yet, she stared straight at her father when she said it. At first, Victor's entire body burned with fury. His eyes caught fire and even Acre had to look away, but not Eclipse. She held his gaze for a long time while a slightly recovered Jackson dispersed the crowd. And when she finally did look away, it wasn't out of fear or shame like normal. It was out of defiance. Then, and only then, did Victor allow the corner of his mouth to twitch up. His daughter had more guts than he gave her credit for. He appreciated her daring nature, despite it complicating matters between them.

Eclipse had no idea what a bomb she had just set off, but Sean did, and he feared for his sister's life. He ran to get her a new bow as an excuse to get away before tears of frustration hit his eyes. No one understood Eclipse better than Sean and he knew that she had just figured out Victor's motives behind supporting her. His father was still a human being and at times he showed the blaring imperfections of one. He had gained more and more power year after year of his life till now and he still tried to gain more as he began conquering the southern kingdoms, but he had reached a new point in his life. He was now afraid to lose that power.

By the time Sean got back to Eclipse's booth, he was totally composed, and everyone was waiting for him. He had only been gone a minute or so, but it had been a long, silent minute except for the twangs of the bows around. Amy was missing shots left and right with great rage written plainly on her face, but everyone knew she wouldn't dare use her telepathy again. The fact that Victor looked calm again told Sean he had come up with a plan and the smile on Acre's face told him that the scientist had put a bug in Victor's ear. That made Sean feel better. If Acre had a say in Victor's plan, then he knew it wasn't going to hurt Eclipse. In fact, it would probably help her in the long run, but the scientist knew how to make it *seem* like it would hurt her so Victor would agree. He handed Eclipse her bow with a slight wink.

Jackson called all nine targets up and gave the order to fire at will. Eclipse stood at the ready, breathing evenly. There wasn't a nervous bone in her body this time. Finally, in a split second, she drew an electrified arrow and fired at the center target. The corner of her mouth twitched up.

*Perfect.*

Partway to its destination, the head deployed its darts, and eight targets violently shook and fell as they were hit by them. Then the arrow sunk into the center target's chest, and it fell backward onto the ground. Eclipse turned around and stared straight into her father's eyes. He did his best to look unimpressed, but it was getting harder after the day she'd had. Her face bore the same rebellion it had moments ago but this time, he didn't let it bother him. Instead, he broke the heavy silence resting on them all by clearing his throat.

"Private, you will spend the rest of today's archery time in the drill room."

He glanced at the end of the building where the drill room was supposed to be and had to do a double-take. *That's right*, he thought, seeing the demolished pile of materials that used to make up the drill room.

"Nevermind," he corrected, impatiently. "just stay here and practice on your own until we get the drill room rebuilt. You'll have an extra hour of archery practice every day. However, I also want you to join the Logans in the weight room for an hour each day and you definitely need more time in the gym's drill room. Acre, can she survive losing three hours of sleep to extensive practice?"

Eclipse looked pleadingly at her trainer. She was already exhausted at the end of each day with eight hours of sleep. She didn't think she could take working with only five. She also didn't understand how much this would help her in the future. Instead, she felt betrayed by her trainer as he answered.

"I think she can, Excellency! I'll start her off tomorrow. But, if I may, why is she training with the Logans?"

"I want her using a 200 lb. bow as soon as possible. So, Eclipse you will wake up two hours earlier and go to sleep an hour later. This will be your schedule after you get out of the Enhancer as well..... if you ever get into the Enhancer that is. Our deal from earlier still stands."

He lowered his voice for the last part, but Sean still caught it. *What deal?*

"Yes, Excellency."

Victor tried not to grin at how unwavering she said that.

"Well, then, I guess I'll go assess the damage at the end of the building."

He turned to go, then stopped and looked back.

"Oh, and Eclipse?"

"Yes, Excellency?"

"You're going to run your penalty laps with the Logans during lunch."

"Yes, Excellency."

And that was it. Victor continued walking and Eclipse turned back to her practice. The only one confused was Sean. He watched his family members act totally natural, but he knew at least one of them had a devious scheme. He looked at Acre. The scientist was smiling after Victor but when he glanced at Sean, his face went back to normal and he jerked his head toward the front of the building, beckoning the boy to walk with him. Sean complied.

When he was sure they were out of Eclipse's hearing range, Sean finally spoke up.

"What just happened?"

Acre burst into a chuckle, obviously pleased with himself, and the boy just stared at him. What had Acre pulled off that he couldn't see? Finally, the scientist calmed enough to explain.

"Anyone can be fooled into believing anything, Sean, even your father." he said quietly. "Victor thinks it's her personality that everyone loves and he's right. She's just enough of him to be totally different than him. So, I convinced him that exhausting her would change her personality. And it very well may, but it will take a long time. She adjusts too well for this to actually work. And in the meantime, she'll become the best warrior in the country, probably the world. Now, he threw in the whole training with the Logans. I think it's because she will never physically be equal with you guys, so it keeps her from thinking she has conquered the world...... yet."

"Wow." Sean said numbly, staring ahead.

Acre's brow creased and a frown found his lips. Sean wasn't as excited as he would have supposed. After all, he had just saved his sister's life, most likely. He thought he deserved a little recognition for that at least. He sighed.

"Alright, what's wrong, Sean?"

"Well," the boy hesitated. "are we really any better than Victor if all we do is twist and bend things to fit our desires like he does? I mean, she's just a kid, Acre! What if we're turning her into a villain? Even if she lives long enough for Victor to die, she may turn out to be just as awful as him if we don't invest into her life differently. She'll turn into, well....... a monster."

That's when Acre got it. Sean was looking at Eclipse as his sister, not as a tool. Acre pursed his lips and thought. It was true. He pressured that girl just as much as Victor did, so he really was a lot like the promontory. He needed her to be a weapon and only really cared about her because she was turning out so well. Of course, he couldn't tell Sean this; the boy would end his life if he knew the plans Acre had for Eclipse. He shared a lot of things with Sean, since they spent most of their time arguing about how to raise Eclipse, but he always managed to lie his way into the boy's good graces. If there was one person he never wanted as an enemy, it was Sean Monohue. He told him his actions were necessary for his sister's protection and that he cared deeply about her. Acre had been successful so far, but Sean was starting to guess at certain things he preferred remained hidden. All in the name of his baby sister.

Sean loved her. He had loved her since her birth, hoping that one day she would be able to make a difference in the world, for the better. He always wanted to help raise her as well as he could to think for herself without rebelling out loud. He had tried to teach her an underlying theme of good morals unlike her father's. He had saved her life behind the scenes on several occasions. Sean loved her more than life itself. What hurt the most is that she would never hear him say that or say it back to him.

Acre knew what teaching her about love would mean. It would introduce weakness to the confidence she had in herself. Right now, she thought her only duty was to Victor, but she had the ability to think through problems. All Victor had to do was push the right buttons and make her mad enough to lose her sense of duty, which he would one day do unconsciously. If he taught her to love and care for people, then she would feel obligated to, and Victor would have something to use against her. He couldn't risk that, for her sake, but Sean couldn't understand........ not yet.

"I had to save her life, Sean. I came up with the fastest and surest way to do it."

"Alright." Sean sighed.

"Alright what?"

"I'll play along, but someday, I *am* going to tell that girl I love her."

# CHAPTER EIGHT

It seemed to Eclipse that lunchtime wanted to be late today, but it finally came and with it, the first chance for Acre to inspect her wounds from the gym. She burst in through his lab door.

"Acre! I've got ten minutes to be at the track. Can you fix my back?"

Acre calmly looked up at her and retracted his lenses.

"Well, hello Eclipse. It's so kind of you to let me eat my lunch today."

Eclipse flinched. Acre was the closest thing to an actual father she had, and she felt terrible that she was such a burden to him. The reprimanding sarcasm reminded her that other people still had time to eat today. Almost every day, she needed his help healing something at lunchtime. She had gotten into the habit of just skipping her mid-day meal. However, Acre still needed food in the middle of the day. Eclipse bit her lip, but she really could not stand the pain anymore.

"Acre, can't you eat while I run? I won't need you at the track."

The 58-year-old scientist sighed. It wasn't that he ever planned on not healing her. He just wanted her to mind her manners and he never babied her, so he made it seem like a chore, but in reality, he worried she might die by Amy's hand in the gym over these next ten days. He opened a drawer in his desk and pulled out a tube that looked something like a telescope. He turned around to see her struggling to get the sweatband Sean had given her off her head. She already had it out of her hair, but the blood had painfully dried it to her forehead. Acre reached over and grabbed the headband from her hands. Only the stuck part remained on her head.

"Stand still." he instructed.

Eclipse grit her teeth and squeezed her eyes shut. She knew what was coming. As if pulling a bandage off a much lesser wound, Acre quickly ripped the band off her skin, ignoring her slight gasp. Then he raised the large end of the instrument in his hand up to the wound and pushed a button on the smaller end. A small yellow light scanned across the mess of blood and scab. Within seconds the light, which was a healing particle construction beam, had fully healed the wound. He did the same to her eye and lip.

"Anything else?"

"My back hurt a little in archery."

Acre spun her around and used the x-ray beam on his tool to scan her spine. He almost gasped.

"It only hurt a little?" he asked suspiciously.

"No," she confessed. "it hurt a lot. Especially when I drew back."

Acre healed the injury and spun her back around

"Better?"

Eclipse stretched her shoulders a bit.

"Yeah. What was wrong?"

"You had a hairline fracture on your spine. Chances are if Amy had hit you again in the range it would have snapped completely."

Acre swung around in his spinning chair, threw the healer back into its drawer, and slammed it shut moodily. The fact that he was so close to losing all his progress and having to start over made him furious. Eclipse walked up to him cautiously.

"Acre?"

"What?"

"You can eat now."

Acre couldn't help letting out a grin. He turned around and looked right into her hazel eyes for the first time since she entered. He placed his hands on her shoulders and sighed.

"What were you thinking in the range? You behaved well in the gym when your father yelled at you. Why did you get angry when he was finally siding with you?"

"Because he *was* siding with me. If he's gonna start taking my side, fine, but I want to earn it. It shouldn't be because he wants to please the damn crowd. He did start using my name today, at least." she ended proudly.

Acre furrowed his eyebrows and thought back through the day. She was right, he called her 'Eclipse' today! Multiple times! He felt a ball of nerves forming in his stomach. So, Victor was warming up to her. That could ruin everything! He tried to hide his fear from Eclipse.

"Alright. Get down to the track."

She nodded and ran towards the door.

"Eclipse!"

She turned around just in time to catch the apple he was tossing to her. The corner of her mouth twitched up and she nodded. Then she spun back around and closed the door on her way out. She had three minutes to get to the track, so she had to run the whole way to make it. From the window, Acre watched her run down the street away from the science tower with a nasty frown on his face.

Eclipse got to the track just in time. A few of the Logans had already started. Naturally, Sean would have waited for her. He always did when she had to run penalty laps with them. The track was one-fifth of a mile so fifteen laps meant three miles. That didn't bother Eclipse. She enjoyed running with the Logans. She saw them as her brothers but saw her real brothers only as colleagues. It was annoying for the men. They would all have willingly died just to make her smile.

"Well, hello Eclipse!"

A broad-shouldered man greeted her. Actually, all the Logans were weightlifters so broad-shouldered was a poor way to describe any of them. He was tall with a toothy smile and messy blonde hair. This particular Logan was Shane, Victor's oldest son.

"Hey, Shane. Where's Sean?"

Shane's smile faded ever so slightly. He and his brothers all loved Eclipse dearly. They had each been involved in raising her more than anyone assumed at her birth, but Sean was significantly more... special to her. Maybe it was the fact that he was one of her archery instructors and that was her favorite exercise. If that was it, Shane felt bad for Aidan, her throwing instructor. A slight pang of jealousy invaded his heart when he thought about it too much, but there really was nothing he could do. He shook the feeling away as the drill master ordered his heat to run. Series ran in heats of ten, since that's how many fit across the track. One of the other guys, a dark-skinned Logan with bright green eyes named Harrison, backed down to let Eclipse run with Shane, since Sean wasn't there.

"I don't know." he answered his sister as they started to jog side by side.

Each member of the series had to jog neck and neck with each other but stay in their own lanes. This required Eclipse to run more than jog since all the Logans were over 15 with much longer legs. Thankfully, the guys always gave her the innermost lane. They were all waiting for their turns in the Enhancer when everything they were training for now would be easier. The Enhancer could only amplify what was already there. It upgraded the senses that any given human developed on their own. Eclipse could go in at ten and she was the last Emily. The Logans were waiting till she got out to start their own enhancement since they had to be twenty, but unlike the Emilies, they had no limit on how young they would have to be. Some were in their thirties. Eclipse couldn't be older than 12 because she had to be enhanced before her mental development reached a certain stage. On the other hand, Acre could physically enhance an eighty-year-old if he wanted. When Eclipse came out, he would simply reprogram the genetic synthesizing serum. It would take Eclipse a month and the Logans only three days. All the Logans had a natural sympathy for the girls, but especially Eclipse. They all had a sense of familiarity and camaraderie with her and tried to support her all they could.

"Hey, I heard about the gym." Shane knew everyone had by that point. but he wanted to get her take on it. "How are you holding up?"

Eclipse shrugged. It wasn't that she didn't like Shane, she was just still mad about the incident, especially since Acre told her it could have killed her. Truth was, Eclipse didn't plan on dying for a long time and Amy was endangering that plan. She gave the vaguest answer she could.

"I'm fine."

Shane knew her well enough to drop it at that but he never really got a chance to talk to her and they were both used to keeping their pace, so he simply changed the subject.

"So, you got your black bracer last Tenthday?"

Eclipse's lip tugged up at the corner. That was the closest thing to a smile she had. Archery was her pride and joy. She was good at it and enjoyed it. That was a pretty rare combination for anyone, let alone her. Shane smiled as he saw her grin. He had picked the right topic.

"Yes. It took the promontory a ton of convincing to issue it, but I got it. Jackson says I'm the first person to ever get one."

"You are. It's unlikely for anyone to get a black bracer, but a ten-year-old? That's legend in the making. What did Acre have to say about it?"

"He made some remark about being more impressed if I got A's on his tests."

Shane chuckled. Acre really struggled sometimes with not rewarding Eclipse. It was his own rule, that she not be praised when she did well except to be told that she was performing her duty well. He was just awful at following it. All her brothers thought he truly loved her like his daughter but couldn't admit it. Shane sighed with amusement before changing the subject yet again.

"So......... you ready for the Enhancer?"

All signs of life faded from her face. She remembered the conversation with her father earlier and grimaced. Not in pain or fear, for that matter, in anger. It was a new feeling toward Victor. She saw his actions in the range and knew how to beat the system. As long as she was a favorite with the people, he wouldn't kill her. Her mind couldn't quite say he was afraid to kill her, but she now knew he was aware of how it would hurt him to do so. And suddenly, she wasn't as afraid of him. Even rulers aren't totally without accountability.

"Eclipse?"

She jumped slightly. She totally forgot Shane's question in her deep thoughts. He sensed she needed a gentle reminder and repeated himself. By now she really didn't care about what he was saying. She was trying to stay alive!! Surely, he understood. Her only answer was a shrug. Shane felt his cheeks getting flushed with frustration. He wanted to stop running and shake her! *Why won't you talk to me?!?!?!?!!* *I'm your brother*.......... *I care about you.* *I want to help*.......... *I love you.* His head screamed so loud it made his eyes water. At least, that's what he wanted to believe caused it. His heart ached. Love was a dangerous thing in Chrosia. Victor knew it drove people to do things they never would otherwise, so it was rather... discouraged. Every marriage was arranged. Failure to comply was punished by death or torturous imprisonment, depending on how public the act was.

Even kids were discouraged from spending too much time at home with their parents. Shane grew up normal; no strong attachments to anything really. In the 28 years he'd lived so far, he had avoided falling for any girls, not even allowing himself to be attracted to one. Then at 18, he held a little, sleeping baby in his arms for the first time, three days after her birth. At first, it scared him, holding an infant, then something happened. She woke up and stared right at him with big, beautiful green eyes. He saw something there he had never seen before. He saw innocence; pure, simple, un-corrupted life. Then she started screaming bloody murder and Acre took her from him, but he stood asphyxiated, those eyes still in his mind. Right then, he vowed to keep that look in his sister's eyes. He vowed to love her above all else in his life.

That's what made him cry as he ran. She would never love him, or anyone, the way he loved her. She would never know how much her stiff attitude and replies stabbed his heart. Or how much he just wanted to hold her in his arms when she got hurt or scared or had to face hours and hours of their father's anger. She couldn't understand her emotions. Acre taught her to thoughtfully respond to everything from an incredibly young age. Logic had to rule her actions and thoughts. Everything she did was systematically thought out, even if it appeared to be done on an impulse. Her mind just had to work that fast. And it's true, she could think and act faster than most people twice her age, and still get better results. But she was just so... Shane thought hard, looking for the perfect word to describe it. Then it hit.

She was a machine. A weapon.

She had no feelings, only capable of doing what she was told by whoever had their finger on the trigger. And right now, Victor had her in his hand. She was insensitive and brutal. Despite her genius and all her potential, she was a mindless killing machine. She believed she thought for herself, but it was all a lie.

As they finished running Shane made a momentous decision. Eclipse had farther to run than him, so she continued to run as his heat stopped. She figured the next heat of Logans would catch up to her anyway. Shane watched her for a second and then took a deep breath and called after her, jogging to catch up. She kindly stopped and jogged in place, waiting for him.

"Eclipse." he said again when right next to her.

"Yeah, what?"

He took another deep breath.

"I want to tell you something."

"What?" she repeated a bit impatiently.

*Here it goes.* Shane thought before answering.

"I.......... I............"

*Love you!!!!! Say it, dammit, say it!!* his head screamed, *I love you!!!!!* but the words wouldn't come. It could endanger both their lives. Instead, he chose a different angle just to get her thinking.

"I think you're beautiful."

Eclipse froze mid-step and cocked her head curiously at him. It wasn't often that someone used a word she didn't know, especially her brothers. They always seemed to avoid using words she didn't know. In fact, they all seemed to have some sort of speech impediment. Each of them had moments of stuttering like Shane just did, but normally they ended up saying something she totally understood. This time he used a new word.

"Beautiful?" she asked doubtfully. "What's that?"

But Shane was shaking his head before she even finished.

"I can't tell you. I just need you to know that. Someday you'll understand it, but I can't explain it to you. It's a good thing, though. You're just going to have to figure it out on your own. And Eclipse?"

"Yeah?"

"You can't tell anyone in the whole world I said that to you. Ok?"

Eclipse's brow creased in confusion. Her eyes squinted suspiciously. And Shane knew her next question before she asked it.

"Why?"

"Just promise me?"

She eyed him curiously. This was a new side to her brother. He wasn't secretive at all, normally. Now, suddenly, he was acting like this was a matter of life and death. What she didn't know was how true that actually was. She looked into his eyes, like she had as an infant, but couldn't convince herself. Secrets were forbidden in Chrosia, even for the promontory's kids. Shane sensed her hesitation and feared for her life, and his own. If she told their father or Acre, they would be furious and end them both. Shane knelt in front of her and grabbed her shoulders, making her stare deep into his eyes and hear every word he spoke.

"Sean! If Sean told you not to tell anyone, would you listen?"

Eclipse hesitated but gave a reluctant nod. Shane felt that piercing stab of jealousy in his heart again, gulped it down, and tightened his grip on her shoulders. It was more important for her to stay safe and keep this to herself than it was for him to be her favorite brother.

"Tell Sean then." he prodded. "If he tells you not to say a word to anyone else, you will listen to him, right?"

"But Shane........"

"Eclipse."

His voice gave no room for argument. Eclipse hesitated again. Then she thought of the range and the gym, and her anger burned. In a swift act of rebellion, small as it was, she made up her mind.

"Yes. If he says not to tell, no one will ever hear of it."

Shane sighed with relief and let her go. He stepped back, fighting to convince himself to leave, but she stood frozen, staring into his eyes, trying to read what was driving him right now. Was he afraid? Maybe a little. Or angry? Or... what? She knew others were irrationally driven by emotions, but she normally could at least tell which one it was. This time... she just couldn't. The next heat of Logans was running towards them and she knew she had to go soon but couldn't move. What was this new side to him??? Whatever it was began to drive her crazy. Shane stared right back into her eyes as the Logans passed him. Then they reached her, and she knew she had to start running to keep up. She jogged backward a couple of steps to keep eye contact and then broke away and spun around. Shane watched her for a few seconds before turning around and taking off himself at a brisk jog towards the range. He had to talk to Sean before she did. Deep down he felt his little brother would understand. Of all the people in the world, Sean saw and knew Victor's treachery. Being forced into watching his own mother die gave him little respect for her murderer.

The entire training complex took up four square miles. It was systematically divided into four sections with each square mile having its own purpose. The complex was in the capital city, roughly half a mile from the promontory's fortress, a building demanding both respect and attention. The fortress was Chrosia's most impressive landmark. Like most fortresses of the day, there was a large outer wall that protected the inhabitants from siege weapons. This one surrounded the building in a large circle and was designed to allow guards passage through its defenses. The gate was a simple arched doorway through the wall and into an adjacent tunnel which led to the actual castle's main entrance. There were three other tunnels that led from the wall to the castle, forming a large x with the building in the center. These tunnels connected straight into the outer wall tunnel of the fortress.

The most impressive item in the fortress's design was not its blueprints however, it was its very substance. The base of every part of the fortress was pure duranium, a metal far stronger than steel. The walls and ceiling of the tunnels, however, were not any true substance. They were electrical force fields as were all gates and the main portcullis. These force fields could absorb more damage than most structures, but they were arched into tunnels so people could walk through them. The fortress itself was completely built of duranium: tall and formidable, square, and eight stories tall, it symbolized pure power and struck fear into those who were unfortunate to get close enough to see its spires rising into the sky. The four corners each bore their own tower, topped with a menacing steeple. The two in the back rose a few stories higher than the forefront pair. The roof between all these towers was flat with a metal parapet. From the roof ran yet another tunnel, this one formed of force fields entirely, with no duranium base. It ran across the sky in a slight arc and connected directly to the roof of the science lab.

The science lab was basically just a tall tower with no outer defenses. Acre's apartment was a small room on the fifth floor, the same floor his personal lab was on. Eclipse had a small cot in the corner of his lab and that was where she lived. The lab was not constructed of duranium however, it was built of solid steel. Duranium was too valuable to use on every building in the capital. However, the lab had yet another force field tunnel connecting its roof to the roof of the Enhancer just like the lab was connected to the fortress. It was, therefore, possible to walk from Victor's fortress to the Enhancer without touching foot to the ground.

The Enhancer was an amazing feat of architecture. The entire building was a singular machine. Shaped like a dome, it was all one room inside. Four huge cylinders ran up the outsides of the building; they provided the Enhancer with its energy. It was the one building in the capital that was completely self-sufficient. The cylinders turned atmospheric energy into electricity for the machine to run on. And it had to generate massive amounts of that energy for it to function properly. The Enhancer genetically altered individuals to create super-powered energy wielders. Series could be enhanced seven at a time. When it was your turn, you had to access the massive building from the roof, so your journey began in the lab. You were taken into the Enhancer and had an IV placed into both arms and a hose run through your chest into your lungs. Then, you were lifted and lowered into a huge glass tank that stood in the center of the room with several tubes running to it. Once inside, you were strapped to the floor.

The Enhancer altered its victim by infusing a chemically modified serum into every portion of their body. When it was turned on, the tubes delivered this liquid into the tank where the victim lay strapped to the bottom, with no breathing apparatus. This was because the liquid had to absorb into every part of the body: the organs, lungs, muscles, skin, bones... everything. The chemicals were designed to soak through eventually, but it took less time if they could work both from the outside in and the inside out. The problem with this was how to keep someone alive when their lungs were filled with liquid. The tube leading into the chest pumped the liquid out of the lungs when they got too full, to keep them from exploding, but there was no form of oxygenation there. Instead, Acre had discovered a way to induce a coma where the victim would no longer have to breathe and the IVs kept the body alive by providing nutrients directly to the cells, including delivering oxygen.

The rest of the building's interior was a supercomputer that controlled the correct formulas and life supports needed for successful enhancement. This technology was what gave Chrosia its superiority in battle as it custom-built their entire army. It had to be protected beyond all measure. The outer wall was built of duranium, then a three-foot layer of solid diamond, and another layer of duranium. It was absolutely impossible to break through, but on top of all that, the Enhancer had a whole separate building located behind it that controlled its security system. This took a huge strain off the energy generators. The entire building had one access point; the tunnel leading to its roof, and security systems could block that off in the case of any emergency. It was programmed to do so as it deemed necessary.

Those three buildings and the armory, a massive building across from the fortress, were set apart from the training complex by about half a mile. The first section of the complex was three buildings arranged neatly in a square mile block. Those were the gym, the range, and a building called the mat. It was designed to teach wrestling, tumbling, weapon-free fighting, and proper falling techniques, all extremely valuable skills. There were also a large assortment of weights and equipment housed there. Across the street, in the second square mile section, was the oval running track, the many barracks and the pool. Right beside it was the third square mile block. It held two stables, each capable of housing 1000 horses. And across the street in the final section of the complex was the riding track. It had several sections and looked somewhat like an onion from the air. Each section, or, layer of the onion, taught a different technique such as jumping, endurance, speed, maneuvering, and vaulting.

It took only a few minutes for the eldest Monohue only a few minutes to jog past it all to the range.

# CHAPTER NINE

Shane burst through the door of the range and froze as six people in his series jumped and stared at him curiously. He quickly composed himself and waved them off, realizing he would have to be a bit more calm about all this, if he didn't want to arouse suspicion. He checked in at the computer and walked toward the end of the room where Eclipse had shot earlier that day. Shane was at a high enough level that he was permitted to carry his weapons with him. Therefore, he was expected to carry them everywhere with him and keep them in perfect condition. This meant performing every activity with them on, except swimming. The Logans were required to carry them above their heads while swimming. This also meant that they didn't need the lockers the Emilies needed. Shane's booth was the same one Amy used so he had a long way to walk. He tried to look calm, but anyone who has tried this knows how difficult it is when you have something to hide.

He couldn't make eye contact with anyone, as if they could read his very soul if he did. So instead, he walked the whole way fussing with his quiver strap and pulling his unstrung bow out to examine the wood. He made sure to keep his eyes down till out of the corner of his eye he read his booth number. Breathing a sigh of relief, he used his foot to help bend his 200 lb. bow to string it. Then he drew it to its proper firing position to test the string. Satisfied, he slowly let the string back to its normal position, took his stance, and fired the first arrow. He hit the target's leg. Shane's brow creased in confusion. He never shot that bad! Puzzled, he checked his bow again. Then he heard the chuckles beside him. Shane looked over at the man to his right. It was his little brother Erican. Erican was 27, with bright red curly hair that did whatever it pleased and a sneaky, crooked smile. Despite being in line for a position in the Logan corps, Erican was small. Strong, definitely, but his shoulder width was only about half that of Shane's. His entire face was littered with freckles. He often lifted sunken spirits simply with a grin. Right now, however, Shane was not in the mood.

"Oh shut up!" he snarled. "It's only my first shot."

Erican put his fist over his mouth and cleared his throat to muffle his snickers as Shane fired again, once more with poor results. This time Erican couldn't help himself and roared with laughter at Shane's confusion. His older brother turned red in the face and shot him a nasty look. Erican just laughed all the harder. Shane continued to fire, hitting to the right of every target, until his quiver was empty. He shot an annoyed glance at Erican, who was leaning on his bow like a walking stick watching with the utmost amusement. As the final arrow missed its mark completely, Shane lost it.

"What the hell?!?!?!" he fumed.

And his brother just chuckled beside him. Shane turned and glared at him.

"You know something, Erican. Spill it!"

Erican snorted desperately and shook his head. He was always in the mood for a good joke and Shane had just provided the perfect opportunity.

"Well," he answered, turning to fire his own bow. "Eclipse and Amy had a huge face-off in here today, in which Amy cheated, of course. So, Eclipse cursed that booth to failure forever. I guess you are just destined to shoot poorly from now on."

He somehow managed to tell his tale with a completely straight face and serious, unwavering voice. Most people would call out a blatant lie like this, but unfortunately for Shane, Victor highly encouraged belief in the supernatural. If you are trying to rule by fear, the unknown is an amazing ally. Everyone in Chrosia believed strongly in superstition. It was taught from a very young age and little reminders were spread through the land in the rare newspaper story. So truly, it was not Shane's fault that he believed his younger brother in this instance. His face paled a bit and he turned back to his targets and looked at his arrows strewn across the ground, all in places he hadn't meant to put them. There was nothing he could do! Changing booths wasn't allowed. Yet he'd never pass another archery test as long as he lived. He sunk to his knees in frustration. This was definitely not his day.

Just then Sean walked up and stood next to Erican. He watched Shane for a while before firing a questioning glance at the redhead. Erican just shrugged and went back to shooting before his grin gave him away. Sean stood in silence as Shane sighed heavily from the ground and finally couldn't take it anymore.

"Shane?"

His older brother jumped at the sound and looked up awkwardly at Sean.

"What the hell are you doing?" Sean asked.

"I..... I don't really know?" Shane muttered.

Sean rolled his eyes.

"How do you make it through every day alive? Someone should have killed you for stupidity years ago."

Shane's face flashed angrily, and he pushed up to his feet. Who was this little shrimp to call him stupid?

"Oh yeah?" he shot back. "How come no one's killed you for being late all the time?"

Sean's face flushed a bit in return.

"I'll have you know that I was working with Victor to help figure out what it will take to fix the damage caused by Amy and Eclipse earlier."

Shane gave in with a shrug. He couldn't argue with that, but something else caught his ear. If Sean and Victor were working on a solution for Eclipse's curse, then he would be able to pass after all.

"You guys can fix it?" he asked eagerly, "How?"

Now it was Sean's turn to be confused.

"Why is it so important to you?"

"Well," Shane hesitated. "I'd like to pass this bracer. And I can't right now."

Sean just stared at him blankly. Shane decided to help jog his memory.

"I shoot in Amy's booth, remember?"

Sean still just stared.

"My booth is cursed?" he tried uncomfortably.

He thought this would be relatively difficult to forget. Finally, understanding dawned on Sean's face and Shane relaxed a bit. Then, inexplicably, Sean reached over and smacked Erican across the back of the head....... *hard*. The unsuspecting victim gripped the back of his head with both hands and doubled over in pain.

"What the-----"

"Oh, don't even, you little shite. Seriously? That's not something to joke about."

It was Shane's turn to stare confused at Erican as Sean walked past.

Shane stopped his youngest brother and looked back and forth from him to Erican.

"What.... what just happened?"

His gaze landed on Sean, who, once again rolled his eyes.

"What's going on with your shots, dumbass?"

Shane glanced back at his arrows and shrugged.

"They all veer to the right." he answered.

"And Erican said that booth was cursed right?"

"Yeeeeees?"

Shane wasn't catching on at all. Sean closed his eyes in exasperation and drove his palm into his forehead. There was no way this was supposed to be this hard.

"Shane." he said slowly. "Look at the back wall."

Shane looked to the left side of the building and grew furiously red. There was no left side of the building! His arrows were veering to the right because of a slight breeze blowing through the opening left there.

"Oh." he gulped and glanced embarrassed at Sean. "Sorry."

Sean just closed his eyes and nodded his acceptance. There was definitely something wrong with his older brother's head. He went to Eclipse's booth and strung his own bow, shaking his head in exasperation.

Shane walked over to Erican, who was still rubbing the back of his head.

"You alright?" he asked as Erican looked at his hand.

"Well, no blood so I think so." he smiled.

"Good." Shane answered and proceeded to wallop Erican across the back of the head even harder than Sean did.

This time, the red head fell to the ground, cringing in pain. Shane picked his bow off the floor where he left it in his despair and collected his arrows, placing them back into his quiver. He returned to his spot and began all over again, this time adjusting for the breeze.

"So, what really happened today?" he asked Sean in between shots after a while.

"Eclipse finally put Amy in her place."

Sean couldn't help but grin as he remembered the look on Amy's face. Shane grinned and glanced over at Erican. He was on his feet, but walking away. Shane's grin vanished. Getting him to leave was 90% of the reason he hit Erican, the other 10% being that he deserved it. He needed to be alone with Sean for a bit. As soon as his brother was out of ear shot, he turned around.

"Sean, I need you to do me a favor."

His brother froze. He knew his brothers' tones better than anything in the world. And this one was as serious as Shane got. He walked over to the rope barrier that separated them and leaned on his bow, trying to act casual.

"Hmmm?"

Shane took a deep breath. He was fairly sure that Sean, above all people would have no issue with undermining Victor, but he wasn't positive and with this sort of thing, it was imperative to be positive. He had no choice now, though. He had to convince Sean to tell Eclipse to keep it a secret.

"I took a pretty big chance with Eclipse today."

Sean's eyebrows furrowed immediately and he pursed his lips. He didn't like people messing with his sister, but he just nodded to Shane, waiting for him to continue.

"I told her that she was beautiful."

His brother's chin hit the floor. That...... that was....... perfect! Someone had finally planted a seed of doubt in Eclipse's mind! That was a start of something wonderful, he knew. Now she would question things and see things that, though she wouldn't understand immediately, would all come back to her in the future. He looked at Shane, who stood staring at his glaringly obvious smile with confusion. He thought Sean would be mad at first, until he explained. He looked like he had just had the best day of his life!

"You....... you're not mad?" he asked cautiously.

"Are you kidding?!?!?!" Sean asked. "I'm grateful to you!! Saved me a whole heap of trouble."

Shane just stared.

"What?"

"I've been trying to think of a way to plant little seeds of doubt in her mind forever, Shane. I was thinking about telling her I love her......... you definitely saved me from jumping in too fast. So........ where does the favor come in?"

Shane stopped catching flies with his mouth and stuttered back his answer.

"I just.... I need you to tell her not to say anything when she asks you about it. She won't believe me unless you back it up."

Shane bit his tongue as he saw the look of pride on Sean's face.

"Well you can count on me." he said cheerfully. "That girl is the best chance this country has."

Shane managed to swallow his jealousy and breathe out a sigh of relief. He couldn't believe how cooperative, even excited, Sean was about this. He had expected reluctance....... maybe a bit of resistance. Then Sean's last words hit home. Best chance this country has. What did he mean by that? Everyone knew Sean was mysterious, but he wasn't normally so blatant. The four brothers were in an interesting situation. They knew since their father had stopped breeding himself that he already knew which of his children would be his successor. None of them were really dying to have the job, but it was the one bit of tradition Victor held onto. They didn't want it to tear them apart though, so they just never talked about it. They all simply assumed that the other four siblings would fight it out after Victor died. But here was Sean, basically saying that he believed Eclipse was going to rule next and he seemed thrilled about it! Shane stared at him. Why didn't he want the throne? Of all of Victor's kids, he had the most pain in his past caused by the current system of government. Why wouldn't he want to have the power to change things?

"Hey, Sean?"

Again, the tone reader heard his seriousness. He stopped firing and looked back over to his brother. Shane wasn't known for being brilliant, which was Victor's main problem with him, but he could be very....... profound at times. Sean waited patiently for his most recent revelation.

"You've never really wanted the throne, have you?" he asked.

Sean smiled gently in return.

"Never encompasses a lot, Shane. There were times I wanted it and would have done anything to get it, but not for a while now."

"When did you want it if not now? This is your prime."

Sean's smile faded into a distant stare. He wasn't looking at his brother anymore. He was looking at a younger version of himself sneaking into the range late at night with evil bent upon his heart. It was two years after his sister was born.

*"Did you really think you could get away with this?"*

*Eleven-year-old Sean jumped and dropped the bundle in his hands. Where was that voice coming from? It was dark and he could see no one. Suddenly, a torch was struck and Sean stood staring up into Acre's face. He couldn't move.*

*"Well?" Acre pushed as he walked closer.*

*Sean regained a little of his sense.*

*"I...... I don't know what you're talking about!" he cried defensively.*

*Acre raised an eyebrow and knelt down beside the boy without breaking eye contact until Sean had to look away. That meant shame, the scientist knew. He slowly looked away to untie the bundle on the floor. Inside the brown cloth lay a rather large dagger for the boy. Acre held it up before Sean.*

*"Then perhaps you would like to tell me what you had planned for this?"*

*Sean stared at the dagger. It looked more frightening in someone else's hand than it had seemed in his. It glinted in the torch light and made him tremble. The courage he needed to drive that dagger home into Victor's chest was fading. His will faltered. He had to look at the ground to murmur out his reply.*

*"Hunting." he lied.*

*Acre's eyebrow rose again but he nodded and wrapped the dagger back up. Everyone needed a back-up plan. The boy could be his, if trained properly. Sean looked at him suspiciously. No one would've bought that answer. Why was Acre, the brightest mind in the country, accepting it?*

*"Walk with me, Sean."*

*He rose back to his feet and turned toward the range's back door. Sean stood his ground in fear. The scientist finally turned and he jumped slightly at his gaze. It wasn't harsh or angry, it was just a gaze, unreadable and patient.*

*"Last I checked, my dear boy, walking required some movement of the lower body."*

*Sean finally found words to reply.*

*"Where are we going?"*

*Acre smiled deviously and turned around before answering.*

*"To teach you how to hunt."*

"Hey, you ok?"

Sean's head snapped back to the present as Shane spoke again. He remembered the question which brought on the memory and answered.

"I needed to learn how to hunt." he muttered.

Shane stared confused at him as he went back to practice. Hunting? What did hunting have to do with ruling? He opened his mouth to ask for an explanation but never got it. Someone came up from behind him and smacked him on the back of the head before the words could escape. He spun around angrily with his fist drawn back, only to see Erican jump slightly with surprise and hold his hands up defensively.

"Whoa there, big guy! I didn't realize I was interrupting anything. And I'm sorry about the prank. It wasn't my place to tease you like that and it won't happen again.......... today." he grinned, holding out his hand for a truce shake.

Shane rolled his eyes.

"Just today?"

"C'mon Shane." Erican explained pushing his hand out a little farther. "That's already a lot to promise."

"Fine"

Shane gave his hand one groggy shake and turned back to his targets.

Erican drove him crazy sometimes, but he was his brother. And these four brothers had learned to stick together over the years. They were stronger together than any of them were alone. In Chrosia, it was always good to have some allies.

"So, what were you two donkeys discussing in so much depth?"

Shane froze in his draw and shot Sean a frantic look out the corner of his eye. He didn't want his brother to give up their secret to the other two boys yet. He wasn't as sure where they stood with his father as he was with Sean. His younger brother fired an arrow before calmly answering. He didn't even look away from his target.

"Oh, just the occurrences at the gym this morning."

"Really?" Erican was none the wiser. "Why the hell would you wanna talk about that? It sent shivers up my spine just to hear about it. Do you think Victor is serious?"

"You have any doubt he is?" Sean replied dryly, slicing through the heart of another target.

Shane truly wasn't the brightest of his brothers and everyone knew it, including himself, but he only just now caught on to what Sean was doing. As understanding dawned on his face, and he went back to firing arrows with adjustments for the wind. Sean couldn't help but roll his eyes. Shane was worried about Eclipse not being able to keep a secret when he could barely do it himself. It shouldn't have been hard for him to join in on changing the subject, but he had looked around awkwardly for several moments instead.

There were certain flaws Victor saw in each of his sons that prevented him from settling on an heir. Shane's was his intelligence, or lack thereof. Erican's was his size. He was a shrimpy 5'7" which drove his 6'9" father mad. Sean's was his blatant rebellion. Aidan's was his dark, pessimistic personality which made him abrasive. And Eclipse? Well, Eclipse was a girl.

But as is often true in a family, each had a gift to counteract each other's flaws. Sean was brilliant, Aidan was loyal to a fault, Erican had a smooth, like-able personality, and Shane was huge. And Eclipse? Well, Eclipse was a girl.

This made them a great team. They didn't always remember that, but what family does? They also didn't realize to what extent they were unstoppable together. Sean could see it coming, but he had to slowly work his sister into it. Shane had unwittingly just laid the foundation for her transformation. Sean grinned to himself. It was one of Shane's accidentally brilliant moments. She was beginning to see through the fog of lies around her. There was one thing Sean didn't see coming. Eclipse was loyal, almost to perfection. She followed her father's every word as if he was the Ancient himself. She may not like him in any way whatsoever, but treason was far beyond her reach. She would proudly give her life if he said it was necessary for the good of all. Sean didn't realize at the time just how loyal his sister truly was.

Erican was babbling on about something and Shane was grinning like a fool for discovering Sean's deceit all by himself. Sean had to focus extremely hard to give the slightest heed to Erican's words. His mind was far away.

"-----for example, what does Amy learn after cheating like that? She learns to rebel. Father might just be cutting down his own tree if he encourages her too much. She's the Dark One, true, but she's a clever Dark One. It wouldn't surprise me if she just cheats her way through beating Eclipse all next week. I mean seriously, what can Eclipse do against telepathy? She's rather helpless in the arena against Amy until she is enhanced, but she can't get enhanced unless she beats Amy........ which she is incapable of if she doesn't get enhanced first. How does this make any sense at all? I think--------"

"I think you should shut up!!!" snarled Sean suddenly across Shane's booth.

Erican's mouth dropped open in shock until Shane jerked his head to something behind him. The red head spun around only to see his little sister staring at him. Most would expect her to be furious with him, but her look was different. She had heard his last few statements and sadly, she knew he was right. She stared at him because she had never heard any of her brother's say one bad thing about her and somewhere inside of her, a new emotion boiled. It wasn't anger. She knew anger all too well. It wasn't hate, either. Or determination or loyalty or rage or confidence. She had never felt this before. Somehow, she had always thought that her brothers had no doubt in her abilities, but this moment was proving her wrong for the first time in her life. It was hard to swallow; her eyes blurred, but she wasn't sure why. She watched all the color drain from Erican's face and she did know that look. That was fear, but fear of what she wondered. She wasn't angry and she would never attack a superior without direct orders from an even higher-ranking officer, but it was definitely fear. She had no idea that there was a fear of hurting someone beyond the point of repair.

Eclipse didn't say anything to Erican. In fact, she calmly broke her gaze with him and walked to her booth. Sean silently stepped out of her way. All three of her brothers stared at her as she finished buckling on her knife belt. She could feel their eyes penetrating her skull and knew she had to stop it. They were beginning to get on her nerves.

"Alright, where's the blood?" she asked solemnly without taking her eyes off her belt.

Sean caught on first, as usual, broke into an awkward chuckle and looked away. Shane followed suit, though not understanding why, and Erican managed a slight smile before turning his eyes. It was an old joke between the siblings. Once she had come to lunch with blood running down her face like crazy, acting like it was totally normal until the boys' staring at her made her blow up and yell at them to 'quit it'. Ever since then, if one of them stared at her too long, all she had to do was ask where the blood was, and they understood that she was no longer on display. It normally was a sign to them that she was ok.

Erican suddenly decided he was ill and needed to take the rest of the day off. No one was allowed to apologize to Eclipse so he had nothing he could say to her. He unstrung his bow and put it back in his quiver and fetched the arrows he had shot while mumbling something about feeling sick to his stomach and never looking up from the ground. Eclipse didn't know it yet, but she was very compassionate and felt awful for the poor guy. He was right and she knew he never meant to hurt her. She had simply overheard him when she wasn't supposed to. Her eyes followed him longingly as he walked away

Eclipse turned back to the task at hand and pursed her lips. She hated throwing knives. Sean knew what was going on in her head. This was the one sport that Amy fairly beat her at. If she was constantly forced to focus on how Amy bested her, how was she ever going to be confident that she could defeat Amy in the gym? He walked up behind her and rubbed her arms. A feeling washed over her. She wasn't sure which one, but it made her feel safe.

"It's only an hour, Eclipse." Sean said softly. "Take it one minute at a time."

Eclipse turned around. Sometimes there were things going on in her own head that she couldn't explain. Sean was one of them. He always treated her like she was more than what anyone else thought of her. Sometimes she wanted to just blurt something out to him as her emotions boiled forward. But she didn't know the words to describe her feelings. The best she could do was guess at it and hope he understood.

"Sean.... I..... respect you...... a lot."

Her own words sounded broken and confused, but he smiled brightly at her and she got the feeling he knew exactly what she wanted to say, even if she didn't. Suddenly, a familiar voice cleared its throat behind them and Eclipse groaned inwardly. She enjoyed spending time with all her brothers, but she also hated having one as her throwing instructor. They always got upset with each other during practice because neither of them knew what to do. She didn't like being mad at her brothers and wished Victor would place someone she already hated as her throwing instructor. Instead, she turned around to face Aidan who came walking toward her with an exceptionally fake grin. What made it worse was that Aidan didn't smile, ever. She knew he was trying to be encouraging, but it was so out of character for him that it had the opposite effect.

"You, sir, are late." Sean informed him.

Aidan shot him an annoyed glance but refused to get back at such a trivial statement, mainly because he had no real excuse. Then Shane unwittingly gave him just the weapon he needed.

"Like you weren't." he called out as he continued to shoot.

Aidan's eyes brightened as he flipped his head back to Sean, whose Shane-aimed dirty look confirmed the statement.

"Sooooo, you were late, huh Sean?" he purred out sneakily. "Should I penalize you?"

Sean grimaced. Technically, he and Aidan were the same rank, but his brother was an instructor right now and he was just another soldier practicing. That meant he could technically penalize him. Sean didn't like people extorting power though, so he tried to start a fight.

"You could indeed, slim, but 1) I was late on Victor's orders and 2) I could fire right back by penalizing you for something stupid in archery tomorrow." Sean shrugged, seemingly carelessly.

Unfortunately for him, Aidan kept his cool all too well.

"Blondie.... it was a joke. Lighten up Seanny." Aidan walked by Sean, tussling his hair, and stopped by Eclipse.

He waited for Sean to retort, but turned to see his little brother walking swiftly back to the front of the building. Aidan pursed his lips into a slight grin. It was far too easy to mess with the youngest Monohue boy.

"Alright, here we go again." he sighed, turning back to his sister. "Fire away, Eclipse."

The first target popped up and she flicked out a throwing knife and hit it square in the head. It bounced off the metal dummy and fell harmlessly to the ground. Aidan frowned thoughtfully as he went out to get her knife for her. He couldn't figure it out. Why couldn't she stick a single knife in years of training? It was improbable on every level of logic, but it was somehow true. So, he tested everything he tested everyday once again. She had good form and stance. She moved fluidly and naturally. And she threw hard. He had seen her throw rocks and knock out animals. He knew the power she could put behind a throw. He picked up her knife and balanced it on his finger right where the blade met the handle. It was perfectly level, beautifully balanced. So, what was her issue? He walked back just as puzzled as ever and handed her knife back.

"So," she asked begrudgingly. "what am I doing wrong?"

Aidan rolled his eyes.

"Eclipse, you have asked me that every day for five years now. What has been, and will always be, my answer?"

"You don't know."

"Precisely. So exactly what information do you think I've gained in the last 24 hours that will somehow change that answer?"

Eclipse's face reddened in frustration. He didn't have to be so sarcastic about it.

"Well, how am I supposed to know? You're the instructor. *You* should've figured it out by now. What kind of instructor doesn't know his trade well enough to answer a simple question?" she demanded, throwing her hands in the air with frustration.

"It's NOT simple!!!!!"

Aidan had never yelled at Eclipse before. His volume stopped her in her tracks. And each immediately felt remorse. They were in an awkward situation. They couldn't show that remorse. Aidan was honestly just having a terrible day. Half of his frustration was because of something going down at the Elite barracks and he was just taking it out on her because he couldn't take it out on the person that was truly driving him crazy. So, they stood awkwardly looking around at anything but each other for a minute before Aidan cleared his throat.

"Ummm..... well........" his mind search frantically for words. "Maybe just keep trying?"

"Yes, of course."

She knew he felt bad about yelling at her and decided to put it in the past with a bit of relief, actually. She hated how people got awkward and unnatural around her. It was annoying. It was like they were constantly scared of her, but she knew that wasn't it. They were scared of Victor. She didn't understand it all, yet, but she knew everyone was hiding something from her under penalty of death if Victor figured out they spilled the beans. In short, she couldn't wait till she could read minds.

After about fifty minutes Aidan began to believe he was more exhausted than Eclipse. She threw every single knife with incredible precision but all of them bounced off harmlessly. He instructed her on new and old methods and techniques and still they hit the floor. Finally, he just plopped down crisscross on the floor and puffed out his cheeks thoughtfully. Eclipse just stood and waited for him. She knew he was frustrated and so was she. She had tried everything. Different sizes, different shapes, long and short, double bladed, short throws, distance throws....... everything! It was infuriating. She was supposed to be the crowned jewel of Acre's Emily series and she couldn't stick a knife to save her life. It was even more aggravating that Amy was an expert at it. Amy. The name bored holes in her confidence.

What if she couldn't beat her, like Erican had said? What if she was doomed to die at ten? All her talent would be wasted and Amy would make general. A shiver ran through her spine. That's what made her fight so hard; the fact that failure put her enemy in command of 500 enhanced assassins. She knew most of the Emilies were good people, but they were afraid of Amy. Someone who always demanded that she got her desires was a formidable foe, but a good ally. They all agreed with her because they were followers and she was a leader, a miserable one, but a leader all the same. Eclipse knew that if she could beat Amy, she would be the leader and the followers would be on her side. The problem was how to beat her. She collapsed on the floor next to Aidan. She knew he was always painfully honest. It makes a pessimist a great friend every once in a while.

"Do you think I can do it?" she asked, looking straight ahead at nothing.

Aidan jumped slightly and pulled his face out of his hands. He held his breath for a second, debating and then sighed.

"No, I don't." her look of dismay made him continue. "Do I think that cuts out any throwing weapon? No. Eclipse, you have good aim and a powerful arm, but some force in this world does not want you to stick a blade. I just need to find some other weapon that will replace your knives on your belt."

He looked over to see her shaking her head and watching her fingers twiddle in her lap. She wasn't talking about sticking a meager knife anymore

"No. I mean do you think I can beat Amy?"

That one hit Aidan square in the head. He had never heard her doubt herself out loud. And he was the instructor of her worst sport. He thought for a bit. Saying yes would give her false expectations but saying no would crush any chance she had. He hated Amy as much as anyone, but he saw no way an un-enhanced human could beat an enhanced one. He looked at her. She sat playing with the threads in her shirt waiting for his answer, with wide, anticipating eyes. He really did care about her and wanted to say exactly what he meant but if she had already given up, he couldn't do a thing in the world to help her. If she was cocky, it was her loss. Finally, he knew exactly what he needed to say. He was just a second too late.

"Your speed in answering isn't very reassuring." she mumbled.

He rolled his eyes and pursed his lips.

"I think it's up to you. Your attitude toward the fight is half of the fight, Eclipse. If you walk in there feeling beat, she'll win every time. If you walk in there full of yourself, she'll beat you again."

"So, what am I supposed to do?"

"Walk in there with confidence in who you are and what you're capable of. It's the best you can do and that means you'll fight your best."

He pat her on the shoulder and pushed himself up off the floor.

"I think we are done for today. You should move on to your next activity."

She nodded and stood up. Aidan awkwardly pat her back one more time and helped gather her knives from the floor. It was quiet for a minute then the question every mentor hates to hear reared its ugly head.

"Aidan?"

"Hmm?"

"What if my best isn't good enough?" she asked.

He stopped and looked her square in the eyes.

"Then you take that bitch down with you."

# CHAPTER TEN

Duke slammed his pencil down on the desk and buried his face in his hands with a long moan. He hated these tests. They were impossible to solve.

"Thank you for sharing your opinion. Now continue with the test."

Joey didn't even look up from his own paperwork and his voice showed no sign of surprise. As it happened, he saw his son do this on a regular basis, so his voice barely went beyond monotony during these episodes. Duke, on the other hand, often continued to express himself fervently.

"Why do I have to take this stupid test every single week?!" he demanded.

Joey continued flipping through his own papers, barely paying his son any attention.

"First, a test cannot be stupid. It is an inanimate object. Second, I never give you the same test twice. And third, if repetition bothers you so much, why do you ask me that same question every week?"

Duke's face flushed. He knew what his father was doing. He was refusing to get angry at him. Duke hated that. He wished Joey would just blow up sometimes and yell back. It infuriated him that the old man never lost his decorum. To be honest, it infuriated a lot of people. He slumped down in his chair and pouted, glancing toward the window. It was a beautiful day and he was stuck inside the stupid castle doing stupid strategy tests.

The study was the quietest room in the house. It was the only door at the end of the hallway which stretched out from the entrance to the suite. It was big enough for both Duke and Joey to have their own workplaces. They had matching desks made from the best wood in the kingdom, but they were ancient. Duke's was cracked in several places and missing a drawer and Joey's had blocks of wood for all four legs. Still, they were beautiful, unique, and quite functional. They sat side by side in the stone-walled room, each with their own candelabra. Every day, Joey and Duke sat together as they each attended their own business until Duke finished, when he was permitted to go outside and do drills with his friends. After drills he would come home and they would review his work for the day. Occasionally, he did very well, but most the time he refused to focus and failed almost everything Joey gave him.

The doorbell rang and Duke sprung out of his chair so hard it flew backwards and tipped. His chair looked as though it was made of twigs compared to his father's solid oak one. He ran right in between the two desks crying out in excitement.

"I'll get it-------"

Duke stopped in his tracks as his throat lost its air supply. Joey had caught his cape as he darted past and used it to pull his son back a few steps. The boy took a couple deep breaths when his father finally released and looked at Joey scornfully. The strategist was still looking at his desk!!!

"Haven't I told you not to wear this ridiculous thing in the house?" Joey pointed out, monotonous as ever.

Duke's face flushed in anger and he opened his lips to mouth off. Just then Joey did look up and his face told Duke to shut his clapper before he even started. His son snapped his jaw shut. He pursed his lips and plopped back down in his chair as Joey removed his glasses and rose to get the door. Duke sat silently and motionless until the study door closed behind his father and then muttered under his breath when he knew it was safe.

"Tyrant."

Joey opened the door to find a cheeky 12-year-old boy with brown curls piled on the top of his head. He gave an ear-wide grin and hopped through the doorway as Joey gestured him in.

"Hey there, Sir Rogers!!!! Where's Duke at this lovely afternoon?" he piped.

Joey smiled. The ball of excitement before him was none other than Alex's son, Antilles. He was a bright boy and a gifted archer, even at 12, but he had too much energy for the old war strategist. Joey was always happy to see him though.......... for brief periods of time.

"Duke is finishing his strategy test, but I'm sure he'll be done soon." Joey replied a bit bitterly.

He knew right now that Duke was laying on the floor listening through the crack in the bottom of the door to see who was at the door. As soon as he heard Antilles' voice, he would rush through the rest of his test to escape into the world of weapon drilling and training with his best friend. Sure enough, only seconds later, he heard the study door swing open and slam shut again as his son shot for freedom. Duke ran up to them, holding his cape. He wasn't going to get caught that way again.

"Hiya Antilles!! See ya Dad!"

He grabbed his friend's arm and pulled him towards the door.

"Duke?"

Joey could see the exasperation in his son's face as he slowly turned around.

"Yeeees?" he asked slowly.

Joey sighed. It was a lost battle.

"Did you finish the test?"

"Yes sir."

Joey's eyes slit suspiciously.

"Every question?"

"Yes sir."

They stood silently facing off and finally Joey just waved him and Antilles out the door. The huge grins on their faces was the only thanks he got. Antilles did at least try to say goodbye before Duke slammed the door, leaving Joey standing alone in the hallway. He sighed. This was as peaceful as his life got, really. He knew as soon as he went to grade Duke's test that it would be a horrid mess so he just stood in the hallway. It was quiet and he had nothing to do there.

It was times like this that reminded him that he was in his fifties. He hated the idea of getting old. War and death made everyone feel much older than they are. Joey now knew that even if the world managed to survive this crisis in the future and once more live at peace, he would never see it. All he could do was try to leave his best legacy to the next generation. He sighed one more time and walked wearily toward the study door.

Duke and Antilles on the other hand were tearing down the steps as fast as they could. They reached the bottom and ran out the massive oak doors to the left without a single glance into the Great Hall. There were seven more steps just outside that led into the large circular courtyard. It was paved with cobblestone and always abuzz with people, walking to and fro. The courtyard acted as a main atrium for several important buildings.

First, was the castle of course. It was considered the head of the circle and immediately to its right sat the infirmary where Alex worked. He treated soldiers and civilians there. Beside the infirmary was a massive building. It was the military cafeteria. It was designed to seat 2000 men for a meal. And next to it, even further around the circle, was the garrison. Unlike its northern neighbors, Central Liberty didn't have specialized soldiers. In times of war any eligible man was allowed to join the army. If you could ride, you were trained as cavalry, if you could shoot, you were an archer. If you were bad at both, you were infantry. Most people didn't get a choice. They were put where they were needed and where they excelled. Volunteers were always welcome, but in times of war, everyone demands pay.

Beside the military complex was the stables, holding up to 500 horses in stalls. The stables were far enough around the circle that they were across from the castle. Behind the wooden building itself, was a large field that followed the very edge of the plateau, completely fenced in and split in half by a second fence line. The trained cavalry horses were kept directly behind the stables in the left-hand side of the fence. The right-hand side stretched out beside the left till it reached the eastern edge of the plateau and was significantly larger. It held the cow herd used to feed most of the capital.

Beside the stables and in front of the livestock field was the outdoor range. Not being as technologically advanced as Chrosia, Central Liberty had fifty very simple straw targets with bulls-eyes painted on them lined up in a row. The lanes were separated by simple fencing. Beside the range was the armory, a rather large building with every sort of medieval weapon, once again displaying Chrosia's superiority in warfare.

Next to the armory, the cobblestone turned into a dirt road that led to the primitive village down the eastern side of the plateau. It was the only accessible way to get to the courtyard as the land wasn't a sharp drop there, but rather a somewhat steep hill. Horses and men alike could easily approach the courtyard from this route. The town was large for Central Liberty, but small compared to just about any Chrosian city. It was always bustling with vendors, travelers and, of course, thieves. The rest of the area was covered in grass or sand or cobblestone. In the distance you could see Mount Dragonesta, a long-dormant volcano. It was nothing more than an iconic landmark, now.

Antilles and Duke had just reached the armory, when the former burst out in laughter.

"Look at Acelyn over there!"

Antilles pointed so a confused Duke could see what he was laughing at. Acelyn was the Premier's oldest child. She was 11 and honestly the worst rider in the country. Yet at this very moment she was trying to manage a large stallion, who took no interest in her. She sat on his back, kicking her little feet over and over, just trying to get the beast to walk around the courtyard. Instead, he bent his head over and nibbled on the grass growing between the cobblestones, flipping his mane carelessly from time to time. Duke wasn't sure what was funnier, the fact that the horse ignored the rider completely or the color of Acelyn's face. He too burst into laughter.

"Don't ride too fast, Ace!" he called out to the vexed girl.

She glared at him furiously, which only deepened the red on her face and made the boys laugh even harder before entering the armory. Each grabbed a yew bow and a quiver of goose feather arrows. They strung their bows before leaving to make sure they wouldn't need new strings and slung their quivers over their shoulders as they walked out the door, eagerly waiting to see Acelyn's struggle once more. They were slightly disappointed to see that she had got him moving until they noticed he was simply walking where he wanted, grazing and ignoring the reign's direction. They chuckled again and headed for the range.

It truly was a beautiful day. The sun was shining, but not beating down, and there was a slight breeze keeping the perfect temperature. The range was empty, since both boys were on a difficult schedule. They only really spent time with each other and were perfectly happy that way. There was less drama and more fun. They also got to know each other better than most friends ever do. Each was brutally honest with the other and both hated archery. Duke hated anything he was horrible at and Antilles considered archers cowards who feared to get their hands dirty in battle. Unfortunately for him, he excelled at archery, which meant it would probably be his career later in life.

Duke watched his buddy draw an arrow and fire in less than ten seconds and grimaced as it struck dead bullseye.

"How do you do that?" he asked bitterly.

Antilles shrugged.

"It's kinda natural now, but don't worry, I was once just as bad as you."

He shot a sidelong glance at his friend before firing again. Duke grinned at the insult. He was terrible and he knew it. But he also knew that it wasn't entirely his fault. He didn't have nearly as much time to practice as Antilles. His smile faded and he moodily shot his own arrow. It hit the target, but on the very outer edge. Typical.

"Damn, I wish I had your life sometimes."

The statement threw Antilles off enough that he missed the bullseye by a centimeter. Duke couldn't help but grin at his friend's face.

"Why would you want my life, Duke? I have to help take care of sick people and all these girls have started annoying me. Mom makes me brush my hair now, thanks to them. I am most likely stuck being an archer which is totally lame-------"

"But at least you get to fight!!!" Duke blurted out. "I'll always stay safe in my office and tell other people how to die. You get to train every hour of every day in how to be a hero. I sit at a desk and learn how to multiply. You have a family. I have an old man who hates my guts. At least you still have a............"

Antilles watched his friend suck in his lower lip before it quivered as his hand instinctively reached up to the wolf pendant hanging around his neck. He knew immediately what his friend was thinking. He still had a mom. Duke wanted a mom more than anything. For some reason, he felt like his best chance of living a non-boring life was to have a mom on his side. Someone to combat the insane toil his father placed before him. Honestly, Duke spent most of his life feeling like an orphan..... and wishing he was one the rest of it. Antilles wisely continued the conversation with no remark to where Duke cut off.

"Have you ever tried just telling your dad that you hate your life, don't want to follow in his footsteps, and simply want to fight for your country?"

"I have told him."

"And?"

"He said," Duke sighed. "'Now that I know what you want, please do as I asked.'."

Antilles whistled. That was quite a come-back actually. Point, Joey. Duke shot him a glare at the sound, not appreciating his enthusiasm. Antilles cleared his throat before continuing.

"Well, why can't someone else be Joey's apprentice?"

"Because the only assigned apprenticeship is through genetics, he would have to ask someone to take his place if he didn't just pass it on to me. And no one, repeat, NO one would want to take his place. So, he never bothered trying. It was just easier to assign it to me."

"Tough bricks, Duke."

Antilles went back to firing. He didn't know what else to say, so he stopped saying anything. Duke was a normal ten-year-old, so when he felt small and aggravatingly helpless, he needed somewhere to expend his frustration. He looked around. Someone had to be having a worse day than him. Turned out, someone was.

Duke watched it all happen before it struck him to yell out a warning. When anyone put their horse back out to pasture, they were supposed to dismount outside the stables and walk them through the stables and then set them free inside the fence. Acelyn was riding toward the gate and got too close for her mount to stand still. He was done carrying a little imp around on his back. He wanted his freedom back. Duke saw him perk his ears up, before starting in a canter toward the fence. Acelyn dropped her reigns and grabbed the saddle horn, screaming more blood curdling than the boys had ever heard. Both of them looked at the other and took off toward the scene, dropping their bows. They knew that horse was going to jump and Ace was going to fall. Neither of them really had a plan, but they had to help. They tried shouting out instructions as the horse began to stance himself for a leap. The boys froze when he jumped. Amazingly enough, Acelyn stayed on and the horse simply stopped to eat while the girl sobbed on his back, not daring to let go of the saddle horn. The jump was fine. That's not what stopped the boys. It was where he landed that petrified them.

The stallion had jumped into the right fence where several hundred bulls and cows just waited to be bothered. And the horse didn't disappoint them. He got just close enough while grazing to bother a particularly big bull with fire in his eyes and smoke in his nostrils. The alpha of the herd. As soon as he gave his battle cry, his herd replied and the chaos began. The boys lost sight of the girl in the riot and had to keep running. Duke, who was the faster of the two, vaulted over the fence just in time to see Ace fly into the air with a particularly nasty buck from her steed as one bull pommeled it in the side. Luckily, she landed in the far-left corner of the fence so she was thrown out away from the stamping feet of horse and bull. Duke sighed in relief. She could just calmly climb out of the fence now, but she didn't. In shock, she laid on the ground and stayed there, hugging her knees and bawling. He tried yelling at her over the ruckus but as the screams of the furious animals got louder, she buried her head in her arms further and cried even louder.

Duke finally realized he would have to make it to her. He took a deep breath and ran as fast as he possibly could along the fence, praying nothing noticed him. Ace didn't even hear him coming until he grabbed her arm and yanked her to her feet. He had to tear her arms away from him as she tried to hug him and practically threw her over the fence to the peaceful left-hand field. He didn't quite make it so she lay over the fence on her stomach screaming and crying until Antilles came up on the other side to help. He grabbed her hands and pulled till she tumbled over on his side, knocking him down. But the bull and the stallion were still at it as Duke tried to climb over next.

The bull threw the horse into the fence and it shattered. One of the boards smacked Antilles right in the face as he managed to get up, grab Ace and force her to run away with him. They both made it out of the corral. Duke was not so fortunate. The fence threw him back into the mess of overly excited livestock and he shot right into the hock of a young calf. The creature screamed in pain and fell with an injured leg. Duke rolled away and desperately crawled through the violent forest of hooves. He finally made it out and stood up, trying to figure out what happened. He shook his head. The world seemed to fade for a few seconds and his ears rang louder than any bell. Something was messing up his vision, turning it blurry and white, as if fog was blocking out everything else. As he blinked over and over again, he began to make out something. At first, it was a huge black blob, but the more he focused the more his thinking came back. The blob began to move towards him and his heart skipped a beat as he realized.......... the bull was charging him!!! He bolted toward the nearest fence he could see and scrambled over it. Thankfully, the charging bull couldn't corner fast enough to follow right away. The boy could barely see five feet in front of him as he dropped to the ground, struggling to re-orient his sight.

It is odd how the mind works. Part of Duke knew exactly what was going to happen next, but couldn't relay instructions to his body fast enough. He had five seconds. In the first, he realized that the fence was not going to stop a raging bull if it charged again. In the second, that he was on the edge of the plateau and the backside of the corral. The third, that when the bull broke through the fence, they would both end up tumbling down said plateau. Fourth, he needed to move. Fifth........... he was too late!!! The fence impacted his back with a loud crack.

He fell. Ground, sky, ground, sky, all the way down the steep incline. His arms reached for any hold. He heard the bull tumbling after him with angry snorts and screams of pain. And his mind stopped trying. It screamed between his ears as the painful bumps and bruises formed themselves against the ground. He tumbled to the very bottom, landing sprawled out on his stomach, barely holding onto consciousness. Any good fighter is taught to stay awake until someone gives them medical attention, so Duke lay, trying to focus on not sleeping, even though he wanted to so badly. He was losing the battle. Slowly his mind was fading out and all his thoughts dying, then a familiar snort saved him. Dukes eyes shot open as the heavy breathing next to him continued. He slowly forced his head up and looked forward. The bull was on his feet again, stomping a hoof and blowing through his nostrils in fury. Duke could see the whites of its eyes. He could feel the heat from its nostrils and only one thought raced through his young mind now.

*I'm dead.*

The bull reared to stomp his front hooves onto Duke's face and the boy just closed his eyes, ready to accept his fate. But thundering hooves never hit his body. And Duke managed to open one eye to look. The bull had stopped!!! He was looking past him, up the plateau from whence they fell. Duke watched it hopefully. Maybe it would leave him alone? Maybe he would live? He propped himself up slightly and opened his other eye. The animal shifted his gaze back to him for a moment and then back up the plateau. He hesitated only a second longer before turning with a flip of his tail and a snort.

Duke watched him bolt away and began to breathe again. He managed to smile and even chuckle with joy as he rolled over onto his back. That was closer than he ever wanted to be to death again. He slowly sat up. How his head hurt! It felt like it was quaking in pain. In fact, all of him felt like it was quaking. Puzzled, Duke looked at his hands and feet trying to figure out what was going on. Then his head made the connection. It was the ground. The ground was vibrating!!!! That could only mean..... the boy slowly looked up the slope. Then he jumped to his feet, ignoring the blinding pain in every muscle of his body.

The entire herd thundered toward him.

Duke froze just long enough to realize he couldn't outrun the stampede in any direction. He searched anxiously for a sanctuary. Where could he hide from a stampede????? The only other thing near him was a large boulder sticking out of the base of the plateau. There was just enough room for him to hide under the edge of it if he could only make it there in time.

He bolted for it and tried to slide into the crevice but in his confusion, landed a few feet short. He desperately crawled as fast as he could into safety, crying as he heard the stampede getting closer. Seconds later, he jumped and screamed as the first of many sets of hooves leaped off the rock behind him and landed inches from his face. Duke screamed as loud as he could, covering his ears with his hands, just trying to block out his own fear, and couldn't even hear himself over the racket. It was loud, it was terrifying, and it seemed to last forever.

Then it was over. The pounding stayed in his ears, the tears flowed freely down his cheeks and the herd slowly vanished from sight, but Duke didn't move. His body felt numb and empty. His heart beat faster than he even knew it could. All he could do was lay still and sob, partly from terror and partly relief. It was the type of weeping that only happens when you honestly lose control. His lips trembled violently and his body shivered as if it was cold. He sobbed over and over and tried to get some air into his lungs through his gasps. Duke bawled on, so much so, that he only barely heard the familiar voice calling out to him.

It seemed like nothing but another thought in his head at first. It barely pierced through the fog of noise in his ears. The ringing and the sound of his own heartbeat were enough to muffle it out. But it continued to cry out his name and finally he heard it loud and clear. He forced his eyes open and a familiar form stood less than five feet away, calling his name at the top of his lungs. It was Joey.

"Dad!"

It was more of a croak than a scream, but it was loud enough. Joey spun around and sprinted over to the rock and fell to his knees. He swept his crying boy, who was still trying to crawl out of his hiding spot, into his arms. After sliding down the entire length of the hill, he was exhausted, but Duke was alive and tight against him. Joey's relief brought tears to his eyes. They sat there for countless minutes, father and son held in an unbreakable embrace. It was a true moment for them. The love they both had for each other shone through for a brief second, and then other emotions reared their ugly heads. When your child gets hurt, you always blame yourself as a vent for your emotions, unless of course, you can blame your child. Joey pulled Duke away and wrapped his hands around his face. Duke knew the look well. He was angry.

"What the hell do you think you were doing?"

Duke trembled slightly as Joey yelled at him.

"Do you realize you could've been killed? Why can't you just obey me for once in your life? This is why I set up rules!!!!! To teach stupid kids like you how NOT to do stupid things like this!"

"Dad, I.........."

Duke barely got the sounds out of his throat before Joey gripped his head tighter and shook it.

"I don't care!!" he yelled even louder. "You are in huge trouble, mister! Poor Acelyn fainted and Antilles is still unconscious. All because of your STUPID, IRRESPONSIBLE GAMES!!!"

The last three words came with three hard boxes on Dukes right ear. The boy was in shock! How could his father hit him after what he just went through!! He just stood crying in pain and anger, too upset and tired to even begin to explain. Joey stood up and pushed him away from him.

"Get home NOW! Clean up and get into bed. And yes I know it's only 1:00. Now go!"

Duke tried with everything he had to run away. He could barely see and his foot kept slipping as he staggered around the plateau toward the town. From the town ran the only way back up the steep hill to reach the fortress again, a dirt road. He stumbled and tripped his way back to the courtyard right in front of the fortress where the fountain bubbled away. With every step he cursed Joey and despised him more and more. When he finally reached the fountain, he splashed off his hands and face, not caring that he missed half of each. If his head had been straight or his ears cleared, he might have heard Alex and Ed calling to him from the infirmary door, but he probably would have ignored them anyway.

His head was struggling to control his body and his mind was so full of hate, he couldn't even think. His anger and spite drove him to fight up every step in the castle, not knowing how many people were calling after him asking if he needed help. He was going to prove that Joey was evil. He was going to show him!! As soon as he got home, he was going to set his study on fire. He was going to destroy everything. He slammed into the suite's door, not realizing he had even made it home yet and forced his way inside where he tripped over his own feet and fell to the ground. The pain shot through his entire body and he screamed so angrily and unintelligibly that Alex heard it in the courtyard through the windows. Duke just stayed on the floor and furiously kicked the door shut behind him. It felt so good not to move. To be silent and safe. He would get his revenge later. Right now, he just wanted to sleep..........................

Joey reached the fountain several minutes after his son and immediately knew something was wrong. He wasn't sure what gave it away. Probably the fact that everyone stared at him as he walked into the courtyard. He walked calmly to the far side of the courtyard where Alex and Vantage were sitting on a bench, tending to their children. Alex was helping Antilles get a drink, since most of his head was bandaged and the Premier was holding his weeping daughter, who had just come to. Joey went and sat right next to the Premier. He was still furious, even though he had no idea why. He was sure it was Duke's fault. What with his constant disregard for rules and rebellious attitude. He guessed he was angry that his son had pulled these two innocent children into his shenanigans and gotten them hurt. He was a politician, though so he hid his anger.

"Ace?" he whispered softly. "Can you tell me what happened?"

The little girl nodded and wiped the back of her hands across her nose and cheeks, trying to stop crying. She tried to recount the tale, but every two or three words she had to gasp or sniff or rub her eyes again. Joey patiently waited for her to finish.

"I was...... riding and...... it bolted and..... I.... dropped....... the..... reigns" she paused to cry a little longer, "Duke....... he..... he jumped....... in and....... he......."

Poor Ace broke down crying. Joey pat her on the back and thanked her. He didn't want to stress her out anymore, so he got up to leave, perplexed.

"He saved her."

Joey looked uncomfortably at Antilles, who couldn't even see him. If this was all true, he just punched his son in the head for no reason. He tried to stay calm as he spoke.

"How so?"

Antilles spilled the whole story. When he realized Duke wasn't with them, he had turned around just in time to see the bull push him over the edge. He knew he couldn't do anything, so he dragged Acelyn into the courtyard, before his head injury finally knocked him out, and told his father about Duke. All Alex said to Joey was that Duke had been in the bull pen and was now being targeted by a stampede. And of course, Joey ran after to try and save his son. But he had no idea it was originally a rescue mission on Duke's part. When Antilles finished, Joey plopped back on the bench and rubbed his face.

"Dammit" he muttered.

Alex knew that look. It was guilt.

"Oh no." he sighed. "What'd you do, Joey?"

Joey just looked up at the doctor and shook his head with a roll of his eyes before burying his face in his hands. Alex got the gist.

"Joe, I know you have this thing about not apologizing to your son, but you owe him one this time and you can't deny it."

Joey was mortified by the very suggestion and his jaw dropped in horror.

"But an apology gives him something to hold over me-------!"

"Oh for the love of barmaids, man!!!" Ed jutted in angrily. "Your son just saved my daughter's life and you are worried about apologizing because you punished him for no good reason???? Grow a pair, sir!"

Joey knew they were right but one other thing was bothering him.

"What if he never forgives me? What if I just ruined his life forever?"

"Oh don't worry, Sir Rogers." Antilles piped up. "He already thinks you are ruining his life!"

Joey shot Antilles an irritated glance as Alex very gently smacked his son on the back of his head. Then the two men set off to go see Duke, Alex to examine him and Joey to be a good father.

As they walked up the stairs the two friends were glad to have some time to talk. Joey had some serious questions and Alex had some serious advice to give. Joey broke the ice.

"Alex, I want you to be completely honest with me."

"Always, Joe."

"Do you think Antilles is right? Does Duke hate me?"

Alex hesitated. He knew that Antilles thought Joey was too strict and expected too much from Duke, but he also knew that Antilles respected Joey a great deal. He got the idea that Duke strongly disagreed with his father on a lot of things and that Joey was a stubborn old ass about it. But did Duke hate Joe?

"It's wonderful that you have to think so long." Joey said dryly.

"Well, you said you wanted a truly honest answer, Joe."

"And it's taking you so long because you don't know how to put it nicely, right?"

"No, because I had to think first. I don't think he hates you, but I do think he hates your job. You decided the day he was born that he would always do things your way and do what you want. Well, then what makes him Duke, if he has to be Joey? Y'know?"

"So, you think I'm a bad father, huh?"

"Of course, I do." The doctor chuckled.

"What the hell, Alex?"

"Joe, I still think *I'm* a bad father. I'm never quite sure about what I'm doing."

"Oh? And what if I tell you that I *am* sure, Alex?"

"I'd say you're slightly over-confident, my friend. Think about it, Joey! You just punished your ten-year-old son for saving someone's life. His entire outlook on decision making has now shifted to either doing the right thing no matter what, or doing what everyone wants him to do to stay out of trouble."

"Well, surely he'll understand my point of view?!?!"

"He's ten. And you went a little crazy. I'm fairly certain kids have no idea why their parents are crazy sometimes. Maybe when he's a parent himself? He might understand then? I'm sure his kids will anger him some day. And they won't understand why he gets mad when they get hurt, anymore than he understands why you do right now. It's a parent's lot in life, I suppose. Look, you wanted total honesty........."

"My mistake." Joey muttered under his breath.

".....and that's what I'm giving you. You expect perfection from Duke in an imperfect world. You've always told him to stay out of that field, but wouldn't it have been wrong for him to do so today and let Acelyn get hurt, or even killed?"

Joey pursed his lips thoughtfully. He couldn't refute Alex, but he also knew his son's attitude too well. He was the type of kid to have an 'I told you so' dance. Apologizing to him would make his day.

"I just don't want to grovel at his feet." he muttered.

"Then don't. Treat him the way you would treat me. Just apologize."

"But then that will give him the edge he needs to undermine my authority!!"

"Well, honestly, Joe. Maybe you should rethink your authority."

The war strategist shot his friend an angry glare.

"Careful, Alex. Our friendship may be at stake here."

"It's because I'm your friend that I'm saying this. I honestly think Duke wants to be a soldier, not a war strategist. He's not cut out for a desk job. He can't stand the fact that there are politics to war that decide who lives and who dies. He's a bit old fashioned and thinks the best warrior should always win. Why don't you just look for a new apprentice and let your kid be himself?"

"Alex........ I've been looking for one for 35 years. No one wants the damn job!"

Joey began to open his front door. Alex reached out and pulled it shut, making his friend meet his unwavering gaze.

"Joey, if you've asked everyone else, why won't you ask your own damn son?"

"Because I'm 52 years old!! And we *will* be at war with Chrosia soon. You know that. When I die, it's his responsibility to step up if I have no other apprentice, so he needs to be prepared to fill that position."

"Joe, Victor chooses the careers of his sons. How can you stand to have anything in common with that man?"

Joey's eyes narrowed with anger.

"*You* are here to make sure my son is alright. *I* am here to make sure he does the right thing. Don't overstep, Doctor."

The men glared into each other's eyes until Alex looked away with a sigh. He should've known better than to try. He pushed open the door and walked in.

"Well, he's not alright, you stubborn ass." he muttered.

Joey watched anxiously as Alex knelt beside his prostrate son. He could see Duke breathing, but there were no other signs of life on his body. The doctor checked his pulse and shook his head.

"I'll get him to the bed. You go get my bag from Drew, unless you don't trust me around your son." Alex commanded spitefully.

Joey bit his tongue and walked away. He didn't have the energy to fight anymore.

ΩΩΩΩΩΩ

Duke woke with a sudden jerk, like a violent shiver. He couldn't see very well but it was definitely dark in his room and hazy, even with the torches on the wall lit. That meant it was evening or later, which in turn meant that he missed all of his practice time and it was back to studies if he got out of bed. With a slight moan he simply shut his eyes and tried to go back to sleep. It was dark and cozy. The fire cackled quietly across the room. Then it was brilliantly bright. He was shooting with Antilles at the range and all was well. They were laughing and joking. And it happened. The sky turned red as blood and the wind tore whole buildings away from the ground. The boys turned, fleeing for shelter. And there it was. A noise neither had ever heard before. It was like a little girl's scream, floating through whatever pitch suited it at that moment. It was eerie and haunting. It sounded as if organ pipes had voices and none of them got along well with other members of its own instrument. It paralyzed Duke. He turns around slowly and everything goes still as he faces the target.

Silence.

But only for a moment. Then the scream again. A massive bull plows through the target at which Duke stares. Its blood-shot eyes scream murder. The ring in its nose bursts into flames and black smoke pours from its ears. Tall as a building, Duke finds himself at eye level with its knees. They bleed profusely, dripping blood all the way down its razor-sharp hooves, which glint dully in the red light. He scrapes the ground and screams out again. The noise rips through eardrums like a knife. And he looks straight at the little boy in his path. Duke watches him charge. The sky melts and drips over his head. He sees it coming closer and closer as the blood drips into his eyes. And then...................

Joey ran as fast as he could. He had never heard his son scream like that. It was absolutely terrifying. He burst through Duke's bedroom door and straight to the bed, grabbing the boy's shoulders, trying to wake him up. It didn't matter. Duke screamed and screamed, switching between wiping blood from his head wound out of his eyes and holding his hands over his ears. He thrashed uncontrollably as Joey pulled him into a hug.

"Duke!!!! Duke, stop!!!"

Hiding panic in your own voice is the hardest thing any parent has to do when consoling a terrified child. They have no idea what to say or do. The best thing is to wait it out......... and say what every parent does.

"It's gonna be ok. It's not real. It's just a dream, Duke. It's gonna be ok."

After several minutes Duke finally heard his father and calmed down. It was only a dream. He was sitting in his own bed in his room. He heard the fire burning again and there was no bull. No Antilles. And no wind. There was, however, blood dripping into his eyes and there was Joey, holding him in a tight embrace, waiting for him to awaken. But there was always Joey. He was always there. And even though he was trying to do right by his son now, Duke saw it entirely differently. He pushed his father away, slammed back into his bed and pulled his fleece blanket all the way up to his ears.

Joey had the most hurt look on his face Duke had ever seen, but it didn't matter. The old man thought he was being comforting, just trying to help. He knew he was wrong earlier and was trying to make up for it, but the look on his son's face as he shoved him away was a deeper wound than the boy knew. Duke looked remarkably like his mother and it was the same look she gave him the first time he hurt her. It was their first fight and he knew he was wrong, but too proud to admit it, so he drew it out as long as he could. Things escalated. She was yelling soon and both of them were saying things neither of them truly meant. Then it happened. He reached out and slapped her.

Then that look, the same one his son flashed at him now, tore through his heart. It was a look of pain and betrayal. The fight stopped right then. He fell to his knees begging for forgiveness, but she ran from the room, crying. Of course, she eventually came back in to wipe the tears from his eyes and forgive him wholeheartedly. It was the last fight they ever had. He controlled his temper for the rest of their marriage, but that look stayed frozen in his mind. So, he knew the right thing to do with his son at this very moment when he saw it once more. He knew he should apologize and ask forgiveness. He knew............ but he didn't. He stayed silent and stared at his son.

Then he made a fatal mistake. He stood up and walked away. No apology, no regret....... nothing. He simply left his son with blood dripping down his forehead into his eyes and onto his bed. He gave up on being a father and became a boss. Nothing more, nothing less. And Duke was left to come to his own conclusions. He saw the life he hated, forced on by his father. He saw the punches he received earlier that day for doing the right thing. He felt alone and unwanted. Desperate for someone to come in and care for his wounds, or hold him and actually mean it. Duke felt afraid, like the fear he felt staring down the bull. Those eyes. He could see them watching him in every dark corner of the room.

And in his mind, Joey was the bull.

# CHAPTER ELEVEN

Sean pushed his food around on his plate in silence. He and his brothers hadn't spoken at the dinner table in a whole month, but tonight their nerves were all higher and tighter than those past forty days. A pin dropping could've set off the argument of the century, so no one spoke, no one coughed or sneezed, and no one made eye contact. They all stared at their plates picking at their food in silence. Unfortunately, when there are only five parties at a table and four are silent, it gives the fifth entirely too much time to talk.

"You four" Victor said as he wiped his mouth with the gold threaded napkins. "are pathetic. She only has one more night. And it's just Eclipse. If something does happen, she's easy to replace. I'll get you a servant girl or something else you can worry about. Like...... I don't know.......... a dog."

The brothers watched Victor throw his napkin down. As angry as they were with him for equating their beloved sister to a dog, they knew he was getting tired of their attitude about it and they definitely knew better than to get him angry. Everyone in Chrosia knew better than that. They exchanged subtle glances and all started to eat. They still didn't feel like talking, but they knew that's not what bothered their father. Thing is, none of them knew what was bothering him. He had just gone a whole Eclipse-free month. That should have put him in the best mood ever.

In truth, Victor was ever so slightly worried about his daughter. She had shown great promise the week before her enhancement and he was considering inviting her into the family, maybe. He suddenly wanted to raise her himself, maybe it was because he was getting older and still had no heir, or because she was proving to be a pocket-sized version of himself. Only problem was that Acre warned him against it. He said if he didn't continue to raise her the way he had her whole life, she would lose the qualities Victor was finally willing to accept. So, instead of going with his gut and being there for his daughter, the promontory fell for his scientist's ploy.

The only bad thing about metal structures is how they respond to certain weather conditions. It was always possible for lightning to cause an issue, such as electrocuting everyone in the building. Thankfully, Acre designed an insulating force field which kept the lightning at bay around the capital city on nights like this one, when rain poured from the sky in buckets, heralded by its dear friends, thunder and lightning.

This safety net was run by a large machine in the middle of the city that basically changed the molecular compound of the air. It was still breathable and allowed rain to fall through it. But it dead ended all electrical currents that did not run along wires. So, the buildings still had light and their generators still functioned. Still there was a slight chance that the field could fail and allow lightning to strike the metal within. So, the four boys knew when Acre burst through their dining room door, out of breath and sopping, something was definitely wrong.

"Victor!!!! It hit! It made it through!" Acre's voice strained over the thunder echoing through the hall.

Victor calmly wiped his mouth again and waited for the noise to end, which took longer than one would expect. A building made entirely of metal resounds a great deal of noise. Acre stood almost jumping with impatience. This was the promontory's new thing. He waited patiently for the other person to get worked up or blurt out more and then, he unleashed his anger. The four boys knew there were many buildings in the capital and that any number of them could've been struck by lightning, but all of them had a sinking feeling they knew which one in particular would get Acre worked up this much. Still, they clung to the hope that they were dreadfully mistaken and waited impatiently for the news. Acre knew Victor's ploy and definitely knew better than to speak again till he did, but the boys could tell it was eating at him to wait.

Finally, it was quiet again and Victor folded his napkin up and looked at the scientist for the first time.

"Calm down Acre. If it was that bad, it would've hit here and we'd all be dead this very second. So, think of your extreme luck while you calmly explain which building it did hit."

Acre bit his bottom lip. He knew he had to compose himself or Victor would just keep interrupting him and waste precious time. Flattery and serenity were his best options at a time like this.

"You are correct, Excellency. I am indeed very fortunate to be alive to deliver this message, since it concerns you personally."

His voice trembled slightly on the last word, so he stopped and watched Victor, hoping he hadn't heard it. The smile on the promontory's face told him he had heard, but he waved his hand for a continuation of the tale.

"Victor, it was not a building that was hit."

"Ah. So many more people should consider themselves lucky. Do tell

Acre," He leaned forward in his chair and glared straight through the scientist's soul, still smiling. "what did the lightning hit that has you all worked up?"

Acre glanced around at the four young faces that stared at him in fear. He gave them the most sympathetic look he could and faced their father again. He knew how this would tear them apart and would rather see the smug look of success on Victor's face than that of pain on any of theirs.

"It took out the security system for the Enhancer. The machine locked its own door and refuses to respond to me. No one can get in..... or out......"

No one moved for several seconds. The hall was silent except for faint sounds of rain drops on the outer walls. The cold, harsh, hand of reality gripped the throats of everyone in the room. Only Acre could see Victor's face drop ever so slightly. If they couldn't get her out, he knew it meant she would probably die. It was a bit of cruel irony, that she would only die once he wished she would stay.

A sudden blast of lightning lit up the entire hall and woke all six men from their realization. The four brothers all moved at once, knocking over chairs as they ran. Victor gave Acre a nod and stood up slowly to follow them. He had to control whatever emotions finagled their way into his cold heart. The boys ran to the roof and into the translucent tunnel that led to the roof of the lab. It was the fastest way to reach the Enhancer, running through the tubes in the sky rather than the streets.

Sean reached the door first and placed his hand on the scanner beside it. On a normal day, when no one was in the Enhancer, the security system would let any member of the leading family in, except Eclipse of course, but access was more limited when someone was actually in the machine. This was mainly because the Enhancer dealt with the very core of a person's genetic makeup. It enhanced properties they already had by a set percentage. The regular was 50%. Interrupting this could kill or seriously mutilate the person inside. Unfortunately for Eclipse, and Sean, the Enhancer did recognize the presence of an entity within its walls and had locked down accordingly. But the entire outer system was shut down. It was part of the building's inside security programming to make sure no one could get in if there was any sort of security breach on the outside. If it did what it was supposed to, not even Victor's hand would register on the scanner.

Sean desperately slammed his hand down again and again. Each time the machine read access denied, he hit just a bit harder, as if force would change protocol. Finally, he gave up and slammed his fists into the door, beating and pounding as hard as he could, crying out forcefully with each hit. His brothers knew better than to intervene and just stood staring in disbelief, shock running through their veins and showing on all their faces.

By the time Acre and Victor approached, Sean had blood running down his hand and arms.

"Sean!! Sean!!!" Acre was mortified by the actions of the boy and ran over to him. "You have to stop!! Beating your hands to the bone---------"

As soon as Acre's hand touched his shoulders Sean pulled one of the oldest hand-to-hand combat tricks. He grabbed the hand on his shoulder and the throat of its owner and flung him around into the blood-smeared door. Acre gasped. The wind was knocked clean from his lungs as his back slammed into the metal. The hand around his throat didn't help much either. But the thing that scared him the most was the face he was staring at. Sean looked........ vicious, a trait not often associated with the boy. His eyes lit up and for just a moment, Acre saw a younger Victor.

"GET HER OUT!!!"

Thunder roared just above their heads, but Sean was louder. Fear clutched Acre's voice more than Sean's fingers. How could he tell this ball of fury that there was literally nothing he could do?

"That's ENOUGH!!"

For once, Victor stepped in to save the day.

"Release him, Sean and compose yourself. You're acting like a child!"

Acre didn't know if it was the tone of voice Victor used or the fact that what he said was true that hit home. But either way, Sean's face softened and he realized what he was doing. Immediately the scientist was freed, much to his relief. Acre's hands shot up and rubbed his throat. Sean muttered out a miserable apology before collapsing to his knees helpless.

Victor puffed out his cheeks and blew in exasperation.

"How dramatic Sean. And so very mature."

When he realized the boy wasn't even paying attention to him, he concentrated on making someone else miserable. It helped him cope with the strange feeling welling in his own gut.

"Acre, how long will it take to repair the system?"

The scientist forced his eyes off his attacker to answer, still massaging where Sean's hand had grasped.

"The entire system is fried. It took me over a year to build it, but I think I can manage eight months this time." he croaked.

It was Shane's turn to look up and away from Sean. No one had ever seen him act that way, so the boys just stared at the motionless form of their little brother in disbelief. But unlike him, the other Monohues managed to keep their heads.

"Eight months?" Shane questioned Acre. "That door won't open for eight months? That's only one month short of a year, Acre. We are just supposed to leave her in there that whole time?!!"

"I'm sorry Shane. It's the absolute best I can do."

"Will the Enhancer at least stop tomorrow and let her wake up?" Aidan asked, still staring at Sean. "She could figure out a way to escape if she wakes up."

"I'm afraid not. The Enhancer is designed to continue working if something goes wrong. It'll run until it's out of serum for her specific enhancement."

"Well...." Shane gulped, not really wanting to know the answer. "what will happen then?"

"She'll die."

Everyone turned and faced Sean. His voice was stable as he confirmed what everyone already knew, but didn't want to accept.

"When the Enhancer stops the IV vitals, she'll still be submerged in the infusion chamber, but no air will be flowing through her blood stream. She will wake up just in time to drown....." Sean pushed off the ground and walked past all of them, only stopping to look his father square in the eyes and finish. "........ and we will get a dog."

Though he didn't show it, Victor was uneasy with the look on his son's face. It wasn't normal for him. He was being bold and deliberate. The words sounded more like a threat than a statement. When the boy finally did look away, Victor realized something. Sean was much smarter than he had thought and he had lost a lot in his life, making him dangerously self-destructive recently. The kid knew what Victor was and was not willing to do. He refused to end the lives of his own sons and was slowly drifting in favor of Eclipse. He didn't want her dead, for the first time in her life. She was fiery and talented. She inspired loyalty and she was dedicated to him in a way he didn't quite understand. He had been looking forward to seeing her enhanced.

The next day was torture for the four boys. Sean and Shane stayed at the range all day, mindlessly firing arrow after arrow. Erican sat with his back against the replacement wall at the end of the range whittling a soft piece of cherry wood and Aidan tried to watch all the Emilies throwing knives, all the while flipping his own knife around his fingers. They didn't speak to each other. They didn't make eye contact. And they didn't notice anything around them, even in the slightest. Each was trying to focus desperately on the last time they saw her. They were trying to memorize her face from month old memories that already seemed to be blurring in their minds. It was a living hell.

Erican's small piece of wood slowly took shape as a magnificent dragon. He had started trying to preserve what she looked like, but somehow her eyes turned into dragon eyes in his hand. She had always liked tales of dragons. Her favorite was the legend of the Inferno, an ancient warrior who tamed and rode dragons in the mountain ranges to the north of Chrosia. He remembered talking with her about the legend all the time, including the last time they talked. It made him feel so guilty, that the last time he spoke to his own sister was seven whole days before she would be locked away for a month. Of course, he had seen her after that and said hi, and he was even there when she was lowered into the tank, but their last real conversation was that day.

Two days after Victor gave Eclipse her ultimatum, she skipped her breakfast hour by grabbing carb-bars on her way to the weight room at five in the morning. That was when the Logans worked out so she knew she could unwind a little. After all, it was the one place Amy wouldn't go. She hated the Logans, mainly because they all adored Eclipse and were the only people with the guts to tease her the way she teased others. So, Eclipse knew she'd be free from her nemesis for the next hour and free to talk to her brother openly. She needed his help.

"Hey!" Erican beamed when he saw her. "What's up, kid?"

Eclipse didn't particularly enjoy being called a kid, but it always prompted that coveted little grin of hers when Erican said it. Not today. She didn't even respond before grabbing his hand and dragging him into a corner where no one else was lifting.

"Erican, I need some help, but it's dangerous."

Now most guys hearing that from their ten-year-old sister assume it's a joke, like a spider that needs slain, but Erican knew that Eclipse meant business. For crying out loud, this is the girl who once grabbed a cobra by its tail on a dare. He knew this was about to be something awful.

"Okkkkk?"

He searched desperately for a better answer, but she continued long before he could find it.

"I need dragon scales."

Erican's mouth dropped and his eyes opened wider than ever before, so wide he could swear his lids ripped a bit in the corner. He shook his head a bit, trying to un-hear her.

"EX-cuse me?"

Dragon scales were the most advanced form of armor. There were only about 10 sets of it in the whole world. It was a compact, magnetic, metal armor with several thousand microscopic scales that contoured to the body of whoever was wearing it. It was virtually indestructible and protected the wearer from everything, even bruising, since it fit tight and gave way to no force. For Eclipse to ask him for this, she was basically asking him to steal from Victor, as it was government-issue only. She was asking him to sign his own death warrant.

"I know" she said calmly.

"How can you even ask....."

"I know"

"Are you absolutely insane?"

"I know, Erican."

"NO!" he hissed, "No, you don't know! If you got caught wearing that, you'd be dead and then I'd be dead and then........ *you'd be dead!*"

"You already said that."

"Well, no. I won't do it."

Eclipse puffed out her cheeks and rolled her eyes. She didn't have time for this. It was time to be more........... convincing. She reached up and yanked his ear down to her mouth by its lobe so she could whisper her next words vehemently right to his stubborn brain.

"Listen to me, Erican. I am going to die in eight days anyway if I can't kick Amy's sorry little ass in the gym. Now, I can't do that unless I pull some serious wool over the entire country's eyes. And you're going to help me in the end because this is the only way. So, pull up your diaper and listen to my plan. You are going to steal me that armor, because you are the second most sneaky person I know, and you're going to give it to Amber. Now, because she is the strongest telepath in the series and the best at using her powers, she's going to temporarily erase this from your memory until I beat Amy and I'm in the Enhancer. Then this will have all blown over and no one will care, even if someone does find out, which they won't because I *am* the sneakiest person I know. But YOU won't ever be implicated even if I do get caught. It'll all be on me and my life is most likely over anyway, so no big deal. Are we clear?"

She let him go and he snapped back to an upright standing position, rubbing his poor ear like a viper had bit it. That was the most violent thing he had ever seen her do outside the gym and her fights with Amy. It was certainly the most violent thing she had ever done to HIM and HE wasn't going to stand for it. He stood up tall and stared straight back into her eyes......... for about five second. Then he looked down at his feet.

In those five seconds, he got it. She was fighting for her life. This wasn't some huge rush in. She had weighed all of her very few options and knew that this, whatever it was, was her only chance. She wasn't really angry at him, she was desperate. He took a deep breath and shook his head. Then he looked into those eyes once more. The begging plea for help finally tipped his scales.

"Ok, I'm in." he groaned, knowing a certain someone was going to hate him for agreeing to this. "But under one condition."

"Anything." she agreed, with a very slight sigh of relief.

"If you are caught. You have to tell them it was all my idea. That I made you do it."

She was shaking her head before he even finished. She knew what that would lead to and didn't want to be the cause of her own brother's death, even if it would save her own life.

"Absolutely not. If I thought there was any chance of this failing, I wouldn't even ask for your help. I won't let you die for me."

"And I won't let YOU die at all. It would be too much of a burden and I would rather take my own life. Plus, you can't do this without me, so you need to learn that all deals require compromise and sacrifice."

She hesitated, which almost made him cry right there and then because it meant she actually cared about him. In reality, she was simply running through her plan in her mind again, making sure no possibility was ruled out. At some point in everyone's life they have to decide who they can count on. Eclipse was out of options. It was either give up, and let Amy steal her life directly upon her death, or take huge risks and fight back as hard as she could for as long as she could and take her own life back. So, she banked on herself.

"Agreed." She groaned miserably.

Erican raised an eyebrow at her response.

"Do you swear on your mother's grave, Eclipse?"

It was the oath she held most sacred and he knew it. She nodded.

"I swear it on my mother's grave."

But Erican still wasn't convinced.

"Swear what, Inferno?" he coaxed gently.

It was his pet name for her. The name of her favorite legend. He called her it when it was just the two of them. Her lip twitched up for a brief second before she cleared her throat and direly whispering her next words.

"I swear on my mother's grave that I will blame you if I fail."

Erican nodded solemnly and they just looked at each other for a while before she said an awkward goodbye and accepted a short hug from him for the first time. As she headed off toward the range, she suddenly felt sick. She had just wagered her own brother's life to save her own. Was she turning into a worse monster than Victor? No, she was going to succeed, which would mean Erican wasn't in danger. Failure was no longer an option. Her brother's life depended on it.

Erican's mind snapped back to the present when his knife slipped and cut his thumb. As he shook and sucked the blood away, he couldn't help but grin. She had been right, of course. No one figured out and she beat Amy because of their little arrangement. His memory of the whole conversation had come back slowly, starting a week after she was placed in the Enhancer. At first, in dreams and flashes, then it all just hit one day. He swore he would never ignore her for a single day again, much less a whole week. And now as he stared at his creation as evening set in, he felt it all hitting harder than ever. He may never be able to hug her a second time.

The last bell of the night rang and he glanced around himself. His brothers were all there with him. None of them spoke or even looked at each other, but being there for the next man was enough for the four of them. Erican took the tip of his knife and dipped it in the cut on his finger and carved just a bit more, using his blood as an inkwell to dye the wood as he carved. Then the four of them walked out of the range together, but when they reached her locker, Erican stopped. He opened it and set his little carving in before walking away. His brothers all watched him go before daring to glance in the locker. The carving was a truly fantastic work. It was only about six inches tall and four wide, but it was beautiful. The dragon was rearing on its hind legs with its wings spread out. And stretched out across his back and wings, carved in lovely red letters it read Inferno.

# CHAPTER TWELVE

It wasn't long before Acre came forward with a solution. Naturally, all his focus was on repairing the Enhancer. Not only because Eclipse was vital to his plans, but because Victor would be furious if she delayed his plans simply by being stuck in the building he needed to enhance the Logans. His original idea had been to simply find a way to get past the security *into* the Enhancer and shut it down. The problem was, he had designed the building to be impenetrable and the security system, infallible, so when his security system malfunctioned from a lightning strike, it took quite a toll on the scientist. His inventions never failed, so he literally had no backup options. There was no way around the system and if the building *happened* to be punctured or the system detected any irregularity at all, security would shut off the machinery. That was what Acre couldn't afford to do. Not only would it take months to override the system and get the Enhancer up and running again, it would kill his beloved Eclipse instantly. When anything set off an alarm, the Enhancer immediately flushed every bit of its chemical agent into the current subject, the strain would overload the body's functions and wake the subject up, just in time for them to basically explode. Acre imagined it was a horrible way to go. Any dealings with DNA went as such. The subject either came out stronger, or dead, their last moments spent in utter agony.

Acre's new idea was still quite risky, but it was his only shot at saving Eclipse. The computer system that ran the security was wirelessly accessible to any computer through an extremely difficult and time-consuming process. It would take months to safely hack the system and even more time to shut it down if he was to avoid detection. Normally, he could hack something by introducing a virus, but that wasn't subtle enough in this situation. His database on the security system computer ran a constant virus scan with absolutely no loopholes. Now, if he could hack that database by slowly and painstakingly changing its function and properties, he may be able to authorize a system shut down. But he would have to do it slowly. Otherwise the computer would discover his presence and signal an alarm. It might do so anyway, but this was their only hope. He presented the idea to the leading family one evening about a month after the big storm.

"What do you think?" he asked at the dinner table, after giving a detailed explanation.

Five sets of eyes stared blankly at him for several minutes before someone finally spoke.

"I literally have no idea what you just said." Victor responded with a careless shrug, "So, I couldn't care less what you do. Just don't destroy my building."

He continued to eat, hiding his concern that she had been stuck so long. His sons had a few more questions.

"Is it safe for Eclipse?" Sean asked.

Acre bit his bottom lip before answering.

"I'm not going to lie. I honestly have no idea if this will even work, but it is the safest option for the building and your sister."

"Well, what does that mean?" Shane scoffed. "That you wouldn't save Eclipse if it would hurt your precious building?"

Victor's quick glare at Acre told the scientist he needed to be careful here. If Victor knew that he could get in without damaging the building, he might be more than happy to kill Eclipse for it. Acre had promised him this was the only way to save the Enhancer. It was the only reason the promontory was on board with the plan.

"Shane, the needs of the many must always outweigh the needs of the few. If the building died, so would our way of life. The consequences would not be so severe over the death of one child. This is the only way to save the Enhancer. It just so happens, it might save Eclipse too."

The only one satisfied with that answer was Victor. He nodded his approval and kept eating. Meanwhile the four boys stared in furious anger at the scientist. They all viewed him as a coward, unwilling to stand up to Victor for anything, even the child he basically raised. One by one, they all shook their heads in disgust and went back to stabbing their food angrily. All but Aidan, who was far more skeptical than his brothers and saw through the ruse. He had spent time with Eclipse and Acre and knew there was something there. He wouldn't say love, but definitely something. He continued to stare at the scientist until Victor was completely distracted. And then he saw it. Acre winked at him.

The next day, Aidan couldn't focus. Just like every day for the last month, he was thinking about her. He decided to let himself hope that she would be safe and make a full recovery from all this. It was the only way he could deal with his guilt. It turned out that Erican was not the only person Eclipse had come to for help. Now, they were not at all close, he and his sister, but he loved her just as much as the rest of his brothers. Their personalities just never clicked. Aidan was a pessimist and only spoke blatant truth. She didn't always like to hear what he said. He taught the one form of combat she couldn't stand and he could never help her succeed at it. But they got along, just not as well as she did with the other three. Their last day together nagged at him constantly.

He had another crazy scheme that he hoped would help her. In throwing practice that day, he gave her a new weapon. It was basically a double-edged blade sharpened into a point at both ends. There was no handle to bounce harmlessly off the target. She looked at it, flipping it around to see every bit of it, before she looked doubtfully at Aidan. He picked up on her skepticism.

"What?" he asked. "*Something* on that will stick. There's no wrong way to hit the target."

"I guess."

She wasn't convinced, but Aidan had another student calling for help.

"Ok, just try it?" he pleaded. "Even Sean got it to work, so practice with it a bit and I'll be right back."

She shrugged in agreement and her targets were put up. She was never so disappointed to see the metal dummies rise up on her range than when she was at throwing practice. She shrugged her eyebrows doubtfully at the knife in her hand but started 'trying'. She needed Aidan on her side to ask him for a favor as soon as he got back. It was awkward though. She couldn't grip it well because all of it was sharp. It flew faster because it weighed less and it cut her hand when she released. And STILL, it didn't stick. The familiar ting of the metal bouncing off metal pissed her off.

By the time Aidan returned, she had hurled the ten knives he left with her wildly at different targets in frustration. Her hands were a bloody mess and not one of them had stuck.

"What the hell did you do?" he groaned, seeing her hands.

"I listened to you!"

It was the snappiest she had ever been with him, and he did not appreciate it. All he ever did was try to help her and all she ever did was blame him for her own failures in throwing. Everyone was stressed out beyond belief with her life on the line and no one was thinking straight.

"I can't help it if you suck at throwing!" he snapped right back. "I can leave you to figure it out on your own though! I won't be such a thorn in your side anymore."

"Fine! I may just live longer now."

"Pfffftt." he snorted. "Not if your gym scores have anything to say about it."

He immediately regretted it. Her face turned that horrid red color that told everyone she was furious while her eyes lit on fire. Her brother winced ever so slightly and mentally braced for what was coming............ but she bit her lip. Technically, Aidan was her superior and she refused to get in any more trouble than she was already in by screaming at him. So, she closed her eyes and counted to ten. It was a trick Sean taught her to control her anger and decide if it was worth getting the last word in. Apparently, this time, it wasn't. She needed Aidan's help. She breathed in and out trying to muster up every bit of control she had. Fortunately for her, Aidan didn't know her very well. He saw her close her eyes and watched her start regulating her breathing and thought she was going from furious to about to cry. It broke his heart, thinking he had caused her to almost cry and guilt filled every part of his body. His frustration went away and he sighed.

"Eclipse I didn't mean to be an asshole. I'm just frustrated and tired of you blaming me for your inability to stick a throw."

He put an arm around her shoulders till she looked up at him.

"Let me know whatever I can do to help, as usual."

Though she had no idea why he suddenly changed his mind, she definitely liked it. The corner of her mouth twitched just a bit. She did need something only he could get. Aidan was one of Victor's Elite bodyguards. He had access to information and resources no one else knew existed. He wasn't thrilled that he spent his life following around his father, but it kept him in the know, especially when it came to government secrets. Nothing made him happier than uncovering conspiracies and routing out someone more intelligent than himself. There was a particular drug that Acre invented to assist with his job and Eclipse needed some of it.

"Do you mean that?" she jumped on his offer.

"Well..... within reason, yeah? Why?"

Suddenly, he wasn't so sure he read her right before. Her next statement reassured his doubt.

"I need a vial of Tryke."

Aidan's eyebrows shot up in surprise and he backed away from her. There was no way she could've said that. No one except Acre and the Elite even knew Tryke existed! It was a military secret and it was impossible to get without Victor knowing. Tryke was a drug developed to aide interrogations. It caused hallucinations and confusion when even the tiniest drop was mixed in food or water. The smell itself was often enough to make someone woozy. But its most despicable attribute was the ability to change one's personality. It could mellow out the meanest of people and aggravate the calmest. If administered properly, the subject wouldn't even realize they were drugged. It was still in its experimental phase, which simply meant they could use it on anyone they wanted but no one was allowed to know about it beyond those that administered it, Victor, and Acre. Aidan had only just learned about it himself and he knew there was no way Eclipse should know.

"I..... I um, have no idea what you could be talking about."

He couldn't have convinced a five-year-old with that lie, but it was all he could think of saying. She squinted her eyes and looked right at his face.

"You can't lie to save your life."

She knew he had used Tryke earlier that very week to help calm down a PTSD patient who had valuable information to give Victor. She also knew he was under penalty of death if he spoke to anyone about it. It was horrible to ask him to risk his life for her, especially when so much could still go wrong with her plan. But she had already put Erican's life on the line. Now, she had no choice but to follow through. Her mind was racing. She was tired and unable to sleep. Death was in all her dreams, and worse, failure forced itself upon her. All she wanted was to win and to live....... but mostly win. And she felt miserable asking for help, but knew she couldn't manage on her own. This awful plan wasn't even hers. She found it on a piece of paper slipped under her pillow. It took her a whole gut-wrenching day weighing all the consequences to even consider it. Then logic won. It was her only way out, it was just.......... she didn't know. It made her stomach turn and her head swim. She never felt like this before.

"Are you completely insane?" Aidan hissed at her through his teeth. "I don't even know how you know about it or what horrible thing you are planning to do, but ABSOLUTELY not!!"

"You don't understand----"

"What I understand is that you are in way over your head. We are talking about things that even I didn't know about till last week. There's no way I'm going to have anything to do with this."

"Bu-"

"No buts. End of discussion, Eclipse."

He shook his head and started walking away. He turned back to deliver one more crushing blow in his anger.

"Yknow....... I thought you were better than this."

Eclipse didn't know why, but suddenly her eyes watered, just like when blood dripped into them at the gym. She watched him storm away from her and he refused to speak to her again before the big fight with Amy. It made her incredibly angry with him. How could he turn his back on her the first time she earnestly asked for his help? She always thought her brothers were all on her side.

That night, she collapsed into her cot with a huff of anger and an unfamiliar burning sensation in her eyes and chest. She was barely there five minutes before a knock on the door made her groan. She was tired. Her new schedule was almost too much for her to handle and she just wanted to sleep. Instead, she begrudgingly rolled out of her cot and stomped toward the door. She hadn't even reached it before the knocks resounded even louder and more impatiently. Eclipse opened the door with a roll of her eyes, but maintained respect in case it was someone important.

It was not.

The hooded figure before her was about four or five inches taller than herself and their cape was drenched in mud from his waist down. She knew it was raining out, but unless this person had been running through woods, the cape shouldn't have been so filthy. All the streets in Holux were paved with metal. Whoever this teenage urchin was, she wasn't interested in getting acquainted. There were far too many important matters on her mind.

"What?" she snapped, hoping to get a rise out of the figure that would at least give her a gender to work with.

"May I come in?" a distinctly adolescent male voice replied calmly.

"Acre isn't here." she answered impatiently.

"Well, that's good cause it would be super awkward if Victor's best friend was here to see me commit treason against him."

Eclipse looked the figure up and down suspiciously. This could be a trap. If Victor was beginning to suspect her, he would try to catch her in the act to present to the world a reason she needed to die. The boy calmly raised the toe of his right foot and scratched the back of his calf with it. He was in knee high boots, practical and flat with decent tread. His clothes were all black and, like his cape, splattered with mud from the waist down.

"May I come in?" he repeated, shifting his weight to his other foot and repeating his scratching motion from earlier.

"I'm not interested." Eclipse replied sternly and slammed the door in his face.

She didn't make it more than three steps away before the desperate knocking continued. There was no way she could sleep with that racket, so with an annoyed growl, she yanked it back open.

"You need to leave!" she warned.

"I can't." he replied, scratching at his wrists and forearms now with gloved fingers.

"And why the hell not?" she demanded.

"I'm kind of dying, actually."

Eclipse let her jaw drop slightly in shock before the figure collapsed onto the floor unconscious. She stood there staring at him for a very long time. Of course, some part of her wanted to help someone in need, but far too much of her upbringing had taught her to never, ever trust a stranger. Especially one who claimed to be a traitor. If they weren't faking it to trap someone, most likely they would get caught and tortured till they named every single person who ever helped them. Eclipse knew better than to risk her life for the random boy outside the lab and she slowly closed the door and walked back to her cot.

She felt sick to her stomach as her rear hit the edge of her cot. She knew it was most likely a horrible test from her father........ but what if it wasn't? What if there was someone dying outside her room and she couldn't muster the courage to help them. What if he was just lost and delirious? What if his family was out looking for him in the woods he must have come from? Eclipse glanced toward the door again as her gut flipped. What if she got up to help him and it cost her very life? Then again, could she live with herself if this was real and he died because she was scared of her father?

With a great heave, she pushed off her bed and strode toward the door, swinging it open as fast as she could to try and catch the boy in a lie. He was in the exact same position his fall had left him in. Eclipse bit her lip and looked up and down the hallway outside. It was silent for several minutes. Then, she made a momentous decision, grabbed the boy's arm and dragged him into the lab as fast as she could. She slammed the door behind them after one more glance in both directions.

Then, she realized her mistake. The lab door had a lock on it, but she couldn't really use it since Acre had the only key to the lock. She figured it would at least buy her some time if she could hear him entering, though, and twisted the deadbolt with a shrug. Her heart was rapidly pounding in her throat now, as the gravity of what she was doing continued to weigh on her mind. Still, the boy didn't wake up and arrest her, so she had to assume she was doing the right thing as she unraveled his cloak from his body and set it aside.

He was probably only a few years older than her, with the greasiest, most uneven hair cut she had ever seen. And she had grown up with Erican! It wasn't really curly, just crooked and jagged. And it was wet, so it lay plastered to the top of his head like some sort of rag. Eclipse carefully rolled him over on his back with a nasty grimace at his hair and started looking for the problem. There wasn't any blood she could see in the darkness and with a groan, she realized she would have to turn on a light. First, she walked over to the window and shut the curtains, hoping they were enough to block the light from reaching the street below, then she flipped the light switch.

It would have made her gasp if she was any other girl in the world, but as it was, Eclipse only raised her eyebrows in shock. Everything the dark had led her to believe was mud, was actually blood. It was pouring from his boots and forearms. She begrudgingly removed one of the boots, only to see a long, wide gash down the length of his calf. The other boot slipped off to reveal the same thing and Eclipse knew she had to move fast. She jogged over to Acre's desk and found the healer. It was the first time she had ever touched it herself and it felt heavy and expensive in her hands, if not a little frightening. She rushed back to the boy and knelt beside him.

Now that Eclipse knew she was past the point of no return, it became far easier for her to help the stranger. Either she was going to get caught and sentenced to death, or she would get away with it. The faster she healed the boy and got him out of the lab, the less chance she had of getting caught. She quickly removed his gloves, rolled up his sleeves and pant legs and spent an entire five minutes trying to get the healer to work. It finally projected the familiar beam she had seen Acre use so many times on her and she healed the long slices in his calves and arms. It was like someone had specifically cut him to make him bleed out and leave a trail wherever he walked. The gashes were large, rough and wide, like a dull ax blade had caused them. She couldn't help but wonder what happened to this boy as she finished and used his cape to wipe off as much of the blood from his skin as she could.

When he didn't instantly wake up, Eclipse began to worry that something else was wrong. She didn't know a lot about anatomy, but she knew that she would have to look for any other problems. The easiest way to work that out was a brief pat down. Hopefully, that was all the farther she would have to go, since anything more would be awkward and inappropriate. She briskly pat from his shoulders to his wrists and then over his chest and stomach. Nothing felt out of place, at least she didn't think it did through his layers of clothing. He was incredibly skinny and wiry, but that was normal for Chrosian commoners. Then, she moved to the outside of his legs, not daring to reach in between them any higher than his knees. She definitely didn't know enough about that sort of anatomy. When she couldn't find anything, she started back at his torso and took a bit extra time feeling around.

Finally, something caught her attention. There was a small, hard nodule sticking out of the right side of his chest. She groaned, but reached inside his many layers of drenched clothes to feel it better. Whatever the object was, it wasn't attached to his body at all and in confusion, she pulled it out of his tangle of clothes and frowned.

It was a small diamond vial. She stared in horror at the label. Tryke. Eclipse rose to her feet quickly and her eyes darted around the room in a panic. There was literally no chance that this random peasant just happened to have a vial of the very drug she needed for her scheme. Victor knew! This had to be a trap! She spun around looking for anything that might be a spy in disguise. The room looked normal, but that didn't abate her fear in the slightest. She had to leave Holux, and she had to leave now. It may already be too late. Eclipse made a move to dart for the rest of her clothes, since she normally only slept in her tank top and pants, but was frozen in her steps as the boy stirred on the floor. Panicking and desperate, she snatched his cape off the floor and wrapped the vial tightly inside as he slowly sat up.

If there had been any sort of mirror in the lab, Eclipse would have been able to see how incredibly guilty she looked to the boy who rubbed his arms and looked up at her curiously from where he sat on the floor. She was standing awkwardly still, paled to her very core, both eyes rounder than the moon and both hands death-gripped a bloody cloak. The boy looked from her face to his cape and back before carefully pushing up to his feet and steadying himself. When he finally looked back at her, she stepped away in fear. He cocked his head to the side.

"You really think I'm going to hurt you after you just saved my life?" he mused with a toothy grin.

Eclipse winced slightly at the awkward smile. His teeth were crooked and oddly spaced and one of the front ones was larger than the other. It matched his horrible haircut and his spindly form. Still, she realized, he was waiting for her response.

"I don't think you could hurt me if you tried." she stammered haughtily, unwilling to let him see her nerves rising even as her voice quivered.

The boy shrugged and shook both his hands through his hair to separate the dripping locks and peel them off his face. Eclipse didn't even realize that it was possible to make his hair look even more ridiculous until he stopped and grinned at her again. It hung intrusively over the right side of his face

"Well, I guess we will never know since I'm not going to try." he smiled.

"I know." she answered defiantly, making sure not to back up as he stepped toward her again.

She still leaned away enough to make him pause with his hand outstretched.

"Are you keeping my cape as a souvenir?" he pushed, shaking his hand.

Eclipse thought about the vial of Tryke hiding in the tight folds of the cape and reached an instant decision. If this boy had stolen Tryke successfully, he *had* to need it far more desperately than her. She bit the inside of her cheek and shoved his balled-up cape into his outstretched hand, removing any chance of her getting the drug she needed to beat Amy. He tucked it under his arm and looked her up and down again.

"I honestly thought you would leave me to die out there for a second." he muttered distractedly.

"Why?" she snapped. "Should I have?"

"Oh, absolutely."

Eclipse let her jaw drop in contempt. She had just saved this boy's life, at great risk to her own, and returned his stolen property even though she desperately needed it. What did he have to be so disappointed about?

"Well, I didn't." she scowled, folding her arms.

Suddenly, it struck her that she was wearing very little of anything and her hands instinctively rubbed up and down her bare arms. She was in a form-fitted tank top with thin straps and a tight pair of pants with bare feet poking out beneath them. It was the least amount of clothing anyone had ever seen her in, besides that one, horrible time, and it made her nervous in front of this stranger as he continued to twist his head curiously to the side and stare at her.

"Who are you, anyway?" she blurted out, trying to distract him from her appearance.

"My name's Peraxlkine," he replied, bemused. "but most people call me Axl since that's a damn mouthful. And you're the royal princess---"

"Eclipse." she interrupted quickly, having never liked being called a princess. "My name is Eclipse."

"I think the entire country knows your name." the boy grinned. "Not that I like to be the bearer of bad news."

The two just stared at each other. Eclipse wanted so badly to ask about the Tryke, but she didn't want him to know she thought about stealing it from him. She didn't even want him to know that she knew about it, to be honest. Instead, she waited for him to start the conversation this time. Her arms had relaxed, now relatively certain this boy wasn't going to turn her in to Victor. She stood still, staring at him with them gently crossing her stomach and her hands resting in her elbows. Waiting, just waiting on him.

"Don't you want to know what happened?" he challenged after a bit.

Eclipse hesitated. Knowledge tended to get people into trouble in Chrosia. If any of the telepaths read her mind, they could see what she had already done this evening, but if she knew that the boy was a traitor, it would make it worse for herself and him. She would be tortured till she told everything she knew about him. She already knew his extremely weird name, because she was stupid enough to ask for it. Anything else might be a horrible liability for them both.

"I want to know," she said slowly, holding up her hand to stop him as he opened his mouth to explain. "but I don't think that would be a good idea for either of us."

He snapped his mouth shut and nodded understanding curtly, *almost disappointed*, she thought. They stood in awkward silence for another few minutes before he suddenly puffed out his cheeks and blew some of his ratty hair out of his face with a huff.

"So.... do... you just..... want me to.... leave?" he asked, awkward and impatient.

Eclipse couldn't figure out why this strange boy was so upset with her, but she nodded.

"I think that would be best."

Axl nodded thoughtfully and rolled his eyes before walking toward the door dramatically. It would have seemed far more defiant if he hadn't walked straight into the door because the deadbolt didn't let it open. Eclipse snorted slightly and the corner of her mouth drew up as he forcefully turned the dead bolt back and paraded himself out the door, leaving it gently swinging on its hinges. It took Eclipse a few minutes of confused puzzlement before she walked over and gently closed it. She had no idea what just happened and knew she didn't have time to figure it out. There was a massive pool of blood that streaked to the door in Acre's lab. She had to clean it up before he got back or she would get caught. Thankfully, the lab had a sink and tons of cleaning supplies. After a while, Eclipse decided on bleach and warm water, filled a bucket with both, and grabbed a rag. She was on her hands and knees scrubbing some stranger's blood off the floor when the door flung open and scared the color right out of her skin.

"YOU DIDN'T TAKE IT?!?!?!" an exasperated Axl cried as he stormed back into the room with his cape back on and his fist shaking around something clenched within his fingers.

"Of course, I didn't take it!!" Eclipse responded nervously, climbing to her feet and rubbing her wet hands on her tank top. "I can't take *that*!"

"Why the hell do you think I'm here?!" Axl prodded with a demeaning tone.

"I---I---" Eclipse stammered, trying to get on the boy's level. "I don't know! I thought you were dying!"

"I was!" he pushed. "My job was to almost die so you would help me out, find the Tryke and take it for yourself! I never *dreamed* that you wouldn't take it!"

"Job?" was all Eclipse could get out in her shock.

Axl growled and rolled his eyes all the way back into his head, before looking at the floor. He turned around to close the door and then continued his explanation to the bewildered girl before him. Eclipse just watched him as he snatched the rag off the edge of her cleaning bucket and started scrubbing up the floor like it was no big deal.

"Yes, job." he replied bitterly. "My instructions were to cause myself some horrific injury, come all the way up here begging for you to help me and make sure the Tryke was easily accessible to you. Then, you were supposed to steal it and I was supposed to run off pretending I didn't even notice. So, imagine my surprise when I get down to the street and put my cape on, just to hear a *full vial of an extremely illegal drug bounce off the damn street and alert every guard for two miles that I have it.*"

He scrubbed furiously at the floor and rung out the rag. Then he looked up at her and shook it accusingly toward her with a grimace.

"I had to kill two men because you couldn't play your part correctly and take the damn vial, *like anyone else would have*!!"

Eclipse just stared at him with her chin dropped to her chest as he dipped the rag back in the bucket and kept moodily wiping the floor. This was all a ruse? Whatever for? She had to know.

"Well," she demanded weakly. "why...... why wouldn't you just deliver the Tryke to me like a normal person would have?"

"Because our mutual friend *rightly* assumed that you wouldn't trust help from a stranger and was hoping that you would just take something you desperately need to survive." he snapped back, moving on to the streak where she drug him into the room.

Eclipse was so flabbergasted by everything going on that she shook her head to help her think straighter.

"Who is our mutual friend?" she asked.

Axl threw the rag onto the floor and rolled his eyes so far up, his chin tilted backwards too.

"Don't ya think if he could tell you that, he would have just brought the damn vial himself?"

"I don't know!" she cried furiously, frustration cracking her voice. "I don't know what's going on! I was just trying to do the right thing!"

Axl slowly stood up and looked at her with a frown. She shifted her weight between her feet and looked at the floor. This.... wasn't what he was expecting. His employer had warned him that Eclipse was a vicious fighter and would do anything to get ahead of Amy this next week. Axl had watched the two girls duke it out for years, now. Eclipse was by far the more talented of the two, but when Amy exited the Enhancer, the dynamic changed. She could win every fight by cheating, since that was legal, but it was the only way she could win. Still, Axl was beginning to think his employer was wrong about Eclipse. He decided to try a different approach.

"You did do the right thing." he said quietly.

"Then, why is that so damn horrible?" she groaned.

"It's not your fault." Axl coaxed. "The world is a horrible place right now and you aren't really being taught the truth about it all."

Eclipse watched the boy reach into his shirt and pull out a small metal object. He gently tossed it to her, and she caught it without looking away from his eyes. It was a metal pin, that much she could tell from her fingers running over it. Eventually, she decided it was worth taking a risk on Axl and she looked down at the pin. It made her brow furrow.

The metal was dyed red and fashioned into the shape of a dragon surrounded by a circle of its own flames. The red dragon was Victor's sigil, so it was well known, just as it was well known that only one group of Chrosians wore the pin she held. Eclipse looked up at the boy in fearful confusion.

"You're one of Victor's Elite?" she whispered.

Axl nodded and carefully stepped toward her. She didn't back away, but he could tell it was more from paralyzing fear than courage. A lump was moving up and down her throat as she tried to swallow it. It wasn't that she was too afraid of him, but the Elite were sworn to Victor's service. Axl had a duty and responsibility to tell Victor everything about tonight. She glanced back at the pin and felt her eyes burn.

"Can I at least get a head start?" she asked calmly. "Like ten minutes before you tell him?"

Axl grinned and took his pin back. She looked up at him miserably.

"I don't have to tell Victor a damn thing." he responded. "The Elite aren't just his protectors. We are sworn to protect the entire royal family. Like it or not, princess, you are part of that family. We have stepped between Victor and his kids multiple times. It's actually a large part of our jobs. I'm not the first Elite to commit treason against the promontory for the good of one of his children and I highly doubt I will be the last. And you can trust me, because if Victor were to figure out that I was giving you a vial of Tryke without his consent, I would be in a hell of a lot more trouble than you."

Axl held his closed fist out and waited for her to place her hand under it. She was still hesitant and he knew his ploy to keep Acre busy was dying out.

"Take it." he ordered kindly, but firmly.

Eclipse held out her hand and he dropped the vial into it before grabbing the bucket and rag and walking out of the room. She listened to him scrubbing the floor outside the closed door for a few minutes and heard him get up and leave afterward. Then it was just her, a vial of Tryke, and a tiny sense of not being so alone in the world. She couldn't help but grin at the label before walking back to her cot and tucking it into her pillowcase. She was almost there. Only a few more people to convince.....

# CHAPTER THIRTEEN

Shane's last talk with Eclipse was three days before the big fight. Shane was kindly left out of the instructions on her paper, but he was her riding instructor. When she walked up almost an hour late to the stables that day, his stomach took a turn for the worst. She was in awful shape, hadn't changed since her time in the gym with Amy or anything. Her clothing was shredded and bloody and her wounds were still very obvious. Normally, she had Acre clean up her wounds and changed clothing before archery. Well, it was now six hours after archery *finished* and he figured she was losing way more blood than most other people could stand.

And yet, she was still walking. He had noticed this recently. No matter how hard she got battered and beat, she completed every single activity each day. But this was the first time she was late this week for anything. And definitely the first time her body was so destroyed. He immediately knew something was wrong. She was walking as if she couldn't feel a thing, even though he was sure there were at least a few broken bones. There was only one excuse. She was drugged. Not enough to mess with her head, but some extremely strong pain killers were at work and she had overdosed at some point.

"Curses upon curses, Eclipse!" he hissed at her as she drew near. "What did you take?"

Naturally he expected some sort of drug to be her answer, instead she looked at him puzzled and in shock.

"How did you know?"

She reached into a satchel at her side and removed one of the healing cylinders Acre always used on her.

"I was going to put it back." she muttered, offering it to a very confused older brother.

He took it slowly and took a breath for his next statement, but hesitated first.

"So.... wait. You aren't on drugs?"

It was her turn to be confused by his statement.

"Nooooo?" she drawled. "Are *you* on drugs, Shane?"

"No?" he guessed.

All this was highly irregular. She normally didn't even talk to him this much.

"So.... you aren't sure if you're on drugs?" she tested.

And Shane shook his head, trying to erase this whole conversation and take control of the situation. He didn't like how she ended up interrogating him. He didn't want her playing him.

"No, of course I'm not on drugs, Eclipse. I thought you were because you aren't even acknowledging the fact that you are seriously injured. Why didn't you at least use the damn healer?"

"I did."

Shane shook his head again. None of this was making any sense. Why was she still bleeding if she used the healer? She sensed his confusion and offered up an explanation.

"Shane, I took the healer from Acre's desk this morning because I have no free time in my schedule anymore. I don't have the time to keep running back to the lab. I used it right after the gym, when I got to archery, but the rest of the Emilies stole my clothes and hung them on the flagpole."

She paused to mutter 'so immature' and then shook her head to push the feeling off.

"So, I'm completely fine, but I'm in my clothes from this morning still. I didn't have the time to go change. I thought you knew I stole the healer when you asked what I took. But you meant drugs?"

Shane nodded, desperately trying to sound as reasonable as her with his answer. He failed miserably.

"I thought you drowned out the pain to make it through your day."

She raised a condescending eyebrow at him.

"I had a broken leg and shattered kneecap. You seriously thought I'd be able to walk like that?"

She watched his face redden as he focused extremely hard on rubbing dried blood off the healer in his hand. He searched for a way to once again get the conversation off his incompetence. He chose the obvious detour.

"Well, what do we do here? You stole a piece of equipment you aren't allowed to have till your training is complete."

She bit her lower lip and rolled her eyes. She knew he could turn her in for discipline, but she also knew her brother.

"Seriously? I need it more than anyone else by my calculations---"

"I agree."

"---and it's not like Acre will miss it if he doesn't nee---wait, what?"

She heard his words a little late. He smiled and held the healer back out to her.

"I agree."

The corner of her mouth twitched up as she took it from him and placed it back in her satchel. He winked at her and decided to give her a more positive subject to consider as he gave her a leg up onto Herald, her training steed.

"So, have you decided on a companion of war?"

In Chrosia, generals of a series were allowed to select one highly trained animal to be their companion. Its purpose was to discourage mutiny among the rest of the series, so they were naturally terrifying. Shane knew Eclipse was planning to be the leader of her particular series and that she had a natural hand with animals. They got her and she got them. She definitely would have already selected a type of companion in preparation for the decision she was sure she'd get to make.

There were nine options. All of them bred to be insanely loyal. First, the chupacabra, a large hybrid of a wolf and lizard whose head was level with a full-grown man's chest when it stood on its four, dangerously clawed paws. It could rear to a full height of nine feet easily. Second was a dire wolf. Just as large as the chupacabra and equally loyal, it presented a less ferocious look. Thirdly, a winged lion, genetically bred to have one, and only one, master to obey flawlessly. He also made a great scout. Fourth was a cockatrice. Cockatrice were bird-lizard hybrids that could stare someone to death. Though no bigger than a hawk, they had second eyelids that hid their death stare until ordered to kill. Their eyes were mesmeric, pulling even the wisest person into a deadly staring contest, which basically blazed holes in their brain through their eyes with an invisible ultra-violet light beam. Fifthly, was the infamous enfield.

Genetically combining five animals was a horrid chore for the breeders, but the result was an extremely majestic creature with the loyalty of a best friend; a lion with the head of a ferocious fox, front legs like eagle talons, hind legs with the speed of a greyhound, and the fluffy tail of a wolf. The sixth creature was a gagana, an extremely powerful eagle with duranium fused into his beak and talon glands at birth. The creature evolved as it grew to be able to fly with the extra weight of metal talons and beak. As a seventh choice, generals could choose the low profile hydrus.

It was a tiny snake that would climb into a human's body through any cavity available and eat their insides until it got so full, it exploded the victim. Kiladrt were a hybrid of a bear and a tiger. The body was very similar to a regular bear but had the teeth, legs, tail, and claws of a tiger along with the unique orange stripes. The ninth choice was a wolf sized black widow spider with its web secretion disabled.

Eclipse had met every one of these creatures several times. They roamed in the forest where she learned to hunt and, sadly, she had killed most of them at one point as part of her training. Scientists originally bred and genetically altered animals to create each of these wondrous creatures, but now they bred on their own in the wild and were captured as infants or eggs for the military when a new general needed a companion or when a general's old companion passed. Beyond that, they simply added to the natural wildlife of Chrosia and were beginning to migrate to the rest of the planet as well. Unfortunately, all but the gagana, cockatrice, and dire wolf were now solely enemies of people. They were more feared than dragons. Especially since dragons had not been seen in thousands of years.

Eclipse had always had an obsessive fascination with dragons. It made Shane think she would go for one of the lizard hybrids. And though she never talked to him much, he knew she would talk about animals at least for a small amount of time. And today was all about controlling her mount so they would be at close quarters for the majority of the lesson. Shane hated the lessons when the conversation ran dry. He didn't like silence. She shocked him with her answer.

"Why would I have a companion selected before I even enter the Enhancer? It's illogical to automatically assume that A) I'll live through Amy being....... well, Amy. And B) that once my enhancement is complete, I'll be able to defeat every single Emily and be placed as general."

"Well, it's what you want, isn't it?"

"Of course. But that in no way constitutes that future as factual information." she shrugged.

"Oooookkkkk." his mind raced, trying to find a way to explain to her. "Let's say that you do get there eventually. I know it's not set in stone, but if you were to be made general tomorrow, what would you choose as a companion?"

"But---" she tried reasoning, but Shane was getting rather frustrated and interrupted her.

"Just humor me. Stop talking logic. And while you tell me what you would pick and why, drop your reigns and sidestep four steps alternatively in both directions till I ask you to stop."

That would keep her busy. Side stepping with reigns could be difficult, but accomplishing it without showed real skill and control. Forcing her to talk taught her to move as one with her horse without having to focus solely on him. It was an extremely important skill for a steed-transported warrior. Eclipse puffed out her cheeks, exasperated, and sighed. She knew what he was doing.

"Fine then. If I absolutely have to pick one-" she paused to re-position her heel to a more sensitive spot on her non-responsive horse's side.

"Keep talking." Shane commanded.

He knew she hated multi-tasking. She liked to focus completely on one thing at a time. But riding needed to be a second nature to her, not a distraction from everything else around her.

"If I absolutely had to choose one," she repeated sharply. "I would have to take in many variables and calculate my best match, logically."

"And what are those variables?"

Eclipse shot him a dirty look and he quickly followed it with another response that aggravated her.

"Overstep."

It simply meant her horse took five steps rather than four, but it was enough for her to lose her composure.

"This is ridiculous! I've only just learned side steps and you expect me to be able to perform them perfectly while discussing very complex matters."

"And?"

Shane disinterestedly pulled a non-existent fuzz off his shoulder.

"Aaannndd" she drew the word out to recapture his attention. "it's impossible. Especially on this monstrosity of a horse."

She bounced in her saddle with frustration at her mount as he bent over and snorted around in the dust beneath him for tiny remnants of grass on the track. Her movement didn't even distract him from eating. Shane tried very hard not to smile and looked with mock indignation at his sister.

"Awwww, well that's not fair at all. Herald won't listen to you?"

"Exactly." she concurred, not always being good at picking up sarcasm. "He's a horrid, disobedient beast."

She nodded disdainfully at the back of the animal's head. Shane clicked his tongue in disappointment at the object of her anguish.

"Well, we can't have that. Why don't you dismount and I'll teach him a lesson while you continue your explanation?"

"Very well, but he won't listen to you any better."

Eclipse gladly dismounted and walked over to the fence, continuing her discourse, while Shane removed her saddle....... and the bridle..... from Herald.

"Well, I most definitely would not take a hydrus. They are disgusting, vile creatures who crawl on their bellies in the dirt for a reason, I'm sure. And I don't want something that........" her voice trailed off as she realized what Shane was doing as she talked.

He sat upon Herald's withers and stared directly at his sister while effortlessly guiding the horse's every move. Four steps left, four steps right, repeat. Over and over, without a saddle, bridle, or a single mistake. Herald danced for Shane, with his head bowed elegantly the entire time. Shane held his hands on his hips and never broke eye contact with his sister.

"Well?" he asked, still moving his steed back and forth with nothing but his calves.

"It's an inadequate representation since I had to focus on your question." she pointed out in her own defense.

"Ah yes, I made you think, talk, and ride at the same time. How awful of me." he agreed to humor her this time. "Very well, you may ask me a question."

Herald continued to flawlessly perform.

"All right. Well, I know you never plan on being the leader of your series, so you will have put no thought into your own question. So, what companion would best suit you?"

Shane nodded and began his consideration without missing a step with Herald.

"That is a good question. I also disagree with the hydrus, mainly because no snake can keep up with a steady traveling canter, so it's very impractical. A winged lion would be a chore to feed and I'm not overly fond of any type of cat. That also rules out a kiladrt. The chupacabra and the enfield are just too unnatural for me. Beautiful, but unnatural. So, that leaves us with two birds, a wolf hybrid, and an extremely venomous spider who is known for eating its mate. Ok..... the spider is just a dumb idea for any guy, so nix it. The eagle is too reflective and will give away my position on a sunny day. The wolf takes a lot of work to feed, so I guess I would choose the cockatrice. Even with its bright colors, it's the easiest to care for, can keep up with anything since it flies, lives extremely long, and its ability to kill never dwindles till it dies itself. Definitely the cockatrice."

Shane stopped Herald and pat his neck in approval. Eclipse stopped looking at her brother a long time ago. Instead, she was desperately watching Herald's feet, looking for a mistake. A couple times the horse did get a little sloppy and tried to overstep or cheat by not crossing his hoof over properly, but Shane always corrected him instantly and Eclipse had to admit she had been wrong. Her brother saw the slight look of dismay in her eyes and knew he had proved his point. Shane dropped his happy go lucky act and dismounted.

"Eclipse, right now you don't understand why it's such a big deal, because you focus too heavily on the present and not how life now applies to the future. If you don't learn how to control a horse naturally and with great ease, while doing other things, then if you ever get attacked in the future while you are on horseback, you won't be able to fight and ride at the same time. I'm not trying to make your life any more miserable than it already is. I'm trying to help you have the skills to conquer anything that comes at you in the future."

His solemn tone embedded into her ears as she stared into space past him. She did need to think about the future and not just focus on the moment. Her life depended on future acts. She had three days to beat Amy and if her plan failed, she had no intention of dying by her father's hand. Her future was more important than her past and her present put together. The last day of this week was going to be the most important of her life.

"A kiladrt." she muttered distractedly.

Shane forgot he had even asked her.

"Huh?" he asked.

Eclipse snapped out of her own thoughts to respond.

"A kiladrt," she looked at him. "I want a kiladrt. They can run just as long and hard as horses. They have an intense sense of loyalty to their masters and they are excellent hunters with their own special set of camouflage. But I want a white and black striped one. It's rare, but I like it better than the orange ones."

Shane smiled at her. She always learned quickly, though she never verbally admitted to her mistakes. Her returning that fast with an excellent answer to his question told him that she was thinking about her future for a change.

"Good choice. Now, tack up Herald and let's try this again."

After that lesson, Eclipse's attitude changed drastically. She worked with him every day with more effort than he had ever seen her put into riding, but she talked with him less. In fact, she talked with everyone less.

Since she had been in the Enhancer, Shane had traveled a lot. He was looking for a reputable kiladrt breeder or captor that could find a white one for when she got out. Eventually his 'reputable' had to be switched to 'sketchy and illegal'. Then, he found a breeder, whose description was the same, but he bred white and black kiladrt with great precision and skill. He agreed to tell Shane every time he had a litter and hold one for him at the right time, as long as Shane paid extra for the infant. He also genetically engineered his animals to live longer and stay in their prime an extended number of those years. He had one that was fifty from his father, that he still used to breed and that still behaved much younger than its age. Unfortunately, the females could not be altered this way, so Eclipse would get a male cub.

Shane never stopped believing that she would get out, be fine and kick ass. And now she was trapped for even longer and every day her chance to live continued to drop. He received letters from the breeder every few months and each time he wrote back saying not yet but soon. And now as he opened one of these letters in his room and read that there was yet another litter on the way, he struggled with how to answer. As usual, he started writing and thanked the man for his understanding and cooperation and continued to say that it was again too soon but then he paused. Should he tell the breeder to drop it and move on? Statistically, it was impossible for Eclipse to live through this. Should he call the whole deal off and apologize? He sat pondering long into the night, almost till the rooster crowed and then he finally decided. He thanked the man again and told him to keep him informed, that the time would come eventually.

If he gave up on her now, he would never forgive himself.

# CHAPTER FOURTEEN

Sean was the only one who knew it all. Eclipse told him her entire plan when she got the letter under her pillow. In fact, she went straight to him thinking he had left it for her. And she was going to tell him no. But she was wrong.

"You seriously think I put this under your pillow?" he asked after reading the whole set of instructions. "This is some insanely illegal bull shite. I wouldn't let you do any of this. It would get you killed!"

"I know. That's why I brought it to you, to make sure it wasn't yours. You are the only one I know who would have the guts to pull this off."

She plopped down on his bed. Sean had become an expert at sneaking her into the fortress during their lunch break. Everyone knew except Victor, but no one cared, the servants all liked Eclipse.

"So, if it's not from you, who did this?"

Sean looked back at the handwriting. He was sure he didn't recognize it. He thought through everyone who would openly be willing to help Eclipse. It wasn't Acre's, Jackson's, or any of his brothers'. But it WAS someone's and not only did they have extensive knowledge of the intricacies of Chrosia's political system, they had information about stuff Sean wasn't even aware of, which was rare. He knew every rumor about anything and looked into it all. Sadly, he was finding that more of his theories were becoming reality.

The worst part was how well the plan was formulated and how very specific the instructions were. He thought it would actually work, but he couldn't think of using his baby sister as a guinea pig. No matter how fool proof their plan seemed, the writer of this letter had no idea of the real outcome. They were willing to kill Eclipse for an experiment. Maybe one of the Elite? They were always meddling in places they didn't belong. He'd ask Aidan about it later. Right now, he had to convince his sister it wasn't worth the risk.

*But she's going to die anyway.* Sean swore in his mind. There was no safe or sure way out of this for Eclipse. She would either die a winner or die before she even got a chance. And, he supposed, it may be possible that it worked and no one ever found out. He sighed, knowing what he had to do.

"I don't know who, but they are a genius."

"What?"

Eclipse jumped back up to her feet.

"You actually think I should try this?"

She ripped the paper out of his hands and pointed to it.

"I would be killed!"

"Only if you got caught----" Sean calmly replied before she interrupted.

"Of course, I would get caught! I'm under surveillance every day and night. Someone will report me. I mean I have to get three other people to break the law and get killed too."

"IF you get caught." he injected forcefully.

"I will, Sean. Aidan follows the letter of the law and he won't give that up for me. No one would. I'm not worth everyone else risking their lives----."

"WELL YOURS IS OVER IF YOU DON'T TRY!!!" Sean yelled at her.

It made her jump slightly, and she deliberately took a step back. Her brother calmed down and ran his hands through his hair before continuing.

"Eclipse, listen to me. You don't realize how many people want to see you beat Amy. None of the Emilies want her as their general, but no one can beat her. You are their last hope. And whether they follow the letter of the law or not, all your brothers will stand by you. So, yes, I think you should try it. It's your last hope."

"What's hope?"

Eclipse had never heard that word before. Sean's eyes widened in horror. He forgot! That was one of those words he wasn't supposed to say in front of her. Not that he minded disobeying, but how do you describe hope to someone who runs on logic?

"Ummmmm." he racked his brain. "It's when you hope for something good to happen in the future."

"You just used the same word to define the word." she pointed out philosophically. "That makes even less sense."

"Ok, ok." Sean waved his hand to hurry up her explanation. "Fine then. Hope is when you expect something good to happen, even when logic is against it."

Eclipse gave him a puzzled look, before looking back at the paper in her hand. She was raised with logic, science, and practicality. Why would someone expect something logic told them was not going to happen? It still made no sense, but she was more interested in the letter. She would remember that word though. *Just like beautiful.* She didn't understand either of them, but she knew they were important, if only because they had been hidden from her.

"So," she sighed. "I'm actually going to do this?"

She looked up at him for his answer, hoping he had changed his mind, but he just shrugged.

"Eclipse I can't tell you what to do on this one. But here's my advice. If you do decide to follow that," he nodded at the letter. "you have to be all in. Don't take no for an answer from anyone. Believe that it'll work and follow the instructions to the letter. If you adjust anything, the entire plan will fall apart and then you will get caught. Understand?"

"How am I supposed to make this decision?"

She plopped back down on the bed and stared at the paper holding her only chance. Sean smiled and crouched down to her eye level, gently raising her chin.

"Do you want to live?" he asked her softly.

She looked from his eyes, back to her paper, and back to his eyes.

"I want to beat her. After that, I'll consider death."

"Then do it."

And he watched her plan unfold for the next week. The next couple days in the gym, she let Amy win and throw her around with her telepathy the entire time. She came within seconds of death every time the buzzer rang and spent no time on recovery. She hit every class on time and stole Acre's healer to help her out, just like the instructions said. She slipped a tiny drop of Tryke into Amy's drink at lunch every day and asked Amber, who was happily in on the whole thing, to tell her miserable horror stories every night. Amber and Amy were both in the barracks together, so it was easy to fill Amy's mind with horror even if she wasn't talking to her, but near enough she could hear. Amy stopped sleeping two days in, when the Tryke-induced nightmares got too much for her, but she put the same energy into her telepathy in the gym every single day, exhausting her abilities. She looked miserable and no one but Eclipse, Sean and some unknown benefactor knew why. Eclipse wore dragon scales every day to the gym to avoid being killed at least and she drugged herself to sleep soundly each night. In all, the plan was working. Eclipse was well-rested and getting stronger each day and Amy was pushing herself too hard just to be able to beat her nemesis to a pulp, especially with no sleep.

Finally, the sun rose on the tenth, and last, day of the week. It was the day of the big fight. Sean and Acre were with Eclipse, helping her prepare for the battle in one corner of the gym. Amy was trying to push past her exhaustion and stood in the center of the gym while the crowd cheered. This fight was highly publicized. Victor was trying everything to throw Eclipse off. Even after all the times she lost to Amy and the fact that the odds of her beating a telepath were pretty much zero, he was still afraid of her determination. And rightfully so.

Sadly, most of the crowd knew why they were there and they also knew that if they didn't cheer for Victor's favorite, they were basically dead men. So, halfhearted as it was, everyone cheered as Amy waved and tried to look as confident as possible. She could barely stand straight.

On the other side, Eclipse simply received a pat on the shoulder from Acre as he walked away. He didn't know what to say and she honestly wouldn't want to hear it right now, so he didn't even try. Sean on the other hand had a few tricks up his sleeve. The rules in an arena fight were no weapons, but they also stated no telepathy if one competitor was un-enhanced. Sean figured she had nothing to lose if she cheated right along with Amy. Before she stepped out to begin the match, he turned and faced her to hide her from the audience.

"I have to go out there, Sean."

"Oh, I know."

He waved his hand to brush away her incorrect perception of him.

"No, I wanted to give you this........ in case you need a last resort."

He handed her a dagger, just small enough to hide it the secret pocket on her bracer. Her brow furrowed as she took it. It was an unusual dagger. She had never seen such design. It had a shiny metal blade, sharp enough to split a hair, attached to an intricately carved ivory hilt. Where they met was a thin, black, leather strip, wrapped around the dagger multiple times. The end of the strip dangled a small, but beautiful dragon charm, whose emerald eyes matched the gem on the end of the hilt. Eclipse took it gingerly. It seemed familiar as the handle settled comfortably into her hand, but she knew she had never seen it before. It was the most incredible weapon she had ever laid eyes on and it most definitely wasn't Chrosian. The metal confused her even more. Most weapons were a dull gray when they were forged, this one was so bright and shiny, she was afraid it would catch someone's eye.

"Where..... did you get this?" she whispered, still a bit mesmerized.

Sean's sudden movement as he looked guiltily at his feet barely drew her eyes away.

"I.... hope you won't be mad, but........ I kinda, well, stole it." he muttered back.

"From?" she replied.

"Your mother." then he quickly continued as her face grew red with anger. "But it's not what you're thinking! It was after she died. Victor was going to burn all of her things, including the dagger. So, I took it to save it for you. I thought you would want something of hers when you grew up. I was going to save it till you got out of the Enhancer, but I thought you might need it today. You know, for a little hope."

He winked at her as he added the last bit. The prep bell rang and made them both jump a little. Eclipse slid the dagger into place on the inside of her bracer and nodded at Sean. She wasn't mad at him, but she didn't understand what she was feeling. It was like she was stronger with that dagger. Like her mom was there helping her. She felt like she had a chance to win this for the first time this week. She dared to believe it was that word, the one Sean used. Hope.

One look at Amy and Eclipse knew she was exhausted. Her eyes had awful dark sacks under them, and she was in complete disrepair. Her hair didn't look perfect for the first time since Eclipse met her. So, she knew exactly what Amy was going to do. Amy wanted to make it end as fast as possible and Eclipse's only chance was to draw it out. Sean reached the bleachers and watched his sister take a deep breath. She was better than Amy, he knew, and once her telepathy kicked in, she'd be unstoppable, but she had to survive one last time. Then the bell rang.

Amy hit hard right away. She fired orbs left and right toward Eclipse. She felt like each one drained her though. If she could just hit the stupid shrimp once, she'd be done and could go to sleep. But Eclipse knew her opponent. And unlike Amy, she excelled in many different skill trees, gymnastics included. She dodged all of Amy's hap hazard orbs with ease, flips and tumbles as well, of course. All the while trying to move closer to her opponent, she planned every move more carefully than all her shots in archery put together. She used a unique zigzag pattern, knowing Amy wouldn't be able to follow in her current state. The number of orbs and rate of fire slowly dropped as Amy grew more exhausted with each one. Then finally when Eclipse was about ten feet away, she lost it. Amy, tired of her enemy dodging, launched six orbs at Eclipse in one last effort to prevail using her telepathy. Each of them covered an escape route for the young princess. One of them would make contact, no matter what Eclipse did. Amy grinned as they flew, and gasps shot through the crowd. No one had ever been able to fire more than one orb at a time before now. And there was a reason for that.

Thankfully, Eclipse had extraordinary reflexes or her story may have ended there. She saw the orbs and noticed that in her haste, Amy did not fire the lowest ones low enough. If Eclipse fell onto her belly, as flat as possible, she would make it. But laying prostrate on the floor would ruin any tactical advantage. She had to get up as soon as possible. She slammed onto her back and watched the orbs pass harmlessly overhead, then she ended her little move by jumping back up to her feet with a kip, ready to dodge the next round.

Only there was no next round. In fact, Amy was standing still, in the same position she launched the orbs from. Her eyes blinking repeatedly, as if she couldn't see. Such a massive display of power had drained her. She couldn't use any telepathy at all and her head reverberated like a ringing bell. Eclipse grinned and stood up out of her ready position and Amy did likewise after a nervous minute. They stared silently at each other for a few moments. No more telepathy, no more cheating. It all came down to who was the better fighter. And they both already knew that answer. Eclipse glared into her opponent's eyes and saw exactly what she wanted to see. Amy was afraid.

"Do you yield?" she asked calmly.

Amy's entire face contorted with anger. She knew she couldn't win, but suggesting she would go down without a fight? Insulting!!

"Never, you little harpy!"

And so it began. Amy charged toward Eclipse, as usual, and spun into a round house kick. Eclipse swung under her leg and darted behind her to deliver a well-placed knee into Amy's side. The latter doubled over into a roll, to escape the next hit and let her kidneys recover. Eclipse followed and launched at her. She wrapped her legs around Amy's neck and flipped, slamming her enemy's body onto the floor. Amy delivered a powerful throat punch to get Eclipse off of her and both girls scrambled to their feet to face off once more.

It was a long fight, almost a whole two hours of strikes and counter strikes. For though Amy was exhausted, this training was drilled so deep into her, she could do it in her sleep. However, only ten minutes into the battle, she was forced to go on defense. Eclipse was faster, stronger, and far more skilled at hand to hand combat and Amy was too tired to stay on the offense, as she normally did. Her only hope was to tire Eclipse out and throw deliberately painful blows as often as she could. Little did she know, Eclipse was wearing the strongest armor known to man and she barely felt each blow. And little did Eclipse know, Amy was stalling, waiting for her telepathy to kick back in.

Finally, the fight was drawing to a close. Eclipse continued her aggressive attacks and Amy's blocks and dodges got weaker and slower. She knew she was going to have to play her trump card. Amy double back flipped out of the fight and fell to her knees. Eclipse walked toward her, determination to win shining in her eyes.

"Wait, wait!!!" Amy cried out desperately, holding her hands up to block her face from the fists of her opponent. She knew Eclipse would stop, simply because she knew that she was a rather decent person. Eclipse did stop.

"Do you yield?"

Same tone and voice as before, but faster breathing.

Amy peeked through her fingers, at the feet before her. Eclipse was standing off-balance and flat footed. That meant she had no idea Amy was faking and that she wasn't ready to dodge. Amy grinned. It was all too easy. Still on her knees, Amy launched the biggest, strongest orb she ever had straight into Eclipse's face. The entire crowd rose to their feet, outraged. They knew it was allowed and they knew Victor wanted Amy to win, but it didn't matter. It was cruel and spiteful with no class and it enraged them all. They shouted and screamed curses at Amy, who slowly stood, smiling wide. She was exhausted, but that was definitely the winning stroke.

The orb hit Eclipse with so much force that it flipped her backwards by her head and she landed twenty feet away on her stomach. Even as she flew through the air, all she could think about was how stupid she was. How could she think that Amy was going to yield? She had known her most of her life and STILL she trusted her desperate plea for help. There was no one to blame for her death but herself. Her face slammed into the floor and she heard the buzzer ticking. If she couldn't stand before it ticked ten times, she lost and she was dead. She heard the whole room screaming for her to get up but she knew from the pain that her nose and right leg where broken and that several of her ribs were cracked. Her right eye began to swell shut as she stared across the floor and counted down her life clock. Five, four, three, two, one. The buzzer noise hurt her head and the entire room fell silent. To everyone in the room, except Victor and Amy of course, hope died.

From her spot on the floor, Eclipse watched Victor come out and raise Amy's arm in victorious spite. She knew what would happen next. Everyone would cheer for the one they just cursed, in fear of being killed by the one who held her arm. Sure enough, a halfhearted round of clapping ensued and Eclipse clenched her fists in anger at the cowards. In doing so, she discovered two things. Her right wrist was broken and she had something in her left hand. She slowly dragged her face across the floor to turn and look at it. It was the hilt of her mother's dagger. The fall jolted it loose from her bracer and now the gem shown right before her eyes.

And there it was. That strength she felt when Sean gave it to her rushed back. She looked back up at Amy. Her and Victor were both facing the crowd with their backs to her. If she cheated, she could win and end Amy's life, therefore saving her own. It was a long, risky walk and she was broken, but that gem staring at her told her she could do it. If she was caught before she could stab her, though, she would be punished for cheating and carrying a weapon, which also meant death. Her father's stupid laws made sure she would die.

..........her father. Eclipse could almost feel the darkness rush into her head as she realized....... she could kill Victor instead of Amy. No more suffering on his account. No more fear. The crowd wouldn't give her away. *They want him dead, too.* That was all she needed. Between the dagger and her new-found purpose, she found the strength to push up off the floor and draw the dagger the rest of the way out. The crowd's cheering grew sincere and she froze, thinking her father would know she was up. Instead, he and

Amy, blinded by their pride, took a bow and stood to face them again. They thought the cheering was for them. Eclipse sighed in relief and continued to hobble and limp toward her father. She could barely see out of one eye and the other was completely shut, but she knew one thing. She wasn't going to make it. She couldn't move fast enough and the cheering wouldn't hold his attention forever. She looked back down at the knife and knew what she had to do.

She had to throw it. It was a long throw and she couldn't really see. She couldn't use her dominant hand because of the broken wrist. It was a long shot, but it was the only one she had. After flipping the dagger so she was grasping the blade instead of the handle, she raised her left arm to gauge the throw and the crowd cheered even louder. Their support powered her in a way she had never felt before. It was like suddenly everyone was on her side. Maybe they would rush to help her even if she missed. Maybe one rebel was all it took to start a full rebellion. Her mind flashed back to all the times he yelled at her and hit her. All the times he had spurned her and treated her like shite. Anger shot through her whole body and caused her limbs to quake. She closed her eyes to concentrate. It all came down to this. Either she would kill him, or he would kill her. This was the end of one era and the turning point in her own life. She felt it and she didn't know how right she was. Her eyes shot open in fury and felt the weight of the knife balance with her arm. She took a deep breath. Then it happened.

She drew her arm back to throw and.............. couldn't.

The entire world seemed to slow to a dead stop around her and Eclipse dropped her arm as the realization shocked even her. She couldn't kill Victor. She just..... couldn't. After everything he had done and everything she knew, she couldn't throw the knife. Maybe it was because he was her father. And even though he never acted like it, she was his daughter. She didn't care one little bit about him, but the prospect of slaughtering him like an animal behind his back was impossible. Maybe, it was because it was unlikely she would even stick a deathly blow. Throwing weapons were her worst sport after all. Maybe she thought the crowd really was cheering for him and they would kill her if she succeeded. She wanted to scream in anguish at her own weakness, but it would blow any chance she had to live. Her mind sought desperately for a reason. And it finally hit her like a rock. It was what he would do. If she stabbed him in the back, she would be no better than him and only prove that she was just like her father. And she wasn't. And she didn't want anyone to think that. So, Eclipse reposed for a throw, but chose a different target. She couldn't kill her own father, but she COULD win this fight. Without hesitation, she drew her arm back and threw as hard as she could at Amy.

The crowd went ecstatic as it soared into the back of Amy's head with a solid clunk, then they all gasped in horror as it bounced right off and clanked to the ground. The princess watched in anguish as it tumbled away and clanked two more times, bouncing even farther from Amy. The world remained slow-paced for her. And she heard her own knees thud onto the floor and echo through her mind. Then, much like a rubber band under too much pressure, time snapped back for her as Victor spun around and glared at her. The room went deathly quiet. Eclipse met his gaze. She didn't even care anymore. Even as he stomped towards her and drew his sword, she held eye contact. Her time was up. She had hoped for just one knife in her life to actually stick, but her luck was dryer than sand and twice as hard to hold onto. All she had left to do was wait for her death and hear one last sneer from Amy. If only she could hear how powerfully her father's heart beat as he realized he was about to end his daughter's life. He wasn't any more ready than she had been to end his.

But Amy didn't turn around. She stared blankly into the audience and wavered just a bit. Then, just before Victor reached Eclipse, her eyes rolled up into her head and she fell unconscious to the floor. In such a quiet room, the thud rang loudly in Victor's ears. He stopped in his tracks and slowly closed his eyes in relief, though his daughter thought it was exasperation. He turned around to look at Amy. Eclipse slowly leaned around his legs to look and there she saw her enemy, what she honestly hoped was lifeless, collapsed in a pile on the floor. The crowd saw Victor's face and remained silent, unsure of what was to come. Her brothers knew they could save Eclipse if they hurried, so they all ran out onto the floor and knelt beside her, ignoring Victor's death stare following their every move. He realized that though Eclipse had cheated, she had also won, which forgave the cheating by law. The problem was the sword he had drawn. If he didn't swing his sword to kill Eclipse, he would appear weak, but if he did the crowd might react poorly. Their faces, though full of fear, held a new emotion he despised to see. They were hopeful. He knew hope could spark terrible things. If he killed his daughter now, what was to stop them from killing him? He slowly rotated around to face his children.

Brothers and sister sat on their knees, united, and stared at their father. The crowd waited for a sign. Victor fought for a solution in his mind. And Eclipse just stared up into her father's eyes. Of all the times he tortured her, this look was the most terrifying thing she ever saw. His eyes caught fire and his face glowed ember red as his chest heaved in fury. She continued to stare at him, though she didn't know why. All she knew was that he was going to have to look her in the eyes if he was going to kill her. Maybe there was a shred of him that did not wish to murder his own daughter in cold blood. Their gaze lasted so long, that she was almost surprised when he raised his sword none the less. She cursed herself for letting him live and stared in the face of her murderer. Thank goodness for Sean.

"I hardly think a knighting ceremony is appropriate, Father."

He yelled loud enough for the whole gym to hear. He was giving Victor a way out because he saw the debate in his eyes and if Eclipse died, Sean knew he would be next. If nothing else, he would kill himself. Victor froze as Sean went against his own conviction, calling him 'Father' even, and considered his options. There was a sudden understanding between the two of them. Sean would stop rebelling and being difficult if Victor made the right decision, right now. The dictator would have the full support of his youngest son again, as much as it would disgust Sean. That put the nail in the coffin. Victor lowered his sword slowly and raised his own voice.

"True, I guess, she was only doing her duty. Nothing special about that."

He sheathed his sword and walked away. Eclipse watched him and couldn't help feeling victorious over a horrid foe. Then she heard it. One person started to clap. She turned and saw a familiar figure stand and continue clapping, even though he was the only person in the room doing so. His hair and teeth weren't any prettier dry and under lights, but he looked exceedingly proud of her. His hands clapped together faster than anyone's she had ever seen. Axl shot her a wink as others began to join his celebrating.

The clapping started to spread, first slowly and uncertainly, then with power and excitement. The applause shook the room. Shane lifted her up onto his shoulders and raised a fist in the air, stepping right over Amy's body in defiance. And then the crowd knew for sure they were safe and cheered as no audience had ever cheered before. They flooded out of the bleachers and gathered around their precious girl held high upon shoulders. No one could believe it. Eclipse had won.

It took longer to get her out of the gym than it took to heal her wounds. The crowd paraded her right to the lab, without once putting her down. However, Sean did slide her off his brother's shoulders, once they were inside, so he could cradle her in his arms on the way up the stairs. He couldn't ever express his true feelings to her, but he knew that he was so happy to see her alive again that it was all he could do to avoid smothering her. Acre frowned, but had bigger issues on his mind. As soon as she was fully healed, Victor would want her in the Enhancer.

By the time she finally made it to her cot, Eclipse crashed onto it. She could barely see and what she could make out was distorted and blurry. She heard everything going on right in front of her as if it was taking place miles away and simply echoing through a canyon in her direction. She was freezing and her own shivers shot so much pain through her body, she begged Acre to hurry in her mind. Words were not an option right now.

She watched Acre shuffle through his drawers in his desk and find the healing cylinder she had returned just that morning. He seemed angry at Sean. They looked like they were arguing, but all she could hear now was a loud and long beep resounding in her own head. She watched the two of them throwing their hands around and yelling at each other. She watched Sean's hand drop to his sword and rest on the hilt, as it often did when he was furious. Her eyes struggled to stay open and her mind fought to stay awake. She knew as badly as she was injured, sleeping was a horrible idea, but it was all she wanted in that moment...... to sleep. Her eyes began to drift shut, out of her control, her head began to fog.

She caught glimpses of the fight as she slowly forced her eyes open each time they shut, but there seemed to be a bright light behind Sean and Acre. It grew closer each time her eyes opened and started to shine even while they were shut. She decided to leave her eyes shut this time as the light grew brighter. It was so enticing, like it was welcoming her into warmth stronger than the heat of the sun. She longed to walk into the light. Then something clutched her hand.

She opened her eyes one more time and stared right into her brother's eyes. They were fraught with concern and his mouth was moving swiftly. He had to be yelling, but she couldn't hear it. She managed to give him her little grin one more time before her eyes shut again, this time for good. Had she been able to hear, she would have known that her brother was begging her to stay awake with tears burning in his eyes. He knew the dangers of falling asleep and he couldn't lose her now. Not after she was finally victorious. When her eyes closed that last time, Sean shook her entire cot.

"No. NO!!! Wake up, Eclipse! C'mon, wake UP!!!"

She didn't move.

Acre jumped to the rescue and pushed Sean out of the way. He felt her wrist for a pulse..... nothing. He held his hand over her lips to make sure she was breathing.... she wasn't. Then, much to Sean's horror, he yanked her onto the ground and started CPR. His mind sought desperately to remember how to perform such an archaic medical action, but he thought he knew it. After his second set of chest compressions, which he felt her ribs crack under, he leaned down to breathe in her mouth and stopped in his tracks. She was breathing again, and her wrist had a pulse, barely but enough to know she was alive. He picked her up and put her back in bed, then took a deep breath. Sean got the wrong idea.

"Is she....." he paused, trying not to sob. "Is she dead?"

Acre shook his head before he even finished talking.

"No, she's alive. Hand me the healer."

Sean looked around and found the device laying on the ground where Acre dropped it to care for Eclipse. His trembling hand could barely pick it up. He handed it to the scientist and held the older man's gaze as he took it from him.

"I'm so sorry Acre. None of this is your fault."

Acre accepted the apology with a nod and began using the healer to mend his young student's wounds. The fact that she was still asleep worried him. If she fell into a coma, there was a good chance the Enhancer would kill her and he knew that Victor would be all too happy to throw her in any way. On the other hand, being in a coma would keep her from having to endure the terrible side effects of a drug induced one.

Once all her wounds were healed, Acre went back over to his desk with Sean following like a lost puppy. He found his old brain monitor in the back of a rarely used drawer and brought it to Eclipse. He blew off the dust and flipped the switch. Amazingly, the device still worked, and a dull light beam coned out from it to her head. He sighed in relief.

"There's still brain activity and nothing looks too terribly damaged. It probably just shut down to protect her from the pain."

"When will she wake up?" Sean asked anxiously.

Acre's brow furrowed.

"Well, that's just it. She might not. Normally when the brain does this, it shuts off and wakes her up when the pain is gone, but she's completely healed and..... nothing." He looked puzzled at the lifeless body before him.

"So….. what do we do?"

"We put her in the Enhancer, of course!"

Both men turned around, a bit startled to see Victor standing in the doorway, with Axl on his heels. He had managed to calm down, but they both knew one wrong move would end Eclipse's life, for good this time.

"Victor, she might not live through the enhancement right now, and I can't rightly give her a drug IV if I don't know exactly what's going on."

Sean was glad Acre always knew what to say to his father. But his hope faded when he saw the look on Victor's face. He knew what was going to happen right then.

"Acre, I believe I have been humiliated enough today. You have two choices. By this evening either place her in the Enhancer or place her in the pit. Those are your options. Send for me when you've made a decision."

And that was it. He turned around and strutted out without another word. They knew there would be no changing his mind. The pit was the worst jail in the country. It was nothing more than a giant hole dug in the ground with a complicated machinated tower in the center. When turned on, it made a loud screeching sound that deafened most people. Then it would randomly shoot out a couple blades and pikes all the way to the wall and draw them back in when they hit. Many people lost limbs or got non-fatally stabbed. The faster you died, the luckier you were. But the weapons were random and the guards watered and fed you daily. Though it was hot water and salty meat. The entire place was a mental torture house. The bodies were never cleared out but were left to decompose. Before being thrown in, the prisoners were blinded. It was a punishment worse than death.

Sean shuddered at the thought of his baby sister in that place and looked at Acre. They both knew what they were going to have to do. They would have to put her in the Enhancer as is, without the knockout drugs. She might die in there too, but it would be far less painful than the pit.

# CHAPTER FIFTEEN

So now, months later, Sean once again sat at the dinner table with his three brothers and his father, pretending to think of anything except his sister. Acre had underestimated how long it would take him to bypass the security system. Still stuck in the enhancer because of the storm almost nine months ago, he wondered if she was even alive anymore. If she was, he knew an IV was pumping oxygen into her blood stream and her skin and brain were absorbing her telepathy through the chemicals she was submerged in. But he didn't know if she was asleep. As far as they knew she could've woken up the day she went in and laid drowning, but unable to die for almost a full year. Sean would never forgive Acre and Victor if that was the case.

The only noise in the room was the clanking of silverware on plates as each man stuck to his own sober thoughts. Victor had been unbearable for months. Everyone thought it was because Eclipse was delaying his plans for the Logan series. In truth, he was overwhelmed with guilt every time he thought of her. He had forced her into the Enhancer against Acre's better judgment. His only consolation was making others feel miserable. He stuck a large piece of steak in his mouth and forced out a chuckle.

"If the four of you could only see how very unhappy you look." he sighed.

Sean couldn't help but shoot a disgusted glare at the man as he wiped grease carelessly from his lips. He had kept their silent agreement and it gave Victor great joy to hear him call him 'father'. He liked to win. It made him look good to the public as well, like Sean was on his side again. The population was growing more in favor of their ruler, now, as stories of him working tirelessly to free his daughter spread. Of course, his sons knew better. The only thing Sean could do was dream of slitting his throat and letting his blood pour out onto his plate till it overflowed. It lightened his mood.

Acre had spent every spare minute in the security office that controlled the Enhancer, trying to override the system, but instead, he discovered just how impregnable the building was. Naturally, he had designed it that way on purpose, but he surely never thought HE would have to be the one who cracked it. It required a great deal of concentration and Sean was absolutely no help. Acre found it hard to discourage his devotion to Eclipse, but he was causing more problems hanging around the office. Questions like, 'Can't you go any faster?' and 'Aren't you done yet?' definitely got old very quickly. At first, Acre answered gently and truthfully, but after three months, his replies became curt and sarcastic. And he even told Sean it was his fault at one point, that the system wasn't fixed yet because of his incessant talking. It was a horridly nasty thing to say, but it did keep the kid out of the way. However, Acre never forgot the painfully astonished look on the young man's face. After all, he and Sean were secret associates

As for the rest of the world, the Logan series prepared for enhancement, though its last five members had not been found, yet. Chrosia continued its dismal march through life, and Amy Gershon perfected her telepathic powers a little more each day. She had a goal. In Chrosia, the government controlled and arranged marriages. She knew when she got older, they would assign her a mate and regulate their child-bearing. The best mate would be assigned to the best telepath and the general of the series. She had no doubt that would be her.

That meant her kids would continue her legacy as the greatest and the best. Because the Enhancer changed genetics, it was very possible that her children would have her gifts. If she got her hands on the Logan's general, their genetic codes combined would lead to unstoppable offspring. It also meant that they would be the most likely to be personally selected by Victor as his heir, that is, if Amy wasn't selected first. Pretty heavy stuff for a 13-year-old to think of, but she knew the system and worse, how to work it. The fact that Eclipse was either trapped for life or dead played perfectly into her scheme.

Fortunately for everyone, Amy's beliefs were not well founded. One year and three weeks after Eclipse entered the Enhancer, Acre once again burst into the Monohue's dining hall in a state of excitement.

"Tomorrow!!" he cried. "I can get her out tomorrow!"

As soon as he said it, he collapsed at the end of the table into the armed, wooden chair. He missed the brothers of the imprisoned girl celebrating and hugging in joy, because he slammed his head down on his arms, resting on the table, and fell asleep.

After a sleepless night for all but Acre, the six men from the dining hall gathered once more outside the door to the Enhancer. The round platform that lowered into the actual building from the roof was only big enough for one person, so after much arguing, it was decided that Acre would go in first to shut off the machine. Sean would follow to see if Eclipse was alright and because he wouldn't let anyone else go first. It was a long argument that Victor impatiently ended by siding with his youngest son. A sign of good faith between them.

The door finally opened with a loud creak and Sean fidgeted nervously with........ well...... everything, his hands, feet, shoulders, just everything. Acre lowered into the Enhancer. The first thing he noticed was the machinery. It was powering through faster than he had ever seen it go. There was a steady torrent of the blue chemical pouring into the tank, but it never overflowed. That's when he saw her, and his stomach clenched with guilt at the sight.

She was awake. Her body, writhing back and forth in the bonds holding her to the bottom of the tank, sucked up the enhancement solution faster than a sponge and faster than any other person he had placed in here. Acre gasped. The machine was set for seven people instead of one! The chemical pumping through Eclipse's veins should have killed her months ago. He had no idea how long she had been conscious, breathing in water. Drowning, but not being able to die.

But, she was still alive!!! In torturous pain, but alive. Sean came down and took in the situation much quicker than Acre, mainly because he couldn't care less about the science. He jumped off the platform when it was still five feet off the ground and sprinted to the tank as fast as he could, vaulting over the edge and screaming desperately at Acre to shut the machine off. Unfortunately, Sean SHOULD have paid attention to the science. Because as soon as he jumped in, the density of the chemical began to burn his skin, but he swam as though it didn't matter. He slit the cords and bindings with his boot knife, again forgetting science. Her lungs were completely filled with this liquid and without the IV, she truly began to drown. Eclipse began gagging and screaming, well, trying to scream.

Sean's burns were impeding his ability to lug his sister to the top of the tank, so he made one last lunge and grabbed the top of the tank with one hand and with one giant swing, threw her out of the chemical and onto the floor. By this time, Victor had made it down and was watching in shock as one child struggled to breathe and the other tried to climb out of the chemical burning his skin off. Acre finally threw the switch and shut off the machine, and Erican was waiting till it was safe to leap off the platform. The enhancement fluid drained back out of the tank, saving Sean's life, but leaving him completely incapacitated. Erican jumped down and pushed past his father to reach Eclipse, who continued to drown outside of water. She puked out gallons of blue gunk, but never took a single breath till she passed out. Erican started CPR and Shane climbed into the tank and started to pull a moaning and groaning Sean out. Massive chunks of his flesh stuck to the tank and ripped away from his bones. Shane was having trouble grasping him without removing even more. His stomach twisted and he struggled not to vomit. When Aidan finally made it down, the sheer sight of...... everything, made him woozy.

Twenty minutes after her brother started CPR, Eclipse showed no change, though Victor was lucky no one was looking at him. He couldn't control the anxiety showing on his face. Sean had crawled from his spot, laying on the floor, over to the group to watch his baby sister's face, leaving half of his body weight in skin and tissue behind him in a trail. He felt like it was his fault. Like he had endangered her life that had barely hung by a thread when he came in. Tears streamed down each brother's face, trying to stay positive and convincing themselves that her eyes were going to open any second.

And they finally did. Eclipse sat up and heaved out another gallon or so of water, but then she gasped and felt air hit her lungs for the first time in over a year. The feeling was rejuvenating, but what followed was not. She saw Erican, bawling in front of her, right before he wrapped her up in his arms. She saw Shane and Aidan doing the same before they also joined the hug. And then she saw Sean. Eclipse never forgot that moment. Her brother laying on the ground staring at her, trying to smile at the very fact that she was alive, but obviously hiding his anguish. She saw the blisters eating away at his bared muscles and bones as her vision dimmed and her mind receded back into the comfort of darkness, and somehow, she knew.

It was her fault.

Eclipse woke up in her old cot the next morning with a start and a deep gasp for breath, though she wasn't sure what it was that startled her. Her head was on fire and her body felt limp, but she couldn't lay on her back anymore. Just the position flashed her back to the tank and made it hard for her to breathe. So, she stood up with a jerk and then froze, wishing she hadn't. It was like a concussion, but a thousand times worse. Like her brain was bruised and bouncing around in her head, especially when she moved quickly like she had to stand. The pain almost made her pass out again. Slowly, with the greatest care, she sat back down on the edge of her cot. It hurt to even do that. She held her head in her hands and tried to remember what all happened. And suddenly it was all too vivid. The torture of the enhancement, always drowning, never dying, passing out from stress and terror only to wake up, who knows how much later, in the same position. The countless days and nights she spent alone in the dark; it all came back to her and then she remembered her telepathy.

Now, as exhausted as Eclipse was, her sense of curiosity was stronger. Victor would have named this her greatest weakness. Acre thought it was her strongest ally. Curiosity kept her from blindly following orders. And right now, she was curious to see what the Enhancer had done, besides making her mind flop around in her head like a fish. She looked up from her hands. She needed something she could move or do with her mind in the room. A slight breeze blew some of the loose strands of hair out of her face and caught her attention. The one window in the room was open and the cool morning air moved some loose papers about as if they were swaying to music. The left-hand corner of her mouth curled down as she focused all of her mind on closing the window. It burned her head to do so, but she had to know her pain was worth the results. It moved about a centimeter down with a slight creak and she stopped and sat up straight. It worked! She had her telepathy..... and she could actually control it. Unfortunately, her pride became her downfall as she tried to force the window all the way closed. Instead, it shattered with a deafening crash.

Eclipse winced at the sound, and being only five stories high, she could hear the commotion she caused in the streets below. All this set her mind into a whirlwind, but she tried hard to focus on what she couldn't see. She closed her eyes and tried to discern who was saying what on the street. Even with her ears ringing, she could hear so much more than she thought. And her mind was playing tricks on her. At first, she just saw a blurry face. It looked vaguely familiar and there was a buzzing noise like muffled speech. Then, all of a sudden, she could hear clearly. There were two men talking, arguing about how the window broke. And then the picture became clear.

It was Acre. He was talking to a younger scientist, but he was staring right at her. She felt so weird, though. She was angry at Acre, but she was happy to see him. It was like she had two personalities. Suddenly, she got it. She was in the young scientist's head. She jumped up and opened her eyes with a start, once again causing her brain to burst. She ground her fists into the sides of her head and gripped her hair. The picture was gone, the conversation was gone. All that was left was a dreadful irking headache..... and Acre.

Eclipse froze as he walked through the door and stared at his bewildered face. *He knows,* her mind screamed in terror. *He knows I broke the window.* She didn't know how she knew, but it flashed like a showcase in her mind. He turned from her to the window and.....

"No, of course I didn't do it on purpose Acre." she snapped, the sound of her own voice hurting her head, so she lowered it before continuing. "I was merely trying to close it, not obliterate it."

He barely had enough time to turn around and furrow his brow at her before she spoke again.

"Well obviously it worked Acre! That was a rather juvenile observation for such a 'learned' scientist to make. And yes, I'm alright, besides you disconnecting my brain from my spine. What?" she leaned forward as if trying to hear him. "Of course, you're talking to me. There's no one else in here. Who could you be talking to besides me? And no, no I am not. How could I possibly answer questions you hadn't asked yet unless........"

Suddenly, she stopped as the realization dawned on her. He hadn't spoken a word, but he had thought plenty. Even now, she could hear his 'I told you so.' with her mind, not her ears. She had been reading his mind, accidentally, and answering his questions before he even asked them.

"Oh."

She slowly sat back down on her cot. She was about to ask how to make it stop, but her brain sought the answer before her mouth could. Apparently, she just had to focus on NOT reading someone's mind. It took several minutes, and caused her a great deal of pain, but they finally reached the point where they could have a normal conversation.

"Well," Acre asked, sitting down beside. "how did that feel?"

"What?" she moaned into her hands, supporting her head.

"How did it feel to know my thoughts almost before I did?" he asked.

She managed to look up at him and reply with dead seriousness.

"It was rather......... inconvenient."

"You'll get used to it." he chuckled. "But for now, we need to act swiftly. Get dressed while I talk to you."

She slowly struggled out of bed to obey.

"Now Eclipse, I of course, couldn't get your father to give you any rehabilitation time, so your schedule starts like normal today. Except for your running and breakfast times. You're going to skip those--- your shirt is on inside out--- to do a few errands with me. Do you understand?"

"Yes." she answered through her shirt as she pulled it back over her head. "But Acre?"

"Yes?"

"Can I eat something?"

Acre walked up to her, grasped her chin and forced her to look into his eyes.

"Eclipse, you can either eat and let Amy destroy you in the gym today or you can drill till you drop and give yourself the slightest chance of surviving till tomorrow morning."

"Today?" she gasped, eyes wide.

"Yes," he sighed. "Victor has decided to bump up the fight to today, surprise, surprise, but more on that later. Right now," he continued, walking over to his desk and grabbing a roll of paper. "we need to set you up with a weapon arsenal. I think your brothers have some surprises for your 11th birthday."

Eclipse shrugged and strapped on her belt as she walked to the door. When she got there, she froze with her arm stretched out for the handle. Acre grimaced behind her back, realizing what a horrid can of worms he just opened. She slowly turned around to face him.

"It's my 11th birthday?" she whispered.

Acre puffed out his cheeks and blew.

"You don't know yet. It's past your 11th birthday, actually. Eclipse, you were stuck in the Enhancer for a year. The security system malfunctioned. Don't drop your jaw like that, it's not professional. Now open the door and let's get to the armory. Your brothers will meet us there to help you out. Eclipse, you forgot your bracer. Go get it and try to pull yourself together. You have way too much going on to get lost in your own head."

He opened the door and started down the hallway while she went back for her bracer. She jogged one step before she remembered how bad her head hurt, so then she walked, only to realized that her head hurt either way. So, taking advantage of her high pain tolerance, she just chose to suck it up and jog. After struggling against bonds in a tank for a year, she was relieved to discover that her muscles had actually grown, versus the standard atrophy that set in for everyone else. So, she jogged after Acre, trying to tie her bracer on the move. It fit perfectly. In fact, all her clothes fit perfect, which put a question into her head.

"Acre, if I'm a year older, why do all my clothes still fit?"

"We took your measurements while you were asleep and laid out your clothes in the lab. Your other sets in the range and what not have all been replaced too. Didn't you notice this? I mean, there are no patches on this set. Well, now you do, I see, but honestly Eclipse, you need to bring your observation skills back. You're going to need them."

They went down the stairs to the metal-paved streets and Acre stalked off surprisingly fast for an inactive man of 60. Eclipse found that she almost had to skip to keep up and her head was still throbbing awfully, but curiosity won out again and she kept asking questions.

"So, what all can I do?"

"For now, I'd prefer you practice constraining your telepathy so we don't have any more....... accidents. However, you will have to learn to defend yourself from telepathic orbs in order to live through the gym today. Don't bother asking me how to, I'm already answering. Just listen. Your powers are connected to your entire being. They will react to your thoughts and instincts eventually, but you must channel and control them. Your mind will have to work hard to make them do exactly what you want.... and nothing else, but then it will become as easy and natural as breathing. When Amy throws an orb at you, there are several ways you can defend yourself against it. One is to simply deflect it from its course. You can also absorb its energy, but that's a little more advanced. And finally, technically you should be able to disintegrate an orb, but no one has been able to do it so far. You wouldn't have to deal with extra energy from the orb, but you won't get hit. Win/win. I'll try to talk you through it when you have a better handle on your telepathy. That, my girl, is the advantage of having the mastermind as your trainer. But here we are at the armory."

Like Victor's fortress, the armory was made of duranium, the impregnable metal keeping Chrosia's technology safe. It was the same size as the gym, but it held much more than weapons. The armory held robot prototypes and disintegration bombs. These prototypes were almost ready. Eclipse knew that Chrosia had used robots like them in Arcane, but nowhere near this advanced. The plan was to use them in Central Liberty when the time came. Each robot was equipped with a mini disintegration bomb, so if it did come down, it was bad for anyone around. Eclipse always felt the need to give them a wide berth.

Then, they walked past the siege equipment and finally reached the section that held weapons for individuals. Eclipse had only been in the armory once and that was six years ago on Sean's hip. There were racks for swords, shields, bows, and quivers placed in aisles. Then, past those, the walls on both sides were covered in an odd assortment of everything from the ceiling down to the benches that lined the sides. It was like a giant puzzle, a very dangerous one, of metal and wood. Occasionally, someone walked around the corners of the racks or just passed them and moved on through the forest of sharp, pointy objects. Apparently, people were just scattered throughout the room, grabbing swords and sharpening them, or stringing bows and testing them. She followed Acre to the left side of the room where five packages wrapped in brown paper lay on a bench. Acre looked around in confusion.

"Your brothers were supposed to meet us here." he shrugged. "Oh well, I can't help it if they're late and you *can't* be late. Here!" he chucked the first package at her, which she barely caught in her surprise. "That's Erican's."

She looked at it awkwardly. She had never received things for her birthday. Was it normal? Eclipse unrolled the paper and stared in amazement at the contents. There was a thick black belt with six black daggers attached. She unbuckled her normal belt and replaced it with the new one.

"Higher!" Acre instructed.

She looked at him questioningly.

"Get it off your hips and tighten it around your belly button."

She adjusted it and looked down to inspect it better. Two of the daggers lay on the front side of her hips. They were her throwing knives, the blades only about four inches long. The next two lay directly on her sides; they had seven-inch blades. And the final two had foot long blades and sat behind her hips. They all had identical scabbards and handles, and she realized, when she drew one, that they were surprisingly light. The scabbards were black with white laces forming X's up the sides. The handles were metal, wrapped in black leather strands. The blades were fascinating, clear and metal at the same time, and they were sharp already. To sum things up they matched her clothes perfectly and she suddenly had a new confidence with them strapped to her waist. She put the four-inch knife back in its scabbard and reached around her side to try and grab one of the larger ones. It was...... difficult. Acre saw her struggles.

"You have to reach behind with your opposite hand rather than in front. Erican designed it so the scabbard pivots when you draw it correctly. They are easy to quick draw once you get the hang of it."

Eclipse reached her right hand behind her back and grasped the dagger behind her left hip. The tip of the scabbard spun out to the left and the weapon slid out easily. Getting it back in was a little more difficult but Acre pointed out that if she was putting it away, she had better not have a reason to hurry. Her job should be done. Also in Erican's gift, was a pair of knives, only about two-inch blades. They fit perfectly into the hidden pockets in her pants on the side of her knees. When she asked what they were for, Acre snorted his reply derisively.

"Killing people."

The next package was from Shane. It held a black belt just like Erican's, with two scabbards just like the daggers, but they held full length swords, blades about three and a half feet long. They dangled off the belt with a short loop of sturdy, black leather, making it easier to slip them in and out. Eclipse realized now why Acre had her move her dagger belt up, as she buckled her new belt below it. Then, she drew her left-side sword with her right hand and flipped it around in her hands. The swords were like semi-transparent crystals with a tint of silver coloring, just like the blades of Erican's daggers. She had never seen anything like it before.

"Are they glass?" she whispered, mesmerized by the work of art in her hands.

"Diamond." he corrected, very unimpressed. "Imbedded and laced with some duranium. That right there is the strongest blade in the world. Despite the fact that it is only two inches thick, it will deflect and stop any thicker or heavier blades and it slices through most armor. Erican made them especially for you and Shane tested them extensively. I know they are too long right now, but you will grow into them."

Eclipse sheathed her sword, whose handle matched the daggers. Acre reached into the discarded papers and pulled out an odd block the size of a bar of soap and tossed it at her.

"Obviously, you'll need this. No regular whetstone will sharpen those things. There's a small pouch on the belt."

Eclipse picked up the block (she couldn't quite catch it) and stuck it in the pouch, snapping it shut afterward. Then, she opened Aidan's gift. His held two, thin black belts, much smaller than the first two. They each had a small 5-inch-bladed dagger hooked to them.

"Does he expect me to throw these?" she asked doubtfully, pulling one out of its scabbard as if it would bite her.

"Those are Aidan's promise fulfilled. If you press that button by your thumb, you'll see what I mean."

She shrugged and looked back at her knife. That's when she noticed the button on the black handle. She held the blade and pushed the button. With a slight click, the blade fell out of the handle. It turned out to be a double-sided, double-pointed knife. Everything made sense suddenly. The knives were for throwing, but she would simply hold the handle and push the button to release the blade, mid throw. Then no matter how she threw it, something sharp would hit some part of the target. There was only one thing she didn't get.

"Why are the belts so small?"

"They strap around your thighs."

Once Eclipse had gotten her thigh belts on and adjusted them, she reached into Aidan's paper again and pulled out two round metal cylinders, 1½ inches in diameter and 4 inches long. At first, she had no idea what they were, but she knew Aidan would have a purpose. Then she noticed the button.

"STOP!!!"

Acre made her jump and literally every person in the armory looked at them curiously as he jumped up and yanked the cylinders out of her hands. Before Eclipse could even ask why, he showed her. Acre pointed one end of the device towards the wall and pressed the button. A large point shot out the top and a small ax head popped out of it near the tip. Eclipse's face turned pale, well, pale-er. She almost just stabbed herself in the eye. She gave Acre a humiliated look and gently took the pop-up halberd from his hand. The light glinted off the razor-sharp blade. She was very impressed with the whole thing.

"That" Acre stated, taking it from her. "is why Aidan is my favorite of all your brothers. He uses his head to find efficiency and define skill. However, I must admit that Sean's gift is quite ingenious."

As he spoke, he pulled a small lever on the back of the cylinder and the ax blade sucked back in and the cylinder shrunk back to its original size except the point stuck out. He used the wall to push the tip back into the cylinder till the device clicked. He flipped it around in his hands, nodded approvingly at it and set it down on the bench before sitting down himself. Then he looked back up at Eclipse.

She was standing perfectly still, as if frozen, with her mind in some distant place, except of course, she was trembling. Violently, like an earthquake, really. No amount of calling her name or even shaking her could snap it out of it either. Acre just held her shoulders and tried to yell through whatever was going on in her head. Then it got worse. The room started to rattle as weapons began to bang against each other till they were falling off the wall one at a time. People were yelling and running for their lives, hoping a sword wouldn't pierce their brains from above. Acre's eyes widened as he looked around. She was going to bring the building down. He gave her one more good shake.

"Eclipse! ECLIPSE!! Stop it. Just STOP!!" he yelled over the noise. "You have to control it!!!"

He had to pull her aside to avoid a falling spear. He tried a different angle next. He grabbed each side of her head and tried to look into her eyes. They were rolling back into her head. She didn't even know what was going on. She was in shock. Acre had to stop it.

So, he took the spear and beamed her over the head with the butt of it. And then stared at the little girl knocked out on the floor. He had no idea what set her off like that with no warning. He thought back to the halberd. Maybe the light gleaming on the metal looked like the tank? No, she was fine with the swords and daggers. Maybe it was the sound of it opening or closing? Or something he said about the weapons or Aidan or Sean..........

Sean. The last time she saw him HAD to be traumatic. He was bloody and blistered, bawling at the sight of his living sister, his flesh falling off his bone right before her eyes. Acre huffed and collapsed on the bench, waiting for Eclipse to wake up. He was trying to be tough on her today, hoping it would snap her back to her old self, but he had to stop. He knew she woke up at some point, but he had no idea how much it hurt, or what she even thought of all this. He wanted her to win today, but she needed him. He thought her brothers would be the gushy ones so he would have to be the jerk, but her brothers didn't show. She desperately needed help.

When Eclipse woke up, he crouched by her side on the floor and helped her sit up. Which she did, but immediately regretted. Her head was on fire, her mind was racing and her ears rang like bells. Acre knew exactly what to say this time.

"Eclipse, you know that Sean is going to be ok, right?"

She slowly looked up at him.

"How did you......"

"Well, believe it or not I raised you. I know not much sets you off, but if something does, it involves that idiot."

"Is he really ok?" she whispered, trying very hard to hold her head together with her hands.

"Yes." Acre sighed. "The machine progressively strengthens the serum over time, adjusting your body to it. When he just jumped in, well, it chemically burned him rather badly. It's caustic stuff. Nothing a healing booth couldn't handle, though."

Healing booths worked the same way as the hand-held healer, but were used for injuries that needed tissue restored over massive sections of a body. The victim was laid in the bottom and the top closed over them like a coffin. Eclipse nodded and rubbed her eyes, ending by burying her face in her hands. She wasn't able to focus on anything and her reflexes were slow. She couldn't afford this today. If only Victor had given her one day to rest, but no, this made sense. Even after a year, he was definitely still angry about the last time he saw her.

"Eclipse?"

"Hmmm?" she moaned, not bothering to look at Acre.

"When did you wake up?"

She didn't move for a couple minutes. And he was scared to say anything else. He didn't want to set her off again. After a while she managed to answer, but he knew it was hard for her, despite the fact she was trying very hard to hide it. She slowly looked up at him.

"I saw you leave........."

Acre suddenly felt the need to stand up and turn away. She woke up right after she went in. He couldn't tell her brothers. They would kill him. She had already moved off the conversation and he was relieved for it. In fact, she was staring at Sean's gift. It was probably the only thing that got her off the floor to be honest. It was easily as long as she was tall, possibly longer. She picked it up and slowly ripped the paper off. All she saw was the string and a new feeling welled up inside her. If she knew anything about emotions, she would have known it was excitement, but for now, all she knew was to shred the rest of the paper. It flew off to reveal a new set of quivers and a bow about as tall as her. The quivers still crossed each other on her back and their straps did the same on her chest, but they weren't circular like other quivers. They were ovals. This let them lay more comfortably and stick out less off her back.

Attached to the quiver with her normal arrows, the one that protruded off her right shoulder, lay her bow in an odd fashion. The device holding it was bolted to the quiver. She had never seen this type of bow before and she carefully unhooked it from the quivers with a gentle sliding motion and inspected it. She was used to a recurve bow, but this one was far bigger and heavier. It was made of metal and the string looped infinitely around the many cams and knobs that were definitely new for her. There were more pieces to this one bow than all the rest of her weapons combined. It was an odd shape, too. There was a handle in the center and it faced away from her before the edges were bound back by the string. She tried to draw it back and couldn't even budge the string, but the handle was comfortable and easy to grip. Eclipse looked at Acre in confusion. Why would Sean give her a bow she couldn't use? Is this what all bows were like now? Did life change that much in one year? When Acre didn't offer any explanation, she decided on a simple question to get him talking. She had only seen wooden bows.

"Is it...." she hesitated, trying not to sound crazy, "made of metal?"

"Yes." Acre replied. "Here put your quivers on. You can't actually use the bow yet as it's a full sized, 200lbs. draw weight, but he wanted you to see it. You'll get a standard issue one till you are older. Your electrified quiver holds 30 arrows and your regular one holds 60. That gives you 90 lives you're carrying around on your back, so try---"

"330" Eclipse interrupted, pulling her hair out from behind her quivers.

"Excuse me?"

"You said 90 lives, it's actually 330 because I can kill nine people with each electrified arrow, so that's 270, and one person with each normal arrow, so that's 60. 60+270 = 330." she replied.

She wasn't trying to be cocky, she was just trying to get her mind back on track. Math seemed like a good place to start. Acre pursed his lips in exasperation.

"Yes, genius. My point was to be careful who you kill. Now, hand me your bow."

"How's it work?"

Acre took her bow gingerly from her hands and furrowed his brow at it.

"I'm not sure. It's Sean's personal design. He called it a compound bow, or something of the like. It's supposedly more accurate and can fire farther and such. He spent a year trying to build one that actually worked and then he had to find a string that could sustain its power. He was supposed to be here to explain it all to you, but I do know that you should never, ever unstring it. It started quite the fight when Erican did it to help Sean one day. I've seen him use it, but I don't know what half of the gadgets on it are for."

He held it back out for Eclipse to take and she slowly reached out for it. There was something incredibly empowering about holding a bow that was designed specifically for her by her favorite person in the world. She looked at it for a few more moments before Acre took it back and told her he'd hang onto it for her, till she could actually use it. Even he couldn't draw the thing, though.

"Ugh, I have no idea how Sean expects you to use this, even in the future."

Eclipse nodded, but it was obvious her mind had moved on.

"Where *are* my brothers?"

"I've been wondering the same thing, but I think I just got it. Today is the first day that the Logans start the enhancement process."

He paused to make sure she wasn't freaking out. She rolled her eyes and gestured for him to continue.

"And I'm pretty sure your brothers are all supposed to go first together. I bet they are all waiting for me at the Enhancer. I'm supposed to get Sean there in one piece. Don't look so worried. I checked on him earlier today and he looks good as new. Been catching up on some much-needed rest as well, I daresay."

Acre took her arm and gave her a slight push towards the door. As they walked he instructed her to go to the gym and have the drill master set her up for the next hour in the drill room on level ten.

"Ten?" she interrupted. "But Acre, that's the highest level. I can't even handle that on a normal day. And today isn't normal. I can barely hear and thinking is painful and---"

"And Amy has mastered level eight. If you can at least keep your feet on level ten, you may have a chance of surviving today."

Eclipse stopped dead in her tracks.

"Surviving?" she whispered indignantly. "That's it? Don't you think I could do a little better than that?"

Acre swung around and gripped her shoulder with his free hand, the other carrying her bow.

"Your entire series is enhanced now remember? Amy is allowed to use any form of weaponry or telepathy, just like you now can. But you only have 4 hours left to practice. Focus on your telepathy, Eclipse, the rest of your skills will return to you easily, but drill that brilliant mind of yours. Drill it till you pass out and play defensive with Amy for as long as you possibly can. Eclipse, I need you to know something and believe it in the deepest part of your soul. I'm pretty sure that if you give her the chance today, Amy will kill you. Do NOT give her that chance, no matter what you do."

Eclipse nodded solemnly and they walked towards the door once more. Her head spun through all the new information and she realized that for the first time in her life, she was overwhelmed. Her mind couldn't focus and her hands trembled. She was absolutely, totally out of control and that very realization shook her to her core. Following Acre even seemed like an impossible task. Once they were outside, he stopped to talk one more time.

"Never forget, Eclipse, that you beat Amy when she was stronger than you. From now on, you are the strongest. You have more enhancement than anyone alive and your hand to hand is higher than the best warriors of old. I know it and you know it. All you have to do is prove it to everyone else."

ΩΩΩΩΩΩ

Eclipse eventually decided to jog to the gym. Her head still seethed in pain with every step, but she decided she had to get used to it. By the time she reached the door, she was panting ever so slightly and felt like she was about to pass out from the pain. *Dammit*, she thought, *I'm out of shape. I guess doing nothing for a year isn't so great.* She puffed out her cheeks and opened the door. Immediately, her eyes shot around the room in confusion. The building was the same size and the bleachers were still there, but the entire inside looked different. There were little dots on all the walls and the ceiling. She stepped back and glanced at the plate on the door before letting it close behind her. Despite the new look, she was in the gym. She signed in at the computer and then jogged to the man in the middle of the room with a clipboard. She was relieved to find out she knew him.

"Jackson?" she blurted out, before she remembered her place. "I mean, Sir." she corrected as he turned to look at her.

"Well, well, well. Look who's back from the Enhancer. It must have been quite a ride. How are you doing?" His face contorted in concern before she could answer. "Wait, shouldn't you be on bed rest?"

Eclipse staggered a bit and raised a hand to her head. Her brain bounced around in her head as she stood still for just a moment and struggled to answer.

"I...... my father........"

She shook her head to clear her thoughts and almost passed out again. Eclipse continued in a burst of frustration.

"I have to beat Amy today."

Jackson felt his heart bleed a little. He knew there was no way she could beat Amy the day after she made it out of the Enhancer. No one could. But he had no say, not even for his star pupil...... and his favorite one.

"Ok.... well..... where the hell is Acre? He left you like this?"

"Well, I---"

"Say now, look at all those gadgets!"

He spun a very nauseous Eclipse around and looked at all her weapons, analyzing them as her empty stomach began to swish.

"Swords are too long and rather skinny, but they look spiffy on you. And check out those quivers! We should get you a bow to go with those, you know, but you definitely aren't here to show me your gear. So, what can I do you for?"

He stopped spinning her as she came face to face with himself and looked intently at her, waiting for an answer. Eclipse opened her lips to speak, but snapped them shut as bile rose into her mouth. Jackson didn't notice as she gulped it back down. He just thought she was waiting to make sure he wouldn't interrupt.

"Go on kid, don't be shy. Speak up and tell me what you need. Whatever it is, I'll do it. Within reason of course. Come now! Spit it out!"

And she did......... from her hands and knees........... onto the floor........ and Jackson's boots....... for almost five solid minutes. The entire time, he watched in horror and disgust, leaning down to help in between each convulsion, only to back up as it continued. By the end of it, he just stood back in horror and watched her heaving on the floor, not knowing if she was done or if it would start all over if he moved. Soon they were both in the center of a massive blue puddle of vomit. It was extremely awkward for him and flat out miserable for her.

"I need," she heaved in pain, "to train."

"Suuure thing, kid." he answered hesitantly.

He tip-toed through her puke to help her stand back up, wiping his hands off on his pants as soon as he let hers go.

"Of course. You can always ask me for anything. What did you have in mind?"

Jackson wisely waited for her reply this time as she got her first deep breath since she entered the building.

"Acre wants you to set the drill room up for me. Level Ten--" she nodded her head towards the back wall, "for the next 4 hours."

An unhappy shadow shrouded Jackson's face. Eclipse felt a new ball of heat growing in her stomach. The type that meant something bad was about to happen.

"Erm, Eclipse, you know I would. I've always done whatever I can to help you hone your skills, but Amy had the drill room reserved for the whole day early this morning. And if you think she was a pain a year ago, you should meet her now."

Jackson stopped to roll his eyes.

"So, she's in there now?" Eclipse asked.

"Yes ma'am. Now, Jason is over there, well what's left of him is over there. You might be able to pull his teeth to figure out her strategy. Or you can ask the other Emilies on the bleachers."

Eclipse clenched her jaw and then closed her eyes as she realized the extra pressure hurt her head more.

"Fine." she muttered and shambled off.

"Good luck, kiddo."

He waited till she was out of earshot to mutter under his breath, shaking his head miserably.

"You are gonna need it."

Eclipse's eyes scanned the group of six women at the end of the building, searching for a helpful face. She found one in a brunette with peach-colored eyes, Susan Hadlina. Susan was 21, but she still spent most her time with the younger Emilies. She was widely known as a sort of mother to the series. She took no sides, so she helped all sides. Eclipse decided to ask her for help when a thought ran through her mind like a jet. She had an eerie sense that Jason wanted to see her....... and oddly enough, help her, but she couldn't decide why she knew this. She couldn't see him anywhere, but Jackson said he was somewhere in this room. She stopped walking toward the girls and looked around the gym a bit before finding him on top of the left-hand bleachers, with his elbows on his knees and his face buried in his hands.

All the Emilies were trained to be silent when they moved. They were stealth assassins. Their job was to get in, kill, and get out without anyone knowing what happened. By now Eclipse was so used to being silent, that it was natural and happened without her even realizing it. She reached the top seat and stood next to the exhausted trainer, expecting him to talk since he called her, but he had no idea she was there until her patience wore thin and she spoke.

"What is it, Jason?"

The trainer jumped and glanced up at her just long enough for her to see the tears in his blood shot eyes. He had several bruises and cuts on his face and hands and, she could only assume, the rest of his body. It couldn't be easy, being Amy's trainer. She was violent and demanding, with no respect for any other breathing thing's life. If it wasn't against the law and punishable by death, she would probably have killed him by now. Eclipse felt a new sense of........ something for Jason. She couldn't quite put her finger on it though. It was odd, this new feeling, as if brought on by witnessing someone else's plight. She knew Amy was vile. She knew Jason was stuck with her, too. She also knew he was extremely drunk. His breath was noxious, and his eyes twitched in the light. He looked back down and rubbed them before answering.

"Hey."

His reply was groggy as she sat down next to him and waited for him to continue. After a couple coughs and disgusting slurps, he did.

"What are you doing up here?"

"Didn't you call me?" she asked questioningly.

He glanced back up at her in confusion.

"Why the hell would I want to be seen with you? I might as well jump into a volcano."

"I won't hurt you." Eclipse snapped indignantly. "And being burned to death would be an extremely unpleasant way to die. Though, I suppose a volcano's heat would make it incredibly fast."

"I know," Jason said quickly, before she continued with her science lesson. "that you wouldn't hurt me without the order to do so, but Amy would if she ever saw this."

He motioned his hand back and forth between the two of them to demonstrate he was talking about their conversation. Eclipse conceded the point with a shrug of her eyebrows, and they sat in silence for a while. Both just staring at the gym, eager to escape their predicaments.

"She's good, isn't she, Jason?"

He nodded.

"She's been on level 8 in the drill room for the past four months and she's mastered it. The plan was to bump her up to nine today, but she wanted to conserve her strength for the fight."

He glanced at her meaningfully and she puffed out her cheeks with a sigh. It was settled then. She was going to die. After all the times she beat Amy, after living through her father's wrath and the Enhancer, she realized it was all pointless. She got up to leave, hoping to sleep a little more before giving her enemy what she always wanted.

"Eclipse?"

She rolled her eyes and turned around in frustration.

"Yes?" she demanded.

He looked around like a man trying to hide his next remarks. When he was sure no one could hear them he continued in a whisper.

"Amy's been practicing and drilling specifically to beat YOU. You are the only person I have ever seen her flinch in front of, she maybe even fears you a bit. She fears particularly what you may become. I've never seen her work harder than the past year, which makes her dangerous. Stay on the defensive as long as you can. That's what will keep you alive. She is awful at dodging but she has deflection worked out to a science. Keep it physical as long as you can. Also," he glanced around again. "block out your thoughts, or she will simply read your mind and know each move you make before you do so. And even worse, she'll know that I helped you. That could hurt any positive outcome for you if she told Victor. And once she's in there-----"

He tapped his temple and shuddered in disgust as he remembered the feeling of her digging through his mind.

"-----there's no stopping her. Now, I need you to do one more thing for me."

"What?" she joined in his whispering.

"Read my mind."

Eclipse stepped back a little. She had no idea how to do that. She had already read Acre's mind accidentally, but she didn't know how she did it. It could be exceedingly dangerous for Jason.

"I could kill you." she pointed out desperately, though she sensed his mind was made up.

He shook his head.

"Don't care. Got nothin' to live for. Now sit."

She obeyed hesitantly and listen to his instructions, not without glancing around to make sure no one was listening.

"Close your eyes and focus on the darkness."

Eclipse raised an eyebrow.

"Seriously?"

"Do it!" Jason snapped and waited till she jumped and did as he said to continue in a sultry voice.

"Focus on the darkness. Let every inch of your mind be consumed by it.

Think of no one or thing besides your own mind."

*This is insane. He's intoxicated and I should just leave. But I doubt he'd let me and I have no wish to cause a scene.* So, she did as he said. With a deep breath she focused on the inside of her eyelids. In and out she breathed, calmly and deeper than she thought she could. With each breath, she searched the darkness of her mind for..... something, she wasn't sure what. She forgot where she was, and what day it was. She forgot the fight and the gym. She even forgot Jason as he remained silent. She forgot her entire reason for entering this darkness. And then she gasped. Whatever it was, it was the most amazing thing she had ever seen. Its color was blue, but such a pure burst of blue that it made her feel...... alive.

It was like standing on a cliff on a very windy day, letting the sheer force of the wind keep you from falling. And suddenly she felt it, wind blowing her hair off her face, but she didn't want to open her eyes. The object before her was too mesmerizing. It reminded her of a painting she once saw Acre looking at. It was a beach, but the sky was blue and bright, something she had never seen in Holux. And then there was the ocean. It shone and glistened in the painting and now, that perfect, pure electric blue resonated in her mind in the form of a magnificent wolf. One the size of a draft horse. He stared back at her and though his entire face shone the brilliant blue, opaquely darkened with black shadows and mists, his eyes burst with the solid color itself. He looked at her and she looked at him. The connection was instant. Though she didn't know it, he was her telepathy incarnate, her familiar.

Jason heard her gasp and knew she was ready. He leaned in close to her ear and whispered her instructions, trying hard not to break her connection. She heard him as if it came through the clouds forming in the picture in her mind.

"Reach out Eclipse. Look for me and follow me. I want to show you something."

Though she didn't know what he meant, her wolf seemed to. He turned and ran down the landscape her brain was creating very swiftly now. It was the capital city, but more glorious and bright than it had ever been in real life. She realized as she watched her new-found friend flee, that her vision switched to his own. It was exhilarating. It felt like she was flying past familiar buildings and faces without a care in the world. She knew she was searching, but she wasn't sure what for anymore, but the wolf knew. He flew on his paws to the gym and she was helpless to stop him. Once in the door, he slowed and searched. There was Jason, at the top of the bleachers, sitting with a young girl. Eclipse gasped. It was her!!! She hadn't seen herself in so long; this sickly, deathly pale girl couldn't be her.

The closer she got to the girl, the more she realized it was, though. She was slowly walking to her own body, up bleachers, through the mind of an imaginary wolf. It was unnerving as she witnessed her own body shiver in anticipation, waiting for the creature's next move. She opened her eyes and met his own. Both versions of her, the one on the bleachers and the one in the eye of the wolf, clicked into an unbreakable bond. She gazed into her own eyes as the mesmerizing blue seeped into the irises from her pupil, eradicating the hazel color she had been born with. Her eyes were blue for the rest of her life. She waited for the wolf to move even closer to her, but he walked straight through Jason instead.

The entire room changed. It became dark and dreary once more and she heard the noise of crowds cheering and booing. She stood in the center of the gym in her own body, no wolf in sight. The bleachers were filled with mobs of people shouting at her. She spun in circles yelling at them for explanations of their words, both vile and encouraging. No one heard her over their cries, but she heard something new. Footsteps and battle cries on either side of her. She jerked from left to right. On her right was an Emily with bright red hair named Amber. The two of them had always gotten along, even when Eclipse defeated her in the gym. She was the last member of her series she had to face before Amy. They had shaken hands after their fight and everything. Amber even helped temporarily erase memories for her plan before the Enhancer. Now, though, she charged at Eclipse with daggers drawn and murder in her eyes. Eclipse turned to run, only to see Amy charging her from her left with a large sword and buckler. Her glance shot between the two girls and she saw the imminent collision. Her best bet was to duck and cover, so she did. The two girls charged even faster and Eclipse closed her eyes, waiting for the pain.

There was a thunderous noise over head as the two Emilies met, but their attacks were not set against the princess. They passed through her like ghosts and fought one another. Eclipse opened her eyes as it continued and looked up. It was a battle between them, they weren't attacking her. In fact, they were completely ignoring her. It all clicked. This fight, this was what Jason wanted to show her. She could see how Amy moved and fought after a year of training. She stood up and backed away from the shades and watched them. Amber was about the same as the last time she saw her, but Amy, Amy filled her heart with terror. She had always been aggressive when fighting, but now she was good at it. She undercut and over cut like a pro. Her buckler bashed more than it blocked and Amber's right arm was soon dislocated from its force. Then it got interesting.

Sensing her defeat, Amber switched to telepathy and threw Amy back with a forceful burst of power, unfortunately, it shot herself back as well, but she had expected this. She landed on her feet bracing with her left arm and sliding back from the force. Amy did the same and then immediately retaliated with a barrage of purple orbs at Amber's face. Amber rolled to dodge and put up a green ward in the process. The orbs that hit it as she stood up pushed her back and staggered her balance, but didn't harm her. However, they kept coming with rapid fire from Amy and even Eclipse, knowing nothing about all this, knew Amber's defense was weakening. She had entered the Enhancer a few years before Amy and had used telepathy far more than the young blonde, but Amy could still beat her? What chance did Eclipse have? She shook the fear out of her head and realized she was watching the wrong person. Her sight snapped to Amy. She held her hands together, casting the orbs out of both at the same time, but it didn't appear to be affecting her. She smiled wryly as Amber began to falter. How could Amy not be exhausted after several minutes of pounding Amber with her orbs?

Eclipse watched in horror as Amber buckled beneath the strength of Amy's attacks. Her ward was flickering, and she began glancing around desperately, trying to form a plan. Eclipse saw it hit. Amber stood up from her crouched position and pushed everything she had into her shield. It grew in size and strength, till it was almost ten feet tall. Then with one final effort, she threw the entire thing across the gym toward her opponent. Amy's eyes widened and she tried to roll off to the side, but it was too wide and it slammed into her face, pushing her back at a tremendous speed and smashing her into the wall. As soon as it hit, it disintegrated, and it was Amy's turn to fall to her knees. Eclipse furrowed her brow. That was a powerful hit. How did Amy survive that? Then she saw it, there was a translucent, purple field covering her whole body like a leotard. It must be a shell of some sort. It dissipated after that hit though.

Now, Amber was on a roll. She was casting telepathy Eclipse had never seen. The shield itself was impressive, but now there were orbs and weapons flying around the entire room!! Amber was controlling all her weapons with her mind and steering them with her hands. And dirt! She was literally picking dirt up off the floor and swirling it in her cyclone of horror. The twister moved towards Amy and Eclipse knew from her face that it was all she could do to survive. She put her shell back up and ran, sometimes flying as the cyclone picked her up. Eclipse let her mouth drop open as she watched how expertly Amber manipulated around objects, without hitting a single thing she didn't mean too.

Then it turned bad, extremely bad. Amy got thrown out of the twister within feet of Amber and made her move. With a powerful leap, she landed on her enemy's shoulders, placing both her hands onto her head. The cyclone stopped immediately as Amber started to scream and grasp wildly at her head, desperately trying to stop Amy. Eclipse cried out as Amber fell to her hands and knees and charged the scene, drawing her sword. With one fell swoop, she sliced off Amy's head.

The room began to shake and a voice like thunder called her name over and over. Her head began to swirl and burn. She fell to her knees and cried.

It hurt so bad! She squeezed her eyes shut to stop the tears, and clenched her head between her hands, trying to block out the noise and the sights all together. She stayed there crying and screaming till her instincts kicked in and she managed to stand up. The room was still vibrating and there were cracks filled with blinding light opening everywhere. She staggered towards the door, trying to escape, but the entire room spliced into thousands of shards and she whited out.

# CHAPTER SIXTEEN

Eclipse woke up with a gasp. She was on her hands and knees, awkwardly positioned on the bleachers. There were drops of blood on the bench in front of her and she soon discovered it was dripping from her eyes, ears, and nose. Her head hurt like it had in the gym seconds earlier----- *wait* ---- she looked up. She was in the gym, but it wasn't shaking, or slicing itself into pieces. It was still and calm. She forced herself to stand, holding one hand on her head, like that would stop it from spinning and observed her surroundings. The other Emilies were still standing down in the gym on the other side of the building. And Jackson was still in the center, but he was looking directly at her, shaking his head no. If he was yelling anything, she couldn't hear it over the ringing in her ears. She gently shook her head, trying to clear it and her thoughts slowly collected. She was reading Jason's mind. She was watching a fight that happened in the past, one Jason saw.

Jason!

Her neck almost snapped as she turned to see Jason collapsed on the step beside her, unconscious in his own blood. Not knowing what to do, Eclipse looked around for help. No one was near enough to even know what was going on, besides Jackson, but he didn't move to help them. He just stared in horror. Eclipse never forgot that face, the first time someone looked at her like she was a monster. She awkwardly nudged Jason with her foot. He sputtered and looked up, watching her breathe a sigh of relief. Killing him would have been bad. He heaved himself up onto the bench again. She sat back beside him. They were quiet for a bit. Jason was just waiting for the great thank you he would get for helping her at his own risk.

"I told you it was a bad idea." she muttered, rubbing blood out of her eyes.

He shot her an indignant glance and then rolled his eyes and sighed. It wasn't her fault. No one ever taught her manners. He tore off a strip of his shirt and handed it to her for the blood. She took it and wiped as much as she could off. The material was so filthy, she felt like most of it just smeared across her face. Then, they just sat there. Both exhausted, both bloodied and ready to quit. Jackson finally looked away with a disappointed shake of his head. The girls in the gym apparently didn't see or hear anything. Eclipse continued to rub all her blood onto her sleeves when the strip he gave her was proved useless and sighed again. Now that she had been in his head, it was awkward to sit next to him, somehow.

"Soooo...... what now?"

"Now," Jason answered. "you know Amy's new style and know not to let her touch your head."

"Yeah, what was that?" she asked, with new-found energy.

Using her telepathy was exhilarating. As much as her head hurt, she felt alive.

"That was Amy scrambling Amber's brain, but she can only do it while in direct contact with your head."

He glanced at her. The look of horror on her face reminded him that he was talking to a child. He raised his hands to calm her down.

"Oh don't worry, it's not fatal. It just hurts like hell. It only took Amber two weeks to recover. But then you rushed in and killed Amy anyway......."

Jason trailed off and squinted his eyes in contemplation. His voice became very accusing.

"....... Eclipse?" he growled.

Sensing the change and not knowing why it occurred, Eclipse turned to see an extremely angry glare.

"What?"

"Did you...... do ANYTHING in my head?"

Eclipse bit the inside of her cheek, puzzled.

"What do you mean?"

"I mean" Jason hissed, standing up and glowering down at her. "did you change the course of events?"

"Ok, yes, BUT," she stood up and stepped away as his face reddened, "I didn't know it would do anything. I was trying to save Amber and I thought it was real in the moment. The wolf disappeared and I thought I was in the real world again. Plus, it looked like Amber was dying. So, I jumped in and killed Amy, but then it all shattered and disappeared."

"Oh good grief. Of course, it did. You changed my memory, so I didn't have any recollection of events after you killed her."

"So, how do you know that she's alive now?"

"You didn't finish the process."

Her face turned pale.

"You mean to tell me, I have to STAY in a place like THAT if I ever wanted to erase a memory?!"

It was the closest to yelling at him she had ever come, and it made a terrified Jason take a step down and backwards. She looked like Victor. He raised his hands defensively.

"No, no. Just if you want to change a memory. You have to remake an entire new reality for them. Erasing a memory is stupid simple, from what I know at least."

Eclipse stared at him for a minute, and he stared back. And that was all she could stand. No more human interaction for the day, unless of course, she got to beat someone up. She gave an awkward little nod and tried to walk around him. He stepped in her way for one more statement.

"When you get to Susan can you give her a secret message for me?"

"What?"

"Withfetlig."

Eclipse raised an eyebrow

"What?" she echoed.

"Withfetlig." he repeated.

Anything if it would make him let her go.

"Ok," she said slowly "Withfetlig it is."

Eclipse was relieved to be able to walk away from the whole situation. Jackson shot her a nervous glance and looked away in fear as her face reddened. She jogged down the bleachers, strode across the room and gave Susan Jason's 'message'. The older woman nodded with understanding as if there was nothing odd about it, and curious as she was, Eclipse decided to let it go for now.

"So," Susan said clapping her hands after a few minutes of what Eclipse assumed was meditation, "you need to learn some tricks right? Specifically, blocking people out of your thoughts. Well, that's easy enough, just refuse to let anyone know what you're thinking."

Eclipse hesitated, considering telling the older Emily that she was literally just delivering a message and then planned on napping till her death. She chose to give in to her curiosity again. If Susan thought she needed to know more for the fight ahead, Eclipse decided it wasn't her place to disagree.

"That's it?" Eclipse asked reluctantly, trying to pay attention.

Her head still burned.

"That's it. It's not some complicated math equation, Eclipse, it's natural. Use your instincts and be careful what you wish for, because it just might come true. You command some very powerful forces. So, how much telepathy have you used?"

Eclipse glanced back up at Jason and shuddered. Susan saw it and knew what had happened. She pulled Eclipse away from the group and they sat on the bleacher together.

"Ok, here we go. Every time you go into someone's head, it's weird. There's no way around it but you may have learned just enough to survive

Amy. So, what is your familiar?"

"My what?"

"When we use telepathy, it often appears to us as an incarnate animal. What was yours?"

"Oh, a wolf. So, everyone has that?"

"Yup. Mine is a little fish. Consider him your telepathic guide."

"Is it, I mean he, like, a separate entity?"

"Oh goodness, no." Susan chuckled a bit. "You control every move he makes, but it helps us put a face on our abilities. It's kind of a neurological scam. Your brain doesn't quite comprehend what you're doing when using telepathy, so it creates a foreign creature and, in your mind, IT is what uses the strange forces you harness now. You only ever notice him when you are in sync with your abilities. And eventually he fades, unless you are using an extreme amount of power."

"But, I feel like I almost blew both our heads off. How is that in sync?"

"Was the wolf there when things started to go wrong?"

Eclipse let her mouth drop as she thought back.

"No, it left before."

"Exactly, it will stay as long as you are calm and in control. If you panic all hell will break loose. At first, you have to focus on literally everything you do, but it eventually becomes second nature. So, let's get started, hmm?"

They stood back up and Susan called Clarissa, another Emily from the group, to come help. Eclipse positioned herself across from the new member of their training group.

"Ok, Eclipse, the first thing you need to learn is how to throw a basic orb. Try throwing some orbs at Clarissa and she will deflect them. Just try to envision it in your head and it will form when you're focused enough."

Eclipse nodded and took a deep breath, focusing on forming an orb in her hands. At first there was just a blue haze, the same color of the wolf and now, her eyes. It was soothing. Like a warm blanket for her brain. Then it began to swirl in between her hands. Suddenly, it burst into what looked like a ball of blue flames. She looked at it without surprise. Susan was right, it was natural. The orb was the size of a softball now, so she bit her lip, preparing to launch it. It spiraled down and disappeared in a puff of blue smoke as it hit the ground.

Eclipse looked at Susan questioningly. Her teacher had an 'uh-oh' look on her face like a held out grimace. When she felt Eclipse's eyes on her, she let out an uneasy laugh.

"I don't think you threw it hard enough. Um, when is your first fight?"

"Today."

Susan grimaced again and sucked air through her teeth.

"Who are you facing, today?"

"Amy."

This time Eclipse didn't recognize the look on Susan's face. And part of that was because it changed a couple of times in two seconds. First, it dropped deadly pale, then she grit her teeth in anger, and then puffed out her cheeks as if trying to stop herself from exploding, placing both her hands out in front of her, palms away. Eclipse thought she was telling her she was too close, so she stepped back as Susan started talking again.

"We better get to work." she said. "Now try it again and treat it like an arrow, aim and let it fly on its own. Don't try to control it the whole way. You stifle the force behind it that way. I think that's why it spun out like that."

Eclipse prepared to throw another orb. It took 2 minutes just to form it in her hands, but through dedication, she managed to shoot it towards Clarissa. It flew fast and even picked up speed as it went. When it reached Clarissa, she held her palm up in front of her till the orb slowed a bit and then swung her arm around towards the floor. The orb followed the motion of her hand and drove into the floor, disappearing as it did.

"Good." said Susan, a little relieved. "Now do it ten more times."

Clarissa deflected each orb she threw with ease, but it still took Eclipse way too long to form them in her hands. Susan watched with worry. Eclipse would be crushed by Amy at this rate. But, she also knew Amy was impulsive. Chances were that she was probably going to start on the offensive. *In that case, I'm teaching her the wrong thing. Such an idiot.*

"Alright, Eclipse, let's work on defense." She piped up suddenly. "Would you rather absorb or deflect?"

"Can I disintegrate the orbs?"

Susan looked doubtfully at her.

"Well........ technically it's possible, but it would take so much energy that it's nowhere near practical. Disintegration requires you to have enough control of your abilities to disperse the particles of another telepath's energy. So, you would have to have a molecular grasp on your abilities. From what I understand, of course. I've had my powers for years and still haven't figured it out. So, I can't really teach you it. I'd start with one of the other two if I were you."

"Which do you think is better?" Eclipse asked with a nod to show she understood.

"I would say deflection, because you don't have to deal with the extra power in your system like you do when you absorb. Amy uses absorption because she's a cocky show off and likes to look like absorbing more power does nothing but makes her more powerful. But I think you should start with deflection. It allows you to stay focused easier and it takes less time."

"Deflection it is then."

That was all Eclipse said out loud, but secretly, she was determined to learn all three techniques to perfection. It wasn't that she thought she would need all of them. It was because she had been taught from birth that she needed to be superior to everyone else. If something was too difficult for anyone else, it was like a challenge for her to master it.

The last 3 hours of her training consisted of learning how to defend herself. She learned that dodging orbs could affect her ability to focus her telepathy, so it was only an act of desperation. So, of course, she decided to never do it. Throwing orbs became a second nature. She learned how to deflect orbs into the floor or walls, and even managed to absorb a couple. After doing these over and over, her head began to feel better, oddly. She came to the conclusion that it was because she was using the power inside her instead of storing it. She was really only halfway right.

It WAS because she was using her telepathy, but it wasn't about using it or holding it back, it was about controlling and embracing it. When a person was enhanced, their atoms, neurons, cells, and such were all stimulated to do, well, more. She was enhanced beyond just her mind. Her muscles, ligaments, and tendons were built to hold her abilities longer and strengthen them beyond any mortal being's. All her muscles increased in elasticity and since the brain is nothing more than a massive muscle, it was affected like the rest. Obviously, it did not stretch and pull in her head, but it worked several thousand times faster and every cell worked night and day with increased mobility. This not only gave her exceedingly powerful telepathy and unnaturally fast reflexes, it also gave her a powerful headache. The reason using her powers relieved the pain was because it forced her to control all the cells that were bouncing around in her head and focus their energy elsewhere. It was the control that spared her pain, not the rampant use of her abilities.

But Eclipse was not a brilliant scientist and no one but Acre could explain all this to her, so she wrongly assumed that any use of her powers helped her, which was incorrect because anyone knows that the more you use a muscle, the stronger it gets. So, as she continued throwing orbs and eventually objects, around the gym with her mind, thinking it was helping, in reality she was only finding a temporary fix for a culminating problem. But no one knew she was in pain and she would have trusted no one with the fact, even if anyone had bothered to ask. Everyone else had a week off before they had to learn any of this stuff.

As the buzzer heralded the end of her practice time and the beginning of her warm-up before facing Amy, Eclipse noticed the steady trickle, then stream, then the flood of people, walking into the gym and sitting in the bleachers. She looked questioningly at Susan, who sighed before answering.

"The promontory's idea. He thinks people watching your fight today will bring out your full potential. Apparently, we aren't exciting enough for him."

She raised her eyebrows, shrugged her shoulders bitterly and pat Eclipse' shoulder on her way to find her own seat in the bleachers. All of Victor's subjects shared a sense of annoyance with the dictator that none of them voiced, but they all communicated amongst themselves with ease. Eclipse watched her go, knowing full well that the crowd was not here for her. She was pretty sure Susan knew too and just wanted to make her think it was about her. She knew they were here because Amy performed better in front of people. But they also distracted her a little and Eclipse knew it. She took a deep breath and turned with confidence to face her nemesis.

Immediately, that confidence shattered.

Amy was still the tall, beautiful goddess with wavy blond hair and bright purple eyes that she was a year ago, but something else had changed about her. She had always seemed rather impulsive and angry, but not now. Eclipse's heart sank to her boots and flew to her throat all at once. Amy was in full control of herself, and therefore, the situation. She was so calm and confident and absolutely assured of her victory. It made Eclipse feel confident in nothing but her demise. Though she didn't realize it till later, she lost the match right then.

She closed her eyes. The busy talking faded out of her mind. Focus. The stress and frustration of the last 4 hours settled and everything around her seemed to slow to a stop, but she knew it hadn't. She knew her world was going to change very soon and that there was nothing she could do about it. But it all disappeared into a void as she sunk into her telepathy. She sensed Acre, but she was more interested in finding her brothers. For some reason, they were the only ones she cared about being there, but she couldn't find them. Then she remembered. They weren't there because they were in the Enhancer. Just thinking about that room sent a shudder down her spine. It seemed they were only at the top of the Logan's list because her father didn't want them here for this fight. After all, Sean was the one who helped her finish the last fight and keep her head at the same time and Victor probably knew that he wouldn't let Amy kill her if he could help it. One. Person. She sifted through every face in the room. She just needed to know that someone was on her side. Just then, her mind found a familiar smirk. Her eyes shot wide open and snapped to it instantly.

Axl.

She wasn't sure why his presence comforted her, but the second her eyes landed on him, he flashed her the biggest, toothy grin yet. A year later, he still looked absolutely ridiculous and she couldn't quite get over it. It made the corner of her mouth twitch up against her will. He winked in response. That only made her grin bigger and it might have been a chain reaction if the situation weren't so dire. Still, she remembered what he said the day they met. *The Elite aren't just his protectors. We are sworn to protect the entire royal family. Like it or not, princess, you are part of that family. We have stepped between Victor and his kids multiple times. It's actually a large part of our jobs. I'm not the first Elite to commit treason against the promontory for the good of one of his children and I highly doubt I will be the last. And you can trust me.* She did feel as though she could trust this strange boy, even though she wasn't exactly sure why. Maybe today wouldn't be too miserable. Something told her Axl wouldn't let Amy kill her at the very least.

And then Victor walked through the door. Her mind instantly shot to the tall man in a panic as he entered. The room fell silent to her even though everyone was still talking. Even Amy faded out of her thoughts as she turned to look him in the eyes. There was a moment between them, one she didn't understand. He wasn't glaring at her in the usual disgust, but he wasn't smiling either. It was like he was fighting so hard to mask one emotion that he hid all of them. They held each other's gaze for several seconds, then he looked away. It felt like she was just short of understanding something he was trying to convey.

He entered the overview sphere and Eclipse watched it rise to the 50 ft ceiling and when it stopped, everything else started. The starting buzzer rang, deafening her. She heard all of the mass talking, let exhaustion creep over her again, and the headache that ceased only minutes ago, flared back into existence. She staggered in her steps and fell to one knee, gasping for breath. It was too much, all of it. She looked up at Amy and met her opponent's gaze for the first time. Amy knew she had already won. Even as Eclipse' eyes burned into her skull, with anger and hatred stronger than she'd ever felt, Amy knew she was going to be sloppy. Eclipse felt like she could only wait for the other girl to defeat her.

She didn't move, though. Eclipse was used to Amy's impulsive self from a year ago, but Amy had learned a lot in that year. She was learning how fun it could be to draw something out as long and painfully as possible. Better to give her hope and then dash it to pieces. So, she waited for Eclipse to make the first move. Even through all her rage, Eclipse knew she had to stay defensive to win. She forced herself to her feet, staggering under the aches in her body and mind. And as badly as she wanted the pain in her head to stop, through death if necessary, she wanted to take Amy out more. The two stared each other down, each waiting for the other to move. A whole minute of this went on before Amy had enough. She didn't jump straight to telepathy though, she threw a knife at Eclipse. It was dodged with a slight lean from her enemy. At least her reflexes seemed to be working. She didn't bother to retaliate. They began to circle, Amy moving first and Eclipse countering each of her steps with her own.

Eventually, they were spiraling inward towards each other, but Eclipse stayed opposite Amy still. Then, they both stopped when they were precisely three feet apart, each with their eyes locked on the other and their minds focusing in. Eclipse could sense every part of Amy's body trembling with anticipation. She forced herself not to grin and waited patiently. Jackson always said that anticipation could ruin a soldier. Amy would make the first move if Eclipse waited long enough and then she could start on the defensive. She broadened her telepathy's scope and waited for the moment she could use it.

Without warning, Amy pivoted on her left foot and swung her right around at Eclipse's face. More sensing what was going to happen than seeing it, Eclipse dropped into a crouch and swiped her left foot out in a circle in front of her to kick Amy's legs out from under her. A year ago, it would've worked, giving Eclipse a chance to stand and make her next move from a vantage point. But Amy had gained talent and skill over the past year. She swung her upper body backwards, lifting both her legs into a back flip, rather than being tripped and falling on her own ass.

Eclipse cursed under her breath as she pushed up to her feet. Amy drew her sword and buckler. Eclipse knew everything about the buckler, but hated them and shields for that matter. They got in her way, lessening her efficiency and inhibiting mobility. She dual-wielded or used two handed weapons instead. She was also proficient at spears and, of course, archery. Her unique dual wield style wasn't taught in Chrosia, though. Amber had helped her formulate an actual style of fighting and hone her skills at it. It was looked down upon, which of course, is why she wanted to master it. It also just made more sense to her. Once, Acre asked her why.

"A sword can accomplish all the same attacks as a shield. It can block and deflect anything, if you use it right, and it gives you two offensive weapons that can both be used for defense also. It's like carrying two swords and two shields."

Acre had shrugged at the time, but he had also been the first to congratulate her a month later for being the top swords fighter in her series at eight years old. Now, he watched with awe as she drew her new, diamond daggers, swinging them with ease and confidence. The swords were too large and a liability, so she went with the largest daggers. She skillfully spun the one in her right hand around, so it faced behind her and kept the left one facing forward. Acre was also nervous and confused. Why wasn't Amy using her telepathy? She already knew Eclipse would win a sword fight. The brunette was already bouncing on the balls of her feet, ready to go. Acre threw a questioning look at Victor but the taller man was enthralled with the fight. Acre frowned behind his back.

The sword fight lasted three hours, with Eclipse in the lead most of the time, but Amy was about to take care of that. She re-sheathed her sword and triple back-flipped away from the fight before Eclipse had had time to act. Then she hooked her buckler back on her belt and watched Eclipse warily place her daggers back in the scabbards. And they were left staring at each other once again. A loud buzzing distracted Eclipse for a second and she glanced to the side. Massive force fields were rising directly in front of the bleachers and walls on the ends of the building. They rose around the room and closed at the ceiling, locking the two competitors in. Eclipse immediately knew what they were for. They protected spectators and the building from telepathic blasts. She took a deep breath and readied her mind.

First off, she needed to evaluate her physical weaknesses and those of her enemy. She had a black left eye, swollen shut, courtesy of taking a buckler to the face. *Stupid mistake.* Amy's sword had barely nicked her, leaving a 4-inch cut on her cheek. But something was wrong. Eclipse felt....... tired and out of breath. In fact, she was exhausted and even standing up straight was a labor. Three hours of fighting had never left her like this before, normally she could go all day with a specific combination of parrying and attacking, giving herself breathers. Damn Enhancer. She hadn't been able to stay fit for the past year. She mentally noted that she would have to build up to her former endurance. She was stronger but couldn't hold out for as long. The only other thing wrong with her was a puncture wound above her right armpit, annoying, but hardly fatal.

All in all, she decided she wasn't doing too bad for three hours opposite Amy. Then, she observed Amy's condition. Her hair was finally starting to look frizzy and didn't line up in perfect curls anymore, she had a gash across her forehead and a deep cut on her left thigh. During their fight, Eclipse had also managed to dart between her legs and stab her right foot with one of the 2-inch knives from Erican. But now, as Eclipse looked at Amy's composure, staring deep into her purple eyes with her own, she knew none of those injuries mattered. They were trivial, in fact. All that mattered now was which of the girls could control their minds best.

Amy fired 3 orbs at Eclipse, one on either side and one directly at her. Eclipse simply directed the third one into the ground beside her. Then Amy released five, one on each side and three straight on. Eclipse managed to deflect the top two, one with each hand, but the third knocked her feet out from under her. She slammed onto her chest and her neck whip-lashed her face into the floor. She lifted her head up, only to get pounded right in the face with a purple blur. At first, it felt like her neck was going to snap, but luckily she slid backwards across the floor, absorbing some of the force. That didn't stop her eyes from watering or her headache from disorienting her, though. She pushed herself off the floor laboriously, only to get slammed in the chest by another orb, thrown backwards ten feet by the force. Eclipse gasped air back into her lungs and paused, thinking before she moved this time. All in one motion, she kipped up to her feet and telekinetically fired every single knife, dagger, and sword she had at her opponent. There was no use for them anymore. They split and went around Amy without her so much as lifting a finger.

She missed one, though! One of Eclipse's daggers slammed directly into Amy's thigh and the girl fell to her other knee with a loud exclamation of pain and anger. Eclipse saw a chance she never thought she would have and went offensive against every bit of advice she had received that day. She charged Amy with her arm stretched out in front of her. She desperately needed her dagger to fly to her hand. To her surprise, it did. She gripped the handle and ran as fast as she could toward the other girl. Amy was already rising to her feet, though. *Faster!* She commanded her body to obey and her feet shifted into a full-on sprint. Amy tore out the dagger painfully and tossed it aside. Her eyes fixed on Eclipse, who was still almost ten feet away. *FASTER DAMMIT!!*

A loud sound, like a whip cracking, reverberated through the room as Eclipse suddenly disappeared into thin air. The entire room rose to their feet and screamed in ecstasy as she popped up behind Amy. She could have killed the girl instantly, but was too thrown off by what was happening. Had she just……. teleported? Eclipse stood frozen in shock until Amy swung around to drive her fist into her face. More out of reflex than anything else, Eclipse ducked under the arm and drove her dagger into Amy's side with all her strength. It sunk in to the hilt and Amy doubled over and screeched in pain. No one had ever been so mortally wounded in the gym before. She furiously yanked out the dagger and raised it laboriously above her head to drive into Eclipse's chest. Eclipse panicked and gasped, crossing her wrists in front of her to catch the blow on her bracers instead of her chest.

Instead, her telepathy created a massive explosion in front of her crossed arms. Amy shot backwards across the room and bounced off the force field, slamming into the ground with a loud thud. Her shell shattered upon impact with the ground, and she took the force to her wounded side. Eclipse stood gasping for air for barely a second. Amy was hurt, terribly, possibly fatally hurt. She summoned both her daggers to her hands and took off again. She knew better than to teleport behind the other girl again. Amy would be expecting that. Instead, as Amy pushed up slowly off the ground, Eclipse ported into the air above her head. She crashed down on Amy's back and drove both her daggers into her shoulders. Amy screamed as the force brought her to the floor again and the daggers drove clean through her body. They pierced the floor.

Amy ported away to her side of the room, trying to find a bit of reprieve, but she accidentally took Eclipse with her. Disoriented by porting when she wasn't planning it, Eclipse fell off the other girl, leaving her daggers in place. Her panicked mind sought to stop her from slamming onto her back and risking getting stabbed, so it ported her back to her side of the gym. At ceiling height. Eclipse tumbled toward the ground and once more held out her hands to break her fall, knowing damn well her arms were about to break. Instead, pulses of telepathy shot out from her hands and braced her four feet from the ground, so she remained levitated, staring at the floor that most likely would have cost her the fight.

Now, Eclipse was disoriented, and Amy had regained control. The blonde was tired of losing to Eclipse. No one..... NO ONE had used porting in the gym, yet. It was a general understanding that it was just cheating. Even Amy had respected that. Eclipse didn't know of course, but Amy was too enraged to give a damn. She retaliated with something Eclipse had never seen before. It came out of her hand in rippled semi-circles that rapidly grew bigger as they sped towards Eclipse, who had no idea what a sonic wave was. She was still levitated when it hit her with a tremendous power that shot her into the force field. Force fields were built to absorb energy, which is why they can block anything. Most people that fly into a force field die instantly because their life force is sucked right from their bodies and Amy had only survived because of her shell. Telepaths have millions of years of energy to spare and Eclipse was no exception. Her bluish telepathy spread out like spilled water on the greenish field and the entire room echoed with her agonized screams.

Even the hardest heart in the room was broken by her cries. Some just looked away, covering their ears. Others began to stand, as if moving to help, but none got far before they realized there was no way through the field protecting them. Amid the terror and pain, Eclipse managed to figure out what was going on. She forced herself to stop screaming, even though her body still writhed in pain. She sought anxiously for a solution for her problem. She searched through mind after mind in the room, hearing bits and pieces of others' thoughts.

"No, NO!! She's supposed to be this great warrior and all. Well, screw that!"

"Oh, poor child."

"Don't let her win, Eclipse. She can't be our general."

"Come on, Eclipse, get out of there."

Eclipse opened her eyes. That last one was Victor. She could see him just barely enough to know he wasn't smiling, or greedily rubbing his hands together like she had envisioned. In fact, he actually looked a little concerned. One would think that hearing her father on her side might give her the strength to fight back and not resign to her fate, but that wasn't the case. Maybe his attitude could save her? Good thoughts were all she needed right now, right? Did her entire life really revolve around whether or not Victor cheered her on in a battle he could stop at any time?

Suddenly, she was furious. Her stomach churned and burned more than any other moment in her life. He had the ability to shut off the force field directly in front of him, but didn't. He could have given her time to recover, but didn't. He could have even called off this fight last minute once he realized how exhausted she was, but he didn't! It didn't matter to her that he would send her good thoughts, if he couldn't even act upon them to save her life. She should've killed him when she had the chance. No one was going to help her, but it occurred to her that if she could absorb orbs, she could absorb her powers back into herself. She closed her eyes and forced herself to focus her mind on the task at hand. It worked, slowly at first, but then she began to draw it in faster.

Amy threw a hasty orb at her in a panic that she may succeed. Eclipse's eyes shot open and blue flames sat where her eyes once were. The tips of the flames danced towards her temples. The crowd cried out in horror. Amy's orb slowed down and slowly merged into Eclipse with the rest of her telepathy. The pain was gone, Eclipse was burning with fury and more power than she had ever experienced. It was time to stop the charade. She was tired of hiding her anger, tired of waiting for someone else to rescue her. Eclipse levitated herself off the force field slightly and cranked her absorption up to the max. Her energy returned swiftly, but she couldn't stop. She drew in more and more. It felt exhilarating at first, like a drug flowing through her veins. She fought to draw it in faster, to keep the feeling that some part of her was alive. The entire force field soaked into her like water into a sponge. But this sponge was way over its capacity. Her head began to scream in pain and every molecule of her body felt like it was about to burst. She felt it coming. She was losing control. All she could do was fire everything she could at Amy. Everything in her told her to do it, just obliterate her enemy with one shot.

Then she heard it. It was faint and barely audible above the pounding in her head. She heard the crowd screaming and cheering her name. They were on her side, on her side as much as they could be with Victor in the room with them. If she let her powers rage, with no force field active, they could all be hurt, or killed. Eclipse fought to calm down and managed to drop to the floor on her hands and knees. This was her body and her mind, and she controlled them as their master. She looked over at the crowd. They were in slow motion, now, as her mind tried to think through the situation. They were jumping up and down, clapping their hands. She sensed their unity. It was contagious. It was the same feeling Sean had described the last time she fought Amy. What was it called? Hope, it was hope. She couldn't risk ending their hope. It seemed so important to them. She didn't know what she was feeling, though. It felt entirely different than hope; like everyone in the room was depending on her and she knew she was about to fail. She felt......... ugh...... sad, she guessed. It was the best she could do. Acre knew better, though, and he could see it on her face from where he was.

Compassion. She had compassion for those around her. She had compassion for the construction slaves that would be forced to rebuild the gym, because of her. She had compassion on the innocent lives she would end if she brought down the building on Amy. In that moment, she even had compassion for Amy. She didn't really deserve to die, did she? Maybe Victor had her fooled, too. But, in the end, none of this mattered, because Amy had no compassion on her. Eclipse managed to stand, barely harnessing everything inside her and a massive purple orb shot across the room and smashed into her stomach. It carried her out of the building, destroying the door, across the street and slid her from where she landed on the concrete, into the pool it surrounded.

As the water closed over her head and burned her numerous fresh scrapes from the cement, her mind turned on her. It flashed back to the Enhancer, watching Acre leave her to drown, not knowing what was going on. Her heart beat rapidly, and her head flew into a panic. Desperately, she fought to push the water away and scream for help. She needed Acre to turn around and see her, but the more she screamed, the more water she drew into her lungs. The sensation was familiar, but still burned and agonized her chest. She just needed him to see. Only he could get her out. Swimming wasn't even a possibility with the straps holding her down. She thrashed to break them, but didn't rise any closer to the surface. Her own mind terrorized her with all the pain and torture she had endured. She just wanted out. She didn't want to go through this again. She screamed out once more for Acre as he left her in the Enhancer again, without even turning back............

Everyone in the gym rushed outside just in time to see a hundred-foot-tall explosion of water burst out of the pool and fall like rain around them all. It stopped them in their tracks, even Acre and Victor paused as they got soaked. It took them a moment just to collect themselves, but one person didn't pause for even one second. He vaulted over the edge of the pool and inside to the poor girl. Eclipse lay prostrate and drenched on the bottom of the now-empty pool, blood seeping steadily out of her ears and closed eye sockets, with long drops flowing from her nostrils as well. No one else moved to help. They just stood around the edge of the pool and watched his every move. His dark black clothes revealed just how pale Eclipse had grown in the Enhancer.

Victor sighed in relief as Axl checked for a heartbeat in his daughter's wrist. He knew that boy would be useful someday. Axl's gray eyes searched desperately for any sign of life in the drenched girl before him and grinned as he caught the slightest hint of a flutter in her wrist. A curt humph made him turn and look behind him. Amy stood smirking at the edge of the pool, cocky as a bird in mating season. Her hand tightly gripped the gaping wound on her side. She licked her lips, making sure to emphasize her tongue in Axl's direction, before flipping her golden curls and turning around to face her public. At first everyone just stared in horror at her, knowing what she had just done and seeing her reacting so joyously about it. Many frowned, others glared, but only one moved. Amber had had enough by this point.

"You sniffling little bitch!!!" she hissed before breaking into a full out yell and continuing, "You think this is an accomplishment?!!? You beat a half-dead child. BARELY, mind you. And you will rot in hell for it if it is the last thing I do!!"

She raised her hand to strike Amy but a thunderous voice interrupted her actions.

"Is that ANY way to treat your general?"

Amber knew that voice. Everyone did. And it was the only one that could have stopped her. It wasn't fair! Eclipse had been winning despite everything. She had fought well and skillfully. She had it in the bag till she paused to stop from bringing the building down accidentally. Amy deserved to be punched more than anyone else in the world, but she had someone on her side that no one could stand up to. Amber turned around, slowly lowering her hand and glaring at Amy till she could no longer. And there was Victor, staring her right in the face. He could tell that she was considering throwing it all away to tell him what she really thought of him. Her eyes burned with fury and her shoulders rose and fell drastically as she tried to control her breathing. The crowd waited to see what she would do. Amber finally swallowed her anger, her rage, her fury and answered him as Axl drew Eclipse up into his arms and carried her out of the pool.

"No, Your Excellency. I'm honored," she almost choked on the word. "to serve her as our leader."

Victor's smile screamed success as he nodded in agreement. He made some haughty announcement that no one heard and then clapped for the new general, who stood at his side perhaps even more prideful than he. The crowd gloomily picked up his clapping, like zombies with no other choice. Amber looked at Axl who was just looking up from Eclipse's body. The worry forming in his eyes told Amber they were both thinking the same thing.

Amy had won.

Again.

# CHAPTER SEVENTEEN

Eclipse sat bolt upright in her bed. Her head screamed in agony, but she didn't care. She looked around and almost missed him. He sat so still, staring directly at her from a chair across the room, his arms folded calmly across his chest. Her eyes locked on him for a moment, before looking for any other presence in the room. It was just the two of them. She had a feeling that she knew what that meant. She looked back at Axl.

"I lost?" she gulped.

Axl nodded, not moving any other part of his body.

"You lost. She was technically the last one standing." He replied meekly.

"Damn."

She tossed off her blanket and forced her body to stand. It was unstable and Axl *did* jerk slightly when she almost toppled over, like he was going to dive across the entire lab to catch her. The movement caught her eye and she steadied herself just to stare at him suspiciously. He was still the awkward, scrawny misfit she had met before. His neck, arms, and legs were all too long for the rest of him. His hair wasn't as greasy and matted, though. It looked like someone finally taught him how to wash it and brush it, but it still hung intrusively over the right side of his face. He might have grown an inch or so in the past year, but so had she, so she wasn't sure.

"How'd you even get permission to be in here?" she finally demanded impatiently.

"Don't need to ask for permission if no one knows I'm here."

She shrugged her eyebrows in concession and ran both her hands through her tangled hair. The chlorine had dried it out and matted it together in clumps. Even that slight tugging hurt her head, so she gave up after a few strands and started pacing instead.

"You should be resting, Princess."

"It's just Eclipse."

"Not to me, it isn't."

She shot him a nasty glance, which he responded to with a goofy smile. Eclipse rolled her eyes. She was too upset with herself to deal with Axl, right now. She remembered the whole fight and knew how many people she had let down. Amy couldn't win this one; it was all Eclipse had left and she refused to serve under that monster. She paced faster, glaring at the floor, until her rage couldn't be contained anymore. Eclipse suddenly drove her fist as hard as she could into the wall. The metal wall continued its existence unscathed, but her wrist and several fingers snapped. Eclipse wasn't sure why, but her eyes filled with water. She barely felt the pain of her bones breaking, so there was no reason for tears, but they came anyway. Then a whimper that caused her to feel embarrassed in front of the Elite. Still, she couldn't stop. Soon, she was bawling in front of Axl. She had never cried before and certainly not with someone watching. It was mortifying. She leaned her forehead against the wall and tried to stay silent.

She didn't hear him get up. She didn't hear him retrieve the healer from the desk and walk over to her. The first sign she had that he even moved was a gentle tap on her shoulder. Eclipse spun toward him in surprise and shoved him away angrily. Axl didn't even flinch, but slowly walked back up and gently took her right arm in his hands. Within seconds, he had healed her bones and set the healer aside, on her cot. He kept a firm grasp on her hand, though. Both his hands wrapped around hers as she sobbed and wiped her tears away with her free hand.

"I can't, Axl." She groaned miserably. "I can't serve under her. I can't pretend to give her any respect. I'd rather die. I'd rather destroy everything in this world than give her the satisfaction. She has taken everything from me my entire life. She doesn't get this. This is mine. It has always been mine. How could I *lose*?"

Eclipse yanked her hand away from the Elite and turned her back on him so she could drive her fists into her eye sockets.

"Princess....." Axl began gently, but she spun around and screamed angrily in his face.

"ECLIPSE!! My name is Eclipse, dammit!! Don't ever, *EVER* call me a damn princess again!!!"

He stepped away this time, a little shocked at how little control she suddenly had over her emotions. She was known for keeping them in check better than anyone. Still, Axl could somewhat relate to her hating her title. His own name was a curse. He nodded.

"I suppose if the princess I served *ordered* me to use a specific name when addressing her, then I would have no choice."

"Don't make me do that." She whimpered, shaking her head. "Don't make me spit out useless orders just for the hell of it. I hate that kind of authority. I hate everything it stands for. I'll never give any orders after this, anyway. Just call me Eclipse, dammit!"

Axl smiled curiously at her as she realized that was an order in of itself and groaned out loud, but he let it slide without comment. That was good enough for him anyway.

"Eclipse," he began meaningfully. "the only reason you lost was because it was literally the day after you got out of the Enhancer. Anyone would have lost in that position."

"But *I'm* not just anyone." She whined. "I'm supposed to be better than that! I have to be!"

Axl frowned and furrowed his brow.

"Why?" he demanded. "Because Victor says so?"

"Because I say so!" Eclipse cried in frustration. "Screw Victor! Screw Acre! Screw Chrosia! The only thing that matters is that *I* know I am better than Amy! And given a second chance, I would slit her throat before I let her beat me again."

She yanked away from Axl again as he tried to gently place his hands on her upper arms. Her feet carried her across the room to glower down from the open, broken window into the dark streets below. It had to be around midnight. She braced her elbow on the windowsill and leaned her weight against it as tears still boiled over and down her cheeks. If nothing else, the cool night air felt good on her puffy eyes.

Axl watched her in silence for a moment, his head cocked in concern. It wasn't that he minded her plan. He thoroughly believed Amy needed to die. Murder just didn't seem like the Eclipse he knew, even to stop Amy. Still, if she needed support, she would always have his. It was his job.

"You would just kill her?" he asked calmly. "You wouldn't even hesitate?"

"Hesitating is what just let her win." Eclipse pointed out, her voice evening out to a deadened response with no emotion.

"Truuuuuuuuue." Axl pondered, stepping toward her back. "And she would deserve it, no doubt."

Eclipse turned around and met his eyes with her own, making him stop dead in his tracks.

"But?" she asked calmly.

"No buts." Axl shrugged.

"Then what?" she demanded.

Axl looked her up and down. She was in her gym clothes. Her hair was clumped together with dried chlorine. She looked tired, sore, disheveled and filthy, but more determined than he had ever seen her. Axl made a momentous decision.

"Would you like to know how to get that second chance?" he asked with a massive, mischievous grin.

ΩΩΩΩΩΩ

Victor watched the ceremony's proceedings with little interest, though if not with a little pride. Generals were instated in a private ceremony in Chrosia and Amy's was no different. The only people here were himself and Amy, Acre and Eclipse' brothers, mainly so she could rub it in their faces, a couple slaves improving the atmosphere, and Jason, who had the honor of holding the pin until Amy received it. There was no such thing as demotions past a certain rank in Chrosia. If a General failed, they were killed and replaced. So, no one else would hold that pin till Amy died and besides the creator of it, Jason was the only one who got to touch it beforehand. He accepted this honor as a drunk, drug addict though, which displeased Victor, though he couldn't kill him yet. Sources said, he was helping Eclipse in the gym, and Victor needed to know what he told her. Her life might depend on it.

Suddenly, Jason passed out, in his drunken state, angering both Amy and Victor. The promontory was about to send him to the pit, when Shane and his brothers, significantly larger after their enhancement, did the same thing. The two of them watched as the entire room fell asleep and toppled over one by one, till only Amy and Victor remained and they knew what was coming. They turned and looked at the giant metal doors, just in time to see Eclipse burst through, laboring to fling them both open. Her hair hung loosely and messily around her shoulders and she looked a lot less threatening without all of her weapons, but something in her eye warned them both not to piss her off right now. She walked up to them and folded her arms, looking back and forth between the two of them. The triangle was silent for a while, but Victor knew his daughter. She wouldn't kill them. Guessing why she was here, his anger burned against her. He had just managed to rescue her from herself and now she was endangering that because of her pride?

"What in hell do you think you are doing, you ingrate?" he screeched at her. "Guards arrest her immediately!!"

Nothing happened. No one came running, No one grabbed his daughter and tore her away from them. Everything was silent. He looked at Eclipse. She raised her eyebrows as nothing stirred around them and then raised a hand to her ear, mock-listening for the sounds of stomping feet. She shrugged.

"I guess no one is coming."

"What did you do?!?!?" he raged.

"I spared you the embarrassment of people seeing this conversation." she answered unfolding her arms. "I merely put your entire fortress to sleep so the three of us could chat without any interruptions."

"Chat?" Amy growled. "I have nothing to say to a traitorous little snake like you."

"Well, it would take one to know one." Eclipse snapped back before continuing with Victor. "Here's the deal, Victor. I will NEVER serve under Amy. I would rather die----"

"I'll gladly arrange that." Victor interrupted, hurt and angry that she would dare use his first name.

Eclipse narrowed her eyes a bit.

"Oh, I bet you would," she mused bitterly. "but the thing is, you can't actually kill me. Look around you. I just immobilized an entire castle for the fun of it, including your precious Elite. Do you honestly think I would just submit into letting you kill me after that?"

Victor's face changed slightly with realization. She was challenging his authority! Her! An 11-year-old now had the power to stand up to him. Secretly, he cursed Acre. But she was so clever. No one was seeing her insubordination. If anyone saw it, she would have to die, she knew. She had cleverly orchestrated this entire meeting so he could walk out feared and respected by the public still. But he had to listen to her proposal first. The tiniest amount of pride welled in his chest and he had to force his face to remain angry. Yet, Eclipse saw him finally understand.

"And now you get it. You've controlled me my entire life and I've never once asked for a damned thing from you. But now I am. As I was saying, I will not be subjugated to Amy. It just won't happen, and if you make her General right now, I will disappear and come back to haunt you. But I know you, Victor. You have to win, so let me present you with a scenario in which you win no matter the outcome."

She paused to test the water.

"I'm listening." he growled, though he was actually excited to hear her plan.

She nodded slightly. He knew he was stuck at this point.

"I want to repeat the battle. If I win, I'm your new General. If Amy wins, I let you kill me. That is, if she doesn't do it for you."

"Which I will this time." Amy snarled.

Eclipse ignored her and stared straight at Victor. He was the only one that truly mattered here. This had to be his decision.

"How, exactly, is that a win-win for me?" he scoffed, trying desperately to sound like himself when he wasn't feeling like himself. "In one of those scenarios, you live."

Eclipse grinned. She knew this would be his response.

"You're right. I live if I obliterate Amy. But think about the last 11 years. It's like I said, I did literally everything you asked of me, with no reservations and no questions asked. I just took out an entire castle of guards, slaves, and Elite, remember? Has Amy ever done that for you?

Think about the applications. As your General, I can get anything you want, whenever you want it, like that." she snapped her fingers in his face. "No more stress between us. I don't want your throne, someone else can have it for all I care. Even Amy, if that's what you want. I can be the strongest asset you have ever had and I want nothing in return. Your bidding will be fulfilled on a planetary scale with no threat to your position. Do you trust *her* that much?"

"Why should I trust you?"

"Because I never go back on my word. I never have and I never will. For example, I promise you no matter what, that when I wake everyone up, none of them will know what changed your mind. They won't even realize that I put them to sleep. What have you got to lose, Victor? If Amy kills me, I'm gone. If I kill her, you have the greatest ally in the world. But if you refuse this offer," she stepped closer to him and glared into his eyes. "I will destroy you. I will take your kingdom by force and put everything I'm offering you now to work against you. I will rip out your eyes and cut off your ears and dice your tongue. Then cast you into your own pit with the thousands of corpses you put there."

Victor tried to hide his shock by raising an eyebrow in amusement. She was being serious. He retained his composure, despite the fear he felt in his very soul.

"I don't think you have the guts." he hissed.

The corner of her mouth twitched up and his gut twisted uncomfortably as he stared into a mirror image of his own determination.

"Would you like to find out?"

Then, she turned around and woke up the room. They all stood in unison and looked directly at Eclipse as she walked towards the doors. Their eyes followed her to the entrance and then their heads all hung. One by one, they began to look back at the ceremony as if waiting for something to happen. Finally, Jason remembered his lines and continued the process. As her trainer, he was in charge of administering the oath.

"Oh um," he fumbled around with the pin in his hands and stepped into position in front of Amy. "Amy Gershon, you will be in charge of 500 soldiers from now on. It will be your responsibility to keep them fit for their positions in the service of this country----"

Eclipse glared into her father's eyes from the end of the room where she stood unnoticed by all but him. Even Amy was moving on with the ceremony like nothing happened. She knew Victor would never give into the demands of a child, even his own. He kept his eyes locked on Eclipse's. The end of the oath was the end of his chance.... and he knew it.

"You will be blamed and punished for their failures------"

Victor bit the inside of his lower lip in anger. He didn't like being cornered. He didn't want Eclipse as the Emily general, it wasn't safe, but she was leaving him with no option. Why was she making it so hard for him to be a good parent, for once?

"You will make the decision to kill or spare those that fail and bring about your own punishment and you will--------"

This was what she wanted, though. Wasn't he a bad parent if he didn't support her?

"Your body and mind shall henceforth be bound to the will of the promontory..........."

"Stop the oath."

Victor pulled out all of his sleaze and all of his experience with lying and manipulation to say this next bit confidently as if it was his own idea. And he knew just how to pull it off. He walked up to Shane and looked him up and down like a collector at an antique shop.

"You don't look very celebratory, my son. Speak up! Why are you so gloomy?"

Shane's eyes darted back and forth for a second, wondering what Victor's game was and then back into his father's eyes. They seemed....... genuine, like he actually wanted to know what he thought. Shane knew better than to trust himself, though. Sean often told him that Victor tried to take advantage of his eldest's limited intelligence.

"Really?"

Victor rolled his eyes impatiently.

"Trust me, you imbecile, you want to answer this truthfully." He growled bitterly.

"Ok?"

Shane hesitated again and glanced curiously at his other enhanced brothers for a moment before making up his mind. If he was going to die facing off to Victor, he preferred it to be in defense of his sister. She deserved that much from him at least. Little did he know, she could hear every word he said and it filled her heart with...... something. She grew much closer to Shane after that day.

"I just.......... I just don't think Eclipse had a fair chance and that you are awfully eager to crown your..... um.... champion. She could do so much better, if you'd just give her a chance to heal."

Amy folded her arms angrily and grit her teeth. Not only was Victor taking Eclipse's side, but Shane was insinuating that she only won because Eclipse was exhausted, which was true, of course. No one was supposed to figure that out, though.

"Oh reaaally?" Victor elaborated, turning back around. "Well, since we are being honest today. Does anyone else think I rushed poor Eclipse?"

The entire room glanced around at each other. This was highly irregular of Victor, acting like he actually cared about their opinions. Slowly, they began to raise their hands, starting with Acre and ending with Jason himself. This did not go over well with Amy.

"Oh bull shite----"

"Silence, Amy." Victor snapped. "Fine. So, she needs a fair shot I guess?"

Heads nodded hesitantly.

"Very well, here's my offer to Eclipse. She has one week to prepare. One more fight, one more chance. *When* she loses, she dies, but *if* she *somehow* manages to win before the beginning of Voidanuar," he met her gaze across the room "it'll be her standing in Amy's place. Now, all of you get the hell out of my sight before I kill you."

The corner of his daughter's lip curved up and she gracefully bowed to him. Acre followed Victor's eyes with his own, but there was nothing but the door, which he rushed to after a few moments. Her brothers were in shock and Eclipse would need to be informed.

He finally found her in the gym, after checking everywhere else first, fully clothed and armed, adjusting the laces on her boots. He still wasn't sure what Victor's game was, but he had to give her the news.

"How do I teleport?" she interrupted his thoughts abruptly.

"Huh?"

"I need to know how to teleport for this battle. I did it accidentally before, but I need it to be far more precise this time."

"How do you know----"

"Acre, I'm a telepath, get over it. You are my trainer, so do your damn job and train me. How do I teleport?" she snapped impatiently

He stared at her for a while, before shaking himself out of his trance. He sighed sadly, but told her what she needed to know. And then she focused and did it right in front of him. She had already arranged with Jackson to have the drill room booked for the next week and she barely waved goodbye to Acre before locking herself in it. The scientist slowly turned around and walked back to the street. What was going on? Eclipse was his last hope and she was turning out just like her father; rebellious, prideful, and hungry for power. He stumbled to the fortress and into Victor's 'council' chamber, plopping down in one of the dusty chairs no one had used in years and wondering what he had done wrong for the last 11 years of his life.

What he didn't know was just how deep her reasoning for challenging Amy went. Axl had told her what she needed to know about Victor, but she had to figure out the rest. Eclipse was not an idiot. She knew from searching through minds at the gym the day of the fight that all the Emilies hated Amy as much as she did. She also knew that loyalty was essential for authority to work. Her father demanded loyalty through fear, but she had seen people rebel against him still. And she noticed how very few people disobeyed Sean and she knew she would do anything for him, but no one feared Sean. Eclipse saw the difference, without ever being taught, it was all about how people were treated. She was a princess to Sean and dirt to her father.

Now as a bright 11-year-old, Eclipse easily hypothesized that if you trust someone, they tend to respond better than when you control them through fear. She also realized that Victor was drawn to Amy because they were both tyrants and Amy, she knew, would abuse any power she got her hands on. The only thing Eclipse didn't understand was why she cared so much about the Emilies. They had all taken turns torturing her for years, yet she wasn't willing to let Amy do the same to them. So, her logic left her confused, though she was confused as to why she was confused. Any normal person would have said that loyalty to an authority sprouted from love and camaraderie between the leader and their followers. But Eclipse had never even heard the word love and would not understand it for years to come. So, without knowing it, she displayed love and compassion for her entire series and challenged Amy.

Acre, of course, knew none of this and merely thought Eclipse was doing everything for selfish, conceited reasons. He would have never guessed that she could understand love and care obliviously enough to refuse to allow her company to suffer at Amy's hand. The poor man was discouraged beyond belief and he spent the whole day mourning his loss, only to mosey back over to his lab like a zombie. He didn't sleep. All he could see when he closed his eyes was his protege lying dead and disfigured on the gym floor, a fate he believed inevitable. She wasn't up for the challenge. After hours of tossing and turning, he finally dozed off.

ΩΩΩΩΩΩ

The day of the rematch came all too soon for Eclipse's brothers. From within the fortress, Shane heard the bell ring and opened his eyes. He couldn't tell if he had slept or not. His mind was too busy skipping from anxiety to anxiety to focus on getting out of bed and getting dressed, so he was a little surprised when he figured out he hadn't forgot anything on his way down the steps. He wasn't rushing, or procrastinating. It was more...... aimless. He knew his schedule and he was doing it. His heart just wasn't in it. He met Sean, Erican and Aidan at the dining room door and the four silently glanced at each other for a few seconds, sharing their thoughts through their eyes. No one wanted to walk through that door, but it was inevitable. Shane finally forced the air out of his cheeks and pushed open the door, then they walked in together.

They didn't get very far before freezing and staring at the sight before them. Amy was sitting at their father's right elbow, who sat at the head of the very long and intricate table. It was made to his every request and, since he didn't mind taxing the life-blood out of his subjects, it was very expensive. Solid silver, polished to a shine and beautifully hand-carved with intricate designs across the entire thing, it amazed the boys that their father had no quell about sitting at it daily. He had killed half the crew that were first assigned to work on it in the first week. Silver was more valuable than gold and diamond, perhaps both of them put together.

"Are you going to stand there all day?"

Victor's question made his sons jump before rushing and fumbling to their seats. It turned out that they had to sit further apart since their enhancement made their shoulders massive, so it was impossible for them to whisper under their breath to one another, now. So instead, they passed a look around between them. They all sat on the opposite side of Amy, determined to ignore her through the meal. Their father made this impossible.

"My sons, I am sure you are all aware that this young woman is Amy Gershon?"

After their disgusted nods he continued.

"Then I would have expected you greet her a bit more...... fondly?"

His stress on the last word was a command, not a suggestion. It was almost hard to believe this was the same man who asked for everyone's opinion ten days ago. Shane pursed his lips and shot a sidelong glance at his brothers to his left before addressing Amy in his best mock-polite voice.

"It is such a pleasure to have you dine with us today, Milady."

"The pleasure is all mine." she returned in a voice just as shadowed.

She hated the promontory's sons.

"But the honor is *truly* all ours." Aidan replied dryly, not without a smidgen of sarcasm.

"I hope you find everything you are looking for."

Erican was by far the best actor of the lot, but he still licked his lips after his greeting, hoping she thought he was sticking his tongue out at her. She got the message. Sean hesitated. He wasn't sure what Victor and Amy were up to and it made him nervous, but after his father shot him a look, he knew he had to say something. They had a silent agreement, after all, and it had kept his sister alive once, so he would play along as long as he had to.

"Good morning." he muttered.

His brothers shared a look of concern. Sean had been different since exiting the Enhancer. He seemed far more serious and less tactful. Maybe the serum wasn't sitting right? Whatever it was, they were afraid it was permanent. Victor did not miss any of his sons' gestures through all of this, but was content to let it slide to simply save him time.

"After all, gentlemen, she is very near to promotion."

He patted her forearm and gave her one of his heartless smiles, to which she gave such a goody-two-shoes grin it made Erican shiver and bend even farther over his plate of food. Shane, however, looked up in the midst of a bite and swallowed quite before he was done chewing. This gave his voice a slightly suffocated tone.

"You don't have any faith in your own daughter, Father?"

He could almost hear his brothers gasp inside their heads. He could feel the lump form in his throat from the look his father gave him. His humorless chuckle made Shane wince slightly.

"I only put my faith in those who deserve it, my son."

As tense as the atmosphere was, Shane couldn't let it be. He sat up and laid down his fork silently. Erican, directly to his left, stared at him with concerned, wide eyes. *Oh please don't.* And Shane knew exactly what he was thinking, but his father had seemed so tolerant the other day. Maybe he was warming up to Eclipse. He certainly was acting strange in the past few days.

"Do you have faith in Miss Gershon, Milord?"

Victor looked up, read his son's expression and sighed. He also laid down his utensil, folded his hands and rested his elbows on the table. Shane could be tedious to deal with, since his lack of intelligence angered Victor more than anything else.

"I see you have very little desire for food this morning and have therefore decided to try my patience to its limit. So, I will humor you for a while, but the consequences may be dire later. I trust you understand that by now. Yes, I have faith in Amy's victory."

"May I ask why?" Shane retorted.

"Why? Because she has done it before. Eclipse has a few abilities, yes, but her mind is slow and disheveled."

Shane had to purposely pull the corners of his mouth into a frown to keep from laughing at the absurdity of his father's statement. Of course, Victor was lying to his sons and Amy. He had no doubt that Eclipse would win this next fight, but he also knew she wouldn't kill Amy. Therefore, his best facade was to offer her the position Eclipse suggested he give her. They talked about it over the last few days and Amy would one day become his heiress, which thrilled her to the core. Victor was on edge because as much as he was proud of his daughter for her bold actions recently, he was furious that she would stand up to him like that. He didn't want to talk about her right now, but Shane wouldn't let it go.

"But isn't it true that Eclipse should be stronger due to her extended time in the Enhancer?"

"Well, it would be," Victor was getting exasperated. "if it wasn't for the fact that her mind was no match for Amy's before-hand. The Enhancer could only bring her to the brink of Amy's power."

Shane looked down at his plate. He knew he could win this argument with logic if he just pressed hard enough, but he also heard the very slight change in his father's voice. Out of the corner of his eyes, he could see Victor glaring suspiciously at him. He waited until his father shrugged slightly and went back to eating. Shane's head spun around in circles. If he continued to stand up for his sister, he risked Victor's wrath, but something was telling him to do just that. He needed to know what changed his mind so suddenly at Amy's promotion. Deep breath.

"I think you're being a bit unfair, Father."

In his mind, his voice sounded much louder and his words far more abrupt than they actually were. Dead silence met his statement, as everyone froze with their forks mid-air or their bites mid-chew. Victor looked out the top of his eyes at his son for a while before sitting up and responding.

"How so Shane Jaspar?"

Shane's head flew into a panic. Middle names are never a good thing to hear a parent say, but coming from *his* father? It was terrifying. His father's carefree tone hadn't changed, but it was dry and had lost all its humor. And his eyes; those dark pits of terror bored into Shane's skull, overshadowing the fake smile he barely wore. Shane glanced sidelong at Erican, whose mouth appeared to be unhinged. He knew Victor was warning him to stop, it wasn't easy to miss honestly, but he also remembered that day at the track. When she had been penalized for the incident at the range. She seemed so hopeless and alone, as if the entire world abandoned her and in that second, he made a momentous decision. He wasn't going to shy away from his responsibilities as her big brother anymore.

"She did beat Amy." he answered firmly. "Often. She just took a little longer once Amy had her telepathy. But she beat her in the end, when Amy was a step ahead of her. You just never gave her a chance, not since the day she was born."

Shane's voice was picking up volume and he, himself, was beginning to rise out of his seat and lean across the table.

"The only way she has ever failed you is by not being as cruel and hateful as you are. That makes her stronger than you say she is and I know-----"

"ENOUGH!!"

Victor's voice echoed through the room as he leaped angrily to his feet, slamming his fist on the table. Shane realized he may have gone too far and slunk back into his seat immediately, eyes riveted on his plate. He felt the blood rush to his face, increasing the pounding of his heart to a deafening sound under the scrutiny of his father's piercing gaze. He took two minutes of this torture. Only then did Victor walk around slowly and stand next to Amy, across from his sons.

"It seems that my sons have forgotten their place in my world."

Aidan and Erican both made gestures to object, but Victor held up his hand to silence them.

"Perhaps we should go over this once more? Now, why was it I needed a fifth child?"

The three boys answered in unison.

"Because we failed you."

"Ah yes. You failed me. Sean? How did you fail?" his disgust was evident.

His brothers turned to look at him, but Sean wasn't even making a move to respond. There was definitely something wrong.

"SEAN RITCHER MONOHUE!!"

He didn't even budge, just stared at his plate like it was something unattainable. Victor was furious. He stomped around the table and grabbed a fistful of Sean's hair, yanking his head backward. That was the first time anyone saw it. His skin wasn't the right color. It looked like the entirety of his face was bruised black and blue. Victor gently released his hair in shock, but Sean's head didn't move from the position he left it in. Aidan reached over and felt for a pulse on his neck. At least he was still alive. Victor sent a guard for Acre and hid his worry behind his anger.

"You!" he barked at Erican, who jumped and glanced away. "can't fight any better than a handmaiden. You, Aidan, waste too much time thinking and studying rather than doing anything worth your time. And you Shane, my eldest, my first hope, how did you fail?"

Aidan could see the muscles in his brother's jaw bulging in and out and he knew how angry he was. Shane managed to hide it in his voice, though. It was even and he looked right into his father's eyes.

"I was born sick." he answered, monotonously repeating what had been barked at him all his life "With diabetes and epilepsy and I don't want your kingdom. I'm stupid and slow, with no chance of being a good leader. That is how I failed you."

Aidan and Erican looked at their older brother with respect and wonder. He didn't cower, but boldly answered, as if he was proud of what he was. It was a rare quality in Chrosia, being proud of being different. And it suddenly hit everyone in the room that he was no longer a boy, he was finally a man, another rare quality in Chrosia. A man with a purpose that no one could crush, with hopes and dreams.

"Your arrogance is disturbing Shane." Victor said meaningfully. "Now, we have a guest, and this is no conversation to have in front of a damn guest."

He walked back over to his plate and then plopped moodily back into his chair with a huff. His eyes glanced up at Sean every few seconds in concern. Despite what just happened, Victor really did care for his sons. Seeing one of them reduced to whatever was going on with Sean right now, was difficult, maybe even painful, for him. He stabbed at his food and anxiously waited for Acre.

That plainly ended the conversation, but Shane knew it would continue later when no one but him could hear, and feel, Victor's wrath. But there was no fear. He started to realize the gravity of what he had just done and he had a feeling that he would have more to say to Victor later as well. It felt like the tiniest flicker of hope, something he hadn't felt in a while. With that in mind and a slight smile on his face, he picked up his fork and continued to eat.

Silence prevailed in the room, broken only by forks scraping plates and an occasional gulp. Victor moved rigidly, enraged that his son would dare to speak to him like that. He should have punished him right there and then, but something stopped him. The way Eclipse had looked at him the other day imprinted itself on his brain. She had been demanding and disrespectful, yes, but she had spoken more to him in that moment than she had her entire life before it.

Maybe he was getting old, but it made him feel like a father to the girl and it affected how he viewed her brothers as well. Victor's anger burned like fire. He was..... interested..... in his daughter. It was the most infuriating thing he had ever felt in his tiny heart. Somehow, that little girl changed his entire family dynamic that he had kept since Shane was an infant. He didn't think he had it in himself to kill any of his children, anymore, no matter what they did. He even regretted those he had aborted, a little. Who knew how many of them would have turned out like Eclipse, fiery and determined to have their way? The guilt and frustration of dealing with these new emotions placed him in a constant dreadful mood.

Jason just picked a really bad time to come bursting through the door. Anyone who wished to see Victor, except Acre, had to wait to be announced, but Jason refused to do so. He strode firmly through the door and stopped just before Amy. He gave no one a chance to warn him with looks or gestures before diving head long into his reason for coming.

"Victor," he was obviously drunk and pointed his finger at the wall behind his target, "I've got a bone to pick with you and you're gonna listen whether you like it or not."

Victor sat straight up, with his jaw clenched tighter than Shane had ever seen, and glared at the man.

"How DARE you?"

"It's as simple as this," Jason stopped to burp. "I quit."

Shane's eyes shot back and forth between the two men. He knew how much danger Jason was putting himself in. He stood up with his hand extended and quietly said the trainer's name, trying to diffuse the situations and give Jason's life a chance. But that's all the further he got before his father jumped up and screamed at him.

"SIT!"

Jason watched Shane jump and then slam back into his seat. The full gravity of the situation hit him like a load of bricks. He knew how this would all end now, but like Shane, he was tired of being a coward. The damage was already done. He decided to go out with a bang. Victor calmly sat back down and listened, telling his sons that Jason's fate was already sealed.

"I am so tired of this torture you call life. It's not. It's a living death and I will not stand by and watch any longer. You are a vain, cruel, filthy bastard and that damned bitch at your shoulder is no better."

Two guards came in and grabbed his arms, but didn't pull him away due to a gesture from Victor.

"I can't deal with that monster anymore! She digs around in my head and forces me to do things like a rat in a lab. I quit, better yet, I defect!"

The reverberation of silence that lingered in the room after that statement froze every living soul present. No one dared take a breath while the promontory glared at Jason. They all knew something was coming, but he had been so unpredictable recently, that they didn't know what to expect. The silence was broken by his chair skidding back across the floor as he stood. Victor strode up to Jason and gripped his jaw with his left hand, his right hand still clenched so tightly around his fork, his knuckles turned white. He drew Jason's face close to his own. The trainer could smell bacon on his breath and began to tremble.

"I'm sure you think you are so brave and so honorable, don't you? That you're doing the world a great favor, being the hero that you are. But, you're forgetting, heroes are those who get to tell their tales and no one will ever know about your actions here today. You may yet out-live me, Jason, but, know this," Victor slammed Jason back into the guards behind him, without releasing his jaw. "you are never going to leave Chrosia."

Then the three boys watched in horror as their father jammed the tines of his fork into the trainer's right eye and ripped it out of its socket, drawing the most agonizing screams from him they had ever heard in their lives. They immediately looked away; Shane at his lap, Aidan focused on making sure Sean was alive, and Erican mistakenly looked at Amy. She just sat there smiling and watching it all, unaffected by the screams and howls of the man who basically raised her as he lost his second eye as well. And then, with a sickening rip, all noise ended beyond a constant drip of blood and a desperate moaning.

Shane forced himself to look up, expecting to see a dead man on the table, instead the sight haunted him to his very last days. Jason was on his knees with his head tipped backwards and his mouth wide open. The muffled screaming gargled out of his throat through his own blood. Shane watched as his father casually scraped Jason's tongue off his fork onto the table next to his discarded eyes, the sockets of which now wept with blood.

His mouth poured out the red substance in equal liberality and the prince found himself desperately holding back vomit. He did this. He pushed Victor too far and his father took out his frustration on poor Jason. He stopped Erican from turning to look, by pulling his brother's head down to his own shoulder. And he looked away in guilt.

Only to meet Amy's gaze. She was grinning wretchedly at him, almost chuckling at his weak stomach. The only thing that could cut through his pity for Jason, was his hatred for her. He just wanted to kill her, right now, right where she sat, but he thought of his brothers and of Jason and realized something about himself. He didn't feel like killing anyone for a long time.

# CHAPTER EIGHTEEN

Acre whistled to ease his nerves as he walked into the mighty metal fortress. Normally, he ate with the Monohues, except Eclipse who never ate with the family, but he was feeling very uneasy for the girl and tried to sleep in to make the time pass faster. It hadn't worked. He felt even more on edge than normal and decided breakfast may help. He never imagined how wrong he was. A guard greeted him at the door to the lab and told him about Sean. He had never had problems like that with enhanced individuals and quickened his pace to the fortress.

Immediately after walking through the doors, he knew something was wrong. The slaves were all doing their work, but silently and exceedingly thorough. Acre stood and watched one maid dust the same banister four times in a row. There was something else that bothered him, too. They were all chalk white and several of them trembled as they went about their tasks. No one made eye contact, and everybody closely resembled ghosts.

Now, the reason for this was quite simply the fact that everyone inside the fortress heard the echo of Jason's cries through the halls, and they all heard them stop, guessing what that meant. Acre, however, had heard nothing and therefore only shrugged and bounded up the stairs. At the top of them one could either go left or right to the next sets of stairs. Acre knew Agony Hill, Victor's pet name for his residency, better than anyone so he turned left and continued up the steps. It was the shortest way to the dining hall. Close to the top, he looked up into the darkness. There was an unusually large amount of clatter coming from the top of the steps, extruding from the dining room door. He stepped up to one of the electronic candles on the wall, but they were spaced far apart. Victor liked the dark. All Acre could see was light coming from the crack under the door and the walls and steps revealed by the flickering circle of light put out by his little wall candle.

The first Acre saw of the three men, which was what caused all the ruckus, was their muted silhouettes in the dark, just outside his circle. They walked into the light and Acre stumbled back against the wall. Two guards were dragging a man by his arms down the steps backwards. They were Victor's infamous Elite bodyguards, the most achieved warriors, and assassins, in the country. They were dressed in all black, hooded so only their grim mouths showed. Acre was used to them; what truly horrified him was the man whose legs they dragged behind them. He knew it was Jason, even though he had no idea how he knew it. His empty eye sockets and mouth spurted blood out over the rest of him. And the sound! The sound coming from his lips was haunting. It was as if a child was sobbing uncontrollably, but as a ghost. His entire body shook and jolted with each wailing noise, which only caused more blood to flow. A long smear of blood followed him down the stairs. Acre had seen this before. This man was missing a tongue. He stared after the trio a long while after they left. Then with a gulp he reached the door and pushed it open, stumbling through and slamming it behind him.

Victor didn't even glance up at the noise, which seemed uncommonly loud to Acre. He continued to jam his unwashed fork into his food and shove it in his mouth, chewing furiously. The three boys on his left resembled the pale figures downstairs, but Amy seemed completely at ease, if not a little pleased. Acre felt a shiver of horror run up his spine and turned to make sure the door was actually closed.

"What do you come as today?"

He jumped at the sound of Victor's voice and spun around to face him.

"A friend, a scientist or......" here Victor made eye contact with Acre, pointing his fork at the mess on the table and continuing disdainfully. "a trainer?"

The scientist glanced down at the table and his eyes slowly moved to the spot. With his eyes locked on the bloody pile he replied.

"A friend Victor. I'm always a friend."

"Then pull the service bell and take a look at Sean."

Acre tore his eyes away from the table to pull a tasseled cord by the door. He walked slowly to Sean, moving as if in a trance. He found his pulse and inspected his skin, which was now a deep purple over his entire body. Acre frowned, finding it increasingly easier to focus on Sean rather than the eyes and tongue across the table from him.

"What's going on?" Victor demanded.

"I'm not sure." Acre mused, unbuttoning the boy's shirt.

"Guess."

Acre glanced up at Victor. The promontory was entirely serious. The scientist sighed and stood up from his crouched position over Sean.

"If I had to guess, I'd say that somehow, he has residual components from the serum in Eclipse's tank and it's mixing with the Logan serum."

Victor slammed his fork down on the table and leaned his head back with a humorless chuckle. Acre continued examining Sean, waiting for the promontory to yell at him.

"Please, tell me, that of all my children, you did *NOT* turn THAT one into a telepath?!" he snapped, looking back to the scientist, who quickly shook his head.

"No, no! He wasn't in the serum nearly long enough for it to affect him that way. I think it's just a bad reaction to several chemicals that are never supposed to be combined. He should be fine once it flushes out of his system."

Victor grimaced, but continued eating. An attractive maid, around 25 years of age, entered the room, nervously wiping her hands on her apron. She now waited for instructions with her eyes riveted on the eyes and tongue on the table. Acre knew her as Hilda, a very sweet and gentle kitchen slave from the southwestern portion of Chrosia. She was obviously terrified, but when Victor didn't address her for several minutes, she reminded him she was there.

"Ye rang, Yer Excellency?" she stuttered.

"Bring up another plate for the scientist." Victor answered moodily.

She nodded and tried to run away as fast as she could, relieved that was all he desired.

"Wait." he caught her as she turned to leave. "Get that shite off my table first."

"O-of course milord. I'll go fetch a towel straight 'way." she answered with a slight gag, staring in horror at the mess.

"Now."

"Aye, Yer Excellency." she said slowly as if each word was disconnected and hard to even get out.

She looked anxiously around her, trying find a towel or unused napkin, anything. She ended up looking at Victor as he took a few more bites before adding a quiet and tentative question.

"How, Milord?"

She barely got the second word out before she realized her mistake. Victor slammed his fork on the table again, making her jump back and let out a slight scream. He glared angrily at her, rising to his feet and yelling so hard spit protruded from his lips.

"Well, you could use your apron, or your dress, or your damned hands for all I care. Just get it off my table!! NOW!!!"

He was yelling so fiercely by the time he was done that even Amy looked worried. Shane watched as Hilda panicked and grasped up all the organs in her bare hands, running towards the door crying in terror.

"Slave!"

Hilda turned around at the sound of his voice, trembling and holding the goop as far away from her as she possibly could. The blood it dripped on the floor was the only sound anyone could hear for a few seconds.

"A-a-a-yy-e?" her voice quivered with her body.

Shane could see the terror on her face.

"Send for General Jackson. I want him here immediately."

"Milord, ye sent out the last courier this mornin'. It may-----"

"THEN LIFT YOUR WRETCHED SKIRTS AND RUN THERE YOURSELF!!!"

He threw his plate so hard at her that it shattered, slicing her face open in several places, but she managed to hold onto her handful through her screech and run out the door.

"I fail to see why everything I'm saying today is being considered debatable!" Victor cried hoarsely, slamming back into his chair.

He drummed his fingers impatiently on the table, resting his head moodily on his other hand, its elbow propped up on the table. Shane made a mental note to apologize to Hilda later on his father's behalf and Acre thought it best to sit silently and wait for his food, though he doubted he would be able to digest any of it. Amy went back to eating as if none of what had happened even phased her, but to the keen observer, she was ever so slightly nervous. She infuriated the three boys watching her and they all knew why. Her mastery of the passive attitude, something she had only gained in the past year, was oddly familiar to their sister's. The fact that the two girls had anything in common disturbed them. Nothing upset her. Nothing angered her. Nothing made her sick or disgusted or guilty. She did as she pleased to whom she pleased. And worse yet, anyone who didn't know her thought she was a saint. How could anything that beautiful be so deadly?

Amy was flawless, perfectly toned skin with no blemishes or scars. She was tall and thin, but not unattractively so. Her lips were always moist and soft, hiding her pearly white teeth. Her features were picture perfect, an elegant nose, with bright purple eyes that always seemed to glisten. And her hair was a wonder. It was thick with large blond curls that rippled down to her mid back. It framed her face perfectly with each strand. It took her less than five minutes to look like this daily. No 13-year-old ever looked so angelic.

As Shane watched her, he realized that the only thing that could lower his disgust was thinking about how Eclipse was different. Two years younger than Amy, Eclipse was almost five inches shorter. She wasn't as small-framed as Amy either, but definitely not overweight. Her neck was long with an oval head stuck awkwardly on top of it and her skin was normally tanner than Amy's, but the Enhancer had left her a pale shade. She had a small gathering of light freckles on her nose and cheeks, nowhere near the amount as Erican, who was literally polka dotted with them. No one had ever truly seen her smile, but she had a pleasant face even without it. Her nose was well-centered if not ever so slightly hookish. Her once hazel eyes had been turned by her telepathy and now they shone brilliantly blue, almost a mystical color. They were far too large for her face, like giant doll eyes that delved deep into whatever they caught in their gaze. And her eyebrows were somewhat bushy. She had always seen her hair as her one redeeming factor because of its glorious curls, but the Enhancer had all but straightened it. It left her hair slightly wavy and that's it. Her hair was down to her waist now.

Jackson interrupted his thoughts, marching boldly, but respectfully into the dining room. Hilda had showed up bawling and out of breath at the gym. She miserably warned him about Victor before sending him off to the fortress. Jackson could work the system like no one Shane had ever seen. He knew how to kiss up to Victor and get what he wanted at the same time. Victor trusted him as much as his mind would allow him to trust anyone. When there was a problem he couldn't trust Acre with, it was always Jackson he turned to. He came right up to the end of the silver table and gracefully bowed.

"You sent for me, Your Excellency?"

"Where is Eclipse right now?"

Victor was out of formalities. His abruptness startled Jackson just a bit, but he recovered quickly and answered professionally.

"I just left her in the drill room, Excellency. She's been in there since yesterday morning. *Early* yesterday morning."

Victor looked up at Acre briefly and then at Jackson for the first time.

"How is that possible if you have to run the control room?"

The control room was a raised room built into the gym that held all the equipment and setting controls for the building. It could set different levels in the drill room for each ability, telepathy, strength, invulnerability. And it controlled the speed and difficulty. Like the range targets, the weapons and enemies in the drill room were metal shards formed into bodies with magnetism, so they could actually hurt the trainee if they weren't careful. Of course, anyone could simply train too hard and injure themselves, which is why an officer, normally a trainer, had to run the controls and judge how the trainee was doing and increase the difficulty by degrees. Jackson ran it for Eclipse most of the time since Acre was often too busy. He shifted his weight uncomfortably from one foot to the other in front of Victor right now.

"Well, erm, she's been controlling the box herself for a couple days now."

It was Amy's turn to look up in concern.

"What?" she asked breathlessly.

After a slight nod from Victor, Jackson turned to her.

"She kept telling me that I wasn't increasing the difficulty fast enough and, naturally, I didn't listen to her since it's against regulation. So, she took over the controls with her telepathy, pushed me out of the booth, and raised it straight up to ten. Been there all day yesterday and all last night. I think Axl has been in there keeping an eye on the controls so she doesn't break anything. She couldn't keep him out the way she tossed me."

Amy's mouth dropped to her chest. No one, not even her, had made it to level ten yet. Amy could hold at level 8 for a few hours but that's it. Her look made Jackson terrified to see Victor's, but to his surprise, the promontory was smiling. He leaned back in his chair with his dead, empty smile, chuckling.

"She's an idiot." he muttered, too impressed with Eclipse to make up any other excuse for his grin.

Midnight was soon approaching. Victor had put a time limit on this fight. Eclipse had 24 hours till the beginning of Voidanuar. There were nine months in a year on Asylum; Darkmoon, Aetherraise, Fayerien, Trahinter, Solstice, Taras, Previnter, Kaysor, and Enfernas. Each month had exactly 40 days, or four weeks. In the exact center of the summer month, Solstice, there were always five days revered as some sort of a holiday by everyone. The sky blackened and no light shone from sun, moon, or stars for five whole days. Those five days were Voidanuar. There were thousands of theories and religious stories based around this time, but the only thing that mattered right now was if Eclipse could beat Voidanuar's unstoppable timeline.

Shane stood at the end of the main street, by the fortress. The starlight glistened off the metal walls of the buildings down the rest of the street and the dull red streetlights did little to comfort him. The gym, though filled with a thousand Logans and Emilies, sat silently to his left as he walked along. The bright light from within cast its ambiance on the dark street. The air felt close and cold, deathly quiet with anticipation. There were no crickets or owls, and no wind released the tension. The only thing that broke the silence was gentle plinking as the first raindrops of a storm fell to the metal below.

The same still silence greeted him as he walked through the gym's doors. It was as if all of nature and man alike felt the approach of the dim outcome of the coming battle. Shane walked towards the overlook orb where his family and Acre stood waiting. Sean was missing yet another fight, since Acre had him moved to the sick ward in the lab. His skin was almost entirely black, now, and the scientist was getting worried. He wouldn't wake up.

"Acre, you have five minutes to get her out here." Victor said forcefully.

Acre nodded and walked toward the drill room, in a trance, feeling every eye in the room following him. He reached the door, glanced to both sides uncomfortably and stretched out his hand to knock. Before it touched, the door slowly cracked open with a gentle click. Acre looked around again, before pushing it open the rest of the way with his fingertips. He spun around as soon as possible to shut it behind him. Then, he sighed and leaned his forehead against the door.

"Eclipse, it's time."

There was no answer and Acre slowly turned around to see her. He never forgot what he saw. She was on her knees and elbows on the floor with her forearms wrapped around the back of her head. Acre could easily see her left ear, since her low braid was pulled over her right shoulder. He stared at that ear in disbelief and crept closer to her, inches at a time, but there was no doubt in his mind. Blood was pouring in torrents from that ear, pooling beneath her head and drying in a line on her neck. There was too much on the ground to have all flowed from the ear, though. He knelt down, reaching out a trembling hand to place it on her shoulder. He couldn't bring himself to do it. It froze above her, shaking and paralyzed at the same time.

"Eclipse?" he whispered, praying she would respond.

After a couple seconds, she did, drawing out a sigh of relief from Acre. She sat up slowly until she was on her knees and turned to look at him. He tilted his head sympathetically. Blood was dripping out both ears, not just the left, and her nostrils and the corners of her eyes. She wiped the blood from her lips with the back of her hand as she glanced at him, waiting to be yelled at. He just shook his head and lifted her up to her feet. She took a deep breath and met his gaze dead on. And his whole opinion of her changed. Her eyes glazed over, but something told him she was far from dazed. In fact, she looked focused and confident, carrying herself proud and tall. She straightened her shoulders and tilted her chin ever so slightly up. What really convinced him was her voice, though. It was sure and clear, full of quiet strength. Acre could do nothing but step out of her way to the door.

"I'm ready, Acre."

It was an absolute statement that needed no answer as she walked past his gesture towards the door. Upon her entering the gym, her brothers noticed the difference. It was the first time they had seen her this alive, carrying all her weapons and wearing her full outfit, but none of it looked half as threatening as her eyes. She burst out of the door wiping blood away from her, well, head, with her sleeves. She ignored the entire world, the crowd, the cheering, her brothers trying to wave, and glared direly at Amy, standing tall across the gym, waiting for her.

Amy's smirk faded as their eyes met. She knew that look. One of them was going to die today and for once, Amy began to think it wouldn't be Eclipse. She shut her eyes and tried to dig into her opponent's mind, but got nothing. She opened up her eyes, perplexed, then shut them and tried again. Nothing. Now, she was visibly uneasy. She knew from experience that even she could only block certain circumstances, but not everything in her head. She couldn't even sense the barrier that kept her out. There was just nothing; she couldn't even register Eclipse's breathing. Amy Gershon, Victor's pride and joy, stood shuffling her feet and clearing her throat under the gaze of his daughter. And his daughter wasn't relying on luck anymore, she was a master.

Just then the clock struck midnight, and the observation orb rose off the ground with Acre and Victor. As the buzzer rang, Eclipse raised the force field around them with a wave of her hand. After all, she had kicked the technician out. Amy shifted slightly farther away from her. She couldn't sense anything going on in the brat's head. Stealth was a telepath's best weapon, and Eclipse was about to use it. This time, she didn't wait for the other girl to make the first move. She slowly formed a softball sized orb in her hands, letting everyone in the room, including Amy, believe that she still struggled with the simplest task. Amy carelessly brushed her curls off her shoulder and took a couple steps back toward Eclipse, who grinned and charged in return. She sprinted four steps and did an aerial, firing her now beach ball sized orb directly at Amy. On its way to her, it seemed to splinter apart into many shards, something no Emily had even thought of yet. Amy could only barely deflect them all around her, just in time to feel a blast of wind shoot her onto her back ten feet away. She kipped up, only to have Eclipse calmly flick her finger from 30 feet away and knock her feet out from under her. She was disguising all of her telepathy now. No flashy colors or even visible energy, but the same amount of force. Amy knew that no telepath could sustain this for long. It drained their power immensely. However, lucky for her opponent, she didn't know that Eclipse had learned a lot in the past week.

Amy used a telepathic blast to push herself off the floor, flipping through the air and throwing a massive orb upon landing. Eclipse took a deep breath and shut her eyes. Time slowed around her as she breathed out and opened them, stretching her right arm out straight. The orb slowed to a dead stop before her fingertips and the entire room watched as it remained in stasis. Then, with a noise like sheep shears snapping closed, it disappeared. Amy took a couple disbelieving steps forward and her jaw dropped. The crowd gasped and stared at the air in front of Eclipse as she lowered her arm slowly. She had just disintegrated Amy's orb while everyone watched. The corner of her mouth twitched up nastily at the blonde.

Eclipse fired several large orbs at Amy, not even having to wait for them to form like before. Amy regained her wits just enough to deflect the first two, but the last three pounded her in the chest in rapid succession, throwing her back into the force field. Amy found herself in the same position she had forced Eclipse into the day before. Her shell withstood the draw for mere seconds before shattering. She desperately tried to fight her way out of the trap, but it seemed fruitless. How had Eclipse managed it?

That was it. She couldn't hold back her screams anymore as the field drew her purple energy out. It felt like someone was stretching her like wool being carded into fibers. She couldn't take it. The pain was excruciating, but the humility was far worse. Her pride and her ego forced her to believe that she could handle anything Eclipse could. So, Amy decided to take a page from her opponent's book. She began to absorb all the energy around her, glaring angrily at Eclipse and screaming at her as loud as she could. She drew in the force field, overwhelming every system in her body, but she had a point to prove. She couldn't stop now.

Within seconds she had sucked in the entire force field and fell to the ground on her knees. Eclipse sprinted towards her. Amy couldn't handle that amount of energy and she knew it. She had to stop her before she killed everyone in the gym. Amy was gripping her head, rolling on the floor. Just before Eclipse reached her side, she lost it. It was like a disintegration bomb went off in the gym. A gigantic purple sphere spread out around Amy. It covered the area at an alarming rate and the spectators panicked. They stood up in the bleachers, trying to push and shove higher or towards the door, basically getting in each other's ways as their lives flashed before their eyes. Eventually, all there was left to do was stare at their oncoming doom. They watched it take over the bottom steps, splintering the bleachers into a million shards with a thunderous noise. It rose up, and the bleachers' foundation began to shake and fall. The crowd clutched each other or anything else they could find. The floor of the gym was shattering much like the bleachers. Acre cried out as he watched the destruction from the overlook sphere. Victor watched, vaguely interested.

Suddenly, a blue blanket of telepathy spread over the purple one and ran along what was left of the structure. It rebuilt the bleachers and held the shards together, stabilizing the building. The purple stopped expanding and stayed inches from the crowd. Everyone peered around as best they could to see what was happening. Those that could see were amazed. Eclipse was trembling with her arms spread out to her sides. It was obvious that she was controlling the blue; not only did it stream out of her fingers, but her eyes had the exact same color of flame flying out of them. It was eerily beautiful, as if she had changed into a mythical creature. The flames were wild and dancing, flaring higher every time she had to exert more energy. The entire building quaked as the ball of energy started to slowly shrink. Her eyes flamed more and more as the purple closed in back around Amy. The bleachers remained intact, surrounded by a blue casing and the floor rebuilt as the orb went along, always back down, closing in on Amy. Eclipse was bawling with the pain it caused her to hold everything together, blood spurted once more from her eyes, ears, and nose.

It hurt so much. She wanted to let go of the bleachers and the floor, but through the weird blue haze in her eyes, she looked at the faces in the crowd. They were terrified, looking at her with a new awe she had never seen before. She clenched her teeth and eyes and groaned in agony with the last bit of energy she had focused on collapsing the sphere and controlling its implosion. It cascaded back in on Amy, forcing a huge crater to form in the middle of the floor and leaving her in the bottom of it. The bleachers began to shatter and fall as she lost control of them, but the screaming crowd made her reach back over and hold them again, sobbing blood in pain. After only a few seconds, she had the entire building stable, besides the crater. The people slowly began to walk down the bleachers, staring at Eclipse in disbelief. She, on the other hand, looked from one to the next in frustration. Her eyes locked on Shane.

"GET OUT!!" she yelled at him, "GET OUT, YOU IDIOT!!!"

It snapped Shane out of his awe and he regained his leadership skills. He turned towards the crowd, encouraging them all to leave calmly but quickly. Harrison began to herd them out as well, helping Shane get the ball rolling a lot faster. Eclipse watched the masses filter out the door to safety. Her father and Acre also landed the sphere and walked out. Once the gym was empty, she released the building and fell to her knees, gasping for breath. She was exhausted to the point where falling asleep right now sounded better than winning. It took part of the ceiling landing right next to her hand to get her back up. Eclipse managed to stumble over to the crater and peer inside. Amy was barely moving, having just now woken up after the bump on her head. Eclipse looked around the gym, as it crumbled around her. Now was her chance to kill Amy and be done with all of this. Drawing her mother's dagger, she slid down into the crater and grabbed Amy by the throat. She was still half unconscious and did nothing to fight back. Her eyes were rolling around in her head like marbles. Bruised and bloody, all the orifices on her face hemorrhaged. Her clothes were tattered and torn. All in all, she was more pathetic than anything Eclipse had ever seen.

Eclipse drew back her hand with the dagger and tried to force herself to dig it into Amy's temple. Everyone knew she had the right. No one would question that. Most people even wanted her to do it. She wanted to do it, but something still stopped her. She stood there with her hand drawn back for several minutes as the building came crashing down around them. She tried to focus on all the pain from the other day. She focused on Amy's words in the past and her apparent new bond with her own father. All of it made her angry, but not enough to kill her. Eclipse threw her back onto the ground with an angry cry of frustration. She just wanted this to stop, tired of all the insanity. A beam crashed into the dirt beside her, reminding her that they were both about to be crushed to death. She looked around, just trying to come up with a plan. Her eyes ended on the blade in her hand. Would her mother have been disappointed in her, right now? Was she weak?

Shane gathered everyone back away from the gym as it crumbled into pieces before their eyes. He anxiously scanned the dust and debris for his sister, for any sign of life really. The heavy rainfall didn't help his search. There was nothing as the mess settled down and the air cleared. Shane's heart sank as he and his brothers ran towards the rubble. They didn't even make it before a big blast of blue energy shot Amy up out of the garbage and she thudded into the ground behind the crowd. They all turned around with gasps and exclamations as Amy hoisted herself off the ground and onto her hands and knees. Shane kept his gaze on the gym's remains. Within seconds Eclipse rose out of the rubble and levitated herself gracefully over the crowd, landing on her feet by Amy, who was still gasping for breath.

With a wave of Eclipse's hand, Amy flew back into the air, upside down, till they were face to face. Amy groaned in pain, followed by a haughty laugh.

"Give up, Amy. Give up and you can be second in command. Keep this up and...... well........ I think you know."

Amy smirked and spat blood onto Eclipse's face. The rain quickly washed it off.

"Can't kill me, can you?" she laughed diabolically. "I knew it. You're weak. So just put me down and let's keep fighting. I will not submit to you. You don't have the guts to do what's needed."

Eclipse raised her eyebrows and the corner of her mouth twitched up smugly. She rolled her eyes back in her head and stretched out her arm. In her mind, her wolf friend danced into Amy's body and ran along her skeletal system. Eclipse gripped every bone he touched with her telepathy. She opened her eyes and glared into Amy's terrified ones. She knew Amy could feel her power grasping at her very life force. Her body began to tremble with the pain.

"You wouldn't." she struggled to whisper.

And that was all it took. Eclipse clenched her hand and teeth at the same time. With a sickening crack, Eclipse shattered every single bone in Amy's body, except her spine and skull. The splinters began to penetrate organs and muscles, causing Amy to splutter more and more blood. With a cry of agony, she writhed and Eclipse dropped her onto her back. She walked up to her and crouched down beside her. She paused.

"Are you afraid to kill me?" Amy muttered, through the blood pooling in her mouth.

"Are you afraid to die?"

Amy managed to turn her head enough to look in Eclipse's eyes. She was dead serious. Amy had a choice to make right now.

"I give up." she whispered.

"So they can hear you, bitch."

Amy took a horridly ragged deep breath and belted out as loud as she could over the storm.

"I GIVE UP!!! YOU WIN!!"

Eclipse grinned her little grin and snapped her fingers. Amy fell unconscious and Eclipse turned to face the soggy audience. Right out front were Acre, wearing the biggest smile ever, and Victor, with the biggest scowl ever. At first no one moved. Many were looking at Victor, not wanting to upset him by clapping or cheering. It was almost more terrifying for Eclipse than the fight itself, that deathly silence. But it only lasted a minute or so, because then every single Emily and Logan cheered out at once, as loud as they could. The rest of the crowd soon joined in. Only Victor remained silent while her brothers jumped up and down with their fists in the air.

And Eclipse just stood there, ignoring everyone around her but one. She stared down Victor. She knew he had to declare the winner still and she knew it was burning him up. His eyes were livid and without reading his mind, she knew what he was thinking. It was the angriest she had ever seen him. Acre caught glance of their staring contest and stopped clapping. Something was up between them, but he couldn't figure out what. She just seemed to be waiting for his next move.

Victor raised his hand to silence the crowd. It happened almost immediately and then all eyes were suddenly on him rather than Eclipse. Drenched, yet standing tall, he let the sound of the rain dominate the streets for a few, gut-wrenching moments. In truth he was a little impressed with how ruthless Eclipse had behaved. Considering her promise of total loyalty, he decided it may not be such a bad thing that she won today. He strode slowly up to his daughter and stopped in front, still glaring at her. The crowd didn't breathe for the next few seconds. Even Eclipse felt a nervous lump in her throat, and she was the one who knew the most about what was going on. He was just staring at her, like a wolf stares at meat. He reached out and gripped her right wrist. She couldn't help but gasp just a bit as he pulled her closer to him. Eclipse lost her confidence looking into his eyes once more and feeling his hot breath on her face. In one quick terrifying move, he spun her around till she faced the crowd and raised her arm in the air.

"I give you, your new General."

The noise was explosive. Victor dropped her arm instantly and strode away toward his fortress. His two Elite guards had to follow, but the shorter hooded figure managed to slip something into Eclipse's hand. It was dense and cold, definitely metal. She knew better than to look at it in front of so many people. There was only one Elite who would pass her trinkets so blatantly. She received her ridiculous amount of praise before extricating herself to the lab. She wanted to be the first one to tell Sean, even if he couldn't really hear her.

Once she safely made it into the room where the healing booths were stored, she quickly closed the door behind her with a sigh. Her back collapsed against it as she took several deep breaths, soaking wet, exhausted and sore. Most likely, Acre would be bringing Amy up here soon. She only had a few moments. Eclipse moved to rub her hands up and down her face and remembered that her right fist was desperately clutching something. She pushed off the door and stared down at her hand as she slowly opened her fingers. Her lips split into a grin, both sides of her mouth twitched up and pulled away from her teeth into her first true smile.

Axl had slipped her the pin Amy was supposed to receive for making general. It was a useless trinket, now. Eclipse would get one specifically made for her. Amy's was a metal circle with a bejeweled black widow spider, her familiar. Acre would most likely have Erican design hers. He had a head for design. She wasn't sure how Axl knew she would appreciate having Amy's in her hand, but she truly, honestly did. Eclipse clenched her fist even tighter than before around the pin. She closed her eyes and focused her telepathy on destroying it. It took a few minutes.

Then the entire pin melted in her grasp as she opened her flaming eyes and let the molten metal drip out through the cracks in her fist.

# CHAPTER NINETEEN

Duke chuckled as Antilles fell flat on his ass with a sound that definitely bordered on a squeak. He placed the tip of his wooden greatsword in the ground and leaned on the handle with both hands as his friend pushed miserably back up to his feet.

"You alright there?" he asked, still stifling giggles behind his smug grin.

"Of course, I am!" Antilles retorted. "My ass burns every time I land on it and my head is still ringing from that last hit, but I am *peachy*. Where's my damn sword?"

Duke nodded to the other wooden greatsword, where it landed when Antilles took his tumble, and the indignant curly-top went and fetched it. They both continued sparring with everyone else in the courtyard. It almost wasn't fair. Antilles was an archer. He was built like an archer and he was good at archery. Duke was a swordsman in the very depths of his being. He was well-centered and a bit stocky and he was damn good at swordplay. Antilles knew he was only sparring with him so they could spend time together. Duke belonged with someone who actually stood a chance against him, who could help him get better. Antilles was not that guy.

A quick pirouette removed Duke from the range of Antilles' swing and the blond thought for a moment about just waiting for him to regain his footing, but this was sparring. He was supposed to be teaching Antilles as much as he could, so he swung the blunt side of his blade gently into the other boy's kneecap and brought him to his knees instead of decking him entirely this time. Antilles groaned and Duke helped him up.

"You *are* getting better, I promise." Duke stated as encouragingly as he could, but Antilles burst into laughter.

"Don't you dare patronize me. I suck and we both know it. It's like you with a bow!"

They both laughed together before Antilles waved off at the rest of the men who knew how to use a sword.

"You should go practice with someone else for a bit. Not that I don't like all these lovely bruises you've left for me, but I think it's time someone returned the favor and we both know I'm not up to that challenge."

"You sure?" Duke grinned. "And I avoided your face just for the ladies."

"Yeah, yeah, yeah." Antilles replied dryly, waving him off toward the other soldiers still. "The best thing you can do for me 'ladies-wise' is not stand so close to me, Mr. I-am-going-to-be-twelve-feet-tall."

It was true. At 13, Duke was already several inches taller than his 15-year-old friend. He had dusty blond hair and blue eyes and Antilles was honestly angry that he didn't seem to be entering an awkward teenage phase. Instead, Duke skipped right by the awkward and went straight to handsome, at least in the eyes of almost every girl in the capital. It was annoying, but Antilles decided to take it with a grain of salt. After all, Duke deserved a win every now and then. It was nice to see him happy whenever he could muster it.

Antilles watched as Duke nodded mockingly toward him and then jogged off across the courtyard, looking for a spare partner. Eventually, one of the older men switched out with him and took a break on the edge of the fountain. Then, Antilles got to watch his friend face off to a more experienced foe. He was still good, only getting hit here and there and never losing his footing, but this at least made him sweat. The archer chuckled to himself and headed toward the armory. He was sore. In the past thirty minutes, he had taken a good beating and gotten in maybe one lame hit. Still, Duke tried not to rub it in too much.

Antilles leaned back against the armory after chucking his sword through the door. No one was going to yell at him for slacking. Everyone already knew that he would end up an archer. That meant he only had to have a basic understanding of swordplay. He had that. Duke made sure of it every day they spent dueling each other. So, instead of consistently getting his ass handed to him, Antilles decided to lazily gaze around the courtyard.

Vincent was out barking orders through his desperate gasps for air. Antilles bet the bastard couldn't even reach his sword if the handle tilted just right under his fat folds. He never drew it and practiced with the men. He just walked through the soldiers, huffing and puffing, and pointed out their flaws with enough derogatory names to fill Clara's swear jar in minutes. He had never heard Vincent give anyone a compliment.

The men all got nervous around him, each wondering if this was the day they were randomly selected to tremble under his berating spit-storm. He chose one person a day to screech at and then everyone else stayed in line as best they could afterward. Of course, everyone stayed in line as best they could anyway, but Vincent liked to imagine it was all due to him. Today, he picked some poor sap who had only just signed up a couple weeks ago.

Antilles was skilled enough to drown out the screaming and keep looking about.

It was a bit chilly today, for the 30th of Solstice, normally the warmest month of the year. They had just finished the first week after Voidanuar, which normally consisted of a great deal of clean up. All respectable individuals stayed home for the five days and avoided trouble by lighting every single candle in the house. Of course, there were still those who decided to roam the absolute darkness and they tended to make messes. No one knew who did what, though, so everyone was assigned different clean ups after the fact. Maybe it wasn't the most efficient way of doing things, but it held with tradition and kept all the zealots from both sides satisfied and peaceful, for the most part. There was obviously a spike in crime during the Voidanuar. Complete darkness coupled with people hiding within their homes was always an easy event for criminals to take advantage of.

This year was easy, at least. A little bit of vandalism and a lot of piss, but not much else. There were no murders, rapes, robberies, or kidnappings this year. That in of itself was impressive compared to earlier years. Antilles once had to help his parents scrub a ritualistic murder scene off the cobblestones in the courtyard. He shuddered. Maybe the world was growing closer together as Victor tried to tear them apart.

There were already rumors of skirmishes happening in Dormiat. Alex said Joey was trying to get the council to send their allies aide before the war started, but they were dragging their feet due to 'procedural complications'. Victor might take offense to the fact that Central Liberty would stand with one of his enemies and redirect his anger toward them. In other words, by the time the council chose to do anything, Dormiat would have already fallen to Chrosia. Joey was fighting for them, though. The council had been in session for an entire month straight, including through the Voidanuar. He refused to let anyone go home until they reached a firm decision on Dormiat. He needed to know what sort of lifelines he was allowed to throw their way when the time came. And the time was definitely coming.

Antilles sighed and looked up into the sky. He needed to focus on something happier. Vincent, Victor, Voidanuar, and violence were dragging his spirits down through the dirt this afternoon. It was a shame, because the weather was desperately trying to make it a nice day. The sun was up and blazing, the breeze was combatting the heat, and there was very little humidity. Normally, Antilles could stand still in the courtyard and wind up pooling sweat down his back, but today, it wasn't sticky enough. He grinned gratefully at the sky and folded his arms over his chest, wondering what this evening would hold, despite it only being 1500.

"You know you're supposed to hide the crazy, right?" Duke panted, wiping sweat from his brow. "You aren't supposed to flaunt it by smiling at the clouds."

"What clouds?" Antilles laughed, waving his hand up and around. "It's clear as hell today."

Duke grinned and tossed his sword into the armory. Then both boys moved off toward the fountain to avoid the massive mob making their way toward their location. Everyone else had to put their practice swords away. Duke and Antilles always bowed out early to make sure they dumped theirs first. That way, they got to the fountain for a drink first, as well. Then it was time to run with the masses. Today was different, though. They both got a free ticket out of running because it was Acelyn's birthday. They were helping Clara set up decorations in the great hall. It wasn't exactly exciting, but it beat running in the dead of summer.

The boys walked into the hall to find Clara already handing out orders to a bunch of other unlucky young men. Acelyn was turning 14 this year, which was special in Central Liberty because it was the age courting typically began. Marriage wasn't legal till a girl was 16, but courting was different. There was no physical involvement and a highly preserved idea of innocence. So, every girl's 14th birthday was a massive celebration, but the Premier's only daughter was certainly going to have an over-the-top party. It was almost like celebrating a national holiday, based on all the preparations. Antilles and Duke shared an eye roll before getting close enough for Clara to snag them

"Oh boys! I have been waiting for you all afternoon! What took so long?"

"Swordplay, mom." Antilles grinned. "You forgot swordplay again."

Clara furrowed her brow and listed off the daily activities of her son in her mind. When she reached swordplay, understanding dawned on her face and she nodded happily to the two of them.

"You're right, of course! Silly me. Anyway, I have a special job for you young gentlemen. Ace is expecting a party, of course, but we are trying to surprise her with as much as we can. Ed is sending her off on some sort of surprise scavenger hunt to find her clothes for tonight. He's asked the two of you to escort her and keep an eye on her."

"We're babysitting?" Antilles asked, trying to hide his downcast frown, but Clara saw it and smacked the back of his head gently. "Isn't she technically an adult today who doesn't *need* babysitters?"

"You're spending time with her." Clara replied dryly. "It can't be that awful. You three are all friends, right?"

The boys both nodded bleakly, knowing that Clara wasn't going to accept any other answer. She nodded curtly in approval and gently pushed both their shoulders toward the stairs.

"Good. She's waiting for you up in the Premier's quarters. And you are going to have to guide her so she can keep her eyes closed. Again, I'm trying to surprise her as much as I can. Thank you, boys!"

Duke and Antilles stepped in stride together, both uncomfortable with their task. Ace was nice enough, but she was as girly as they came. She cried a lot and worried about her appearance and gossiped. Neither of them had really gotten along with her for the past year, despite being inseparable friends before then. Maybe it was just because of their schedules. They were far busier as teens than they had been as kids. Still, the two of them decided to accept their lot in life. Again, it was better than running or whatever Joey would want Duke to do instead.

They should have known better than to even think Joey's name. It always seemed to summon him. Sure enough, as they reached Duke's home, the door opened and Marcus stepped out angrily and spun around to yell at Joey, who stood behind with a grimace.

"You know I'm right, Joe! Dammit, you've known I was right for a decade, now. We aren't in control of the situation anymore!"

"And whose damn fault is that?" Joey snarled in return. "I trusted you to keep your mouth shut, Marcus! But no, ye had to go and spew our entire plan right out of yer shite hole!!"

"I did what I thought was right!!!" Marcus boomed back. "If you don't like the fact that I still have morals, then you go right ahead and leave me out of everything from now on!"

Marcus stormed across the hall and slammed his door after entering. Both boys stared at it, asphyxiated. They had never seen Marcus so angry. In general, he was the more reasonable of the two brothers. Duke almost jumped when Joey found a different family member to yell at.

"Duke Justice, aren't you supposed to be running!!?!?" Joey snapped angrily. "If you aren't using the time I give you to train, then why the hell should I keep letting you have it?"

Thankfully, Ed and Acelyn walked down the stairs just then and interrupted the entire situation.

"Ah! There you two are!" Ed chuckled, firing a warning glare at Joey. "I thought you were just dragging your feet. Are you quite finished with them, Joey?"

The war strategist squinted in confusion and glanced around the four people outside of his door. No one was sure if they were supposed to remain silent or explain. Finally, Duke sighed.

"I'm helping Clara today, Dad." He reminded his father, who suddenly remembered and softened a bit. "She said she cleared it with you like six weeks ago."

"She did." Joey answered shortly and waved Duke on before turning back inside and adding one more instruction. "Just make sure you all stay out of trouble and whatever."

The door shut and Antilles instantly looked at the Premier.

"Damn, you made it just in time, Your Honor." He rolled his eyes toward the door that just shut.

"Timing is everything." Ed winked at the boy, tapping the side of his nose, and then gently pushed a reluctant Acelyn their way. "Anyway, you three should get going. This is the first clue and there are four more once you figure it out."

He wrapped his daughter's hand around a small, folded piece of paper and then kissed her nose and told her to have fun and be safe. Antilles and Duke rolled their eyes in sync again and then the three teens walked back down the stairs. Ace closed her eyes when she was told and bounced excitedly when Clara made a big fuss over her on the way to the door. They didn't talk until they were in the courtyard and then Antilles broke the silence.

"Alright," he mumbled. "where are we going, Ace?"

"How the hell am I supposed to know?!" she snapped right back, hearing his annoyance.

Both Antilles and Duke glanced at each other and then shot Acelyn the most exasperated look they could. She blushed right up to her scalp and cleared her throat with an embarrassed giggle. She waved the note in her hand slightly.

"Oh…." She gulped. "I guess I do have the clue."

"Noooooo" Antilles drawled with wide eyes. "Really?! Well, isn't this just going to be *great!*"

"Hey!" Ace cried in frustration. "It's not like I asked for you either, moss head!"

"That's it!!"

Antilles threw both hands in the air and tried to walk back into the hall to tell Clara he couldn't handle the prissy little princess today. Instead, Duke caught the end of his cape and held on with one tight fist while smiling at Ace. He had always liked her, despite she and his best friend hating each other recently. Antilles grabbed his own cape with both hands and tried to yank it out of Duke's grip, but couldn't even get the bigger boy to budge. It was uncanny how solidly Duke could hold his ground.

"Listen, Ace," Duke explained calmly. "why don't you go ahead and read your note out loud and I will help you figure it out. Antilles will go and saddle a few horses----"

"I don't want to ride in front of you two again!!" she begged instantly.

Duke had to bite his tongue to avoid either laughing or yelling, especially since Antilles scoffed as loudly as possible. Then he turned around and tried to grip his cape over his shoulder, yanking on it with all his might. His entire body was leaning desperately away.

"That's fine." Duke growled, more upset that Antilles had almost escaped than at Ace's attitude. "You can ride on Chompers with me if it will make you feel…… safer?"

He wasn't exactly sure if that was the answer she was looking for, but she smiled gratefully, so he assumed he said something right. Maybe Joey's constant reminders to be civilized were rubbing off on him, despite him thinking Acelyn was being just a bit difficult today. She and Antilles had butt heads ever since the corral broke when they were younger. Still, Ace had been very kind to Duke after all that, so maybe he just thought he owed her that same courtesy. She took a deep breath and let her smile widen.

"You're such a gentleman, Duke." She nudged him, twisting her toe in the dirt. "I'd love to ride Chompers with you. And I don't mean to snap at him. He's just so difficult."

"I'm…. right…. here!!!" Antilles panted angrily. "Lemme go, Duke!"

Neither boy realized what would happen if Duke did as he asked, but the younger boy suddenly felt guilty and listened to his friend. And Antilles proceeded to immediately fall forward onto his chest, just barely catching his face before it drove into the ground. Duke gasped through his teeth and moved to help him up, but Antilles jumped to his feet before he even took the first step. The mortified boy looked like he was about to scream at Duke. Instead, Ace's laughter filled the air. She laughed so hard that a snort escaped, silencing her instantly. Then Antilles got to laugh as both her hands clamped over her mouth.

After that, the three of them were finally ready to head out. Antilles happily jaunted off to saddle Chompers and his own horse, leaving Ace and Duke to read through Ed's clue as they slowly followed him. The first one led them to the oasis. They rode there at an easy pace, knowing this was supposed to take a while. Ace and Antilles argued the entire time and Duke tried to mediate. He didn't like it when they fought, but it seemed to be the only hobby the two of them could enjoy together. Ace sat behind him on Chompers and clutched tightly around his waist till her knuckles and hands were white. She hadn't been comfortable on horseback since getting thrown into a mess of deadly cattle. Still, Duke didn't mind. It was actually kind of nice. He felt like a knight of old, protecting a damsel in distress.

The note at the oasis was stuck to a tree with a dagger and it sent them back into town. There was a quaint little butcher shop just at the base of the plateau. The butcher had a thick accent and a pretty daughter, but he also had a clue for them, as long as they used the secret phrase from the note at the oasis. It was a cypher and it took all three of them to figure it out. Unfortunately, that required Antilles and Acelyn to stop fighting for a few minutes. This was the longest part of the entire scavenger hunt. Duke's head hurt by the end of it. He was the one who eventually figured it out, while simultaneously keeping Ace from clawing Antilles's eyes out with her fingernails. She threatened to do it twice in fifteen minutes because he 'breathed too loud' while she was thinking. Of course, once he knew it bothered her, he did it on purpose.

After the butcher gave them their note, Acelyn cried for about 30 minutes because Antilles called her fat after she called him 'moss head' again. She didn't seem bothered by the rest of the insult, which was 'you fat, nasty, prideful, bitch of a demon', but the 'fat' bit stuck. Duke desperately tried to pull her attention back to the task at hand, partially because he didn't like to hear her cry, but mostly because he had no idea what a 'farcardo' was. After getting tired of him asking her, Ace angrily told him it was what she used to call Mount Dragonesta before she could say 'volcano'. They were about to head west when Acelyn also let them know there was no way the clue was at the volcano. She wasn't allowed that far away from the castle. Duke groaned and re-read the clue. At least Antilles was being quiet, now. He felt like an asshole for making her cry on her birthday.

From then on, it got a little better. Antilles sucked up all the pride he had in his body and chose to be nice. Acelyn figured out that the clue was directing them toward the safest place from the volcano, which was back up the plateau. Apparently, her family had a plan if the mountain ever erupted. They were all supposed to meet at the bell in the center of the courtyard. After several minutes of searching, Antilles found a note stuck to the inside of the massive bell. He still thought the entire thing was lame and stupid, but he was trying to make sure she didn't show up at the party bawling and ruin it for his mom. Clara was trying so hard to make this special for her. Central Liberty didn't have many causes to celebrate anymore.

The note in the bell sent them back down the plateau to a tavern, The Sultry Barmaid. The owner, a man named Filch, had a note from the Premier that allowed Acelyn to have her first mug of mead. Duke and Antilles were both given one as well, with a wink from Filch to Duke. Technically, the legal drinking age was 14 and he knew Duke was a year short. Still, he didn't make him feel outcast at all and the three actually got along for an hour or so before Filch told them they were supposed to go back up to the infirmary. Clara was going to meet them there around 1800. The three kids jumped up and ran outside. It was already quarter till. Clara wouldn't like it if they were late. They would have to move faster than a trot. Acelyn clenched her eyes shut and plastered herself tight against Duke's back for the whole ride, but they made it with about a minute to spare. They all three stumbled through the door into the McNeilson's kitchen, only to realize Clara wasn't there yet. A collective sigh escaped their lips just as she burst in behind them.

"Oh, darlings, I hope you haven't been waiting around for too long!" she cried. "I got held up and lost track of the time."

"I can't believe you would be late, Mother!" Antilles scolded with a grin aimed toward Duke.

The other boy laughed, but not because of Antilles. Clara spun him around and smacked his rear indignantly, ordering him and Duke to get cleaned up and dressed in the clothing she had laid out for them in the back room.

"And don't come out till I call you!" she snapped, pushing them both through the door and slamming it after them.

"Damn, this sucks." Antilles said as soon as he was sure she wouldn't hear them.

"Huh? What?" Duke replied.

He hadn't really been paying attention for the past few moments. It had been a long three hours and he just wanted to drift off and sleep, honestly. He knew he still had to go to this party, but he was somewhat dreading several more hours of faking adult behavior.

"This whole thing!" Antilles pressed. "So, Ace is turning 14. I get that it's a big deal to her, but why do I have to care so damn much?"

He yanked off his clothes and tossed them off to the side as Duke followed suit. They both used the basin of water to wash up as the younger boy finally revealed his true opinion.

"I think it's honestly a waste of time." He shrugged. "I mean, we are basically at war, or will be soon. Shouldn't everyone be a bit more focused on that? At least girls only have one 14th birthday."

Antilles shot him a sheepish grin and they each pulled on the fancy clothes that they both instantly hated.

"At least they don't have puffy collars like Vincent's." Antilles elbowed Duke till they both laughed.

Vincent definitely did dress in a ridiculous fashion, but since he never had to fight, it made sense for him. The boys were still uncomfortable in their silk shirts with slits down their chests, but it was easier to handle since they both got to make fun of each other. Their pants were comfy cotton and then they each had tall boots that folded down. In the end, they both looked very dashing and hated every second of it. Especially because Clara yelled through the door to remind them both to brush their hair. Duke didn't mind. He had a simple crew cut, so he just ran the boar bristles over his head and then shrugged, guessing that was good enough. Antilles scowled when he passed the brush to him, though. His hair was curly and full of knots and mattes. Brushing it out would do two things, hurt like hell, and make it puff out to the sides in a frizzy fashion that he absolutely hated.

By the time he finished, Duke had to bite his lower lip to avoid laughing. It took Antilles one glance at him to know he couldn't keep his hair like this. He cussed and dunked his entire head in water. After drying it, Antilles shook his fingers through the locks to loosen the curls back into their normal placement. And he tossed the brush away when Duke playfully held it out to him again. He shot it a look of disgust. Clara called them out as Duke laughed at him and got punched in the upper arm for it. It didn't hurt

Duke, but Antilles shook his hand when the other boy turned around to leave.

They walked out into the kitchen and Clara hurried them out with her. The whole point of a big party for the 14th birthday was a representation of a girl turning into a woman. It was the first time they wore a ball gown and were allowed to fashion their hair in a mess on top of their heads. No one was supposed to see the girl until the big reveal to the entire party. Clara carefully hid the boys' eyes as they groaned and complained about the old tradition. They had almost made it out, when Ace stopped Clara in her tracks.

"Clara, wait!"

The kindly woman turned back and looked at the girl, who suddenly flushed bright red and cleared her throat.

"Um.... could you.... maybe.... leave Duke for a second?"

"Oh, of course, deary!" Clara replied cheerfully, unsure why Ace would want this edit so suddenly, but happy to help her in any way. "Duke, why don't you stay here and talk to Ace while Antilles and I make sure the hall is ready. Just be sure to make it in by seven, Acelyn dear. That's when it all starts. You have about twenty minutes. And make sure you keep your eyes closed, Duke!"

Ace waited until the kitchen door closed behind Clara and Antilles and then even longer, till they both heard the infirmary door slam. It was almost like Clara wanted them to know that they were alone. Duke's nerves skyrocketed as he gulped and made sure his eyes stayed clamped. Acelyn sighed dramatically in relief.

"Oh, you can open your eyes, Duke." She reassured him. "I don't mind."

"Yeah, but I think Clara might kill me." He warned.

Ace laughed.

"I won't tell her if you won't."

Duke grinned and opened his eyes, still a bit hesitantly. Ace beamed at him as he did so and looked her up and down. She was in a fancy, silken, lavender dress. It had two very thin straps holding it up, making Duke wonder why the dress wasn't heavy enough to rip them. It certainly looked like it should have. There were several layers that made it far wider than her body at the bottom. Her black hair was pinned up in a bun with a wavy tail hanging over her left shoulder. She shrugged in embarrassment as he stared at her until he could force words out of his mouth.

"Damn Ace." He whispered after clearing his throat several times. "You look so old!"

The hurt look on her face instantly alerted him to his mistake and he shook both his hands and his head, trying to explain.

"Not old like *old*." He cried desperately. "The good type of old. Like a grown up and all that stuff."

She still looked a bit displeased, but grinned kindly and wrung her hands together.

"I know what you mean, I think." She stepped toward him a bit, making him gulp again. "It's something nice, I'm sure. You've always been very nice to me, Duke."

"Well.... yeah." He rubbed the back of his neck bashfully. "I try at least. I'm not always great at it."

She smiled at him.

"I think you're better than you think, honestly." She giggled. "I was hoping you would sit in here with me till I had to go into the hall because...... I'm a little scared. All of this is scary."

She sat on the table and rubbed her own arms, hugging herself. Duke scratched the back of his head and sat next to her. They were quiet for a bit before he spoke.

"Ace, I really don't think you have anything to be scared about." He said slowly, making sure to listen to himself so he didn't sound like an idiot again. "I've never really been to one of these before, but I doubt anyone has ever looked----" he waved up and down at her. "---like that. It's...... pretty damn amazing."

Ace smiled at her lap and leaned against his shoulder, careful not to ruin her hair. That was what she hoped he had been trying to say earlier. It was nice to be proven right and complimented all in one. It didn't calm her nerves much, but she let her dangling legs swing for a bit as she nuzzled into his shoulder. Her hand slid forward and held his tight between them. With a gulp, Duke spoke again.

"I think we only have about five minutes, Ace." He coaxed. "Clara will kill me if I make you late."

She nodded and they both slid off the table together. Duke smiled at her and turned to leave, but she kept hold of his hand and turned him back to face her. Her other hand grasped his free one and she gently swung both his arms as she tried to explain why she wanted him here.

"Duke, I know you didn't have to be so nice today. If it had just been me and Antilles, I might have cried all afternoon. I know we don't talk as much as we used to, but I miss you. I miss being your friend. We used to mean so much to each other and be so close. It's not fair that Antilles gets you all to himself just because he's a boy. I'll even try to behave around him if it means we can be friends again. Just please try..... for me."

"Ace, we've always been friends!" Duke cried in surprise. "I wouldn't change that for anything. I've just been busy. I'll try, though. I'll try to be.... less.... like that."

She smiled and braced off his hands so she could stand on her tiptoes and kiss his cheek. At least, Duke thought it counted as his cheek. It was kind of on the corner of his lips. When she pulled away, his entire face flushed red and he tried to ramble something about them really needing to go, but she already knew, and his nervous mumbles fell on deaf ears. After a gentle squeeze from her hands to his, she took off, gathering her skirts and turning around to wave one more time at him before rushing off to her party. Duke slammed down in one of the chairs and tried to come to grips with what just happened. It took him a while. Far longer than he meant it to. Then he cleared his throat, stood up with a deep breath and headed for the great hall.

The party was well underway by the time he slipped through the door. He was trying to be inconspicuous, of course, but one person saw him, since he had been looking for him the whole night. Duke carefully entered a conversation with nearby soldiers to try and blend in when he saw Joey glaring at him. A quick side-glance told him he was unsuccessful and Joey wiggled his finger in a 'come hither' fashion. Duke groaned, but obeyed.

"Where have you been?" his father demanded when he sunk into the chair next to him at the table.

"I was doing a favor for Ace." Duke responded, carefully avoiding lying.

Joey raised his eyebrow in suspicion, but let it go for tonight. This was a party and he and Duke had to get along for the time being. Of course, that wasn't going to stick, though. As soon as he realized that Joey wasn't going to question him any further, Duke decided to try and get some information about the outburst he witnessed between the two brothers.

"What happened between you and Uncle Marcus earlier?" he asked before shoving food into his mouth.

"None of your damn business, Duke." Joey snapped, not unexpectedly. "I've taught you better than to dig into the affairs of others. Especially your elders."

"Sorry." Duke mumbled and went back to eating.

It was easier just to apologize and move on. Otherwise, the two of them would fight for a few hours, it would escalate, and he would still lose. Instead, his eyes searched around the room. The party began with a feast, like all good parties do. Acelyn was drowning in attention at the head table, which most likely thrilled her. So many young men kissed her hand and doted on her new appearance, Duke honestly began to wonder if she would even know who he was after tonight. He wasn't sure why that mattered so much to him. Even Clara made sure Antilles said something nice, which must have killed him to do. Then Alex, Clara, and Antilles all came and sat with the Rogers. Marcus was mysteriously absent from the entire affair.

If nothing else, Duke and Antilles were both grateful for the food. Home cooked meals of this proportion were hard to come by, but Ed had made sure to pull all the stops for his little girl. Excellent mead, roast boars, baked potatoes filled with bacon and cheese and an assortment of greens everyone knew better than to look too closely at. Still, it was all delicious and once the waiting staff cleared the dinner plates, they began serving custard tarts to each individual. These crumbly little cakes were so rare that this was Duke's very first one. Antilles had several over the past few days as Clara helped the chef perfect his recipe, so he was a bit sick of them and let Duke have his as well.

After the meal, there was supposed to be a dance. Neither of the boys wanted to dance. It wasn't that they didn't know how, unfortunately, both of them had been taught since they were part of the council's families. In general, it was because neither of them liked dancing with girls they didn't know. Ace was the only one their age who lived in Feldon's Peak, the rest of the young women they saw were the daughters, nieces, and sisters of important lords. So, it was either dance with older women they knew, who still treated them like little boys, or force themselves to meet new girls, who might find it offensive that they would even speak to them. After all, Antilles and Duke were the sons of the council's doctor and war strategist. It wasn't like their families were actual nobility. Sometimes, the children of the lords who ruled their own fiefs were particularly rude to them, trying to set themselves apart. Duke and Antilles were more than happy to remain invisible and established themselves with the men moving the tables out of the way, once they were cleared. Then the band began to play and they tried to mix in with the soldiers who attended for one reason or another.

It was still exciting to watch, though. Despite the fact that neither of them would ever admit being interested in girls, they both enjoyed watching them dance, all dressed up and flirtatious. There was something intoxicating about it; the way they moved, their hair, their dresses, their laughs. It was contagious. Even the soldiers around them would point out their favorites and whisper their desires into each other's ears. The boys didn't bother trying to hear what they said. Both of them knew enough about men and women to have a pretty clear guess and neither of them were yet over-joyed with the idea of settling down with a girl. They were more than content to just stare and let their imaginations do the rest.

Unfortunately for Duke, he was very handsome, even as a slightly bashful 13-year-old with no idea how to talk to girls. So, when one of them approached him and gripped both of his hands, pulling him toward the dance floor, he shot Antilles a desperate look and hoped his friend would save him. Instead, the archer burst into laughter and waved. Duke was sucked into the dance within seconds and to the end of his days, he had no idea what all the girl said. She was pretty, he knew that, with her brown hair and honey eyes, but she talked so incessantly, he could only nod and hope he didn't mess up the dance.

Libertarian dances were performed by groups. Each person had a partner, per se, but they weren't always dancing with them. Sometimes, they switched for a brief moment and gripped some other lady's hand in a quick spin. Other times, they bowed to the person beside them or switched places. It was all very difficult to follow if you hadn't been trained how to do it at some point. Duke still had to focus desperately on not slipping up his turn each round. If he messed up, their entire group would be thrown off and the awkward, painful, realization would soon hit that it was his fault. In practice, it was bad enough, Duke couldn't imagine the humility if he fumbled at an actual event, Still, he held his own fairly well and even received a compliment from his partner, whose name was apparently Roxanne.

She offered to dance the next song with him as well, but Duke told her he was a bit tired and moseyed back over to Antilles, who had the widest grin. He knew he was going to be tortured for this all night before his best friend even opened his mouth. Antilles never got the chance, though.

If the doors to the great hall could open any more violently, Duke had never seen it. They both flew open with a kick from the figure who stormed through them seconds later. It was an entrance that demanded attention and reaction. The band stopped playing mid-strum. Everyone stopped talking and dancing only to gaze upon the small figure gliding deliberately toward the head table where most of the council now sat.

It was a woman, Duke was willing to bet his life on that, despite her hidden features under a turban wrap. She wasn't tall or stocky enough to be a man. She was dressed in the uniform of a Dormatian monk, meaning she was a soldier in their army. He didn't know the ranks well enough to guess how important she was, but her orange robes twisted and wrapped about her figure in the most functional way one could divine for such clothing. She took long strides and even breaths, but no one was looking forward to hearing whatever report a Dormatian might have to give on this night. There was only one thing this unscheduled visit could be about.

The monk approached the table and glared out from under her turban at the men before her as she came to a halt. Tradition would be to bow, introduce herself and explain her visit calmly, but she didn't bear the presence of one who valued that tradition any longer. Instead, she spoke even before removing her head ware.

"I had to see it to believe it." She said calmly, with a healthy portion of spite. "My whole ride up to this castle, everyone was speaking of a celebration occurring and I thought 'No! No, the councilmen know better than to celebrate with the world in its current state. No, there must be some mistake.'"

Her voice was level and cool, even though it certainly sounded like she was more than willing to kill them all. Ed was the first to recover, considering she was ruining Acelyn's special day with her intrusion. He slowly rose to his feet and pressed his fingers down on the table so he could lean on them meaningfully.

"We try very hard in this country not to let Victor win before there is even a fight." He explained. "Maybe the world is dark and dreary right now, but it is our job to promote hope and continue living our lives to the best of our ability. We cannot blame Victor if hope and goodwill die out. That will be on all our heads. That being said, who *the hell* do you think you are, soldier? How dare you storm into my Great Hall and accuse me and my council of apathy to the state of this world?"

The woman reached up and removed her turban, which was apparently wrapped around a hard helmet since it thudded loudly onto the floor where she discarded it with a toss. Her brown hair cascaded from where it had been rolled up inside and fell to her knees, easily. In Dormiat, it was a sign of shame to cut one's hair. It was often used as punishment for minor infractions and sins against the monasteries, which were both the religious center and military outposts of the country. The longer a soldier's hair, the higher ranked and honored the individual was.

"Do I look like a common soldier, Your Honor?" the woman demanded breathlessly. "And do you honestly believe I care one bit about this party? It is some poor girl's 14th year, is it not? Perhaps the young girl standing directly behind you, hiding in your robes?"

The woman turned away from the table and waved about the room with her gloved hands. Everyone grew silent as she raised her voice for all to hear.

"This is how 14-year-old girls spend their time in your country?" she mused arrogantly before turning back to the table. "Would you like to know how little Chrosian girls spend their time? They topple entire governments in one night."

The room responded with silence as everyone awkwardly hugged those they cared about as far away from this crazy woman as possible. She carelessly grabbed mugs from the horror-struck councilors until she found one with mead left in it. She chugged it and searched for another, chomping meat off a leftover boar leg as she looked. Everyone just waited.

"That's right." She finally continued, after gulping down everything in her mouth. "One little girl, one night, and it all came crashing down. Tell me, councilors, have you ever seen an entire infrastructure obliterated in 12 hours? This girl...... she could materialize out of thin air. Pop into a room and then vanish like she was never there. She started with the lords. 1,074 lords had their throats slit within hours of each other. Then she cycled back through and murdered their families. Next was their individual courts. With the entire country in an uproar, she came through once more and took down the monastery leaders. No one even knows who is next in line for anything anymore. The commoners, the servants, the monks, any damned person left with legs and a will to live, are all heading for the capital, which is the one place this Maiden of Death left intact. So, why don't all of you tell me once more what is so important for you to celebrate."

It was Joey's turn to stand up and hold out his hand to stop the woman. Normally, he would be absolutely thrilled to hear someone trying to force the council into making a decision about Victor, but this wasn't the time or place. And Acelyn certainly didn't deserve to have her entire night ruined by an unstable monk who......

Joey stopped and sat down instantly. That drew the woman's attention even more. She glared at him, looked him up and down with a confused frown and then waved him on.

"No please!" she snapped. "I'd like to hear what you have to say."

Joey pursed his lips together and stood back up. Maybe he was still angry with Marcus from this morning or maybe he was frustrated with the council. Maybe he just wanted to pick a fight. Whatever the reason, he decided to speak his mind.

"I was going to ask you to leave or have your breakdown somewhere else, on your own time, but maybe you're right. Maybe we should all be more concerned over what is happening to our north. I *do* know that what you're describing is impossible. There's no way a single girl could accomplish what you're implying. And there's certainly no reason she would wipe out all the lords and not take the king down with them. This is obviously a ploy from your own king's court to solidify his tyrannical power over his people. But sure, let's blame it all on an imaginary child from Chrosia and make it everyone else's problem as well."

Joey pushed off the table and strode toward the staircase, waving a few guards after the monk. She glanced angrily between the guards and his back as he reached the bottom of the stairs. Just as Duke turned to follow his father, who snapped impatiently to get him to do so, the monk spoke up again.

"I saw her!!!" she screeched. "I watched her kill!! Her eyes erupted into blue flames, and she uses diamond swords and blows heads off!!"

Suddenly, everyone in the room began to calm down or get angry. They could only hear the ravings of a madwoman that interrupted their celebration and ruined a perfectly good night. She was desperately spinning in circles, looking for just one face that believed her. The guards were about to grab her and throw her in prison, the people were beginning to relax and laugh, mocking her. She was arrested kicking and screaming about how stupid they all were and how they'd see she wasn't lying. Meanwhile, Joey and Duke walked all the way home, completely ignoring the rest of the party, which started back up several minutes after the monk's cries couldn't be heard any longer.

Joey opened the door and let Duke walk in ahead of him. Then he followed and slammed the door so hard, it made his son jump. Joey walked around him and to the end of the hall, crashing into the chair at his desk and Duke just stared. He had never seen his father so upset with a foreign diplomat. And it only got worse. Joey delved into his bottom right drawer and removed a large bottle of whiskey. He didn't bother getting a glass, just sucked a large gulp right out of the bottle and then glanced up at Duke.

"Get in here." He demanded.

Duke didn't dare disobey. In fact, he practically skipped right into the study and sat in the wobbly chair opposite his father. However, he forgot it was wobbly. So, when he dropped his rear into the seat, it tilted dramatically to the left before he was perfectly balanced and he toppled right back out of it, rolling on the floor a bit. For almost two years, he had kept the secret chair deformation from Joey, but as he jumped back up to his feet and rubbed the back of his neck, Joey glared at him.

"The hell was that?"

"Uhhh….." Duke admitted nervously. "Remember a couple years ago when you were expecting that Chrosian diplomat? Well, I thought it would be funny to shave down the leg of the chair and I forgot about it till now, because I haven't sat in it since then."

Joey groaned and rolled his eyes up to the ceiling. Then he waved at Duke and scoffed.

"Ladies and gentlemen, the future of this great nation."

"Well, I don't have to be." Duke grumbled before raising his voice. "What's pissing you off today, anyway? You've been nasty to everyone."

Joey grimaced and chugged more from his bottle.

"None of your business." He growled.

"Maybe it is!" Duke snapped. "You want me to do your damn job, don't you? Well maybe you should teach me something useful for once."

Joey gulped down yet another guzzle of whiskey and snorted at his son.

"We both know you don't give a shite about what I have to teach you. You just want to know what's going on so you can use it against me in the future."

"Damn." Duke responded spitefully. "Once. I've done that once. And maybe you shouldn't have hit mom in the first place, asshole."

Joey chucked his now-empty bottle at Duke's head. The boy dodged it easily, having learned over the years to duck. Joey sneered in what could only be disappointment and dug out another bottle.

"Fine, you want to know why I'm pissed?" He asked after another dreg. "You want to know the awful truth about politics?"

"Is it that all politicians become miserable alcoholics with nothing to live for?" Duke spurned and Joey growled through his grit teeth.

"No, smart ass. It's that politicians control what people believe. What if I told you that I know for a fact that every damn word the young lady down there said was absolutely true and I still made her look like an insane bitch in front of everyone? What would you have to say about that?"

Duke rolled his eyes and scoffed. His arms folded rebelliously over his chest and he shook his head.

"Look, if you don't want to take me seriously, fine. Pardon me for trying to take a damn interest in your life. I thought that's what you wanted. I'm going back downstairs. Drink yourself to death for all I care, I'm not getting Alex this time when you don't wake up."

Joey stood up and slammed his bottle down on the desk, making his son jump yet again. Duke should have run right then. He knew better than to pause. It gave Joey time to dart around the desk and grab the front of his shirt in his fist. Duke's spine was slammed against the wall within seconds and the back of his head bounced off the stone with the force. Joey leaned forward and got in his face. Duke tried to gag on the scent of his breath, but couldn't manage it through the fist digging into his throat.

"Listen to me, you little shite!" Joey spat at him. "I'll die when I'm good and ready and it won't be because of your stupidity! And you think I'm lying about the girl? I'm not. There are girls in this world who bear the power she spoke of, easily. And instead of siding with her and inciting panic, *well-deserved* panic, mind you, I chose to defame her to the entirety of the council just to keep these pathetic, simple-minded imbeciles happy for a few more years before they all die!"

Joey tore his son away from the wall and threw him down the hallway. Duke tumbled a bit, but eventually managed to push up to his hands and knees, gasping for air. He glared at the old man as he went back to sitting in his chair and drinking. Duke knew he only released him because he was about to pass out. Joey had learned to hide all his abuse over the years. His son stumbled up to his feet as the war strategist kept talking.

"The only thing I can't figure out is why this 'Maiden of Death' would leave the king and his court alone. If you are going to topple a country's government, why leave it's center untouched?"

Joey stared at the map on his desk as he tried to figure it out. Duke thought about staying frozen right where he was and hoping his father basically forgot he existed. Eventually, Joey would either tell him to go away or pass out from drinking and then he could just leave at his leisure. He had learned not to just walk away. Every time he did, Joey reacted the same way he just had. If Duke managed to escape, it was worse when he finally got home. It was better to wait for his reaction right now, than come back to his wrath later. So, he waited while Joey finished his bottle again and tossed it away with an aggravated yell.

"Dammit!! I just don't get it!!"

Duke rolled his eyes and walked back to the doorway, leaning on the door jamb.

"That's because you are thinking like nothing more than a politician."

He said dryly.

"And I suppose you are going to think like more than a stupid little boy right now?" Joey challenged angrily. "Don't tell me my business, Duke!"

"I'm not!" the boy finally snapped, tired of the demeaning tone his father was using. "This has nothing to do with your damn business. This is basic stuff that any soldier would understand! If every single person in a leadership role suddenly died by some supposedly mystical force, what would the Libertarians do? They would panic and flock to the safest place they could think of. If this girl, or demon, or whatever, left the king and his court untouched, the Dormatians would automatically assume that he has some sort of immunity to her or something like that. The entire country is going to flock to the capital, assuming they are finally safe once they make it there. Then, if this girl is smart, she can wipe them all out in one fell swoop. Chrosia has the damn numbers to do it and we already know that's Victor's final goal after Arcane. She's not thinking like a strategist, she's thinking like a fighter. That's what you're missing, because you haven't been sober in over a decade and it's killing your ability to think."

Duke pushed off the wall and shook his head while turning around to leave as Joey stared up at his back from where he rested his forehead in his hands. He forced his mind to focus on everything his son had said, not just the insults at the end. It actually made sense. He sat up and fought for the words to stop Duke from leaving angry. He wanted to tell him that he was intelligent and he was probably right about everything. Instead, he just watched him leave without saying a word.

Duke stomped out of the suite and down the stairs. He hadn't decided how he was going to react to what just happened, yet. He wanted to punch something, but he already felt the tears welling up in his eyes. He stopped on the bottom step one floor down and collapsed onto his ass, sobbing into his fists. It was less painful than punching the stone walls in the stair way and no one was around, anyway. Or so he thought.

He didn't hear her walk up, but when she sat down next to him, he only jumped in embarrassment till his eyes met hers. Ace had somehow managed to escape her own party to come up and find him. She grinned sadly at him and wrapped her arm around his shoulders. Her hand gently stroked his upper arm and Duke gave in. He laid his head down on her chest and kept crying. It didn't make sense and it didn't change anything, but when she turned to face him and wrap her hands around his head, holding him tight against her chest in a hug, Duke felt better than he had for years. She kissed the top of his head and whispered in his ear.

"This friend thing goes both ways. I'll always be there for you, too."

# CHAPTER TWENTY

Axl casually stared at the devastation around him. Millions of women and children lay dead at his feet, huddled together and bleeding out in rivers across the keep floor. He couldn't believe Eclipse did all this by herself. It was so out of character for her. He waded through the bodies and blood, back to the entrance of the keep. The door was shattered into pieces that still somehow hung from the hinges. Axl passed through them with a determined stride. He had to talk to her about this.

His mind wandered back to three years ago, when Victor sent him to fetch Eclipse from her cabin in the woods. She had moved out of the lab on her 12th birthday and lived in a little cabin with Adamere, her black and white kiladrt. So, it didn't surprise Axl when he knocked on the door to her cabin and the kiladrt roared on the other side of it. Eclipse opened the door a few seconds later.

"Axl?" she raised an eyebrow. "What are you doing here?"

She leaned against the door and glanced around behind him. He was used to this response. She always thought he was bringing trouble with him. The first few months she lived in her cabin, he did somewhat torture her by sneaking around outside at night, refusing to announce himself. He was just following orders, but she eventually caught him last month, with a certain amount of cheating. They had been some kind of acquaintances ever since. However, he didn't often visit her during the day. Never, actually. He made it perfectly clear that they could only spend time together at night. Standing on her doorstep at noon even felt wrong to him, despite having a legitimate reason to be there.

"Victor wants to see you." He explained. "It turns out I'm a better messenger than a bodyguard, so I'm the unlucky fellow he sent to fetch you this time. And he wants you to bring Amy, of course."

Eclipse groaned and pushed off the doorframe, waving Axl into the cabin. He hesitated after catching the glare Adamere was aiming his way, but eventually slipped in past the kiladrt. The beast didn't really like him, which was disappointing, because he wanted to throw his arms around that fluffy neck more than anything. Eclipse had been eating lunch, but she set her plate on the floor for Adamere, knowing she wouldn't have time today. He chomped down on the odd mixture of bland meat and veggies without hesitation. He was used to this.

"Why does he need Amy every single damn time?" Eclipse grumbled rhetorically as she grabbed her cape and swung it over her head.

Axl grinned as she strapped on her quivers and made sure her compound bow was on its hooks. She had been able to draw it for a couple weeks now, due to the strength she had from the Enhancer and an intense workout routine she committed to ever since she got out. Eclipse hadn't changed much in the two years since she beat Amy at her own game, but then again, nothing ever really changed in Chrosia. After ordering Adamere to stay in the cabin, she followed Axl toward the fortress. They walked in silence for a bit while she shot an order to her Colonel. Then, she glanced at him.

"You're being quiet." She stated.

"I was just waiting for you to break the silence. Figured you had to shoot Amy a quick mind message."

Eclipse shrugged her eyebrows and kept walking like she didn't really care. Of course, she and Axl had known each other long enough by now for him to know that she wouldn't have bothered to ask if she didn't care at all. She wasn't one to play games. Alternatively, Axl loved games. He lived for them. Getting to know his charge had been one of the most time-consuming games he ever took the time to play. Deep down, he thought she was actually a fun person. A fun person who didn't like anyone, but to each their own. She had an air of responsibility and intelligence about her that seemed fitting for someone far older. For example, they were walking to the fortress rather than porting. She didn't jump into things. She thought them through and made calculated decisions. Maybe this was just procrastination, but he doubted it. They reached the fortress several minutes after Amy, who stood impatiently waiting, tapping her foot and keeping her arms folded.

"You told me to meet you here 20 minutes ago!" she snapped. "What took you so long?"

"I sent you the message twenty minutes ago." Eclipse answered dryly. "I didn't tell you I was sitting here waiting for you. I had to walk here from my cabin."

Amy rolled her eyes, but didn't push it. After all, she was just a Colonel since Eclipse won their duel two years ago. Being second in command wasn't good enough for the blonde, though. She still wanted to take Eclipse's position, by force if need be. No matter what, she was about to enjoy entering the fortress wall with her, because Victor hadn't quite warmed up enough to Eclipse to give her access. However, Amy was a frequent visitor. The Elite on duty let both Axl and Amy walk through with no hassle, but stopped Eclipse with the butt of his spear. Eclipse rolled her eyes spitefully over to him and waited for his explanation, knowing what it was already.

"Name and request for entry."

"Come on, Steven." She replied bitterly. "Everyone knows my name and Victor himself sent for me."

"I don't make the rules, princess." He sneered.

Axl frowned. The Elite didn't like Eclipse. They hadn't since she got out of the Enhancer. All of them enjoyed the little moments they got to humiliate her, mainly because she couldn't do anything about it. She outranked them, yes, but they answered directly to Victor, which meant she still had to take their abuse with a grain of salt. Everything she said to any of them could easily be reported to the promontory as a threat to his authority. Eclipse and Victor had a deal. She would never challenge him again.

"Eclipse Monohue." She groaned. "And I'm here because, like I said, His Excellency summoned me."

He typed her name into the computer and searched through the list of expected invitees. Eclipse knew he was taking his good old time, since she watched her name pass by several times, but she bit her lip and waited. Amy grinned from the other side of the gate and Axl tried to look nonchalantly around the courtyard. Eventually, Elite Steven decided to tap on her name and nod her toward the fortress. She scowled at him before taking off with long strides. Amy shot him a wink that Axl didn't miss. He'd talk to Steven later and Steven would regret it.

Eclipse led her two companions into the dark fortress, opening the doors for herself and letting them swing shut so the other two had to catch them or get beamed in the head. She was obviously stifling her bad mood already. It was just a bad time for Erican to pop out from behind one of the massive metal pillars and scare her. She didn't scream, but she did jump and instinctively punch him in the face. Axl snorted and then burst into laughter as a mortified Eclipse turned red with anger.

"Dammit, Erican!" she snapped crossly. "What the hell?"

Her brother had both his hands cupped over his nose, so he caught most of the blood, but several drips were still making their way out.

"Hello to you too, Eclipse." His muffled voice responded. "Father is up in his library and he wanted me to tell you and send you to him. Also thought I'd let you know that this doesn't seem like a normal meeting. You haven't done anything recently, have you?"

"Not that I know of." Eclipse frowned. "The Emilies have just been patrolling as guardsmen in Holux. Maybe he wants us to handle Voidanuar this year?"

"Nah, he already assigned the Logans to that." Erican shook his head, finally removing his hands and just wiping away the blood on his sleeves while they talked. "Worse yet, he placed us under Alan's command for the whole damn thing. I'm really hoping he isn't planning on making that a permanent set-up. Alan would make an absolute shite Logan."

"He would." Eclipse nodded vaguely, pulling her healer out of its holster and handing it to Erican. "Here, fix your damn nose. I'll head up and see what he wants and then grab it on my way back out."

"Mk. Have fun." Her brother grinned mischievously.

"Right." She muttered.

Axl, Amy, and Eclipse made it the rest of the way to the library without any other interruptions. It was on the top floor of the fortress, so they had to leap up several hundred steps, but all of them were used to the physical activity. Two Elite stood outside the library door and demanded that Eclipse give them her name and request for entry again, despite letting Amy and Axl through with a nod. She didn't even bother to argue this time and just did as she was told. Soon enough, the three of them were standing at attention right inside the door as Victor and Acre whispered together, hunched over a map on the only desk in sight. Victor finally glanced up.

"For individuals who can teleport," he began, keeping his lips pursed as well as he could. "it took you all a long time to get here."

"We were delayed at the gate and the door, Your Excellency." Eclipse bowed stiffly and hid the anger in her voice quite well, Axl thought.

"Why?" Victor demanded.

"I had to sign in."

The promontory nodded slowly, knowing she hated being singled out for menial tasks like that, but unsure of how to change it without showing her favoritism. Instead, he let the whole thing slide and waved the three of them over to the desk, pointing out something for them to look at.

"General, we believe it is finally time to progress further into the south." He explained, his finger tapping Dormiat. "And I think this would be an excellent chance for you to prove the worth of your series."

Eclipse raised her eyebrow and looked down at Dormiat. It was the smallest of the southern kingdoms, sitting between Central Liberty and what used to be Arcane. The Emilies hadn't been combat tested, yet. Mainly, they had been handling small inconveniences Victor had. So, it made sense that Victor would start them on a lesser threat. Of course, Dormatians were also known for their prowess in battle and they were proud of their seemingly undefeatable army. The army wasn't run by the government, instead that power fell to their religion. The monasteries were the real powerhouses, training their people in martial arts as a form of meditation. Eclipse had studied their culture for a while, finding it intriguing.

The Dormatians believed that war was a religious experience only meant for those who had been enlightened enough to be deemed worthy of killing in the name of their god. That meant they accepted both men and women, trained them day and night, and then once their hair reached a certain length, it was said that the Ancient considered them her tools on Asylum. Religion could convince people to fight a thousand times stronger than fear. Their eternal souls were linked to their actions on the battlefield, so they didn't often let a defeat stand without a violent and devastating rebuttal. Still, Eclipse knew her business.

"When do we start?" she asked, looking back up at Victor, who raised both his eyebrows.

"Well, I would think you'd like to start by asking what is expected of you." He hinted darkly.

Her brow furrowed and she glanced between Victor and Acre.

"Is this *not* a Cleansing?" she replied very slowly and deliberately.

She didn't want to sound like she was questioning her father, since that violated their deal, but she was pretty sure she already knew what was expected of her and the Emilies. Cleansings were easily one of the most-taught tactics in Victor's army.

"It is." Her father retorted, just as carefully. "But there are ways I prefer my Cleansings done. You should be concerning yourself with those preferences, Eclipse."

"Of course, Your Excellency." She answered, straightening back up to attention. "Whatever you desire, we will do to perfection. What are your commands?"

Victor nodded approval and hid a smile in a glance to Acre, who rolled his eyes. Then, the promontory turned back to his daughter and began his explanation.

"Very well, Eclipse. I'm sure, by now, you know that our greatest asset is fear. Fear controls our own people and fear prevents our enemies from striking. Of course, with any amount of fear, you have to have balance between it and what appears to be mercy. As such, when I attack a new country, it matters how it is done. It's not just about winning, General. I expect greater things from your corps, *especially* your corps. You've been quite an expensive lot to deal with."

Eclipse nodded, still waiting to hear something she didn't know yet. Maybe Victor had specifics in mind and he was slowly getting to them, in his very own long, drawn-out way. She waited patiently, despite every second stuck listening to him feeling like daggers scraping along ice.

"So," Victor continued after her nod. "I'd like to know how you would accomplish all of that in Dormiat. If I approve of your plan, you will be free to begin enacting it right after Voidanuar. If not, Amy will formulate the Emilies's battle strategy."

Eclipse didn't even need to glance over at her Colonel to know she sneered her direction. Of course, Amy didn't think Eclipse would have a plan formulated quick enough to satisfy Victor. Axl knew better. Eclipse talked about Dormiat a lot over the past month. She had already guessed that it would be Victor's next target and she had been studying for this moment. She had every single book, scroll, or note that Acre could scarf up for her sitting on her nightstand at this very second. Not that she knew Victor was going to ask for her opinion, she just wanted to be prepared if he was vague on his orders. Having to voice her strategy out loud made her blood turn to ice. What if she was wrong? What if he hated it and gave Amy control over their mission instead? Axl watched the color drain from her face as she forced her lips to reply with as much steady confidence as she could muster.

"First, I would destabilize their government. Since they use a very basic feudal system, that would be simple enough. You take out the 1,074 lords and their entire courts, the commoners would begin to panic and turn to the monasteries both for religious guidance and military protection. You take out the highest-ranking monks at each monastery, then the rest of the soldiers will be as lost and confused as the commoners."

"This sounds like it would take too long." Victor warned her impatiently. "I want them defeated in three years or less."

"Oh, I could do all that in one night." Eclipse waved him off. "The idea is to cause nation-wide panic, right? If I spread it out too long, people would expect where I was going to hit next. Take it all away in one night and no one knows how to react."

Victor raised both his eyebrows, but let her continue without interrupting for now.

"Once the government toppled, commoners and soldiers alike would either defect, allowing you to show mercy, or march to the only fief that wasn't affected, thinking it was somehow protected from us."

"I thought your plan was to kill everyone in one night?" Amy snapped, trying to poke holes in everything she heard.

Eclipse closed her eyes and rolled them so no one saw, but she answered calmly.

"I said I'd kill all the lords, Colonel. Keep up. I'd leave the king and his entire court alone. That way, *like I was saying*, every Dormatian would move toward the capital, thinking it was safe from us. With all their forces congregated, the king will most likely order a pre-emptive strike on Chrosia's southern border, since that's what his religion teaches, which the Emilies will be there to stop dead in its tracks. Then, we would spend a few months attacking along all the borders of Dormiat to push them together even more, and catch those who are too proud to run or switch sides. After a year or so, the entire population will be huddled together at the king's capital, firmly believing they are safe there. That's when we wipe them all out in one attack. It shouldn't take more than one year," Eclipse told Victor, before quickly adding. "unless you want it to, Your Excellency."

Acre had his lips pursed to keep from grinning as he and Victor focused on the map intently. The promontory was rubbing his chin, deep in thought. The strategy was sound, maybe brilliant, but he wasn't willing to admit it, yet. And he certainly wasn't going to say anything in front of people. Eclipse lifted her foot and scratched the back of her opposite calf. She didn't like these long silences. Victor didn't really yell at her anymore, but she always expected him to, still. And as embarrassed as she was that Erican made her jump earlier, she hated it far more when Victor startled her. Normally, because he made fun of her afterward every time he did. Her newest goal was never being startled by jump-scares. It was proving harder than she originally thought, though. Finally, Victor sighed.

"I like it." He mused, as if he was just as surprised as everyone else in the room. "I'm giving you the three years, anyway, because the longer you can let people stew in their fear, the better, but you may start enacting your plan the day after Voidanuar. You will have till the Voidanuar after your 16th birthday to accomplish the Cleansing. I'm assuming you will be the telepath who wipes out the government officials next week?"

"I wouldn't trust anyone else with the task." Eclipse nodded. "I like to make sure shite is done right."

Victor let the corner of his mouth curl upward in amusement and then nodded toward Axl.

"I'll leave that to you, then, but since this is your first real assignment, I'm going to have Axl tag along with the Emilies wherever you go. He will be reporting directly to me."

"I will?" Axl raised an eyebrow suspiciously, before remembering his manners. "Your Excellency?"

"Yeah." Eclipse grimaced at the Elite before turning back to Victor. "Am I getting punished for something, Milord?"

Despite wanting to burst into laughter at Axl's sudden indignation, Victor kept a straight face.

"Is there anything you deserve to be punished for, General?" he asked complacently, glancing out the top of his eyes at his daughter.

"Not that I'm aware of, Your Excellency." She responded. "That's why I was asking, just to make sure."

Victor nodded curtly.

"Then, in that case, no. It's not a punishment, just a precaution. You never know how a unit will do in their first battle. Axl is just going to be my eyes and ears. You can consider him a glorified messenger if you'd like."

And she had at first, Axl grinned as he remembered their first few months on the march. He refused to call her 'Eclipse', opting for 'General' instead, out of respect. She did not appreciate it. It took her so long to convince him to stop calling her 'princess' when they were kids, that she considered it a horrible regression. As such, she ordered the Emilies to call him 'Elitist Peraxlkine Mop-top' every single time they addressed him. It got old incredibly fast. About two months after she single-handedly destroyed the Dormatian government, Axl finally broke and asked what it would take to drop the titles and go back to just using their names. Her response was diabolical.

She told him she would drop all of it and redact her orders if he got on his knees and begged her in front of the women. He refused. Another month later, he finally broke and fell to his knees, begging as loud as he could, in front of all the Emilies. Eclipse shrugged and changed her orders, then berated him for 'being so dramatic'. The entire thing was just a ploy to embarrass him, or punish him, and it worked on both counts. Ever since then, though, it had just been 'Eclipse' and 'Axl'.

Axl could hear the massive party the Emilies were throwing long before he reached their camp. They had settled down just a few miles outside the capital city of Dormiat, in preparation for this last battle. With the Dormatians all but extinct, and Victor's orders carried out to perfection, the telepaths were all ready to begin the ride home tomorrow. As such, this was one of their last nights to party outside of Victor's reach. He was sure they were all desperately trying to get drunk and enjoying their time together.

*The singing and dancing might be a bit over the top.* he mused as he entered the camp. His brow furrowed curiously as he watched the girls interact. They seemed exceptionally..... close. He catalogued it in the back of his mind, winked at Amber when she waved at him, and continued toward Eclipse's tent. She had set up a small distance from the rest of the Emilies so it would be easier for all of them to find her if they needed her. Axl's bemused grin vanished when he heard the sound of Amy yelling at her general. He frowned. She couldn't be happy with Eclipse's actions today. He slipped through the flaps to Eclipse's tent just in time to prove himself right.

"You had no right to take all the glory from the corps!" Amy screamed at Eclipse, who calmly poured herself a mug of something before responding.

"Amy, there is no glory in slaughtering a flock of sheep. I fail to see why a keep full of women and children holds any either. Go celebrate. We set out for Holux tomorrow."

The blonde growled and huffily stomped out of the tent, jamming her shoulder into Axl on her way. He didn't even flinch. Axl waited for Amy to leave before zipping the tent closed behind her and turning back to face

Eclipse. She wasn't looking at him, instead opting to lean on her wooden dresser with both hands so her head could droop all the way down to her chest. Axl didn't have to see her face to know how miserable she felt. Every once in while, she would lift one hand to sip tentatively at her drink. Axl stepped away from the door and cleared his throat. With Amy gone, he could finally ask Eclipse about the keep.

"Why *did* you do it?" he finally asked quietly.

Eclipse drained her mug in one gulp and ignored him while she poured another. It had been a long day and she just wanted it to end without more drama. She decided to pull rank to make sure that happened.

"My decisions are my own and you have no right to question them, Axl." She replied darkly.

He sighed audibly and Eclipse grit her teeth. She knew he was rolling his eyes dramatically behind her back. And she knew he wasn't about to let this go and leave her in peace. They had spent too much time together for that. Victor had sent Axl as a backup plan in case Eclipse failed, but of course, she did incredibly well, so he didn't have much of a job. Instead, she and him had become friends and a strong force on the battlefield. Then this past year, they spent their time together fighting and barking at each other, out of absolutely nowhere. Eclipse didn't want that right now. She turned around and leaned back on her dresser so she could make eye contact with him, hoping that would help him understand that she didn't want to talk about this. Instead, Axl's brow furrowed slightly.

"Are you alright, Eclipse?" he stepped cautiously toward her

Eclipse scoffed and put her mug back on the dresser behind her.

"I'm fine." she snapped, folding her arms defensively. "I just finished a war for Victor. I successfully defeated an entire nation with 500 women. I should be on top of the damn world."

"But...." he pressed.

"Don't do that, Axl."

"What?" he shrugged.

"That!" she moaned. "That whole digging around for information thing you do. You already know what I did, and you must know I don't want to talk about it. What do you want me to say? That I disagree with my orders and regret my oath to Victor? Because that is just a great way to get killed."

"Only if someone hears you." he said softly, stepping toward her again.

"Yes, so I should just sit here and talk to one of Victor's Elite about it." she replied bitterly.

He cocked his head to the side and stared at her like a hurt puppy.

"That's not fair, Eclipse." he whined. "Have I *ever* told Victor something you said to me in confidence?"

"I don't know." Eclipse squinted suspiciously at him and kept her voice taut and dry. "Have you?"

Axl grit his teeth and tried to stay calm.

"You know *damn* well that I wouldn't betray you to Victor! You're just lashing out at me because you don't want to face the truth about yourself. About what you just did in that keep!"

"Axl, leave me alone." she warned hoarsely, but it was too late, he was on a roll.

"And let's just skip the fact that Amy has been pestering you about it ever since and you're scared she *will* get you in trouble with Victor."

"Get out!" she yelled, pushing him slightly, but not enough to make him move.

"And let's not forget that today is your 16th birthday and you always turn into a bitch on your birthday----"

Eclipse pushed him hard this time. If he hadn't grabbed her upper arms, he would've fallen out of the tent flaps into a heap, most likely taking the whole tent with him. As it was, she tore herself out of his hands and punched him in the jaw instead. Axl turned his head with the force of it and spat blood out of his mouth. She gulped slightly when he turned back to glare at her. They had been fighting a lot recently and it always ended with them hitting each other till one of them gave up. She knew what was coming. Axl drove his own fist right back into her face and she spun and fell against her dresser behind her. Tears stung her eyes, but didn't drop as she stayed bent over it for a moment, then pushed off into a spinning kick. He dodged it, knowing every single move she used in combat. They had been fighting side by side in Dormiat for almost three years.

Axl easily kicked Eclipse's knee out and she gasped slightly as she fell, but she was just as quick to recover and delivered a solid punch to his femoral artery. His leg buckled. He only stumbled back one step, but it was enough for her to get back on her feet. He swung his fist at her while regaining his balance and she ducked under it before stomping on his foot and jerking her elbow up, so it connected with his chin. Axl knew that her next move would be to shove him out of the tent, so he took a chance and wrapped his arms as tightly as he could around her stomach. Through a bit of dumb luck, he managed to encase both her arms against her torso and keep them there. She kicked her feet out in front of her and tried to wriggle away, but Axl held tight with everything he had.

"Lemme go!!!" she screeched vehemently.

Eclipse jerked back and forth with all of her might, just trying to escape his arms, but Axl held on until she let out an enraged scream that shook the tent. If anyone walked in on them in this position, it could easily be misconstrued, so he released her with a shove that allowed her to stumble forward and catch herself on the dresser again. She banged her palms off of it and turned back around with her fists clenched. Axl held up both of his hands.

"Stop!" he ordered, shaking his hands slightly. "Just stop it, Eclipse!"

"Or what?" she sobbed, trying not to let tears fall. "What are you going to do?"

They both stood staring at each other, panting slightly after their scuffle and waiting for the other one to move. Axl thought about just leaving her alone. Instead, he forced himself to calm down enough to talk rather than yell. He was tired of fighting, but he just *had* to know why.

"What the hell is this?" he demanded angrily of her. "We got along just fine for two years and then this past one, we've been at each other's throats more than the Dormatians! What happened to us, Eclipse? I thought we were supposed to be friends!"

"Well, you thought wrong!" she yelled, barely keeping her tears back. "I don't know what happened, but apparently we aren't friends. I guess we never were!"

Axl scoffed and rolled his eyes to the side, resisting the urge to bring up all the times he ever helped her. Instead, he threw both hands into the air in defeat before running them both over his head and through his hair. Eclipse felt a ball of guilt building in her stomach before he even opened his mouth, but she stayed angry to avoid it.

"Fine by me, *princess*!!" he snarled, spinning around and unzipping the tent.

The zipper got stuck on the canvas and he angrily jerked it around until it came loose, growling and cussing. Then, he turned back to look at her.

"Fine!" he repeated, as if she had said anything since his last one.

"Fine!" she tossed her shoulders up in a furious shrug.

"FINE!"

Axl stomped away before Eclipse could say it again and have the final word. Eclipse stood staring at the flaps to her tent as they blew in the breeze with her fists clenched and her teeth grit. She hated everything that just happened. She hated it every time it happened, but she could never stop it. Axl infuriated her! He didn't need to be such a know-it-all asshole all of the time. She bet he was even going to storm back in here after a few minutes, just so he could rub her face in the fact that he walked away first.

She wasn't entirely wrong. Axl did suddenly burst back through her tent door, turning around to instantly zip it closed behind him. She only caught a glimpse of his face, but it worried her. He didn't look angry anymore. He had stormed out, desperately trying to figure out why he and Eclipse would start fighting a year ago after getting along so well before then and why neither of them seemed able to control themselves around the other. He made it about ten steps before he suddenly figured it out. Unfortunately, he wasn't sure she would agree with him, so he stared at the zipper a long time before mustering the courage to move.

Axl spun around and drew up to Eclipse with one long stride. His right hand flattened on her lower back and his left gripped the back of her head. He pulled her into a kiss, ignoring her grunt of surprise. Her palms immediately fought to push his chest away and her eyes widened into moons, but the struggle didn't last long. She didn't really kiss back, just stood there and stared at him awkwardly as he sucked on her lower lip. It was maybe the most uncomfortable, ten second kiss either of them could imagine. Then, he pulled away and pushed her backwards, staring directly into her still-shocked eyes. It was her move now, but he had always known, deep inside, that he would have to make the first one. He knew they were close, that they cared a great deal about each other. This kiss was just a gamble that their recent tension was due to both of them finally being old enough to understand what was happening between them, what they really wanted. Eclipse just stood there and stared at him, her mouth moving up and down silently as she fought for a response. Axl waited several minutes and when nothing happened, he got embarrassed and turned to leave.

"Happy Birthday, Eclipse." he mumbled miserably.

She finally dove toward him and caught his arm before he opened the tent again. Eclipse spun him around and he immediately held her waist with both hands as her hands gripped either side of his face. She kissed him this time, and they didn't stop for several minutes. Her lips moved in synchrony with his until neither of them could breathe. Then she pushed away again and gasped for air. Conflict twisted her face in horror. She couldn't even bear to look at Axl. She spun and braced both her hands on the dresser behind her. Even that couldn't hide the rapid rise and fall of her shoulders as she fought to control whatever was happening inside her right now. Axl had stumbled backward with that last kiss and couldn't move since it ended. He just stared at her back, waiting. For what, he wasn't sure.

"I need you to leave." Eclipse finally choked out through the pounding in her chest and ears.

She couldn't even hear the words she spoke and almost wished they weren't the ones she was thinking. Leave? She didn't want him to leave! She wanted him to come up, spin her around and smash his face into hers again. But deep down, she knew. This was one of those things that just couldn't happen. That never should have happened. She needed it to go away.

"Yeah........" Axl replied breathlessly, the pain showing on his face when she couldn't even turn to look at him. "........ of course........ I'll leave."

He stumbled out of the tent, leaving Eclipse alone with an array of emotions she obviously didn't understand. Her face was pale, blotchy, and bright red, all at the same time. Her mind couldn't even force itself to ask what just happened. It was too busy trying to crush the muscles bouncing around in her chest and making her ribs ache. She seemed unable to catch her breath and jumped violently when something rustled the tent flaps behind her. She spun around with sword in hand.

"Dammit, Adamere!"

Eclipse sheathed her sword and clutched at her chest as the massive kiladrt trotted into the tent and stretched, yawning before curling up in a ball on the ground. A couple months after she was promoted to general, Shane had presented her with the kiladrt cub. At the time, he was only six weeks old, but already the size of a large dog. Now he was 5 years old and a ferocious ally to her. He never left her side for long. Eclipse scratched his ears mindlessly and then walked over to her cot. She sat down on the edge of it, still gasping and shivering like she just wasn't sure what happened.

The tent flaps rippled again after several minutes and she jumped back up to her feet as Axl zipped them shut and began pacing back and forth in her tent, careful not to disturb Adamere. The two of them had grown very fond of each other since the days when he would growl at Axl every time he was within earshot. Adamere didn't even bother to look up at the visitor. Eclipse fiddled with her fingers, staring intently at them, and listened to his desperate footsteps. She flinched slightly when they finally stopped, and his voice sliced through the silence.

"You kissed me!" he cried, before jolting at his own volume and lowering it to a hiss. "Like I know I kissed you first; and that was basically exactly what I thought it would be! I kissed you and you were in absolute shock and I feared for my life because I totally thought you were going to stab me--- I get all that. Bu-bu-but then *you* kissed *me*!!! I didn't expect that!! I thought I'd kiss you and you'd kick me out because you were completely disgusted by me and honestly thought you'd kill me, like I said, but NO! You grabbed my face and kissed me right back with eyes closed and everything and honestly that scares the living shite out of me because I don't know what to do with that. Obviously we need to talk about it because I don't even know how I am supposed to act around you and I think you need to know how to act around me and maybe you don't even want to see me ever again in any way an----"

"STOP TALKING!" Eclipse suddenly screeched, holding both her hands out in front of her.

Axl hadn't so much as taken a breath since he started talking and his incessant, rapid babbles were making the entire situation worse. He clapped both his hands over his mouth in response to her and nodded fervently, realizing just how much had spouted out without him realizing it. They stood in silence, staring at each other, both on the verge of hyperventilation.

"We..... *do* need to figure this out." Eclipse finally led slowly as Axl nodded emphatically in response, not daring to remove his hands from his mouth. "Obviously...... none of this was supposed to happen. We head back north tomorrow morning and this can't..... this just can*not* ever be something..... something we even *remember*, much less actually discuss, in Holux. I....... I think we just need to accept a version of tonight where this didn't happen. At all. None of it. None of this happened."

She finished so definitively that Adamere did raise his head. His human friend normally only spoke with so much command when she was about to enter into battle. He glanced curiously over to the only other human in the tent and cocked his head to the side. Were the two of them going to fight again? Axl's hands slowly dropped to his sides, and he shifted his feet in the dirt. He looked dejected, but forced himself to nod along with whatever she wanted.

"That....." he hesitated sadly. "..... would be the smartest thing to do. I'll go back to my tent and you will never hear about this again, since that is what you want. That *is* what you want, right?"

"It's the only way this can go." She whispered guiltily.

Eclipse watched him sulk over to the tent flaps and felt like she might throw up. He unzipped them and paused before leaving, turning around one more time.

"I....." he paused and then sighed. "I think I'm going to head out tonight, General. That should give us both some time apart to..... figure.... things.... out."

Axl bowed slightly and left her alone again. Eclipse plopped down on her cot and stared straight up at the inside of her tent. Her temples pulsed furiously with each gulp she took, and her skin felt numb and achy. She walked over to her dresser and poured another drink with shaky hands. It took her a few minutes to drain it, she wasn't sure how long. Then she spent some time cleaning and sharpening her weapons. Then brushing Adamere, then drinking, then back on her cot, where she started. Eclipse had no idea how long this went on. Time felt like a disillusioned concept as her mind refused to think about what happened this night.

Then, Eclipse suddenly stood up and deliberately walked out of her tent. It was the middle of the night. Only the moons and stars rested in the sky. She glanced at them for a few minutes before hesitantly taking her first steps away from the tent. The Emilies were all asleep by this time, either exhausted from the day or their celebration after the day. Still, she carefully kept her profile low, blending into shadows and freezing at the slightest noise. Soon enough, Eclipse made it to where Axl's tent had been pitched, even farther from all the other girls' tents than her own. She glanced around.

There was nothing. He hadn't left a single sign of his camp behind. She doubted she would even be able to find where he had driven the stakes at this point. Eclipse stared at the blank plot of land before her and tried to understand what she was feeling. It was like she hadn't believed he would go. Like she knew without a doubt that he was going to be here when she arrived, grinning at her for falling into some sort of trap. It was a long time before she turned to leave. And even then, she glanced back one more time before heading back to her tent.

She didn't make it. She was close, when her eyes caught a quick glance of something unusual. Eclipse stopped sneaking around and walked up to the campfire the corps had been using for a couple nights now. There were felled logs around the large ring of stones that contained their fire pit, but her target wasn't sitting on one of them. Instead, she sat in front of the log, leaning her back and neck against it as she stared straight up. Eclipse quietly sat down beside her. The red head didn't even startle.

"General." She said calmly, with a nod. "I thought you would be asleep by now, honestly, but no. You don't sleep till all of us are out, do you?"

"Sometimes it takes even longer. Why are *you* still up, Amber?"

The woman grinned.

"A sick obsession with the stars, I suppose." She chuckled. "I like to stare blindly into them like a damned idiot."

The corner of Eclipse's mouth twitched up and she settled down further so she could lean her head back like Amber's. They both stared up at the billions of stars in silence. Eclipse had always liked Amber. She reminded her of Erican, with her bright red locks and freckled face. Plus, she had a sense of humor to match, just like the Monohue boy.

"That one group of stars bears an uncanny resemblance to Adamere." Amber suddenly mused after several minutes, pointing to where she meant.

Eclipse snorted, her grin growing slightly. She didn't answer, but let Amber continue.

"And that one looks like a dragon."

The general barely glanced at it.

"And that one?" Amber giggled. "That one looks *exactly* like a man's favorite organ."

Eclipse frowned and looked where Amber was pointing. She didn't see anything in the stars.

"How would you know that?" she demanded, more curious than angry.

"Oh, come on, General." Amber rolling to face the other girl with a mischievous grin. "You don't *actually* think you command 500 virgins, do you?"

"I would like to believe so!" Eclipse scoffed nervously. "I shouldn't have to remind you all of Victor's orders on the subject. You mean to tell me, you *all* ignore his commands?"

"On that one thing?" Amber snorted. "Yes. Most of us. No one should have command over a woman's body but that woman herself. Don't worry. We are all very careful. I'm surprised you haven't tried anything, yet. I mean, you have a whole house to yourself. We all still share a barracks. I wouldn't know what sex in a bed feels like, honestly. How shite is that for a

23-year-old to say?"

Eclipse just shook her head, unable to even hold a conversation on the subject for several minutes. She could see where Amber was coming from, but if any member of her series were ever caught, it would be the end of them and, quite possibly, her. Victor wouldn't stand for it and she had an oath to abstain from all the things he didn't stand for. Axl painfully reminded her of that mere hours ago.

"I couldn't." she finally answered, still shaking her head. "I wouldn't even know where to start or what I was doing. And besides, I never know how many spies are watching me and I can't risk Victor finding out."

"Oh, but the risk is half the fun!" Amber rolled onto her back again. "Dodging guards and risking everything for one night of pleasure....... the feeling is immeasurable."

"I certainly hope none of you purposely engage in more risk than absolutely necessary." Eclipse scolded. "It's not just about you individually, after all. The entire series could be implicated and punished if even one of you got caught. I won't tell you all what to do with your own bodies, but I truly wish you'd respect each other enough to..... abstain. At least a bit."

Amber sighed and shook her head with a mischievous grin working its way onto her face.

"And what kind of life would that be, General?" she questioned after a moment. "Always doing exactly what you are told, never daring to think for yourself or cross any lines, submitting to every whim of men placed over you by sheer happenstance. Who could live like that?"

"I live like that." Eclipse responded quietly and Amber shot her a glance of pity before responding.

"You think more for yourself than you are given credit for. What you did today.... taking on the burden of slaughtering so many innocents for our sake..... that wasn't something you were ordered to do. It was something you did to protect us. I'm terribly sorry you had to face that alone, General. If it's any consolation, we would have all done it for you, had you not given us the order to remain back."

Eclipse flashed a slight grin at Amber before rising to her feet and stretching. She longingly looked once more to the constellation that reflected her precious Adamere and then responded.

"My consolation is knowing none of you were involved. And knowing you are all talented enough to avoid capture during your nighttime escapades so far. I'm going to pretend that I still don't know, because if I did, I would have to tell Victor. It's part of my oath to him. But if I don't know something, how could I possibly divulge it to my father? Goodnight, Amber. Be sure to get some sleep before our journey home tomorrow."

The girl on the ground gave a half-hearted salute with a wide grin, knowing her general would never breathe a word to the promontory about their discussion tonight. Eclipse nodded back and returned to her tent, where Adamere barely bothered to glance up at her, as close to sleep as he was. She kicked off her boots and scratched his head before collapsing back into her cot. Her mind inexplicably locked on Axl. She frowned. He was gone. Their time together, whatever it was, was now over. She needed to forget him as much as her conversation with Amber. Yet there he was, in her head, making jokes, fighting expertly beside her for three years. Honestly, Eclipse wasn't sure she wanted to forget him. There was something about him. She could hear his voice in her mind and see him laughing while flipping his messy hair out of his eyes. Her brain seemed desperate to focus on his lips. Every move they made.

Eclipse groaned and opened her eyes again. She wasn't going to get sleep tonight, apparently. She rose from her bed and got yet another drink, despite it not actually helping with her nerves at all. Enhanced individuals couldn't get drunk. Their metabolism processed the alcohol too fast. More often than not, they just ended up dangerously dehydrated and exhausted. She never felt any different at all. It was more of a comfort habit. Still, there was no comfort in her mug tonight. She even grimaced at the liquid, like it had lost its flavor in the past hour, somehow.

There was a gentle knock on her tent pole and she gulped down the alcohol in her mouth before choking out 'enter'. Adamere looked up at her in concern as she continued to cough, but she waved him off as the tent flaps opened and someone entered. She covered her mouth and turned to greet them.

"What is it…… *Axl?*" she coughed.

She thought he was gone! It never occurred to her that he might be the mysterious knock at her tent so late at night, not after he said he was leaving for good!! She turned to face the dresser and continued to fight her lungs and stifle her chokes as he explained himself.

"I wanted to be sure that my report to Victor was accurate. So, I need to know whether your corps plans on riding back to Holux or teleporting back…… General."

"We can't very well leave 500 of Victor's horses in Dormiat." Eclipse answered, not meaning to be derogatory, but sounding very so anyway. "Obviously, we will have to ride."

"I just wanted to be sure, General." He replied dryly, picking up on her accidental tone and feeling frustrated by it. "If there is nothing else, I'll take my leave."

She heard his heels snap together before he bowed and Eclipse felt like this was her last chance. For what, she wasn't sure, but it nagged at her. With an inward groan, she turned around and faced him.

"Axl?" she called with a quivering voice, just before he exited the tent.

The Elite turned back and furrowed his brow.

"Yes, General?"

She waved dismissively at him in frustration.

"Drop the whole.... General..... thing. Just for a moment. It makes me feel...... sick...... to my stomach. Not painfully, but like a dull ache."

"That was not my intention, but very well." Axl replied slowly. "What do you need?"

"I feel like we are not being thorough." She hesitated, unsure how to say what she was thinking since she didn't know what it even was, yet. "Like I need to know..... more about..... earlier...... if you'd let me ask."

Axl kept his brow furrowed and his hands folded behind his back in parade rest. His rigid form was bothering her, and she didn't know why, but his stoic tone was worse.

"What did you want to ask?"

Eclipse gulped. She hadn't actually thought of a question yet. Still, one seemed ever present on her mind.

"Why?" she asked, trembling. "Why did you.... erm..... do that..... in the first place?"

Axl looked directly into her eyes for a long time, his face not changing from its emotionally masked state in the slightest. Eclipse could feel her heartbeat racing, but refused to show any more emotion than he was, so she just stood staring like an idiot. The silence and suspense were painful for them both as one fought to be patient and the other fought to find the exact words he wanted.

"That... question.... would require me to be incredibly...... vulnerable." he answered meaningfully, hoping she let it go at that.

"And......" Eclipse drawled. "you feel like you are incapable of that?"

"Yes." Axl said instantly.

"Why?" she demanded, her face reddening.

Axl looked down and ran his hands through his hair before folding them back behind him. Adamere was once again glancing back and forth between the two humans in puzzled amusement. Finally, the Elite had his answer and let his sorrowful eyes meet Eclipse's again.

"Because that feeling you have when I call you 'General'?" he groaned. "Is the same, sick, feeling I have every second I spend listening to you treat this like nothing more than some.... sort of..... everyday, official business. I kissed you for reasons that don't matter if you just want me out of your life. And I really don't want to talk about it anymore if you are going to treat me like...... like...... like....."

"Like *what*?" Eclipse snarled far more angrily than she meant to.

Axl's face softened painfully as he snorted in disbelief, shaking his head at her.

"Like just another burden in your life that you have to impatiently put up with." he answered quietly. "Good night..... General."

And just like that he turned to leave again. And Eclipse let him, yet again, even though her chest screamed at her to cry out after him. He didn't pause and look back this time, but zipped the tent closed without hesitation. Eclipse was left alone in her tent again, feeling the dirt and grass between her toes as they flexed uncomfortably over and over. That had to be the last time Axl stormed in tonight. Whatever chance she had to say anything meaningful was lost now. She might as well try to get some sleep before the Emilies packed up their gear and rode north in a few hours. They only had till Voidanuar this year to make it home. She refused to be late, no matter what did or did not happen between her and Victor's Elite.

Eclipse removed all of her weapons and stacked them against the dresser. She wouldn't be taking the furniture in her tent home with her. They were all things the Emilies confiscated from Dormatian homes over the time they stayed here. They all did it. Eclipse settled for a dresser and all the mead she could find. Other women found trinkets they wanted to keep as mementos or delicacies they couldn't find in Chrosia. She allowed them to take whatever they willed and do whatever they wanted. They were going to be held hostage back in the dank, dark city of Holux soon enough. They deserved some freedom.

Her thoughts were interrupted by yet another ruckus coming from the entrance to her tent. She froze in her steps and hopefully stared through the zipper as it opened yet again. Axl burst back through and charged Eclipse fast with his long strides. She was so caught off guard that she didn't get a single word out before he swooped her up and sat her on the top of her dresser. Then, his lips connected with hers.

She didn't fight it this time, even letting his rough hands grip either side of her face to keep their lips pressed together. That feeling built back up in her stomach and chest. She clenched her eyes and held the front of his hauberk tight in both fists so she could engage deeper in the kiss with him. It was the longest one yet. Eclipse wasn't sure if she was going to throw up or scream. It ended up being nothing more than a delighted moan vibrating in the back of her throat. Axl kissed her till he couldn't breathe and pulled back slightly, forcing her to look him in the eyes as he gripped her chin and lifted it.

"I kissed you...." He gasped, pausing intermittently to press his lips against hers between his explanation. "... because I'm obsessed with you... ...... and because you're the only thing I can think about anymore....... because when I'm near you....... my blood boils..... and my stomach churns...... and my chest aches........ because every second I'm *not* with you physically hurts......... and because I want, no I need you. I *desperately* need you, Eclipse........ right now........ or never."

His voice softened toward the end, as he leaned his forehead into hers and waited for her response. She was shaking, gasping for air and clenching her eyes shut as every inch of her being felt conflicted against itself. Her hands slowly braced on his chest and gave the slightest push, to which he responded by stepping away from her and giving her space. She glanced around the tent in confusion as though she didn't believe her own hands did that. She didn't want space!! She wanted him right back where he was a second ago. Her mind and heart raced against each other to force a decision and her lip quivered.

"Eclipse." He prodded, gently, but firmly.

Her eyes locked on his with another desperate gasp for air.

"I kissed you because I want more than friendship and soo much more than just a kiss, even. And if you can *honestly* say you don't want the same thing, I'll leave and never bother you again. But if you are holding back because of Victor, or duty, or anything beyond your own desire, right here, right now, then you need to tell me. Because the only thing that's going to stop me right now is *you* saying no. Because *you* don't want me inside you."

Eclipse felt like her entire body was on fire. *Inside me? That's where this is going? Of course, it is!* She scolded herself. Her palms sweat and itched as she fought to figure out the feelings torrenting through her body like a hurricane. Her skin felt cold and hot all at once. Her head felt like she was going to scream and pass out. Her chest felt like it was going to explode. Instead, she just sat, sick to her stomach that he was so far away still, and waited till she could force the words out of her trembling lips.

"I'm not saying no." She croaked, and Axl stepped back up between her legs and pressed his forehead back to hers.

She tilted her head, so their lips brushed against each other again, but he didn't dive back in the way he had before. Instead, he gently kissed her lips a couple times and moved over to just under her ear so he could whisper to her.

"Then, what are you saying, Beautiful?"

Her gut twisted with that simple action alone. How was she supposed to make it through everything else? Axl kept kissing the side of her neck, drawing feelings out of her she didn't know existed. His hand slid up her shirt and laid trembling on her side. It was warm and safe, but Eclipse still didn't know what she was supposed to say. Axl waited patiently, though he didn't stop being the biggest distraction she ever had to face. His lips sucked gently on her neck, his right hand held her side and his left hand stroked between her legs, all of it waiting on her.

Eclipse finally shifted her head, so their foreheads pressed against each other again. And even though she could barely breathe, she opened her eyes and stared directly into his expectant ones.

"I want you, too, Axl." She whispered, almost inaudibly. "Right now."

His mouth twisted into a smile, and he pressed his lips back into hers. After a moment, he moved the tip of his tongue firmly between her lips and, even though she didn't realize this was part of kissing, she let it pass. It danced around in her mouth, leaving her with an unforgettable taste when he finally pulled away to help her undress.

They couldn't keep their hands off each other. Of course, it was just a lot of confused making out and groping for a long time, neither really sure how this all worked. They stayed at the bookshelf for a while, then Eclipse stood up and they stumbled around the tent trying to strip the other person and not realizing how many layers they each wore. Axl eventually swiped her feet out from under her when he had finally gotten her down to her tank top. She fell onto her back on her cot with a slight huff of surprise when he came with her. He pinned her arms above her head straddled her waist, all the while kissing her neck and face in a truly awkward fashion. Eclipse suddenly let a panicked grunt escape and Axl instantly sat up off her. She followed suit and wrapped her arms around herself in an embarrassed hug.

"Are you ok?" Axl finally panted, trying to force his eyes to see straight.

He was only in his underwear and so was Eclipse, but she still had her tank top on. It wasn't a great time for either of them to stop, but she felt like she needed to warn him.

"I don't know what I'm doing." she desperately tried to explain.

Axl sat back on his rear and took a deep breath to calm down, then he chuckled.

"Wanna know a secret?"

She nodded and he reached out and held her hand.

"Neither do I, Heartthrob."

"Heartthrob?" she gasped, still trying to stifle her breathing.

Axl lifted her hand to his bare chest and gently flattened it against his skin. Eclipse forced her eyes to concentrate on her fingertips, like it was somehow wrong to look at him, even though she was touching him. She could feel his heart pounding through their connection and her eyes shifted up to his. He gently brushed loose hairs out of her eyes.

"Every day for the past year, it's done that." he coaxed. "When I see you or hear your voice. When I watch you on the battlefield or bump into you in camp. Even when I just think about you……. it keeps me up at night."

"You think about me at night?" she gulped.

Axl laughed.

"Why do you think I've been such an asshole, lately? I haven't been sleeping."

Eclipse let the corner of her mouth twitch up and she relaxed enough for her hand to slide down ever so slightly. She hadn't worked up the courage to touch him yet and it was driving both of them crazy. He seemed so sure about everything and she was terrified. Axl gently leaned back over her till she laid down and stared up into his eyes with her big blue ones. He smiled.

"Eclipse, I may not know what I'm doing, but I know there isn't a single other person on this planet that I'd rather figure it out with. If you need to go slow, we will go slow. You just have to talk to me."

She nodded and traced down his abs to his waistline, her eyes following her fingers. Axl didn't push her either direction, but gently slipped one strap of her tank top over her shoulder. Their eyes connected.

"I'm not sure slow is easier." She whispered, trembling. "I think we need to speed up, honestly."

Axl grinned down at her and did as she asked. It was still awkward and new, but it definitely was easier to jump right in and not think too much about it. They had to figure each other out, that was all. Adamere stared fixatedly at them, which made both of them inexplicably nervous. The one time Eclipse cried out, Axl had to cover her mouth to keep her quiet so no one outside the tent could hear them, but it all ended relatively quickly, as most first times do. Then, the tent grew deathly quiet as both of them realized that every single thing they knew had just changed.

Eclipse rolled out of her cot and quickly pulled her clothes on, at least her pants and tank top, before pacing back and forth, running her hands through her hair in distress. Axl calmly put his pants back with a few bounces and waited for her to scream at him, sitting back down on the side of her cot. She looked over at him five or six times and shook her head each time, unable to find words. Her left hand dropped to her chest to clutch it. Her right still gripped a fistful of her own hair and held on for dear life. She was obviously terrified of something. Axl patiently waited for her to tell him what before remembering who he was dealing with. Finally, he stood up and sighed.

"Are you mad at me?"

Eclipse jumped and turned to face him, her hand still knotted up in her hair. They stared at each other and both gulped several times. Whatever their old relationship was, it was dead. Whatever happened next would change both their lives and Axl was leaving it entirely up to her. Her response to this would determine just how close or secluded they were both going to be for a while and it scared him that she might ask him to leave again. Still, if that was what she wanted, he couldn't argue. Instead, she jogged right back into his arms and jumped. Axl caught her thighs as they kissed again and Eclipse forced her tongue through his lips. He eventually slammed back on the bed with her straddling his hips and she willingly stripped everything back off this time. Soon enough, they both collapsed beside each other and Axl had to stop Eclipse from jumping out of bed again. He just barely caught her wrist before she escaped.

"You don't have to run away every time. It's ok to hold each other for a while after." he pleaded gently. "Just stay here. With me."

Eclipse hesitated but nervously slid back under the sheet with him. She couldn't look at him and laid on her side, facing away and trying to figure out what was going on in her life right now. She was still breathing heavily when Axl gently scooted toward her and propped himself up on his elbow so he could look right down at the side of her face. Eclipse closed her eyes and hummed as he gently stroked the hair off her ear. After a moment, she slid backwards so their bodies were pressed tight against each other. Axl leaned down and kissed the exposed side of her neck.

"You take all the time you need." he whispered in her ear before cradling her entire body in his own. "You never have to run away from me. You never have to worry about telling me exactly what you want. I'll always listen, Eclipse. I promise. I care so much about you."

Eclipse laid awake, blinking and trying not to focus on the feeling in her chest. He was so close. They were both drenched in sweat and sticky, but she didn't even mind. She didn't mind any of this, beyond the fact that they would both be killed if they were caught. Her eyes were locked on the flaps of her tent, though she wasn't sure what she would say to get out of this if someone did happen to walk in. Axl shifted slightly behind her and she felt the reason why and grinned, rolling over to look up at him as he propped up on his elbow again. He gave her a wide, toothy grin as the corner of her mouth stayed up longer than ever before.

"Do I have to have all the answers?" she whispered. "Right now?"

Axl leaned down and kissed her long and hard. Eclipse moaned into his mouth as his hand slid between her thighs. She tried sucking on his lower lip to keep him close, but it snapped back into place when he pulled away to smile down at her.

"You never need to have all the answers with me, Heartthrob."

# CHAPTER TWENTY-ONE

THUD!!

18-year-old Duke Rogers squinted and leaned back, looking at the position of the arrow he had just fired. It was on the lower right-hand edge of the straw target. He puffed out his cheeks.

"You still shoot like a girl." someone said behind him.

He turned towards the familiar voice only to see Acelyn sitting on the left-hand fence that separated his target from the one next to him.

"Like you could do any better." he snorted in reply, trying to hide his nervous smile from her.

"I know I can't." she replied with a careless shrug. "That's why I said what I did."

Duke shot her an annoyed glance before grumbling something about how he at least hit the target every time now. Ace smiled coyly and let the subject drop. She looked around herself. It was a lovely morning in Feldon's Peak. The sun was shining, the grass was green, and it was actually summer, when those things were supposed to happen. What made everything even more beautiful was the secret she held close to her heart. It was the kind of day that just begged for a happy sigh. She gave it one.

While she admired the scenery, Duke also noticed beauty, but his eyes were locked on her. Acelyn's deep black hair fell loosely around her torso in large messy curls that just looked perfect all the time. Her pale skin glowing with happiness and her pink cheeks brimming with smiles. Bright green eyes shone behind her long lashes and a slight breeze blew both her hair and her light orange gown ever so slightly to the south. It was a perfect picture, he thought, only interrupted by the fact that her gaze shifted back to him. He immediately looked around, commenting on what a lovely day it was, and she heartily agreed. He closed his eyes happily. Her voice was just like music. Duke locked eyes with her for a moment and grinned before turning back to his practice. He was so enamored with his thoughts that he didn't hear Antilles come up in the lane to his right until he slammed his quiver into the ground. Duke jumped and his attention shot to the noise.

"What's up with you?" he asked.

Antilles shot him a sidelong glance with his jaw clenched so tight that the muscles in his face bulged out. Without answering, he moodily fired an arrow into the bullseye.

"Today was classification day." he said shortly.

Acelyn slid off the fence and walked over to the one that separated Duke and Antilles. Duke felt a tingling sensation run through his entire body as he realized they were less than a foot apart. Oh, if only she would turn around and face him. He couldn't wait for the day he could feel her lips on his again. That kiss from her birthday still made his face hot when he thought about it. He fought to keep his mind in the present. The two of them watched Antilles sink a few more bullseyes before Acelyn spoke up.

"And you are-----"

"Archery Private." he growled, sinking another arrow.

"What's wrong with that? You're great at archery." Acelyn argued, missing Duke's cue to remain quiet.

Antilles turned to face her.

"What's wrong with it," he answered with heat, "is that archery is a job for cowards. You stand in a high, totally protected place and watch the real soldiers die for their country beneath you."

"So, you'd rather die and be of as little use as possible, than kill 50 men and live to do it again?" Acelyn retorted, slightly angered by his tone.

"If that's what's expected of me, yes!" he answered a little louder.

"Well, it's *not* what's expected of you." she yelled with her hands on her hips. "If it was, you would be in the infantry."

"I would *rather* be in the infantry."

"But you're not, are you?"

"No, that was my point."

"So, stop worrying about it."

"I'm not worried, Ace, I'm just disappointed."

"Well, you shouldn't be angry at least."

"Wasn't angry till you got mouthy with me."

"You call being totally honest and stating the obvious truth, being mouthy?"

"No, I call it being redundant."

That one made her stop for a second and think.

"What?"

Duke had seen this whole routine before. His eyes shifted from one to the other with a calm, almost disinterested tint. He knew they would argue for an hour or so about thirty million things and then make up, forgetting what started the fight in the first place. So, though he heard what they were saying, it really all slipped through his mind. He turned and continued his practice with a chuckle and a shake of his head. In the back of his mind, he still heard what was going on. Of course, the focus had shifted.

"Well, I think your whole family is crazy." Antilles barked.

"Then, perhaps you'd like to forget about last night." she snapped back.

Only then did Duke's ears perk up. Not because of what Ace said, but because Antilles didn't say anything back. He turned and watched. Acelyn had her arms folded and her back facing Antilles, who stood silently staring at the back of her head. The 20-year-old boy took a deep breath and jumped the fence, tilting his head down slightly to look up at her face. He gently took her elbows in his hands.

"Not in a million years," he whispered softly and coaxingly.

Duke watched uncomfortably as Ace smiled and uncrossed her arms, allowing Antilles to slide down them to hold her hands. They stood staring into each other's eyes with giant smiles. Duke had never seen them make up like this before. It looked oddly familiar. Like he had once stood just like this with her. He looked desperately from face to face, a ball of flame growing in his stomach, making him sick.

"Wow, that was quick." he croaked through a severely dry mouth, trying to break the feeling that he was invisible.

Somehow, it didn't work.

"I guess being an archer isn't so bad." Antilles said, rubbing her hands with his thumbs and gazing deeply into those green eyes.

"I'm sure your family will appreciate it." Ace answered biting her lip shyly. "All of them."

Duke felt a sudden need to break up this conversation.

"Well," he laughed uneasily and uncommonly loud, "what family does this guy have a chance of getting?"

He bumped his best friend with his bow jokingly. He continued to chuckle till he noticed four eyes staring at him. The mock laugh and smile vanished. He knew, somehow, he knew, but playing dumb was his last hope that he was wrong.

"What's going on with you two?" he asked, trying to mask his trembling voice.

Antilles exchanged glances with his 19-year-old girl and waited for her nod. She smiled and gave it. He kissed both her hands, making his buddy nauseous with jealousy, and then walked over to Duke and placed his hand on his shoulder. It was taller and bulkier than his own and he had to look up to meet his eyes. Duke was clenching his teeth so hard, he thought they were going to crack, but he managed to keep the same concerned look on his face.

"You know how I told you my family was going to have dinner with the Vantages last night?"

Duke managed to nod through the green haze in his eyes. He definitely knew what was coming now. And he didn't know if he could stand to hear.

"Well, the whole point of that dinner was so our parents could talk and I could take Ace for a walk afterward." he paused to glance back at the beaming girl behind him, "And on that walk, after hours of desperate begging, pleading, and spilling my blood for attention"—Ace elbowed him indignantly and Antilles grinned at her before continuing to Duke---- "the woman of my dreams agreed to marry me."

Duke's world shattered as time slowed to a painful halt around him. His lovely Acelyn was to marry another, his best friend of all people. His best friend. He remembered that he was supposed to be Ace's friend as well and in an instant, he decided those two facts would not change. All the betrayal in the world couldn't end how much he loved Antilles and Acelyn and he was going to prove it. He dropped his mouth a little and looked between two of them. Then, with all the deceit and tact he could manage, he bowed his head, shaking it back and forth in what looked like disbelief.

"Wow….. Antilles…." he said before lifting his head. "…. that's……... amazing."

Antilles cocked his head and squinted his eyes suspiciously.

"Aaaaare you sure? Cause you don't *seem* sure."

Duke realized he would have to step up his game with an inward groan. He forced himself to smile and even laugh before grabbing his friend by the shoulders and shaking him in excitement.

"Of course, I'm sure!!" he lied. "I've been expecting this for years."

"Really?!" Ace squealed with happiness.

Acelyn had desperately hoped this wouldn't cause issues between the two boys. She walked over to join them and hold her fiancé's hand, pecking him on the cheek with those perfect lips. It was the closest she had ever been to him. Duke couldn't help but stare in lust. Thankfully, he recovered before they both looked back at him.

"Absolutely!" he responded with as much excitement as he could muster. "It was so obvious! And I wish you both the best of luck, of course."

"Well, you'll have to do that at the wedding, Best Man."

Antilles nudged him in the chest with his elbow, pushing him back a bit. Then, he grabbed his bride by her waist and hoisted her back up onto the fence, walking up so close they were almost kissing, and just stared into her eyes again. Duke was pretty sure he was drooling, watching them. To touch her like that, to hold her in his arms and run his hands over her body. To kiss her anywhere on that smooth, pale skin. He loved her, he loved her so much it hurt. It made him nauseous again and it was the first time in his life that he was happy to hear the lunch bell ring. He managed to smile before they turned to look at him and he shrugged.

"Damn, there's the bell, guys. I have to go," he began to un-string his bow. "I'm real happy for both of you…. and proud too, of course."

He forced out one last smile before walking around them and picking his quiver up off the ground. He walked away with a sour complexion, before turning around to wave halfheartedly. They already had their backs to him, holding each other in their arms and his stomach flipped as Antilles planted a light kiss on her perfect, red lips. His hand sunk slowly with his heart. Then, he turned and jogged into the great hall, trying to un-see it all. Maybe he was losing his best friend after all.

Duke bounded up the stairs as fast as he could, staring at the floor to avoid contact with anyone. It worked until he didn't see Clara before he ran right into her, making her drop the food tray she was carrying and almost knocking her over.

"Ancient's sake, Duke! Be more careful, deary. You're going to kill someone one of these days!"

Clara watched him fumble around as he stacked the wooden dishes back onto the tray, mumbling some weak apology. She sensed something was bothering the boy. Wanting to turn his mind to something happier than whatever he was thinking, she changed the subject. She simply picked the wrong one.

"Did you hear about Antilles and Acelyn?"

"Yes."

He shoved the tray back into her shocked hands and continued his race up the stairs. Clara stared after him in shock long after he was out of sight. She didn't understand how he could care so little about his best friend's wedding.

"Well, *I* hope they'll be very happy." she muttered confusedly.

Joey was sitting at the dining room table, eating and pouring over some of the tests Duke did earlier in the day. He didn't even look up when he heard his son come into the apartment and walk up to the dining room door, out of breath.

"Go put your gear away and while you're eating, we will go over these logarithms from this morning." he said flipping over a paper.

"I'm not really that hungry." Duke answered flatly, leaning on the door frame and folding his arms.

Joey looked over the top of his spectacles. At 60 years old, he was tired of having his son question everything he said. The boy's face was red and he looked hesitant, like maybe there was something he wanted to tell him. Joey removed his glasses and peered at his son. Duke did seem a little more agitated than normal, but he needed to learn life didn't slow down when he was grumpy.

"I didn't ask." he answered, replacing his glasses and looking back at his work.

He didn't see Duke roll his eyes and swing his head before heaving himself off the door jamb. He shuffled down the hall to his room, slamming the door after entering. Joey flipped over the three minute hour glass beside him without even looking up. Whenever Duke had an attitude about his paperwork, he procrastinated and drew everything out as long as possible. If Duke wasn't sitting beside him in three minutes, he would have to go drag him out. Joey knew that logarithms are not at all fun, but any military leader should have a good head for numbers. Duke did surprisingly well on his formation exams, but mathematics and logic killed him. Joey took off his spectacles, tossed them onto the table and rubbed his eyes, ending with pinching the bridge of his nose. Every problem on the test he took today was wrong, every single one. He didn't know what to do with his son anymore. He was so rebellious, so stubborn, and so aggressive. It didn't help that he regularly told Joey he hated him, either.

About three years ago, Joey was drunk and attacked Duke again. This time, the boy fought back. Joey ended up with several broken bones and his son had to run in a panic to fetch Alex. The doctor probably saved Joey's life, but neither father nor son would tell him what happened. In the end, he was left to assume that Duke beat the hell out of his own father. He had no idea what could spark that amount of anger and hatred in the boy. He was always so docile and kind around his friends. It victimized Joey to his friend and villainized Duke and word spread as Joey took the time to recover. Either way, Joey never hit Duke again. The two had little more than a passive aggressive relationship of painful jabs and insults, but the violence was all but gone.

Joey was already in poor condition for his age, due to his alcoholism. The average man lived to be about 80 but Joey did not, however, feel as though he would. He was sure that Chrosia was going to declare war on Central Liberty soon and they had less than 20,000 active soldiers and those were still spread out among the fiefdoms or assisting their neighbors against Chrosia. Their last scouting report informed the men that Victor had at least double that in his capital alone. At least.

There were also rumors and reports of this Maiden of Death, who could wipe out entire armies by herself. They said she popped in out of thin air and slit the throat of her quarry before they even knew she was there. Dormatian refugees were terrified of her. The council had released the monk from four years ago with a weak apology that none of them were excited to deliver. She had obviously been telling some form of the truth. She disappeared right after with a dire warning that they would all pay someday.

Joey released his nose and glanced over at the hourglass, just in time to watch the last grains of sand fall. He looked hopefully at the door for a few moments before groaning.

"I'm getting too old for this." he muttered, standing up.

He put back on his spectacles and headed out of the dining room. A short walk to the end of the hallway took him to Duke's closed door on the left just before the study door. Joey didn't even bother to knock. The first thing he noticed upon entering was the first thing everyone notices. Duke's room whistled. There was some minuscule hole in the mortar of his brick walls, which was also the exterior wall of the entire fortress. It let air pass through it when the wind blew, which resulted in a low whistle. At least that's what everyone thought, though no one could find the hole or stop the noise.

The second thing Joey noticed was that his son had not put his things away as he had been told. Instead, he had hung his quiver over the back of a chair, sitting just to the left, and laid his sword across the seat. Joey looked across the room at the wooden wardrobe he had given his son specifically for his weapons. Its right door stood wide open from earlier that morning. Beside it was his clothing wardrobe, with both doors and the drawers beneath them wide open with clothes lying in, on, and around them from days past. Joey rolled his eyes back to his immediate right. On a pure marble pedestal, a birthday present from Marcus which looked like a miniature Doric column, sat a large bronze basin of water. The maids were kind enough to bring it up the stairs every morning for Duke, mainly because all of them were attracted to him. He was tall, broad-shouldered, handsome and funny. His blond hair was cut close to his scalp, except the top, which was a little longer, and his bright blue eyes sparkled when he grinned. Plus, he was completely uninterested in all of them, so that made them try even harder for his attention. He was supposed to return the basin before lunch. This he rarely did, despite his father's continual reminders, so Joey looked at it in un-phased frustration.

Finally, Joey looked at Duke himself. He was lying in his bed, fully clothed, on his right side, facing the wall, the same one with the door. Joey squinted his eyes and walked up to the bedside. He stood staring down at his son, waiting for an explanation. Duke neither moved nor spoke. Joey folded his arms across his chest and sighed with exasperation.

"Are you going to get up?" he asked calmly.

"No."

"Are you sick?" Joey asked, raising an eyebrow to his son's former answer.

"No." Duke answered shortly, knowing that he couldn't tell his father that he felt sick over a girl.

"Are you sure?"

"Yes."

Joey took a deep breath and changed his tone from an inquiry to a command.

"Then you *are* going to get up."

The old man turned and walked towards the door. He stopped by the basin to turn and check for his son's obedience. He hadn't moved.

"Duke." he warned.

He watched the teen's side rise and fall with a deep sigh.

"Fine." he grumbled, without moving. "I'll be out there whenever...." he paused, realizing he had no intention of moving and didn't want to promise such. "....... whenever I feel like it."

"Fine." an outraged Joey replied after several moments of bewilderment.

His moderate tone surprised even himself, since he felt as though he was about to explode. He shook his head in anger, which once more put the basin in his view. His eyes locked on it. Then he lifted them to his still motionless son as a plot formed in his head. A two-in-one discipline just to save time. His face split into a slight smile at his own cleverness. He picked up the basin and tip toed over to the bedside once more. With one more look at Duke, he threw the water over his head.

Duke very suddenly decided to get out of bed. He rolled off the edge, spluttering and shaking his head. He reached up one hand to rub his eyes and finally managed to look up angrily from his hands and knees and speak.

"What the hell was that for?" he roared.

His father rolled his eyes.

"Oh, well, let me see. *Countless* reasons, of course, but let me pick a few of my favorite. I believe you know that when I tell you to do something, it's not a suggestion, requiring your agreement. It's an order that you reply 'Yes Sir' to."

Joey calmly walked over and replaced the basin, feeling very proud of himself. Duke pushed himself up to his feet with a heave and felt his bed.

"It's all wet now." he cried accusingly, throwing his arm out to the side.

"Yes, it is." Joey answered flatly, folding his arms behind his back. "And no maid is going to suffer for your stupidity. So, you can either change the hay bales out yourself or sleep on a wet, moldy bed until you do."

"And when do I have time to make a bed?" Duke spat vehemently. "You never give me time for anything."

"Nevertheless, you are the only one who may change that bed." Joey turned to leave as he continued. "Now, I believe we have some tests to look at."

Duke drudged after his father, down the hallway and into the dining room. He was not, however, following to display obedience. He chased after his father for argument's sake.

"I don't see why we have to do this now." he growled, wiping his face on his sleeve, which managed to stay dry underneath his body.

"When would you prefer?"

"I don't know, how about a few million years down the road?"

"Well, the way your math scores are, we may very well be doing this for that long."

Duke shot his father an annoyed glance behind his back before answering.

"I don't understand why I can't just be a normal man!"

"Well, in the first place," Joey replied sitting down at the table they had reached by now. "you are not a man, you're a boy, which your behavior should easily prove to you, despite the fact that you are supposedly turning 19 in a couple weeks. And secondly, you weren't born to live a normal life."

"No." Duke said nastily. "My problem is that I wasn't born to a normal father."

"Is that so?" Joey asked disinterestedly, looking over the papers in front of him.

Duke growled angrily and pounded his fist onto the table as it grew into a yell.

"Can't you just listen to me for five minutes? Don't you think there *might* be a reason I don't feel like dealing with this today? Aren't I more important to you than those damn papers?"

His voice cracked slightly near the end.

Joey didn't even look up.

"I've heard every word you've spoken." he answered coolly. "You just haven't said a damn thing in all that babble."

Duke's mouth dropped open in exasperation, and tears of anger welled up in his eyes. He stood gawking while all his thoughts jumbled up his ability to reply. Why did no one love him? Not even his own father could stand to look at him, how could Ace force herself to do it either? Screw the fact that he almost died for her eight years ago! He winced slightly as he remembered.

She had come in to read to him while he was bedridden. Every day. They had gotten very close in that time. She considered him the best friend she had, despite his best friend being Antilles. She would run her fingers through his hair and giggle at her own poorly formed jokes as she told them. She was the only light he had in his life after that. He thought the two of them were meant to be! They certainly got along better than she and Antilles! How did he wind up with Ace after everything? And what about her birthday? And almost everyday since? She constantly hugged him and touched him and kissed his cheek. They spent just as much time together as he and Antilles did. He was almost positive they had both seen each other as more than friends. Was he just the bridge she needed to get to the guy she actually liked? He couldn't even think of their kiss earlier without a little vomit shooting up his throat. He closed his mouth to swallow it and thought of his reply.

"Why is it so hard for you to give me your full attention?" he choked out.

This time Joey did look up, with a huge sigh, and put the pen he was using down.

"Perhaps it's because you never say anything worth my attention."

"So...... I'm not worth your time?"

"No, you're not." Joey answered hotly. "But the council meeting your idiocy just made me late for, is."

Joey stood up, swiped up all of his own papers into a stack and pushed the test over to Duke.

"You will sit at this table," he said, putting his lunch dishes on a tray on the opposite side of the table, "until your test is completely, 100% correct. I don't care if it does take you a few million years. You will not leave this room." he continued, shoving papers into his satchel designed for just that. "until I have checked it over."

He threw the top flap over his satchel opening and finished with a bark. "Twice."

He swung the strap over his head and straightened his clothes a bit. He looked at his son's angry face for a few seconds, even though Duke avoided eye contact. Joey rolled his eyes and walked toward the door. He turned back around and glared at Duke one more time.

"You will learn your place, Duke, even if I have to break you to make you accept it."

Then he turned and left, slamming the door behind him. Duke slammed down into his seat and snatched the pencil off the table in front of him. It snapped in two under his grip. And that was it. He snapped with that pencil. Duke stood up, knocking his chair over in the process and threw the test at the door, after ripping it into a million pieces. The shreds flew around the room without one of them reaching the intended target. He paced the floor angrily, yanking on his hair. He couldn't handle his own life anymore. He just wanted to blow up in fury. He picked his chair up and threw it across the room into the wall. The chair shattered, to his delight. It was the sweetest release he had felt in a long time.

After throwing, and breaking, all eight chairs that sat around the table, tipping over the desk by the door and chucking the tray of dishes across the room; he was finally able to stand still. He observed his destruction, breathing heavily with tears streaming down his cheeks. He didn't really feel any better, just more exhausted and incredibly sore. In fact, looking at all this just broke him even more. He fell to his knees and wept freely. A few minutes later, Joey came in, set a vial of sap glue and a fresh stack of parchment on the table, without so much as looking around the room, and then left again. A second later, he returned to put about forty pencils on the table as well and then walked out, leaving his son to fall onto his side, hugging his knees and bawling.

It was about two hours before Duke could pull himself up off the floor and grab the spare chair from the corner. He slammed it down on the floor next to the table and dragged himself around, picking up the pieces of his test. He dropped them onto the table and plopped down in his chair. There he sat, thinking over the events of that morning for the millionth time. How could everything turn so wrong so fast? This was a new feeling for him. It was gut wrenching pain, headaches like from a cold, and sorrow like death. Death. It sounded so peaceful to just disappear. He didn't even care what was beyond it's cold embrace. Sleeping forever was all he needed. That would definitely catch his father's attention.

# CHAPTER TWENTY-TWO

"I'm sorry, I'm late gentlemen."

Joey sat down in his chair in the council room and emptied his satchel into a messy pile on the table. No one said a word as he arranged his papers and tapped them on the table, straightening them into a neat stack. Finally, he laid them down and looked up with a sigh. Everyone was staring at him. Staring judgmentally, at that. He looked from face to face to make sure before speaking again.

"So....... what did I miss?"

No one spoke, or even changed expression. They still just stared at him. He sought more desperately for a friendly face. His eyes landed on the Premier, who shuffled ever so slightly, enough to give Joey hope that he would talk to him.

"Ed?"

The addressee sighed and shifted uneasily in his seat. The councilmen started to follow his example. Some shifted their eyes away in guilt, others just changed the way they were sitting. Vincent, however glared at him with a smirk of triumph. That made Joey uncomfortable, which was a hard feat to accomplish.

"You didn't miss much, Joe. We are just getting started."

Joey glanced up at Alex, hoping to get a hint. His best friend couldn't even look at him; he was fake reading some paper over and over again.

"Then," Joey slowly shifted his eyes back to Edward. "what is our first order of business?"

"You are."

Joey turned his gaze back towards the voice with a subtle roll of his eyes. Vincent Bosh, Major General of Central Liberty's army. Joey controlled his expression to avoid showing his disgust. Most people disliked Vincent. He was an overbearing Lord of his fief and an intimidating general. Joey personally thought he was a haughty, self-centered snake with no heart and no sense of decency. His language was dreadful and his temper even worse, but he was the only current volunteer for the major general position. No one else wanted to spend their life destroying others and sentencing them to death. Joey stifled his emotions as usual, but he truly did not want to deal with the general today.

"I am?" he asked, turning back to Ed and Alex.

Alex remained quiet, but Ed knew better than to let Vincent answer again.

"Yes, Joe." Ed sighed. "I'm afraid you are."

The strategist looked blankly at the younger man.

"And, what have I done this time?"

"To hell with it, man! It's not you. It's that damned boy of yours!"

Joey snapped his head back to glare right into Vincent's eyes in anger.

"And what about my boy, Vincent?"

"Honestly? Where the devil are we to begin? That little ass is completely out of control." The general threw his hand around while he spoke.

Joey stood up and placed his hands on the table, with precise and meaningful movements. His unwavering gaze fell on Vincent with a fierce warning shining through them.

"I hope you know, General, that your vulgarity is just as unprofessional as your weight." he ignored the sudden crimson color on the angry general's face. "As for Duke, I'll admit that he's an irresponsible adolescent and causes me more trouble than any of you can imagine, but what could he have possibly done to deserve hatred from all of you and earn such a precious spot in the council's official business?"

"Oh, come on Joey. It's not what he's done." Lord Herring Sebastian of Rivenwood fief replied awkwardly. "It's what he could do in the future. Duke is reckless. He is rebellious and we've all had to deal with his anger issues and his attitude. And we've seen his test scores. We believe he is incapable of replacing you. He simply doesn't have what it takes. We want you to choose a different apprentice."

"And I'll take Duke." Vincent confirmed with a nod. "Boy's damn good with a sword and hits like a brick. He can take out all of his rage on Chrosian bastards."

Joey stared at the man calmly until he squirmed and slowly sat back down. His gaze shifted once more to Alex. It was the guiltiest he had ever seen him, pretending to pick at something on the table. That told Joey he agreed with everything that was going on. Then he looked to Ed, who simply shrugged his shoulders and raised his eyebrows. Joey looked back at Sebastian. He looked sympathetic, but also a bit nervous. Everyone felt awful about what they were trying to tell him, he knew. He was older than all of them, by several years and he had been on the council longer than them all. It wasn't the first time Vincent had been against him, but it was the first time the entire council had been a united front against him. And it was the first time they came after Duke at Vincent's behest. Joey would be damned before letting the fat bastard get his hands on his son. Obviously, he couldn't say that to the entire council. He removed his glasses and folded them, tossing them on the table in frustration. Alex, from across the room noticed something he should have seen many years ago.

Joey was old.

Not just physically either, he was spiritually exhausted and mentally tired. His eyes had become beaten and weathered with many cares and even more worries. They were tired and dull, yet stark with emotion when he chose. His speech, though still stoic, lacked the command it once had. Altogether, Alex watched a defeated man state his defense.

"Gentlemen, I will be entirely honest with you, and I'll accept the same in return. My son has failed at everything I ask of him. He is dreadful at mathematics, logic, and statistics, three things vitally important to this position. His character is lacking on many counts and his self-control is atrocious. I believe my dining hall testifies to this at the moment. But there is a reason I continue to fight him on all these things. Beyond hoping that he won't always remain this way, I have seen extraordinary talent in Duke. He has his moments of brilliance, including predicting literally everything that would happen in Dormiat when he was only 13. That means he thinks like whoever is planning Victor's battles. Call it fate, or destiny, or I'll even give you dumb luck, but Duke may be just the man we need if he'll only get his heart in the right place. He's an original. He doesn't think like any other strategists in the south and that could revolutionize the trade, which just might keep Victor on his toes. He could be the one to turn this war around."

Joey looked around. Some men rolled their eyes and some nodded in agreement. One Lord Richard Holden of Farrscore fief answered first.

"We cannot assume Victor Monohue has any plans to attack us. He can have no complaints against us or our country."

"Sure, he can." Alex replied spitefully. "He doesn't own us yet; there's his complaint."

Several councilors, including Sebastian and Vincent, stood and began to argue. The latter two believed Victor would stop with what he had if Central Liberty made peace with him, like paying tribute or something. *Idiots*, Joey thought. Ed argued that Victor was known for not keeping his word and would still attack them. Lord Lawrence Darkson of Doth fief claimed that Chrosia's intent was to claim the world and that Victor would declare war soon. Lord Parker Dawson, the country's leading psychiatrist, simply tried to point out the flaws in everyone else's thought process.

Joey sat down and watched. He had seen all of this a thousand times in the past three years, since the fall of Dormiat. It was tiresome, trying to follow this argument to its end. In fact, he gave up a couple hours in. His mind still dwelt on Duke. Deep down, he knew this would happen. Duke had often caused mischief for other members of the council and Joey had punished him every single time, but it didn't stop him from doing it again, the very next day sometimes. He was an exhausting person to raise. He argued against anything, and his test scores had gotten worse and worse over time. Joey didn't even set much store in tests in math or strategy, but he used them to test character as well. That was how Duke was failing. He was aggressive and angry, undisciplined and selfish. Joey thought back to the day before. Duke had come in late for dinner, again, and when Joey had mildly pointed it out, he had gone into some explanation. Joey fought hard to remember his exact words.

*"Dad, it was a huge honor. The Colonel was impressed with my work at practice and asked to drill me personally. I couldn't say no. It was the greatest hour of my entire life. He offered me a starting position as a sergeant. A sergeant, Dad! That's amazing for someone with as little training as me, but I need more practice time. So...... can I have it?"*

As Joey remembered the look on his son's face at that moment, something struck him. He had smiled, Duke had actually smiled, when he was talking about training more. Joey thought back through the past few years. Duke hadn't smiled for him in so long. He had yelled, screamed, frowned, and grimaced, but not smiled. Joey felt the entire world slip away, the room went silent as everything faded. He sunk into his seat even further as it hit him. His son was miserable. It wasn't just that he had a poor attitude. He hated his entire life. Joey thought back to when he left his son with his torn-up test just hours earlier. Even though he hadn't appeared to look around, he had seen him. It was a miserable sight. Duke looked worse than Joey had ever seen. How could he have left him there? There was no way this was about the test, or even what happened yesterday, when he declined his son the one thing he wanted most in the world.

*"Duke, we have been over this time and time again. You are not a soldier. You are a future council member. You have no right to ask this of me again. No, no, no, a thousand times no. That's it, I'm tired of this. I generously have let you indulge this behavior for a decade. Enough is enough. This is your last week of training. I think you know plenty for your future job."*

The argument had raged on for hours, but Joey ashamedly couldn't remember any more of it. How was it possible that he couldn't remember what his son said just yesterday, but he could remember every word of the council meetings for the past week? He was a terrible father. It only just hit him after 19 years of doing all the wrong things. He was abusive on every level, physical, mental, emotional. The fact that Duke managed to keep it all hidden proved how much better of a man he was than his father. Maybe it was because Joey had run out of whiskey for the first time in years or maybe it was just his old age. Something about the entire council accusing his son set him off. Duke was desperate about something, and he was sitting with a bunch of monkeys discussing rumor.

Joey stood up with a jerk, interrupting the yelling in the room and pushing back his chair. Everyone silently watched him stride towards the door faster than they had seen him move in years. Ed may have called after him, but he didn't care. He reached the stairs and took off running. He thought of that day when Duke almost died, saving Acelyn. He remembered it so clearly. He thought his son was dead for a few miserable minutes and when he figured out he wasn't...... he punched him for it. Joey had just been so happy to see him alive and then forgot that feeling immediately. Within an hour he had turned back to his stoic, authoritative figure; telling Duke what he could or could not do as was his habit. How could he change so swiftly?

Joey reached his suite door and burst through, not bothering to close it before running to the dining room. It was destroyed. Chairs broken everywhere; the contents of the desk spilled out in front of where it lay face down. The entire room looked like a tornado hit. But as he looked around, he noticed something was missing. His son. Joey ran around the room like a mad man, checking corners and looking in the rubble. He even looked under the parchment on the table for Duke in his frenzy. He threw the stack down with an escaped sob and a loud thud.

After searching for hours, in every place he knew Duke would hide: the training fields, the range, and the stables, Joey stopped in the oasis. Feldon's Peak was mostly sand and dirt in summer. It was dry and hot, on account of it being so close to a gigantic volcano, but there was lots of vegetation growing because of the irrigation system running through the city. The most beautiful spot was just outside the city limits. There was an honest-to-goodness lake with trees surrounding it and untamed grass all around. There were crickets and songbirds. It was so peaceful and different than the normal scene. It's where Duke, and Joey for that matter, went when they needed to escape life. Duke had been going there more and more in the past year, Joey realized as he stared down at the water now. He leaned back against a tree and slid down its bark till he was sitting. He would wait here. Duke always came back to this spot. He would sit and wait for his return. A horrid thought brought a lump to his throat.

If. If he returned.

# CHAPTER TWENTY-THREE

Eclipse opened her eyes and instinctively glanced at the flaps of her tent. They were gently blowing in the scorching wind outside. She hadn't slept, but laying still with her eyes closed was as close to rest as it got for her. It was early morning. She rolled out of her cot, grateful Harrison constantly had spares for her, and stood up. Her arms instinctively raised above her head till her back cracked, and she could feel every scar on her body stretching. Young as she was, there were a lot of them. It was easier to ignore them. She quickly pulled on a set of clothes, still working with the same style she wore as a kid. She fastened all of her weapons on, including the dagger she slept with every night, and stumbled out of her tent.

It was already starting to get warm, even though she guessed it was only four in the morning. Hers was the only officer's tent, since the Logans still hadn't chosen a general. That was the only reason she was with them instead of her own series. Victor needed the Logans and Emilies to finish off Ashtar, but he refused to place Sean in charge and that's who the Logans wanted. He put Eclipse in command, instead, leaving Amy temporarily in charge of the Emilies, like she always wanted.

The two corps weren't even in the same part of Ashtar, anymore. Alan Losh, Victor's official messenger and head torturer, had come by four months ago and ordered the Emilies to deal with the Libertarian reinforcements amassing in the east and then return home. There was a rebellion they needed to put down in Chrosia. That left Eclipse in Ashtar with the Logans to finish the job.

Ashtar was a massive desert. Eclipse hated finding sand in literally everything she owned, every crease and crevice, and the heat was unbearable. Her men were tired and ready to go home, too. Victor wanted the war to last, so she was forced to hold them back from wiping through the country in one fell swoop. She and the Logans could easily have finished the entire country off in weeks. Instead, they were stalling, taking out little pieces of the population at a time. It was frustrating, but Eclipse had kept her oath to Victor from when she was 11 and followed his every whim. Well...... almost.

She walked to the well they had set up camp by and used the archaic device to pull a bucket of water up from the deep pit. She wet her hands and wiped them on her face. It was all she could bear to wash her face. Anytime water touched her head, she panicked a little. She could maintain control as long as her face didn't get submerged. The water at least cooled her off. It had been a long night.

"Were we supposed to get up early?"

She didn't even jump as Harrison walked up to the well and whispered in the darkness. She knew he would be up first. Very little startled her anymore. She just didn't care enough to be scared. Eclipse casually turned to look at him.

"No, I couldn't sleep."

He furrowed his brow and took the bucket of water from her, washing his own face.

"That's weird, I gave you enough sleeping pills to knock out Adamere."

At the sound of his name, the large kiladrt meandered out of Eclipse's tent and stretched. He yawned, which sounded a lot like a roar, and shook, trotting happily up to Eclipse afterward.

"I guess sleeping pills don't cut it anymore." Eclipse murmured as she scratched her companion's ears.

"Particularly bad last night?" Harrison asked softly.

She shot him a reproving glance. He knew she didn't like to talk about it. She talked to him when she had to, because he was the Logan medic and occasionally, she needed medical help to deal with it, like not being able to sleep and needing someone else to operate the healer. Plus, he replaced her cot. Thankfully, Sean ducked out of his tent just then and interrupted the conversation. He stumbled to the well with a disdainful look at Adamere. His tent sat nearest to Eclipse's, so he heard the kiladrt yawn and it woke him up. He moodily grabbed the bucket from Harrison and dunked his entire face into it. Eclipse shuddered slightly at the noise.

"Your damn animal woke me up again." he said darkly to his sister.

She shrugged.

"I told you he would when you chose to set your tent up there."

He moved his mouth around awkwardly to mock her and scrubbed his face and hair with Harrison's cape to dry off. She ignored his mood and quickly scanned the camp with her telepathy. They were the only ones up and no enemies were snooping around their borders. She figured she would let the Logans sleep an hour or so longer. With a wave of her hand, her tent folded itself up and ropes tethered the bundle to the top of her ruck pack. Sean looked at her curiously.

"Are we moving out?"

"Father's orders." she nodded. "It's finally time. He wants us back home."

Sean's mood improved immensely. He pumped his fist in the air and actually smiled. Eclipse rolled her eyes at him, but secretly felt the same way. It was too hot and sandy in Ashtar. She missed the wet, gloomy weather in Holux and was ready to get back. Of course, they had to finish here first, but that was easy enough.

The sand crunched behind her and without hesitation, she drew her bow, nocked an arrow, and turned around to point it at the person she hadn't sensed seconds earlier. Alan Losh raised an eyebrow at her. He was a tall, scrawny man with bird-like features. His nose hooked just like a beak and his eyes were small, dark and beady. For just a second, she considered releasing the arrow. Then, he grinned mischievously at her as she gulped and lowered her bow with a grimace. She caught sight of the dull glint the electronic collar around his neck reflected in the low light. She knew it kept her telepathy out of his head, which is why she didn't sense him. Eclipse reluctantly put away both her arrow and compound bow from Sean, which she had been able to draw for 6 years, now.

Alan had started working for Victor when she was in the Enhancer as his head torturer. Apparently, the man had a knack for making people miserable. Eclipse despised him, but he technically out-ranked her, even as a general. Harrison knew why she had issues with him and always tried to help diffuse the situation, but it was hard to deal with a man with no shame.

Eclipse had deeply personal reasons for hating the bird-like man. He was her handler. After each of the Emilies turned 12, their trainers were relieved of duty and they were assigned to a handler. His job was to make sure the girl under him was held to Victor's standards of excellence and, more importantly, celibate.

Eclipse didn't like Alan hovering over her. She didn't like him trying to control her. And worst of all, she didn't like the fact that he actually could control her. Not only did she have to obey him to keep her promise to Victor, but Alan also excelled at his job. He was a miserable, sadistic, creative wretch, but he was a good handler.

"How'd you sleep, Number Two?" Alan taunted as he drew up to the side of the well opposite her.

"Fine."

It was hard to keep a straight face and talk to him, and she dropped the official title since it made her cringe every time it passed her lips. Victor wanted to make sure there was no chance of a relationship developing between a handler and their charge, so their official titles for each other were incredibly mundane and slightly demeaning to the girls. Of course, Eclipse knew that most of the Emilies slept with their handlers at one point. It wasn't like the handler could report himself and then they couldn't say shite about anything the girls did because they had dirt on them. Eclipse would rather die than even think about her handler that way.

Harrison glowered at Alan, who grinned at how uncomfortable he could make Eclipse. Sean watched curiously. He didn't know as much about the situation as Harry, so he wasn't sure why she always seemed to cower around Alan. Yes, he was a horrible person who totally invaded her privacy, but she dealt with their father with more confidence than this. Finally, Alan shrugged his shoulders and said the words Eclipse wanted to hear more than anything in the world.

"Anyway, Eclipse, I have to be getting back to Victor. He expects you and the men home before Voidanuar again. That gives you two months to finish up and one to travel home."

She looked away from him as he walked around the well and whispered right into her ear.

"I'm already dying to see you then."

The feeling of his breath on her ear made her cringe. Then he walked away to where he left his mount. Eclipse didn't move till she heard his hoof beats pounding away on the sand. Then she instinctively looked at Harrison as he opened his mouth to say something.

"No." she warned him flatly and walked away to do her job.

After a few hours of telepathically scanning the entire country, Eclipse located the main mass of the Ashtaran army again. She had employed the same devastating tactics she used in Dormiat, so everyone in Ashtar was gathered in one location. The Logans had been patiently tailing their movements, waiting for Victor's all clear. They were only about 20 miles from the capital city, where the population was staying for safety. Their army was about 80,000 in number and Eclipse only had the 500 Logans. Not that she thought she needed anyone else, though she wished her Emilies had stayed to help. The Logans were very capable and had been bottled up for years. They were ready for a good, long fight, but she knew they needed to be smart.

The hardest part would be the cavalry. The Logans didn't really work well on horseback. They were massive and Victor refused to commission draft horses for them, even for traveling. In other words, they marched everywhere and carried all their own gear, including their tents, on their backs. Right now, she knew the Ashtaran king was calmly gathering his cavalry, with no doubt in his mind that his 30,000 mounted warriors could take 500 slow brutes. Eclipse could telepathically see the soldiers grabbing their spears and scimitars. They were expecting an attack already, which put her men at another disadvantage. She would have to deal with the cavalry to give the Logans a chance. Her eyes opened and she went back to wake up the camp.

They made it to the capital around noon and the Ashtarans were ready for them. They knew the Chrosian's weakness to mounted warriors and had their cavalry stationed right outside their gates, waiting patiently. Shane whistled softly to himself.

"Damn, that's a lot of horsemen."

Eclipse nodded. Their orders were clear; it was a Cleansing. Take out the army and wipe out the population. She glanced from her brothers to the enemy once more. Then she turned and barked out orders.

"We stick together and watch each other's back. If someone gets separated, they're dead. Our only shot is to move as one unit and hold them at bay. Under no circumstances are you to let them break us. I want a solid snake formation. NOW!"

The Logans jumped into action. They spread out in a line, all 500 of them. Eclipse watched them expand to either side of her and waited till they were ready. It was easy for her to give orders after that. She projected them directly into every Logan's brain. Her strategy was simple. Their line would advance on the enemy and wipe them out. Each soldier's job was to make sure no one broke through the line at his location. Eclipse's job was to keep all 500 of them alive. She glanced to her left. Shane drew his great sword and Aidan nodded to her. She looked to her right. Sean drew his bow and Erican, his broadswords. They both nodded as well.

Eclipse closed her eyes as the Ashtarans hollered out their war cry. She had won countless battles in Dormiat, though none with this terrible of odds. She had faith in the Logans, but knew most of this battle would be up to her. Her eyes flashed open and blue flames emerged from their sockets. She ordered a charge and took off toward the enemy army.

All their time at the track, matching their strides, helped the Logans stay neck and neck as they charged across the open field. The enemy horses began prancing with anticipation as they drew down upon them. Eclipse counted down from three and boosted herself forward into a massive jump with her telepathy. A spear from one of the Ashtarans flew into her hand and she landed ten feet in front of their army with the tip of it digging into the ground. It conducted her telepathy for her, and the effects were catastrophic.

A blue beam fired out to both her sides for thousands of feet and held for a second before exploding out in front of her down the entire length of the line. The blast threw every warrior off their horse as they all broke under the force of her telepathy. The ground where the beam held creased into a small ridge and as the Ashtarans struggled to get up and find their weapons, the Logans leaped from the ridge onto their heads. Eclipse left the spear embedded in the ground and jumped up onto the ridge. Archers were about to be a problem.

Sure enough, a sheet of arrows fell from the walls of the city just as she looked up at it. She raised her hand, and an immense blue shield covered her men and caught the arrows as they drove into it. With a flip of her hands, the shield disappeared, and the arrows all turned around to face the archers who fired them. If they weren't completely baffled, they may have thought to duck. She forced both her hands out and the arrows fired back at the Ashtarans on the wall. The archers were no longer an issue. She drew her swords and joined her brothers in the fight.

To her left side, Aidan was throwing knives left and right. Each one hit its mark with ease. They once counted how many throwing knives Aidan wore on a daily basis and his siblings discovered it was over 100. He had two larger blades that snapped out of his bracers with long retractable filament cords attached for when he ran out of knives to throw. He could throw them repeatedly and retract them back to his wrists. The cords were a duranium filament, unbreakable, but thin. Eclipse had shown him that with enough force, the cords themselves could easily slice through enemies, decapitating them if necessary. The daggers were large enough to use in hand to hand combat as well and he also carried a sword and buckler, just in case they malfunctioned, which happened with all technology on occasion. There were even two hand crossbows slung over his back if he needed a further fail safe.

Sean stabbed one enemy in the eye with his arrow before yanking it back out and firing it, eye still attached, into the fray. He and Aidan kept their portions of the line from being overwhelmed by taking out people farther back. Shane gracefully slashed his massive sword back and forth, slicing through everything in his path, and Erican ducked in and around Sean to make sure no one was fast enough to sneak past his brother's ranged attacks.

All in all, her brothers were doing just fine. A little too well, in fact. Other portions of their line were getting bogged down as the cavalry found their footing. Eclipse teleported to one such position and switched her swords out for her bow. In minutes, half the problem was ended with carefully placed electrified arrows and she ported to the next problem area, snapping hundreds of enemy necks with her telepathy. She did this over and over, until the cavalry and infantry were defeated, and they stood at the portcullis into the city.

A wave of her hand shattered the gate and let them through. She and her brothers went in first as the rest of the Logans fell into formation behind them. There were still thousands of men to deal with inside, but she had to get them safely through the gate without funneling them into a trap prepared by the defense. A wave of men charged them as they first entered, and Eclipse snapped her fingers. Their spines broke in half, and they collapsed into piles of flesh, rolling in the direction they had been running. That gave the Logans the time they needed to funnel through the gate and spread out in teams of ten, slaughtering everyone in the streets. Eclipse knew the women and children would all be hiding in the inner keep of the main fortress. That was the only part of their task she was dreading, cutting down thousands of innocents. It was easy to write off killing someone who would happily kill you instead.

They made their way easily to the adobe castle and Sean broke down the door with a flat-footed kick. The king's most trusted men valiantly tried to stop them, but Eclipse overloaded all their brains and their heads exploded. Then they walked into the throne room and came face to face with the king and his harem. Eclipse stopped five feet away and sheathed her swords. The king had over 50 young women crowded around him, holding onto their children for the final moments of their lives. The youngest was an infant in his mother's arms. The oldest was probably Shane's age. Her brothers waited for her command. Why was she hesitating?

Eclipse's eyes met the king's frightened gaze. He didn't look like an enemy, just a man standing with his family, large as it was. He didn't even have his sword drawn. He knelt before her.

"Mercy, Eadhra' Almawt. Mercy, I beg. Anything. We provide anything for lives spared. Mercy, I beg!"

His family knelt as he raised his hands to plead with her. Eclipse walked up to the man and pulled him to his feet. His harem stayed prostrate on the ground. She placed her hand around the back of his neck and looked directly into his eyes. The Logans watched in concern. They were under direct orders from Victor to end the entire royal family. If Eclipse disobeyed, there would be hell to pay. She pursed her lips sympathetically and ignored the look of shock on his face as her dagger drove into his gut.

"You're begging the wrong person for mercy, Your Majesty." she whispered.

His family panicked and the Logans moved to step in and help, but Eclipse held a hand up to stop them and waved her other hand over the large royal group. Their necks all snapped, killing them instantly and painlessly, even the tiny infant. Eclipse muffled her gulp beneath a throat clear. She ordered the entire corps to search the castle for survivors and went to the keep alone. The Logans were good men, she had no right to ask them to bear the guilt she was about to endure. She had managed it just fine in Dormiat. Of course, back then she had Axl.

The door was easy enough to remove. It flew off its hinges with a glance from her. She stepped through and came face to face with over two million women and children huddled close together through the many layers of the keep tower. Eclipse gulped dryly as they screamed, and their children cried. She thought of walking away, leaving them to fend for themselves and hide from Victor. She would never have to tell him, and she could change the memories of the Logans so they remembered her killing them. It would be an easy deceit. But, no, she had an oath to her father, whatever he wanted, when he wanted it, with no questions asked. She stretched out her hand and her eyes flared into blue flames as their screams grew louder.

Her brothers noticed the difference the second they saw her. She looked defeated, tired, like she couldn't take out one more person. They all shared a concerned look. They had never seen her like this before. Word had spread when she returned from Dormiat about what she did, but she constantly said there was nothing to talk about. And she truly seemed fine until her 18th birthday, when her entire personality changed. Muted. Estranged and apathetic. The Logans would have helped her here, of course, but they were all secretly grateful she didn't let them. Victor wasn't even accepting infants into his care anymore. It was death for all. Mercy no longer mattered to him.

The corps stood and surveyed their handiwork. The battle had lasted all afternoon and into the night. It was a magnificent feat, taking out an army of 80,000 with just 500 men and one 18, almost 19-year-old girl, but none of them felt very celebratory. Instead they all sorrowfully followed Eclipse as she walked through the city and back out the gate, over the corpses of horses and men alike, to the ridge she had created. She paused to telekinetically return all of Aidan's daggers to him, then she looked out across the Logans.

"Well done." she told them. "Victor will be pleased. Now, let's go home."

They knew what she was trying to do. If they returned home sulking, Victor would be angry. They had to look at their accomplishment today as just that, an incredible victory over the foes of their leader. Sean forced himself to clap and she nodded at him gratefully as the Logans all joined in. Then they all marched back to camp in the cool, early morning air.

# CHAPTER TWENTY-FOUR

"They're back already?" Victor asked incredulously as the messenger nodded enthusiastically.

He glanced over at Amy and waved the messenger toward the door. Ashtar was supposed to take a few months! Alan had only just returned himself yesterday, after a three-week ride. How were the Logans back already? Eclipse must have misunderstood her orders.

"It just means we can start earlier. Why do you care so much?" Amy demanded as Victor rose to his feet and paced the floor.

She was much taller, now, but still the most beautiful woman in the country. Her blonde hair almost reached her waist, cascading there in large, elegant curls. Her purple eyes shone out as the most remarkable feature on her face, even if she was glaring at Victor, right now.

"I was just expecting a little more time, Amy!" he snapped angrily.

"More time for what?" Acre asked, walking in on the wrong conversation.

"Nothing!!" Victor and Amy growled in unison.

Acre raised his hands up in submission and backed up slightly. Victor rolled his eyes.

"Eclipse is back." he groaned.

Acre furrowed his brow.

"How's that even possible? Alan only just got back yesterday."

Victor shrugged and ran his hands over his head. Acre had never seen him so on edge. He glanced between him and Amy, who was obviously angry at the promontory for something. The two had been in cahoots for years, but normally they agreed. She was the reason Victor pulled the Emilies out of the fight in Ashtar to crush the rebellion, under her leadership. The only problem was that the series was struggling to function under her. They hated her and wished to be reunited with their real general. It was the only hiccup in Amy's plan.

Victor hadn't seen Eclipse in almost a year, since just after her 18th birthday, but they had worked out an understanding relationship before that. She ate meals with them and he allowed her to call him 'Father'. They could even hold civil conversations. They weren't close by any meaning of the word, but Victor was excited by how things were moving that way. Then the rebellion hit and ruined everything. It was obvious that Eclipse was involved since the rebels named themselves Moonlighters after her and claimed she should rule, not him. It meant one simple thing. She was too dangerous to keep alive.

They were trying to save the Emilies by seeing how they worked with Amy in command, but they refused to accept her orders unless Victor backed them up in person. They definitely wouldn't be loyal to her if something happened to Eclipse. So, the entire series had to be eliminated. They had everything set to go down in two months, during the Voidanuar after Eclipse returned, so Victor could deal with the fact that his daughter betrayed him. He was reluctant to act, even after all the blatant proof he had. He still had hope that they could have a relationship. It hurt him that she didn't want that, then it made him angry. He also knew it was his fault. There was a........ situation....... on her last birthday that he could have handled far better than he did and he knew she held it against him still; that she would always hold it against him. The trio walked outside the fortress together and ran into the four Monohue brothers, who were on their way in.

"Where's your sister?" Victor growled instantly.

"Well, we missed you too, Father." Erican exclaimed mirthfully. "Eclipse ported the Logans home and immediately headed for the Emily barracks."

"She didn't think to give her report, first?" Acre asked in surprise.

It wasn't like Eclipse to switch up protocol, even for her series. Generals delivered their reports to Victor upon return from anywhere and then went about their usual business.

"Well," Sean replied slowly. "She left me to give her report because she knew Amy would be with you, Father. She wanted to get the Emilies' honest opinions of Amy's command before she.... erm...... dealt with her."

Amy's face reddened and paled at the same time. She turned expectantly to Victor and placed her hands on her hips. As far as he was concerned, he was about to lose Eclipse forever, so he didn't care about the two girls' petty squabble anymore. He just wanted five minutes alone with her before he sent her off to die. Completely ignoring Amy, he strode past his sons and towards the barracks, alone. No one watching was sure if they were supposed to follow or not, so they stood still and awaited orders, like they were trained.

Eclipse was greeted by her series with several cheers and handshakes. They all jumped out of their bunk beds, where they were relaxing, and made their way toward her, just hoping to shake her hand or pat her back. It didn't take her long to hear the things Amy put them through and stitch them together in a timeline. As soon as they dealt with the aid from Central Liberty, they teleported back to Holux and were sent to crush the rebellion in a massive city named Celnisia. Their orders were to raze it to the ground and kill every person in the city. Amy demanded more of them, though, and commanded them to torture each individual before they died. When the series refused to follow her orders, she punished them all by torturing them with her telepathy.

With no one defending them, the girls had to resign to her punishment. Physically acting out against any superior officer was immediately punishable by death. They continued their silent protest and obeyed the promontory, killing everyone in Celnisia, but they had disregarded Amy for the last five months and only followed the orders that came straight from Victor's lips. As a result, they were sentenced to their barracks until Eclipse got back and decided their fate. Blatant disobedience was not to be tolerated.

Eclipse listened to her soldiers' complaints with great concern. Most likely, Victor would expect her to punish them direly for their insolence, but she couldn't help feeling a little proud that the group of girls who were once too frightened to look Amy in the face, now openly rebelled against her. A lot had changed among the women around her. They were bolder, braver, and just a bit smarter. She would have complimented them if she wasn't furious at their lack of judgment.

"You mean to tell me," she said with a frown. "that all of you thought it would be a good idea to disobey your commanding officer?"

The group silenced the moment she opened her mouth. When Eclipse spoke, they all listened, didn't matter when or why. When she looked angry, they listened in terror. Right now, they weren't sure why she was upset.

"She was only our temporary commanding officer, though." one of the younger women pointed out.

Eclipse rolled her eyes and looked at the girl sharply.

"No, Clarissa, she is my second in command, which makes her your commanding officer at all times I'm not present. Like it or not, she has authority over all of you for that alone. Now, I have to go try to convince Victor that none of you deserve death and I'll be honest, the odds of that are pretty damn slight."

Eclipse turned on her heels and walked toward the door, through the sea of indignant faces. They had done all of this for her! How could she be disappointed in them? A few of the older Emilies understood, though. She was only upset because she didn't want them to get hurt. Eclipse was a spectacular leader, always putting her soldiers first, even when it pissed them off.

The young general left the room and bounded down the stairs to the building's exit. She was clenching her fists as she pictured Amy torturing her own colleagues and thought through the many ways she could make her pay. Eclipse was so focused on her thoughts that she swung open the door and walked straight into her father, who was on his way in at the very same time she was leaving.

It was an awkward moment, as the two ended up in each other's arms briefly. Their eyes met and Victor felt a slight shift in their relationship. It was the first time they even came close to a hug. Then, Eclipse pushed away and bowed, panicked by the way her stomach flipped. She was either scared or furious, but couldn't quite land on one of them. Victor stared at her, not even moving his hands from the position they had been in to hold her arms. She stayed bowed until he snapped out of it and shook the feeling off, then he waved his hand toward her and she stood at attention and waited for him to yell at her for skipping her report. He wasn't even thinking about it, now.

"You made it back far earlier than I thought you would." he said calmly.

"I decided it would be a waste of time to have the Logans walk thousands of miles back to Holux when I could teleport them here instead." she explained. "We were all eager to get home."

Victor was glad she finally figured out how to drop the formalities from their conversations two years ago when he asked. She didn't use titles when addressing him anymore, but only one thing could change the stiff way she stood before him. Victor nodded in response to her and jerked his head toward the street.

"Walk with me, Eclipse."

They were walking for only a few moments before he continued their conversation.

"Porting 500 giants all this way must have strained you."

She shrugged.

"A bit. My head hurt for a few seconds afterward, but that's all."

"And I take it that my orders were carried out in full?"

"Ashtar is yours. Everyone is dead and burned. We made sure of that over the past three weeks."

He nodded approval.

"Excellent. And how did the Logans fare?"

"No casualties. They work well together and follow orders to the letter, but they need their own general."

Victor was already shaking his head.

"Eclipse, we have been over this. I trust Sean about as far as I can throw him and I will not put him in command of an enhanced series."

"I wasn't talking about Sean. I simply said they need a general. I don't think it matters who you choose. They listened to me, after all." she shrugged.

There was the opening Victor was looking for. He needed to hear a confession from her lips, if he was going to end her life over it.

"Yes, well people seem to have no issue listening to you. Can you explain that?"

Eclipse pursed her lips and sighed. She had noticed this, too. Most people obeyed her without a qualm. She wasn't sure why, but she guessed it was for the same reason they obeyed Victor.

"I guess I scare them. I'm powerful and I work directly for the most vengeful man in the world. If you knew that someone could teleport behind you and kill you before anyone could stop them, wouldn't you be worried?"

That, in fact, was exactly what he was worried about right this instant. He tried so hard to see her words as something other than a threat as he cleared his throat and looked at his feet. Thankfully, Eclipse changed the subject, but unfortunately, she chose the wrong topic.

"How did the rebellion fare, by the way? Is there anything I need to finish up, or has it been handled?"

Again, Victor tried to ignore the fact that she went from talking about assassinating him to the rebellion. He felt a small lump forming in his throat as he realized Amy might be right about his daughter's treachery.

"Celnisia is gone as well as its rebels, but I don't believe we cut the head off the snake. They seemed far too organized for a group of peasants."

Victor looked down the street and bit the inside of his cheek.

"If you had to guess," he said meaningfully. "who would you think was leading them?"

She thought for a moment, making her father sweat.

"Well, I suppose it would have to be someone close to you, who knew the schedules of your series and had inside information on the proceedings of the government. They probably live here in Holux and keep close tabs on all of us, watching everything we say and do from the shadows or hiding in plain sight. If you're looking for a specific name, though, I'm not sure. Would you like me to find them?"

"No, that's alright. I have other orders for you."

Eclipse caught the change in his tone, but couldn't figure out why it happened. Little did she know that she just described herself as the leader of the rebellion to an already suspicious father. She patiently waited for him to continue.

"It appears Central Liberty has become a bigger problem than we originally thought. I'm sending you and your series to a large ravine on the border to find refugees they are hiding there."

He found it difficult not to choke on his own words, but she appeared none the wiser.

"Right away?"

Victor squinted at her.

"I thought we had a deal, Eclipse. Whatever I say, when I want it, no questions."

"We do, of course." she responded quickly. "I just thought you would want to discipline the Emilies first. And it will take a moment to get everything mobilized, but of course, whatever you want."

"I'll leave that up to you. You can have a couple days to prepare. I just need to know what you're going to do to Amy."

"What do you mean?"

"Come on, Eclipse. I'm not an idiot. I know what she did to your girls. What are you going to do about it?"

The corner of her mouth twitched up as she stopped playing innocent and looked straight ahead.

"I'm going to demote her."

# CHAPTER TWENTY-FIVE

Amy was not pleased when Eclipse demoted her to a private, in front of the entire Emily series and Victor, who did nothing to stop it. Amber and Clarissa were promoted to cover her position, since the two of them had always run a close second to her rank and power anyway. Then the Emilies prepared to move out to Central Liberty. The plan was to port close to the border and march the last few miles. Victor's information said there were secret caves in the ravine where Chrosian refugees were hiding, under the protection of the Libertarian government. They were going to have to go into the ravine and search for them.

Eclipse wasn't particularly excited to drop into the bottom of a ravine where a primitive dam was the only thing holding back torrents of water hundreds of feet above her head. So, when she finally led her series to the edge of the reservoir, she squinted into the water and shuddered.

"That's a hell of a lot of water." she muttered.

Beside her, Amber nodded. She, Eclipse, and Clarissa had always gotten along, and it amazed the general how smoothly things had gone in the few days since she dropped Amy down several ranks. The series was definitely doing better, and they were all happily content with the new order of things. Since they weren't terrible people, they didn't even lord it over Amy's head at all.

"Why would they store the water for their capital this far away? We are still 150 miles from Feldon's Peak." Clarissa asked softly.

"The climate is unpredictable in the south. They need a steady source of emergency water during droughts, even if it's this far away. Their only other option is a small oasis just east of the plateau. It's not big enough to provide for the entire city. They have basins that gather rain to irrigate their crops, but it dries up without the precipitation. This is their best option."

Amber looked Eclipse up and down with new respect.

"You got all that from staring into a reservoir?"

The general rolled her eyes over to her new second in command and pursed her lips.

"Amber, I filled out an I.S.R. on Central Liberty like three years ago when we first got back from Dormiat. I know a great deal about them."

"Right. I forgot."

Eclipse let out a deep breath and walked past the reservoir and the dam holding it back from the rest of the ravine. There were little slots that allowed some water to make it through and a small stream ran through the bottom of the gorge. She grimaced and moaned, but jerked her head down, with a glance at Clarissa. The older girl shouted out orders to the series while Eclipse levitated herself and Adamere down to the bottom of the ravine. The water only came up to just above her ankles. She forced herself to focus on the feeling of it running over her feet and remain calm. She had enough control by the time her series joined her.

Eclipse glanced up at the dam and felt the same crawling sensation up her spine. She shook it off and telepathically scanned the walls of the ravine. Amber saw her wince in pain and her brow furrowed.

"What's wrong, General?"

Eclipse dug her palm into her forehead and gasped slightly. She hadn't experienced pain while using her telepathy in a long time, years in fact. Maybe she had been overworking it recently. With everything in Ashtar, and then teleporting 500 men thousands of miles, only to port back south to the ravine. It was incredibly familiar, the pain and nausea, something she had felt before definitely and she knew what it was, but couldn't remember the name right now. Alan used it, whatever it was. She fell to one knee as the world spun around and her hand dropped to the ground to steady her. But it hit water instead. She lifted her hand and brushed it off on her shirt. Then she put it back down to steady herself again.

Amber was next. She had been trying to scan with Eclipse, but she suddenly collapsed next to her general, unconscious. Eclipse jumped slightly at the splash from behind her, but she couldn't even manage to turn around and look. Soon, she had no choice as more bodies fell behind her. She lowered to her hands and knees and crawled around in a circle. Her entire series was toppling over and landing in the water beneath. She looked from them to her hands and gasped.

Her hands and knees were sinking in blood! She forced herself up to her feet and rubbed her hands together to clean them off. They burned and she had to stop. What was going on? Her brain ached and she couldn't balance on her own two feet. The water rushing over her ankles seemed louder than normal. She looked down in shock. It was water. But it was blood a few seconds ago. There was a deafening crash to her left, but she ignored it and stared at her hands, flipping them back and forth. There was blood on one side and water on the other. She gulped as the crash resounded down the ravine again. She slowly looked back at her soldiers. They weren't moving, they were melting into the tar at her feet.

"Tar?" she muttered under her breath, looking down again.

Her feet were trapped in the black goop, now. Another crash. The tar started to rise up her legs and she felt it flowing past her knees now, but tar doesn't move; not like this. Eclipse slowly put the pieces together. She was hallucinating, but she was too slow. The crash was followed by another horrifying noise. It sounded like an explosion and a waterfall put together. She slowly looked up at the dam. It wasn't there anymore. Instead a torrent of water was cascading down on her......

....and her series. Forcing the panic rising in her stomach down, Eclipse raised a force field in front of her series and braced it with both her hands. It was the only chance she had to save her girls. She could clearly see the shield she raised, but the water crashed down on her head anyway. She felt it pound her down onto the floor of the ravine and then sweep her limp body, along with the hundreds of bodies behind her, downstream.

The rest was in flashes as Eclipse tried to maintain control under the water. She saw their faces getting thrown around her. Susan's head flashed by and bashed against a rock. She heard the crack of her skull breaking, even in the chaos. Eclipse tried everything to escape: telepathy, teleportation, swimming. She hadn't gone swimming in years, but she still tried. Panic set in and she screamed for Acre to come back. *DON'T LEAVE ME HERE!!* Then the world went black.

ΩΩΩΩΩΩ

Duke heard the persistent destruction of the dam from his hiding spot, the cave he had been living in for weeks now. He ran out to its entrance and stumbled into the ravine, looking to the west and shading his eyes from the sudden light. He couldn't see the dam from where he stood, but it was the only thing that would make such a racket. The water around his knees was growing higher, which meant it was almost broken. Duke had one shot; climb out of the ravine before the massive wave reached him. The dam was still holding on for now. He hit the side of the gorge and jumped to the nearest hand hold he could find. Another crash resounded far to his left. That was the third one.

Thankfully, he and Antilles had learned to climb years ago, otherwise he would have been trapped. He heaved himself up the wall with ease till he was 20 feet up, then the fourth and final blow struck the dam. Duke heard the water crashing toward him and scrambled as far up the side of the ravine as he could before it hit. His arms were burning and his feet kept

292

slipping from their holds. He could finally see the pounding water headed his way and flattened his body as close to the wall as he could, closing his eyes. The torrent missed his feet by inches. He was left hanging onto the side of the ravine as it rushed by beneath him. The residual wind almost yanked him off, but he held on for dear life. He opened his eyes and looked down.

There were bodies! Broken, bloody bodies tossed about in the ravine below his feet. He could hear the sickening smacks as they pounded into the walls and their bones snapped. He shifted slightly to see if he recognized any of them. It only took him two seconds to realize they were Chrosians. No one in Central Liberty dressed so scantily. His eyes darted around searching for survivors, but instead, they just locked on one girl in particular.

He wasn't sure why she stood out to him. She wasn't particularly beautiful or interesting. Her brown hair was plastered to her face and her eyes were closed. Her clothes were torn and blood seeped from her face, but she floated along the top of the water like some sort of mystical creature. He almost fell watching her pass by. She was at the end of the wave, when it was dying down and leaving their corpses strewn behind it. The water rested her onto a small ledge in the ravine and then it continued on its path, as if it knew he was there to help her. The ledge was just under his feet, about 10 feet down. Duke judged the distance and then jumped.

He landed on his hands and knees with a crack as his right wrist broke, but at least he was right next to the girl. After growling in pain he reached up with his good hand and checked for a pulse. There was nothing. Duke had watched Alex resuscitate enough people during practice to know CPR. Even though it shot pain through his whole arm, he crossed his hands over her chest and pumped them up and down, hearing at least two ribs crack under the pressure. He almost panicked till he remembered Alex telling him that was normal. When she didn't improve, he gently sealed his lips over her mouth and forced as much breath as he could into her lungs. Her chest rose and fell with each breath. That meant there was no blockage, he assumed. Air could get in and out. Duke went back to the chest compressions, checking for a pulse every few seconds. Again, nothing. He breathed into her mouth and prayed. He wasn't sure why, but he needed this girl to live.

It didn't escape him that this was not only the first time he touched a girl's chest, but also the first time he placed his lips on a girl's mouth. Despite how focused he was on saving her life, there was a nagging feeling of anxiety in the back of his skull. What if she woke up? He was almost as afraid of that as he was of letting her die in his arms. Would this stranger hate him for touching her while she was knocked out? Or would she be grateful? Would this start something between them? That seemed like a fairy tale possibility. Hero and damsel in distress. There were thousands of tales about that love story. All of them ended the same way, except his own. Maybe she wouldn't even care that he saved her, just like Ace didn't care. Would she ever even realize how close he felt to her as his lips locked over hers again?

He spent ten minutes trying to resuscitate her, feeling closer to her with every second. A vision of a future with this stranger fabricated itself in his mind. What was she like? Maybe she was sarcastic, but in a funny way, not a mean way. Maybe she liked riding and swimming. Those were things he'd love to do with her. His imagination ran wild as he continued CPR. Each compression burned visions of the two of them heading it off over mead or laughing over a dumb joke. Each breath made his heart beat a little faster. What if all of this was only seconds from becoming reality? What if he would finally have someone who understood him, someone who cared? Time was escaping him and he suddenly realized how long he had been trying to wake her up.

Then he knew. She was gone. He finished pumping his hands and leaned down to breathe into her lungs once more. Her chest still moved, but there was no pulse and she didn't wake up. Duke had to face the reality that this stranger was dead. He went to pull away from her, but hesitated. She deserved some sort of send off, right? She could have been someone wonderful, someone amazing. No matter what, she didn't deserve to die alone in a wet mudhole, no matter how she got there. The boy shifted slightly and closed his eyes. He kissed her.

It wasn't long, but it was powerful. His lips gently cradled her lower lip and he let his hand drift around to the back of her neck while he kissed her. He stayed maybe five seconds, before slowly pulling away and cradling her in his arms. That kiss was more real to him than anything he had felt in his entire life. Maybe real enough to wake her up like the stories of old? There was something here, but she needed to live for him to figure out what. She still didn't wake up and his heart wrenched in his chest. Why was he cursed to be alone?

Suddenly, Duke was hit with an overwhelming amount of guilt. At this very moment, he felt more for this dead stranger than he did for Acelyn. She was supposed to be the love of his life, but here he was, kissing a corpse like it was more precious to him than she ever was. The sick feeling in his gut that reared its ugly head when he thought of Ace came back and he clutched his stomach and jumped away from the girl before him. Still, it killed him to drop her lifeless body like that.

Just like that, Acelyn was gone from his mind and he was left staring at the pretty face before him. She looked so peaceful, like there wasn't a care in the world that could bother her now. Why did he feel such a connection with this stranger? He knew absolutely nothing about her, besides the fact that she was a dead, enhanced Chrosian with long brown hair braided over her right shoulder. He gently reached back over to her and straightened out the braid before tucking her stray hairs behind her ears. Something on her chest glistened in the light and he reached out to grasp it. It was a necklace chain tucked into her shirt. He pulled on it till he could see the pendant on the end.

It wasn't very fancy. Just three thin metal rings interlinked with each other. Each one had a name inscribed on it. The center one said Eclipse, the one on the right, Adamere, and the one on the left, Axl. He wasn't sure what it meant, but the chain was long enough to hide deep down her torso. His guess was that she needed to make sure it didn't fly out for any reason. It was a secret, whatever it was. It couldn't be love interests, he decided. No man would be willing to share this beautiful girl with two other guys. Maybe three brothers? Or the names of pets? There wasn't even anything that made him believe this was a gift of love at all. It certainly didn't seem very valuable, just iron rings. Her hair got tangled in the chain as he slipped it off over her head and stared at it in doubt. Still, he understood that a necklace could mean more than it appeared. He personally had one he had worn his entire life. It was his mother's. The metal wolf pendant had large green eyes and fit snugly in the palm of his hand when he was nervous. He had often held it for courage when he talked to Ace. He found himself clenching it tightly now.

Guilt made it hard for him to breathe as he thought of Ace again. He clutched the pendant in his fist and leaned back against the wall behind him. His breath became raspy as he tried not to cry. He wasn't ready to be alone for the rest of his life. The last few weeks had been miserable. He was lonely. He just created an entire fantasy from seeing a dead girl. His eyes shifted back to her face. No worries; no fear, not even a tiny bit of stress. He wanted the peace he saw on this girl's face. He staggered up to his feet and peered unsteadily over the edge of the cliff at the bottom of the ravine. The water had died down to barely nothing. Duke glanced at her one more time, hoping she would wake up. Maybe if she opened her eyes, he could find a reason to live again. When she didn't, he clutched both necklaces and dove head-first to his death.

One hour. If he had stayed with her for one hour, he would have seen her mystical blue eyes blink open and her pupils shrink in the light. Eclipse drew air into her lungs and sat bolt upright. Water had dripped off her hair and pooled under her head, making her jump forward. Almost instantly, she remembered where she was and scrambled to the edge to look for her girls. The corpses she could see were mangled and motionless. She scanned for something, anything, but silence echoed through her head. With a gulp she realized she was the only one left. She reached up to clutch the rings she wore around her neck. It was her safety net, her way of coping with her miserable, infuriating, painful life.

And it wasn't there.

Both hands desperately shot to her neck and she frantically searched for it over her entire torso, taking off her gray over shirt and rubbing herself down again. When she still didn't find it, she slid down the side of the ravine and into the small amount of water still flowing through it. She fell to her hands and knees and searched for her necklace, sloshing around muttering frantically to herself and screaming in rage when she couldn't find it. She was losing her mind and didn't even realize it till she threw a dead, bloody body away and it splashed beside her. The noise made her freeze staring at the corpse.

Suddenly, Eclipse was staring straight into Susan's face. It was crushed on the left side and bloody everywhere else. Her body was mangled and broken and her bright peach eyes stared straight through Eclipse. The general only then felt the sharp pain in her chest, like something was broken. She felt the despair at losing her necklace. She felt the exhaustion from being dead for hours. She felt the misery at failing her girls. Eclipse groaned in pain as she crawled toward Susan and scooped her into her arms and lap. She pressed her head to Susan's forehead for just a few moments, wondering what was next.

Too many emotions tried to force their way into her heart, but one outweighed the rest. She didn't have time to deal with the pain, the sorrow, or the misery. Eclipse slowly glared up at the top side of the ravine to her south. The Libertarians were to blame for this. They were monsters, murderers, and she was going to make each and every soul pay. Ashtar was nothing compared to what she was capable of. She was the daughter of the most ruthless man in history and mastered her craft better than anyone in existence. No one knew revenge like her. No one knew pain like her. Flames ignited in her eyes and heart as her breathing picked up. Eclipse let them burn unchecked.

# What's Next?

You can leave a review on Amazon to help the author in her self-publishing journey.

Ready for the next book? You can find Eclipsing the Flames on Amazon, book two of the To Be Nameless Series. You can also check out the author's website at namelessjaquish.com to see all of her books and check out upcoming announcements in her blog.

Thank you for reading and I hope you enjoyed!

Made in the USA
Las Vegas, NV
27 February 2024

86386288R00184